DANGEROUS
LIES

ALSO BY BECCA FITZPATRICK

Black Ice

Hush, Hush Saga

Hush, Hush

Crescendo

Silence

Finale

BECCA
FITZPATRICK

DANGEROUS LIES

SIMON & SCHUSTER

First published in Great Britain in 2015 by Simon & Schuster UK Ltd
First published in the USA in 2015 by Simon & Schuster BFYR,
an imprint of Simon & Schuster Children's Publishing Division, New York
A CBS COMPANY

3 5 7 9 10 8 6 4 2

Simon & Schuster UK Ltd
1st Floor, 222 Gray's Inn Road
London
WC1X 8HB

www.simonandschuster.co.uk

Simon & Schuster Australia, Sydney
Simon & Schuster India, New Delhi

A CIP catalogue record for this book
is available from the British Library.

HB ISBN 978-1-4711-2508-9
TPB ISBN 978-1-4711-2509-6
eBook ISBN 978-1-4711-2511-9

Printed and bound by CPI Group (UK) Ltd, Croydon, CR0 4YY

Simon & Schuster UK Ltd are committed to sourcing paper
that is made from wood grown in sustainable forests and supports the Forest
Stewardship Council, the leading international forest certification organisation.
Our books displaying the FSC logo are printed on FSC certified paper.

THIS ONE'S FOR MY CHILDHOOD FRIENDS

ACKNOWLEDGMENTS

First and forever, thank you to the Fitzpatrick boys: Justin, Riley, and Jace.

Thanks to Jenn Martin, who works tirelessly behind the scenes so I can focus on writing.

I'm grateful to my team at Simon & Schuster: Jon Anderson, Justin Chanda, Anne Zafian, Mekisha Telfer, Lucy Ruth Cummins, Chrissy Noh, Katy Hershberger, Dorothy Gribbin, Jenica Nasworthy, Chava Wolin, and Angela Zurlo.

A shout-out to Zareen Jaffery, editor extraordinaire.

I owe my copyeditor and proofreader, Katharine Wiencke and Adam Smith, respectively, a thank-you.

Catherine Drayton, it's been a wild and exciting seven years. Thanks for taking a chance on me. Lyndsey Blessing and the crew at InkWell Management: Thank you for your support!

To the many librarians and booksellers who've placed my books into the hands of a reader: consider this a thank-you just for you.

Thanks to Matt Epley for answering my baseball-related questions.

Thanks to Cameron and Rebecca Chin for providing insight into the world of rodeo cowboys and ranch life.

Thanks to Erin Tangeman for helping me with a couple law-related inquiries.

Thanks to Rob Baer for answering my questions about broken ankle bones—even if you did ask for a rather steep cut of the royalties as compensation.

Thanks to Jason Hales, who, I hope, believes in second chances.

Laura Andersen, Ginger Churchill, and Patty Esden: Long-distance hugs have worked surprisingly well at holding our group together. Love you now and always.

Finally, a heartfelt thank-you to you, dear reader. Whether you've been reading my books over the years, or you're taking a chance on me now, it's been a pleasure writing for you. I do hope you enjoy Chet and Stella's story.

1

AN ANGRY RAP SHOOK THE MOTEL ROOM DOOR.
I lay perfectly still on the mattress, my skin hot and clammy.
Beside me, Reed drew my body to his.

So much for ten minutes, I thought.

I tried not to cry as I nestled my face into the warm curve of
Reed's neck. My mind absorbed every detail, carefully retaining
this moment so I could play it back for a long, long time after they
took me away.

I had a wild impulse to flee with him. An alley flanked the
motel, visible from the room they kept me in. Details like where
we would hide and how we'd keep from ending up at the bottom
of the Delaware River with cement blocks strapped to our feet
kept me from acting on that impulse.

The knock grew louder. Bending his head close to mine, Reed

breathed deeply. He was trying to remember me, too.

"The room is probably bugged." He spoke so softly, I almost mistook the sound for a sigh. "Have they told you where they're taking you?"

I shook my head from side to side, and his face, which was crisscrossed with cuts and swollen at the cheekbones, fell. "Yeah, me neither."

Because his body was also bruised, he rolled gingerly onto his knees, searching along the headboard. He opened the nightstand drawer and fanned the pages of the Gideon Bible. He looked under the mattress.

Nothing. But of course they'd bugged the room. They didn't trust us not to talk about that night, even though my testimony was the last thing on my mind. After everything I'd agreed to do for them, they couldn't give me ten minutes, ten private minutes, with my boyfriend before they dragged us apart.

"Are you mad at me?" I couldn't help whispering. He was in this mess because of me—because of my mom. It was trouble with her that had effectively ruined his life and future. How could he not resent me even a little? His hesitation made me feel a deep, limitless anger toward my mom.

Then he said, "Don't." Softly, but firmly. "Don't say that. Nothing's changed. We're going to be together. Not now, but soon."

My relief came quick and sure. I shouldn't have doubted him. Reed was the one. He loved me, and had proven once again that I could count on him.

A key scraped the lock.

"Don't forget the Phillies account," Reed whispered urgently in my ear. I met his eyes. In the seconds that followed, we shared an unspoken conversation. With one slight nod, I told him I understood.

Then I threw my arms around him so tightly I heard the breath go out of him. I released him just as Deputy Marshal Price thrust open the door. Two black Buick sedans idled in the parking lot behind him.

He glanced between us. "Time to go."

A second deputy, one I didn't recognize, led Reed out. With one backward glance, Reed held me in his gaze. He tried to smile, but only one side of his mouth turned up. He was nervous. My heart began to pound. This was it. Last chance to run.

"Reed!" I called out. But he was already inside the car. I couldn't see his face behind the tinted glass. The car turned out of the lot and accelerated. Ten seconds later I'd lost sight of it. That's when my heart really started to pound. This was actually happening.

I squeezed my suitcase handle hard between my fingers. I wasn't ready. I couldn't leave the only place I knew. My friends, my house, my school—and Reed.

"First step's always the hardest," Deputy Marshal Price said, coaxing me outside by the elbow. "Look at it this way. You get to start life fresh, reinvent yourself. Don't think about the trial now. You won't have to see Danny Balando for months, maybe years. His attorneys will tie this case up in knots. I've seen the defense delay trial with excuses ranging from a lost E-ZPass to traffic on the Schuylkill Expressway."

"Delay?" I echoed.

"Delays lead to acquittals. General rule. But not this time. With your testimony, Danny Balando is going to prison." He squeezed my shoulder with conviction. "The jury will believe you. He's facing life without parole, and it's going to stick."

"He'll stay in jail through the trial?" I asked uneasily.

"Held without bail. He can't get to you."

Holed up in a safe house for the past seventy-two hours while I waited for my mother's drug dealer to be arraigned on a first-degree murder charge and multiple counts of drug possession and trafficking, I'd felt like a prisoner.

The last three days, a pair of U.S. marshals had guarded me at all times. Two in the morning, another set during the day, and two more for the night shift. I was not allowed to either make or receive phone calls. All electronics had been confiscated. I was provided a wardrobe of ill-matching pieces a deputy had grabbed from my closet at home. And now, as a key witness in a federal criminal case that was going to trial, since Danny Balando had pleaded not guilty to the charges, I was about to be transferred to my final penitentiary. Whereabouts unknown.

"Where are you taking me?" I asked.

Price cleared his throat. "Thunder Basin, Nebraska." There was the faintest note of apology in his tone, which told me all I needed to know. It was a crap deal. I was helping them put away a dangerous criminal, and in return, they were banishing me from civilization.

"And Reed?"

"You know I can't tell you where he's going."

"He's my boyfriend."

"This is how we keep witnesses safe. I know it isn't easy on you, but we're doing our job. Got you the ten minutes you asked for. Had to jump through a lot of hoops. Last thing the judge wants is for one of you to influence the other's testimony."

I was being forced to leave my boyfriend, and he wanted a thank-you?

"What about my mom?" Straightforward, no emotion.

Price rolled my suitcase to the rear of the Buick, carefully avoiding my eyes. "Headed to rehab. I can't tell you where, but if she works hard, she'll be ready to join you at the end of summer."

"We both know I don't want that, so let's not play this game."

Wisely, Price let it drop.

It wasn't dawn yet, and I was already hot and sticky in my shorts and tank. I wondered how Price could be comfortable in jeans and a long-sleeved shirt. I didn't look at the gun in the holster over his shoulder, but I felt its presence. It was a reminder that the danger wasn't over. I wasn't sure it ever would be.

Danny Balando wouldn't stop searching for me. He was in jail, but the rest of his drug cartel was roaming free. Any one of them could be paid to do his bidding. His only hope was to hunt me down and kill me before I could testify.

Price and I slipped into the Buick, and he handed me a pass-port with a name that wasn't mine.

"You can't come back, Stella. Not ever."

I touched my fingertips to the window. As we drove out of

Philadelphia in the predawn hours, we passed a bakery. A boy in an apron ran a broom across the doorstep. I thought he might glance up, and pause to watch me until I was out of sight, but he kept at his work. No one knew I was leaving.

That was the point.

The streets were empty and shiny black with fresh rain. I listened to the water rush under the tires and tried to not lose it completely. This was home. This was the only place I knew. Leaving it felt like giving up something as vital as air. Suddenly I asked myself if I could do this.

"My name's not Stella," I finally said.

"Normally, we let witnesses keep their first name, but yours is unusual," Price explained. "We're taking an extra precaution. Your old and new names sound similar, which should help you adjust."

Stella Gordon. Stell-a, Stell-a, Stell-a. I repeated the new name in my head until the syllables locked together. I hated the name.

The Buick sped up, merging onto the interstate. Soon, I saw signs for the airport, and at that moment, a fierce ache gripped my chest. My flight left in four hours. I was having a hard time breathing; the air refused to go in—it pushed down on me like something solid. I wiped my palms on my thighs.

This didn't feel like a new beginning. I craned my neck to keep the lights of Philly in view. As the car left them in the distance, I felt like my life was coming to an end.

SUNLIGHT STRETCHED ACROSS THE NEBRASKA MILES,
burning fiery pink-gold through a bank of clouds on the horizon. It was almost sunset, and the land spread out, an expanse of never-ending cornfields broken only by the rising silhouette of a windmill or grain silo.

Gone were the sleek skyscrapers glittering with lights, the historic brick storefronts of the Main Line patched with colorful advertisements, and the lush, manicured gardens and winding roads of the suburbs. No rush of people bustling to catch the subway downtown, or car horns blaring a cacophony of staccato blasts as traffic thickened.

Deputy Price and I passed cattle grazing along the barren highway, swishing flies with their tails, a few raising their large triangular heads to gaze curiously in our direction, making me wonder when they'd last seen a car. I cracked the window. The air smelled green and alive and foreign as it whistled inside. Three shirtless boys, skinny as broomsticks, walked barefoot along the highway, fishing poles balanced over their sunburned shoulders.

I could hear my best friend Tory Bell's voice in my head. *They've sent you into Children of the Corn. Forget about Italian drug lords—I give you twenty-four hours in this place.*

Price said, "School's out. All summer to do what you please. You lucked out."

"Lucky me," I echoed.

"You'll be safe here."

He waited for my response, but we both knew I wasn't safe. Every morning I would wake up wondering if today Danny would find me.

"You'll be living with Carmina Songster. Retired cop. Very capable. She knows the truth about you, and she'll be living your cover story."

"What if I don't like her?"

"Everyone likes Carmina. They call her Gran. The whole town calls her Gran."

"And she's going to protect me?"

Price turned his head, leveling his Ray Ban–shaded eyes with mine. "Some friendly advice. How this summer plays out is up to you. Could be a miserable one or a tolerable one. Hell, it might even be better than tolerable. I know you're angry at your mom—"

I stiffened. "Don't bring her into this."

"Carmina can call her, when you're ready. She has the clinic's number."

I fixed him with a meaningful icy glare. "I said I don't want to talk about her."

"You've got a right to feel betrayed and hurt, but your mom is going to get better. I really believe that. You can't give up on her now. She needs you more than ever."

"What about when I needed her?" I snapped. "I stopped holding my breath for her to get better a long time ago. She's the reason I'm here, not home with my friends in a world that actually makes sense." My breath caught in the back of my throat.

Price held his tongue several minutes before saying, "After I introduce you to Carmina, I have to head back, but she knows how to reach me. Call me anytime."

"She is not my family. You are not my family. So let's not play this game either."

He grew very still, and I knew my remark had stung. He was putting his life on the line to protect me; the least I could do was show a little gratitude. But I'd told the truth. I was a job to him. We weren't family—I didn't have a family. I had an estranged father, who'd turned down the U.S. attorney's offer to place him in WITSEC with me. I was never to contact him again. And I had a mother in rehab, who I hoped I never saw again. Family implied love, commitment, a sense of solidarity. At the very least it implied living together.

We rode the rest of the way in silence. I shifted away from Price, watching the sun melt below the horizon. I'd never known the sun could take up so much space. Out here, without buildings or woods or hills to block the view, the sun wasn't merely a sphere; it seemed to spread like shimmering gold liquid, a fat brushstroke of paint on the skyline. It was as dazzling as it was alien.

After dark, Price turned onto a rural road. Plumes of dust clouded the windows. I jostled in my seat as the tires bounced over potholes. Towering, gnarled cottonwood trees framed the road, and I briefly wondered what it would feel like to climb their thick, sloping branches all the way to the top. As a little girl, I had dreamed of having my own tree house with a tire swing. But I was too old to wish for those things now.

I could just make out the silhouette of a two-story house. It had the biggest lawn I'd ever seen, with more cottonwood trees soaring over the roofline. The lawn gave way to open fields, and past those, I could see nothing but a sapphire sky powdered with stars.

It was almost overwhelming, the sheer vastness of it all. I felt completely alone. I had traveled to the edge of the world; there was nothing beyond this place. A few steps farther, and I might drop over the end of the earth.

Unnerved by the thought, I cracked my window again for fresh air, but the breeze was sticky and humid. Night insects droned in a soft, monotonous rhythm. It was an eerie, empty quiet, unlike anything I had ever heard. Suddenly I longed for the familiar sounds of home. I would never get used to this place.

Price slowed at the mailbox, checking the number against the document in his hand. Having confirmed we had the right house, he pulled into the driveway of a stately white clapboard farmhouse.

The house had a porch on both the main and second levels, two white railings running the entire width of the facade. A large American flag hung down from the second level and rippled gently in the breeze. Several smaller flags staked into the lawn created a pathway from the porch steps to the driveway running alongside the house. Bunches of colorful flowers bloomed from whiskey barrels at the top of the drive.

"We made it," Price said, turning off the engine. He popped the trunk, where my suitcase waited.

I knew I had to get out of the car, but my legs wouldn't move. I stared up at the house, unable to picture myself inside it. I thought of my real home. Last year as a birthday gift—or, more accurately, to apologize for failing to register me for driver's ed because she was too busy getting high, and the timing had just happened to work out nicely—my mom had hired a decorator to refinish my bedroom. I got to pick everything. White-painted bookshelves, a vintage chandelier, Tiffany-blue walls, and a Victorian mahogany desk we'd bought on our last trip to New York. My diary was still locked inside the top drawer. My life was back there. Everything was back there.

As we climbed out of the car, a woman rose from the porch swing and descended the steps, the heels of her red cowboy boots coming down hard on the weathered wood.

"You found the place," she called out. She wore jeans tucked into the boots, and a denim shirt with a few buttons open at the top. Her platinum white hair hit just above the shoulders, and she studied us with snapping blue eyes. "Just enjoying a glass of lemonade and listening to the cicadas. Can I offer you a drink?"

"Now, that's an offer I can't refuse," Price said. "Stella?"

I glanced between them. They watched me with careful, braced smiles. Feeling my head begin to spin, I blinked a few times, trying to right the world. The woman's red boots began to swirl like a kaleidoscope, and I knew I'd lost the fight. Suddenly I was back in Philadelphia, a man bleeding out on the floor of our library, human tissue splattered on the wall behind him. I felt the weight of my mom's head cradled in my lap, strange, hysterical sobs breaking from my throat. I heard police sirens wailing up the street and my own pulse roaring in my ears.

"Perhaps you'd like me to show you to your room, Stella?" the woman said, jerking me out of the flashback.

I felt myself sway, and Price caught me by the elbow. "Let's get her inside. Long day of travel. A full night's rest will do a world of good."

Regaining some of my senses, I ripped out of his hold. "Don't."

"Stella—"

I whirled on him. "What do you want from me? Do you want me to drink lemonade and act like any of this is normal? I don't want to be here. I didn't ask for this. Everything I know is gone. I'll—I'll never forgive her for this!" The words came choking out before I realized it. My whole body felt tight and slippery. I swiped at my eyes, refusing to cry. Not until I was alone and could risk falling apart. I pressed my fingernails deep into my palm to draw the pain out of my heart and focus it somewhere manageable.

Before I dragged my luggage up to the house, I saw the woman's—Carmina's—mouth pinch at the edges, and Price flashed her an apologetic grimace as if to say there was no accounting for teenage behavior. I didn't care what they thought. If they believed I was selfish and difficult, they were probably right. And if I made this summer a living hell for Carmina, maybe she'd let me move out early and live on my own. It wasn't the worst idea I'd ever had.

Price trotted up the porch steps to hold the screen door for me, and Carmina said, "Maybe we'll put off a tour of the house until tomorrow. Bed might be just the thing."

"I can't be the only one who's dog-tired," Price readily agreed.

I wasn't tired, but I wanted to close myself behind a door just as badly as they did, so I didn't argue. I didn't care if it made me look compliant. Carmina would find out soon enough that even though the Justice Department had given me a cover story and a new life, I wasn't going to pretend like anything about this was okay with me.

Inside, the house smelled like rosewater. Dainty flower–printed wallpaper peeled away from the walls, and I caught a glimpse of the sofas in the living room—battered blue corduroy. There was an antlered head of some species of deer mounted above the fire-place. I'd never seen anything so backwoods or tacky.

Carmina led the way up the worn staircase. Nail holes pitted the wall going up, but the portraits had been taken down, and for the first time, I wondered briefly about Carmina. Who she was. Why she lived alone. If she'd had a family, and what had happened to them. Instantly, I shut off the questions. This woman meant nothing to me. She was a government-issued stand-in for my mom until I turned eighteen at the end of August and could legally live on my own.

At the top of the stairs, Carmina pushed open a door. "This is where you'll sleep. Fresh towels on the dresser, basic toiletries in the bathroom next door down. Tomorrow we can swing by the store and pick up anything I missed. Breakfast's at seven sharp. Any dietary restrictions I need to know about? Not allergic to peanuts, are you?"

"No."

She gave a satisfied nod. "See you in the morning, then. Sleep tight."

Carmina closed the door and I lowered myself onto the edge of the twin bed. The springs squeaked an off-key note. The window was open, letting in a warm, muggy breeze, and I wondered why Carmina wasn't running the AC. She wasn't going to leave the house windows open all night, was she? Was that safe?

I shut and locked the window and yanked the blue cotton curtains shut, but right away the hot, stuffy air felt suffocating. I lifted my hair to fan the back of my neck. Then I peeled out of my clothes and flopped back on the bed.

The room was small, barely wide enough to hold the bed and an oak dresser. The pitched roof made the walls seem to squeeze even tighter around me. My eyes traced the patchwork of blue rectangles on the faded ceiling where posters, now gone, had preserved the original paint color. Blue paint, blue curtains, blue sheets. And a dusty baseball glove on the top shelf of the open closet. A boy must have lived here. I wondered where he'd gone.

Somewhere far away, surely. As soon as I turned eighteen, I was going far away from this place too.

Reaching into the front pouch of my suitcase, I pulled out a small bundle of letters. Contraband. I wasn't supposed to bring anything from my old life, any proof that I had come from Philadelphia, and I felt a thrill at this small rebellion—accidental as it was. Call me sentimental, but lately I'd been carrying Reed's letters with me everywhere. The more unstable my home life had become, the more comforting I'd found them. When I felt alone, they reminded me that I had Reed. He cared about me. He had my back. Up until three nights ago, I'd stored the letters in my purse. I'd moved them to my suitcase to keep them from being discovered. Some of the letters were recent, but others were from as long ago as two years, when Reed and I first started dating. Vowing to ration them, I took one from the top and returned the others to their hiding place.

ESTELLA,

DON'T KNOW IF YOU'VE EVER HAD SOMEONE LEAVE A NOTE UNDER YOUR WINDSHIELD WIPER, BUT IT SEEMED LIKE THE KIND OF THING YOU'D FIND ROMANTIC.

REMEMBER THAT NIGHT ON THE TRAIN, WHEN WE

FIRST MET? I NEVER TOLD YOU, BUT I TOOK A CANDID PICTURE OF YOU. IT WAS BEFORE YOU LEFT YOUR PHONE ON YOUR SEAT AND I CHASED YOU DOWN TO GIVE IT BACK (HERO THAT I AM). ANYWAY, I WAS PRETENDING TO TEXT SO YOU WOULDN'T KNOW I TOOK YOUR PICTURE. I STILL HAVE IT ON MY PHONE.

I LOVE YOU. NOW DO ME A FAVOR AND DESTROY THIS SO I CAN KEEP MY DIGNITY INTACT.

xREED

I pressed the letter to my chest, feeling my breathing slow. *Please let me see him again soon,* I silently begged. I didn't know how long the letters would tide me over. But tonight's letter had done its job; the loneliness drained from my body, leaving a deep physical exhaustion.

I rolled onto my side, expecting sleep to come quickly. Instead, I grew more aware of the quiet stillness. It was an empty sound, waiting to be filled. My imagination wasted no time inventing explanations for the soft creak of the walls, shrinking as the day's heat wore off, or the occasional thud on the floorboards. I couldn't shake the picture of Danny Balando's dark eyes as I slipped into restless sleep.

3

THE RUMBLE OF A LAWN MOWER CARRIED THROUGH the bedroom window, which I'd opened in the middle of the night after waking dizzy with heat and bathed in sweat. The whine of the engine grew nearer, passing right under the window, then droned to the far edge of the lawn. I cracked one bleary eye and found the clock on the nightstand.

Annoyance and outrage shot through me. Kicking free of the sheets, I stuck my head out the window and shouted, "Hey! Check the time!"

The guy pushing the mower didn't hear me. I slammed the rickety window shut. It muffled the noise fractionally.

I flipped the guy off. He didn't see it. The first rays of dawn were behind him, illuminating thousands of flecks of pollen and gnats buzzing around his head like a halo as he pushed the mower across Carmina's yard. The toes of his boots were stained green from the grass, and he wore a tan cowboy hat low over his eyes. He had earbuds in, and I watched his lips move to the lyrics of a song.

I dropped a nightshirt over my head and stepped into the hall. "Carmina?" I padded to the end of the hall and knocked on her bedroom door.

The door cracked. "What is it? What's the matter?"

It was so dark in her room, I couldn't make out her face. But I heard the anxiety in her voice and could hear her fumbling for something, clothes most likely, on the floor.

"Someone's mowing your yard."

She dropped the clothes and straightened. "And?"

"It's only five."

"You woke me up to tell me the time?"

"I can't sleep. It's too loud."

Her mattress springs creaked as she settled back into bed. She let out a sigh of exasperation. "Chet Falconer. Lives down the road. Wants to finish work before it's too hot—good for him. Don't you have one of those little music gadgets? Turn on a song and you won't hear a thing."

"I wasn't allowed to bring my iPhone."

"An iPhone isn't the only thing round here that plays music. Try the bottom drawer of the dresser in your room. Now, go back to bed, Stella."

She leaned out of bed and pushed the door closed in my face.

My back went up, and I walked stiffly to my room. I cast an evil eye out the window, watching as Chet Falconer finished another row and swung the mower around. From this angle, I couldn't see his face, but a small patch of sweat soaked through the front of his white T-shirt, and when he paused to wipe his cheek on his sleeve, the hem of his shirt hitched up, revealing a taut stomach. His arms were tan and muscular, and he tapped his thumb against the mower's handlebar to keep time with whatever music he was listening to. He'd obviously started the morning with an entire pot of coffee. Since I couldn't say the same, I just scowled at him. I was tempted to open the window and yell down something obscene, but between the earbuds and the mower, there was no way he'd hear.

I sprawled facedown on the bed and folded the pillow tightly over my head. No luck. The lawnmower continued to whine through the windowpane like an angry insect. Taking Carmina's advice, I jerked open the bottom drawer of the dresser and nearly choked on my laughter.

A Sony Walkman, complete with AM/FM radio and cassette player. I blew dust off the surface, thinking I hadn't traveled to Nebraska—I'd traveled into the previous century.

Sorting through the cassette tapes littering the bottom of the drawer, I read the handwritten labels. Poison, Whitesnake, Van Halen, Metallica.

Did Carmina have a son? Had this been his bedroom before he'd bolted—wisely—out of Thunder Basin?

I chose Van Halen, because it was the only tape that didn't need to be rewound. Hitting play, I snuggled under the sheet and turned up the volume until I could no longer hear the rumble of Chet Falconer's lawn mower.

I wandered down to the kitchen at ten. I followed the smell of bacon and eggs to find my way. I couldn't remember the last time I'd had bacon and eggs. Disneyland, probably, when I was seven, with Mickey Mouse–shaped pancakes. The idea of eating a meal at a table set with real dishes, let alone having someone cook for me, was unfathomable. My go-to breakfast was a skinny latte and whole-grain oatmeal from Starbucks. I ate in my car, on the way to school.

As I entered the kitchen, I found the table cleared and the food gone. Through the screen door leading to the backyard, I could see Carmina on her knees in the vegetable garden, pulling weeds. Judging by the large pile beside her, she'd been out there a while.

"I think I missed breakfast," I said, crossing the yard to her.

"Think so," she said without looking up.

"Did you save any for me?"

"Last I checked, bacon and eggs don't taste good cold."

"Okay, I get it. You snooze, you lose," I said with a shrug. If she thought she was going to make a point by starving me, she was pretty inexperienced at parenthood. I could do just fine on a mug of coffee. Wouldn't be the first time. "When's lunch?"

"After we drive you around to fill out summer job applications."

"I don't want a job."

"School's out, so most of the good jobs have been snatched up, but we'll find you something," she went on.

"I don't want a job," I repeated more firmly. I'd never had a job. My family wasn't old money—we didn't live in a country estate on the Main Line, and I didn't dress effortlessly like Jackie O.—but we weren't living paycheck to paycheck, either. My mom had been a debutante in Knoxville, and while she'd burned through what could be called her dowry, it was important to her to keep up appearances. It just would not do to have me seen in the workforce. My dad was a principal in a venture capital firm, and after he divorced my mom more than two years ago, he left her with enough money that she didn't have to work. Up until a few days ago, I'd lived with my mom in the suburbs, in a beautiful gray fieldstone cottage that sat at the end of a long, tree-lined cul-de-sac. Circumstances as they were, I'd never had the motivation or desire to break a sweat for minimum wage.

And I definitely wasn't used to taking orders. My mom was more like a roommate than a parent; we were often ships passing in the night. I hadn't had someone tell me what to do in years.

Carmina sat back on her haunches and looked at me squarely. "What're you gonna do all summer, child? Sit around and feel sorry for yourself? Not under my roof. Time a girl your age learned to look after herself."

I ran my tongue over my teeth, checking my words. If Carmina wanted a fight, I could give her one. But if she, an adult, was baiting me into a fight, it stood to reason that she had an agenda. Maybe she thought if I could just yell and scream and get all my pain out in the open, I'd suddenly become a new person. One who wanted to be in Thunder Basin for the summer. One who wanted to make Carmina's life easy.

"All right," I said, forcing myself to speak calmly. "What kind of job do you think I can get?"

Carmina frowned, proving I'd guessed right. She'd expected me to fight back, to let my anger out. She'd hoped I would. I had news for her: The cop had lost her edge in retirement. She couldn't read me. And I couldn't think of a bigger victory.

"Well," she said thoughtfully at last, "there's food service. I hear the Sundown Diner is hiring carhops. Or you could work in the cornfields; they're always looking for help. But it's hard, hot work with long hours, and the pay isn't anything to smile about."

"Okay," I said, still cool and collected. "I'll take a shower and get ready."

By the time I'd climbed the stairs to my room, I'd changed my mind about the job. I'd probably hate it, but it couldn't be worse than sitting around the house all day with Carmina. And since I got the feeling she expected me, a bratty teen with an attitude problem, to fail at manual labor, I was invested in proving her wrong. How hard could a summer job be? Flipping burgers was gross, but hardly rocket science. And if I got the diner job, it would have air conditioning. Surely Nebraska had embraced that modern convenience.

I found it a touch ironic that I, the proverbial princess from the castle high on the hill, was being forced to take the disguise I least wanted—that of a poor, hardworking servant girl. I wondered if Deputy Price and the rest of his friends at the DOJ had planned this—to give me a heaping spoonful of humble pie. They probably found it amusing. *Go ahead, boys. Laugh all you want.*

When this is over, you'll still be wearing cheap suits and \
scum of the earth. Meanwhile, the government will have to \
family's accounts, I'll have my money back, and this humiliating \
will be nothing more than a distant memory.

A half hour later I emerged from the bathroom with damp
hair and the cheap smell of Ivory clinging to my skin. I wore cut-
offs and a basic white tee. I'd skipped putting on makeup, except
for a quick dab of tinted moisturizer and a swipe of lip gloss.
Although it was so humid out, I hardly needed either.

Carmina had moved her weed-pulling to the front yard. She
knelt over the flower bed at the bottom of the driveway, tossing
weeds into a bucket. When the porch door slammed shut behind
me, she looked up from beneath her wide-brimmed straw hat.

"What kind of job are you hoping for dressed like that?" she
asked, rocking back on her heels to examine me.

"Don't care."

"You don't care, you're gonna get stuck with the cards at the
bottom of the deck."

"Somebody has to get them."

"You've sure got the attitude down, don't you? Get in the truck,
then."

An old Ford truck with peeling blue paint was parked in the
driveway, and after wrenching the heavy passenger door open, I
climbed in. The insides of both doors were rusted over and the
seat covers had split open to reveal foam cushioning. The glove
box lay open. I tried to shut it, but the securing mechanism must
have been broken, because the door flopped open in the same

position I'd found it. I rolled my eyes and hoped the next surprise wouldn't be a rat darting across my foot.

"Really hoping you loan me this clunker," I breathed cynically as Carmina hoisted herself behind the wheel.

"Buy your own truck. That's what a paycheck's for." She pumped the gas pedal, cranked the ignition, and the engine growled to life. "Bought this truck working my first job. Felt good to be an independent woman. Wouldn't dream of robbing you of the same satisfaction."

"What year's the truck?"

"'79."

I whistled. "You're older than I thought."

"That what you think?" She laughed long and heartily. "Girl, didn't anybody tell you you're only as old as you feel? Judging by your long, sour face, I'm not the one who's got something to worry about."

As we drove down the gravel road that led to the paved street that would eventually take us into town, we passed a two-story redbrick house shaded by a grove of cottonwood trees. There were hanging flowerpots on the porch, and the architecture had the charm of, and potential for, a country bed and breakfast.

At that moment, Chet Falconer rounded the side of the house carrying a rusted toolbox in one hand and a ladder in the other. I still couldn't see his face, but I recognized the low-tipped cowboy hat and white T-shirt.

"How old is he?" I asked.

"Nineteen." After a beat, Carmina's eyes darted to mine, as if she'd suddenly perceived something important. "Oh, no, you don't. Don't you get any ideas. That boy has enough trouble."

"What kind of trouble?"

"There's only one kind of trouble—the kind you stay away from." Carmina said it in a way that let me know she wasn't going to give away more, no matter how hard I pressed. Fine by me. I could be patient. What she probably didn't realize was that in telling me nothing, she'd made certain I would dig deeper into our resident man of mystery.

I watched Chet's arms flex as he hoisted the toolbox onto the porch and braced the ladder against the side of the house. One thing was for sure, he had a nice body. Maybe country boys knew how to work it.

"He does a lot of home maintenance for a nineteen-year-old," I said. "His parents must be slave drivers."

Carmina cast me a disproving look. "His parents are dead. He's man of the house. If he doesn't take care of the place, no one will."

I couldn't believe he had the entire house to himself. In three months, I could be like him. Living alone, in the city of my choice. I couldn't go back to Philly, but there were other places I liked. Boston was at the top of the list. "Where's he going to college in the fall?"

"He isn't."

"He's going to stay here in Thunder Basin and mow lawns for the rest of his life?"

Her eyes broke from the road to meet mine. I saw a flash of something in them. Anger, sorrow. A glimmer of pain. "Problem with that?" she said coolly.

"Yes. It's a loser thing to do. He should get as far away from this place as possible and get a real life, a real job."

Carmina didn't answer, just kept her gaze forward, but I knew she'd understood my insult perfectly. Being a cop in a sleepy town like Thunder Basin wasn't a real way of life. But the fact that she sat there and took the snub with nothing more than a resolute upward tilt of her chin made me somehow feel like she'd won this round.

We spent the next two hours popping in and out of fast-food joints and greasy diners dotting the seven blocks that made up Thunder Basin's downtown. Most of the buildings were either redbrick or whitewashed cinder block. A bulbous water tower and a few grain silos made up the rest of the cityscape. Nailed to one storefront was a handmade sign that read HAIRCUTS, 7.5 OWED. *The tip alone on my usual cut is three times that*, I thought dryly.

I filled out an application at every restaurant, leaving it with the manager. I gave my fake name and my fake Social Security number, which matched the details in my fake passport. Carmina helped me fill out the address and phone number where I could be reached. I checked the boxes for waitress, dishwasher, and hostess—I didn't care what job they gave me. I'd hate them all. I'd spend the next three months doing what I had to, and then I was out of here.

On the ride back, Carmina said, "Anything strike your fancy?"

I stared out the window at the haze of green rushing past in a blur. There was no rise and fall of the road, no hills to be climbed or valleys to dip into. The road was a straight shot, with tidy rows of plants walling me in on either side and a dome of blue trapping me from overhead. I felt like an ant under a glass. Hot, hopeless, doomed. "Nope."

"You should have put on slacks and a blouse."

"Nobody calls them slacks anymore."

"They make a better impression than hacked-off jeans that show half your leg."

I ran my fingers seductively up my thigh. "More than half, Carmina. A lot more than half. Besides, I'm not trying to impress anyone."

She turned to face me, eyes widening theatrically. "You don't say."

AFTER DINNER, CARMINA WENT TO BIBLE STUDY.
I was left at the house, stuck. I didn't have a car. I could only travel as far as my own two feet saw fit. It occurred to me that if I did get a job, Carmina would have to provide me with transportation. It wasn't like I could walk the five miles into town and back. At this point, I'd be happy with a bike. More and more, I was becoming convinced that being employed wasn't such a bad way to pass the summer.

I watched Carmina's truck bounce down the gravel road leading away from the farmhouse. Dropping the curtain in my bedroom window, I headed downstairs to watch TV. If nothing else, it would be cooler on the main level. After TV, I could sit on the porch swing, lick a Popsicle, and listen to the coyotes. Because there definitely wasn't anything else to do.

I climbed down the flight of stairs, and just like that, I was tumbling down into the past.

The traumatic flashbacks were stronger than memories. I wasn't blacking out—I was conscious—but the flashbacks eclipsed my real vision. They felt very real. And they always began in the same place. It was after midnight. I'd broken curfew again. Not wanting to risk waking my mom (Who was I kidding? She was probably passed out), I parked my car one house down from our gray fieldstone. Oddly, there was a white Honda Civic already parked on the curb. The Foggs never left cars on the street. And they didn't drive a Honda Civic.

Shrugging off the oddity, I hurried around the side of the house, rooting in my bag for keys.

As I crept up the back steps, I could smell our boxwood gardens and the newly blossomed trees. Even though I made it a point to never be home, and to avoid my mom when I was, I loved our house, especially the yard. It was my favorite escape. Lounging in the gardens, hidden in the shade of old trees, I daydreamed to music by Ben Howard, the Oh Hellos, or Boy.

I let myself in. The kitchen light didn't turn on. Nor did the dining room chandelier. It never occurred to me that something might be wrong. I assumed my mom had forgotten to replace the bulbs. In the dark, I felt my way toward the staircase. My footsteps were light and quick. If I was lucky, I could avoid my mom until morning.

As I crossed in front of the library's beveled glass doors, I saw her slumped in one of the leather wingback chairs. Moonlight filtered through the shutters, casting her in waxy, white light. Her party favors were spread on the side table, a colorful concoction of pills. I started to feel disgust—

And then—

And then my eyes were drawn to the shadows behind her. I stared at the man's crumpled body in a daze. His limbs were sprawled in funny, permanent angles. I walked closer. I didn't want to, but I couldn't stop. I walked until I stood over him, his vacant brown eyes staring up at me.

A neat hole was blown through his forehead.

I came out of the flashback panting. I fumbled for the switch at the bottom of Carmina's staircase, relieved when light immediately chased away the darkness.

The dead man was in a casket, six feet below grass. And Danny Balando was in jail. He couldn't hurt me. My steps to Thunder Basin had been erased; he'd never find Stella Gordon.

With a hollow shiver, I climbed upstairs and pulled one of Reed's letters from my suitcase. I needed him here with me, reassuring me everything was going to be okay, but tonight I would have to settle for his words. It was infuriating that the Justice Department could rip us apart. They were making it possible for me to be with my mom again, so why not Reed? If I'd had a say, I would have chosen to live with him. It wouldn't have even been a choice.

Estella,

I got in a fight with my dad tonight. It was bad. Now that I'm 17, he's pushing me to enlist. I've been telling him for years that I'm not following in his footsteps, but he refuses to hear. I came to your house to spend the night, but you're not here and you're not answering your phone. Call me when you get this. I hope it doesn't bother you that I come over all the time. I hate being at my place. When I'm there, my dad won't leave me alone. After our fight, he told me if I left he wouldn't let me back in. Well, I left. I don't know what's going to happen now. I used to wish my mom would stand up to him, but she never will. She always retreats, hiding out in bed, using her fibromyalgia as an excuse to not get involved. It's a disease, but it's also her coping mechanism. If she has it to deal with, she doesn't have to deal with us. I wish I had enough money to get my own place. Someday I will. And I'll take you with me.

xReed

It hurt to remember our plans. We were going to run away and start a new life together. Now I didn't know if I'd see him again. He could be in Kentucky or Kansas. I'd never know. Unless I went looking for him.

And I could go looking, because I knew how to find him.

Deputy Price had made it very clear that I should never, under any circumstances, attempt to contact anyone from my old life. Danny Balando and the dangerous men he employed would never give up looking for me. The only way they'd find me was if I broke the rules.

I knew contacting Reed was breaking the rules, but he wasn't in Philly anymore. He was in WITSEC—witness protection. His ties to the city had been erased, and if the U.S. marshals had done half as good a job making him vanish as they had me, I wasn't going to tip off Danny Balando's men to my location by contacting Reed.

I hadn't seen a computer in Carmina's house, and I wouldn't have used it anyway. If I went through with this, I couldn't leave a trail. Earlier in town I'd seen signs for the public library. It was too far to walk there tonight, but I was guessing Carmina stored a bike somewhere in that weathered barn behind her house. I didn't know how long Bible study lasted, but it was safe to assume I had at least an hour.

Swatting mosquitoes as I jogged across the backyard, I swung open the barn doors and glanced around the cavernous space. The air smelled of mildew and hay. And gasoline. I was pretty sure the gasoline smell came from the large automobile hidden under a canvas cover at the back of the barn. I lifted the canvas and saw that Carmina was keeping an old Ford Mustang on hand. The paint was an ugly shade of brown, and there were a handful of dead hornets on the dash, but I wasn't feeling picky. What were the odds I could get it to start?

Carmina had left the keys on the driver's seat, which made finding out a whole lot easier.

After a few tries, the Mustang's engine grumbled to life and the smell of burning oil filled the air. Carmina had forbidden me from borrowing her truck. But she'd never told me I couldn't drive the Mustang.

I knew the way into town—it was a straight shot once I turned onto the paved street at the end of Carmina's gravel road. In town, I found the library easily. There were only three other cars in the parking lot, so I had my pick of stalls. It felt strange not to circle the lot and drive the surrounding streets multiple times, hunting for a space. Back home, I rarely drove into the city, for that reason alone. It was far more convenient to take a train.

At the front desk, I applied for a library card. After checking my passport photo and address, the librarian gave me a temporary card. My real card would arrive in the mail within two weeks. Carmina wouldn't suspect anything—I'd tell her I liked to read, which wasn't a lie.

I found a vacant computer and logged on to the Internet. Soon after Reed and I had started dating, he set up a private e-mail address that we both had access to. Instead of e-mailing each other, we wrote drafts for the other person to find. Each draft got deleted after it was read. Reed had read an article about spies using the technique, and while I thought it was a little over the top, I didn't argue. His dad was military—army. Your upbringing shaped you. We'd used the e-mail regularly at first . . . and then totally forgot about it.

With a few quick keystrokes, I signed in to the private e-mail— Phillies6o@gmail.com. The drafts folder was empty.

I tried not to feel deflated. I'd expected to find a new message, especially since he'd reminded me about the secret e-mail account yesterday morning before we left the motel. Wanting to let him know I was okay, I typed a brief e-mail.

> Arrived safe and sound. Well, maybe not the last
> part. You should see this place. I'd almost rather
> be dead. Miss you. Let me know you're OK.

I read over the words carefully, double-checking that they were too bland to pose any threat to me, on the wild chance anyone intercepted them, then typed a quick P.S.

> P.S. They put my mom in detox. Now taking bets
> on how that will turn out.

I saved the draft and logged out.

I blew out some air. Time to be patient. A virtue I'd never loved, much less embraced.

5

AS I WALKED OUT OF THE LIBRARY, THE SKY WAS black velvet and diamonds. In Philly, nighttime meant one thing: worrying about my mother, who she was with, what she was doing, and if I was going to have to go out and look for her. I stood still a moment, cautiously testing this new darkness. It was so quiet, so uncomplicated, so lovely, it seemed ridiculous to be afraid of it. The warm air tingled on my skin. It smelled fresh and greenly fragrant. The darkness offered relief from the high, hot sun that had stung my eyes all day. It painted the landscape in shadows. I could almost forget the cornfields and the blue, blue sky—I could almost forget I was here.

The parking lot had one remaining car—Carmina's Mustang. I didn't know where the teens of Thunder Basin hung out after sundown, but the library obviously wasn't it. I would have cruised the seven blocks of the main drag looking for signs of nightlife, but Carmina would likely be coming home from Bible study soon. She couldn't know what I'd done tonight.

I turned the Mustang's ignition. The engine made a low chugging sound, but refused to fully catch. I pumped the gas and tried again. More growling and whirring, but the engine wouldn't turn over. I had the windows rolled down, and the car belched thick clouds of foul-smelling smoke. Not a good sign.

I got out and walked around the car, but nothing looked out of the ordinary. The stupid thing had started fine twenty minutes ago. What was the matter now?

"Need a hand?"

I swiveled around. Through the darkness, I made out a tall rangy form wearing Levi's, pointed boots, and a fitted black T-shirt. His dark hair curled around his ears, and he tipped his cowboy hat up, shooting me an easy smile.

"Mind if I have a look?" he continued, gesturing at the car.

I squeezed the Mustang's keys in my hand. I had no reason to trust him. In hindsight, I should have parked under a streetlight. Not that there was anyone around to see, if he decided to drag me into an alley and slit my throat.

"Nope, I've got it covered," I said, striving for politely disinterested. "She usually takes a few tries to start."

He rapped his knuckles affectionately against the Mustang's side panel. "Old cars. Either you love 'em or hate 'em."

"Got that right." I angled myself behind the steering wheel, hinting that I wasn't in a chatty mood. "Thanks for checking on me, neighbor," I added, since it sounded like a small-town thing to say. Probably best to act like a local, so he'd think there'd be someone to miss me if he did drag me into the alley.

I tried the engine again. More coughing and sputtering, but no success.

"Sure you don't want me to give it a try?" he asked, his tone still friendly. And maybe a touch amused.

"Just because I'm a girl doesn't mean I can't start my own car," I said, mildly enough, but my words were underscored with annoyance. Please go away, I silently urged him.

"Your car? Huh. That's interesting."

"What? Because I'm a girl, I can't be into muscle cars?" I challenged.

"Not what I said."

I cranked the key harder. Same low rumble from the engine. It was close to starting, but I couldn't push it over the edge. Carmina was going to kill me. I didn't know how much longer I had until she got back, but it couldn't be long.

I let go of a resigned breath and pinched the bridge of my nose. "If I give you the keys, are you going to slit my throat with them and dump my body in the alley?"

"Wouldn't be smart to tell you if I was."

Instead of laughing, I glared up at him.

He grinned, clearly pleased with his joke. "You're not from around here, are you?"

"What makes you say that?" I wondered if he was going to

launch into the timeworn cliché of how everyone knows everyone else in a small town.

Instead, he said, "Last year I sold this car to my neighbor."

Suddenly I had a bad feeling.

"Carmina Songster," he recalled. "Are you going to tell me why you're driving her car, or should I let you explain yourself to the police?"

Crap.

I pushed out of the Mustang, standing up to him. He had several inches on me, and up close like this, I could see that his eyes were a bright jewel blue. Somewhere between turquoise and sea glass. "It's not what it looks like."

"That's a relief, because it looks like auto theft. What I'm trying to figure out is why you stopped at the library. You're a few blocks short of the interstate. Shouldn't you be hightailing it out of town?"

"I live with Carmina now."

He gave a snort, instantly rejecting the idea. "Carmina hasn't had a visitor in the nineteen years I've been her neighbor, and I already know all her family. So 'fess up. Who are you, really?"

"She's my—foster mom," I said flatly. It was the first time I'd had to use my cover story. If he pressed for more information, I was supposed to tell him how I'd been living in foster homes since my mom died, but I prayed he wouldn't dig deeper. I didn't want to talk about Stella. I was sick of her already. I wanted to go home. To my real home. And while I was at it, I never wanted to see this backwoods wasteland again.

He shook his head distrustfully. "Carmina? A foster parent? I don't believe it. How old are you?"

"Eighteen in August." Three tiny months until I earned my independence. Might as well have been an eternity.

"Why would Carmina take in a seventeen-year-old girl?" he puzzled aloud.

"Maybe she's lonely."

He snorted again. "That lone wolf? Nah. Something isn't adding up. When did you get into town?"

"Last night."

"What's your name?"

"Stella Gordon." I felt glass in my throat when I said it. I hated the name. It was like I was talking about someone else, which I guess I was.

"How long have you been in foster care?" he went on, evidently trying to make sense of my story.

"Since my mom died."

"I'm sorry to hear that."

I shrugged. I felt nothing. My mom was alive, but she was as good as dead to me.

"Where did you come from?"

"Tennessee," I lied. "Knoxville, Tennessee. Ever been there?"

"Can't say I have."

Neither had I. Guess this meant I could say what I wanted about Knoxville and neither of us would be any wiser for it.

And then he said, "But I would have expected a different accent. Yours sounds . . . East Coast."

"Oh," I said dismissively, giving myself an extra second to think up an excuse. "That's because my dad grew up in the Mid-Atlantic. I took his accent more than my mom's."

To my relief, he seemed done grilling me and extended his hand. "Welcome to Thunder Basin, Stella. I'm Chet Falconer."

I frowned. "The same Chet Falconer who mows Carmina's lawn?"

A smile twitched his lips. "She mentioned me?"

"You woke me up at five this morning! See these bags under my eyes? You can take credit!"

"Your eyes look perfectly fine to me."

Before I could wonder if he'd given me a line, he went on, "Tell you what. I'll make you a deal. I'll get this old battleship running, but I need something in return. There's a diner around the corner with two people at a table in the back. One of them is a punk trying to look tough in a leather motorcycle jacket," he added darkly. "I want you to grab a table close enough to eavesdrop, order a cheeseburger so you look like you belong, then come out and tell me what they talked about."

"I see. You want me to spy on your girlfriend? If you think she's cheating, she is."

He ignored me. "I'll have the car running by the time you get back."

"No deal. I'm in a hurry. I need it running now."

"Well, this is gonna take a few."

I blew out some air. "Fine. But you're paying for the cheese-burger."

He gave a sigh of exaggerated patience, then slapped a ten-dollar bill in my palm. "Eat slowly. I want to know everything they say."

"Even the heartbreaking stuff? The parts where she talks about how awful your breath smells and how your mouth overproduces saliva when you kiss?"

He pulled his cowboy hat off and whacked me on the butt. Actually whacked *me* on the butt. "Get going before you miss everything. And I don't have bad breath. Or that other thing."

"You'd better have this car working by the time I come out," I warned.

"Yeah? Or what?"

"Or I'm gonna make you buy me a second cheeseburger. And fries and a shake." I didn't sound ruffled, but if I didn't beat Carmina back, she'd probably make me sit in jail overnight to teach me a lesson. Plus, she'd make sure I never got my hands on the Mustang again. And I couldn't let her do that, because I needed a way to get to the library. I was going to check the e-mail account as often as I could. Reed would e-mail soon and we could begin to formulate a plan to get back together after my birthday. He was nineteen and could legally live on his own; we just had to wait for me to turn eighteen.

"Hold that thought until you've tried the first burger," Chet cautioned with a pirate glint in his eyes.

"What's that supposed to mean?"

"Let's just say the county health department isn't what you'd call fastidious. Fact, jury's still out on whether we have a health department."

I waved his crumpled ten-dollar bill in the air. "Then I'll pass on food and consider this my tip for my stellar espionage skills."

Turning on my heel, I strolled to the end of the block and looked both ways down the street. The Sundown Diner was on the bottom floor of the next building. I recognized it from that morning's job hunt. The outside lights were on now, moths fluttering madly around the bulbs. A blue-and-white striped awning extended over the door.

I swung through the entrance and made a quick scan of the place. Business was scarce tonight. Only two tables in use. A mother with two small boys was seated in the booth next to the jukebox. At the back of the diner, two guys sat hunched across a table, deep in conversation.

Guess I'd been wrong about Chet's girlfriend. He was having me spy on two guys. The one wearing the leather biker jacket looked about my age, maybe a year younger. His brown hair hung in his eyes, which kept shifting nervously around. His companion was several years older, with a beer belly that strained against a Journey concert T-shirt. He sported thick red sideburns and a black head bandanna, and he looked like a hybrid between a Hell's Angel and a redneck. I immediately knew I didn't like or trust him.

"Just the one tonight?" the hostess asked me, fishing through her stack of menus.

"Do you mind if I sit in the back corner booth?" I flashed a smile. "My lucky seat."

"Sure thing, hon."

I settled into the booth. I was close enough that I should have been able to overhear the guys at the next table, but they'd stopped talking when I'd taken my seat. To encourage them to let me fade into the background, I pulled Carmina's Walkman out of my handbag, set it on the table, and inserted the cheap plastic headphones into my ears. *Don't mind me, boys, I'm in my own little world. Now, start talking, and make it fast. I'm on a tight schedule.*

The younger of the two was the first to talk.

"I've got a few grand coming from my parents," he confessed uneasily.

"Define 'few.'"

"Four."

The Hell's Angel scratched the scruff on his neck thoughtfully. "It's not a lot, but it should be enough."

"Once I get you the money, how long until I'm in business?"

"Two weeks. Gotta transport the goods from Colorado."

The younger guy nodded, thinking it over. "Okay. I'm in."

"Not so fast. How soon can you get me the cash?"

Just then a waitress ambled over, standing between me and their table. "Anything to drink?"

"Water," I said, trying to keep one ear trained on the guys' conversation.

"Questions about the menu?"

I hadn't opened the menu. I already knew what I wanted. No matter how hard they tried, they couldn't screw up fries. They were cooked in hot grease. Any lingering bacteria would be killed off.

"A large order of fries, please."

"That it?"

I nodded, figuring I deserved to keep the rest of Chet's money, and she sauntered back to the kitchen.

One table over, the Hell's Angel and the boy were wrapping things up. The boy was on his cell phone texting, and the Hell's Angel was scrounging through his wallet for cash to pay his tab. I knew Chet wouldn't like it if I returned with next to nothing to report, but he'd have to deal. He'd told me to eavesdrop. I couldn't help it if the conversation only lasted a couple of minutes.

"I'll call you when I have the funds," the boy in the biker jacket said, sliding out of his chair and pocketing his phone. As he rose to his feet, he must have sensed me watching, because his eyes flicked in my direction. His eyebrows drew together suspiciously at the sight of me, and I immediately picked up my menu, looking absorbed in reading.

He left, followed by the Hell's Angel, and I decided rather than wait around for my fries, I'd go see if Chet had upheld his end of our bargain. I paid for the fries at the register and hoped my waitress enjoyed them.

In the library parking lot, I found Chet bent under the Mustang's hood. He looked over his shoulder as he heard me approach. Even in the darkness, I could see his hands were smudged with grease.

"Well?" he asked expectantly.

"The kid's parents are giving him four thousand dollars, and he's going into business with the Hell's Angel."

Chet swore under his breath. "What else did they say?"

"Not much. It was a short conversation. The kid hopes to have his business running shortly."

"Over my dead body."

"Just tell me you got the car working."

"Yeah, it was the carburetor. I've got it propped open with a pencil to let air in. See if the engine starts now."

I swung behind the wheel and turned the ignition. Right away, the engine purred to life. I was so relieved, I could have kissed Chet.

Instead I said, "What's the fastest way back to Carmina's?"

Chet dropped the hood and brushed his hands clean. "She doesn't know you took the car, does she?"

I bit my lip. "Can this be our little secret?"

"New girl in town already owes me a favor." He smiled, bringing boyish dimples to his cheeks. "Take Rodeo Road home; you'll skip a couple lights. Carmina never gets home from Bible study before nine thirty. As long as you don't get stopped at the train crossing, you should beat her by five."

Five minutes wasn't quite the buffer I'd hoped for, but it would have to do. I blew him a kiss and roared out of the lot.

At the farmhouse, I was relieved to see Carmina's truck wasn't in the drive. I backed the Mustang into the barn, just the way I'd found it. Letting myself into the house, I flipped on the light. And nearly swallowed my tongue.

Carmina was seated on the sofa, tapping her nails on the armrest. Her features looked chiseled from ice. Her mouth compressed thinly, and it made my heart squeeze.

"I didn't see your truck," I said nervously.

"Sent it home with Mac Hester after Bible study—he's fixing the transmission. Gave me a lift home. Keys," she said, extending her hand.

I gave them to her.

"Apology."

"I'm sorry."

"Not good enough, Stella."

I shifted my weight and exhaled impatiently. "I'm sorry I took your car. It won't happen again."

"Look at me when you speak to me."

"I said I'm sorry," I snapped. "What more do you want?"

"You're coming to church with me tomorrow morning."

I looked her square on. Taking her car was wrong, and I'd apologized. We'd settled the matter, and I wasn't going to let her use my bad behavior as an excuse to exercise authority over me. She wasn't my mom. She was a moving piece in the Justice Department's cover story, and I was going to let her know that I knew it.

"I'm not going to church."

"Oh, you're definitely going to church."

"Are you threatening me?"

"You're under my roof, and I expect certain behavior from you. Stealing my car and only feeling bad that you got caught . . . those things severely disappoint me—"

"Stealing?" I challenged, my defenses automatically shooting up. "I didn't steal your car—I borrowed it! Did I leave town? Did I crash it? No! It's in the same condition as when I took it!"

"Don't interrupt me, and don't talk back to me," she said evenly. "I'm not your mother, Stella. I know that better than anyone. I never had the opportunity of meeting her, but I'd be doing her a great disservice if I let you steal and lie, and get away with it."

I pushed down my shock and humiliation and channeled it into rage. "Don't bring her into this. You don't get to use her to make me feel guilty."

"Starting tonight, you have a curfew of nine p.m."

I made a strangled sound. "What? You can't give me a curfew. I've never had a curfew!" By the time I was old enough to go out at night, my mom was too high to care what hour I came or went. I took care of myself, set my own rules. Who was this woman that she thought she could tell me what to do?

"Curfew stands. And you're joining me at church tomorrow. I can't make you like it. I can't even make you listen. But I'm not going to stand aside and let you run wild this summer. Not on my watch. Maybe I'm wrong. Maybe I'm making things worse. But I'd rather try and fail than sit here, too damn hesitant to act. I hung a dress in your closet. I don't care if you don't like it. I expect you to be showered, dressed, and in the truck by nine thirty. Are we clear?"

I fled upstairs. I slammed the bedroom door, not caring if it was childish. She couldn't make me go to church. I'd call Price. Things were not working out with Carmina. Maybe he could talk to the U.S. attorney's office and get them to overrule their decision to place me in a home until my eighteenth birthday.

They thought they knew what was best for me, but I was better off on my own. I'd been on my own for two years.

Curled up on the bed, I comforted myself with one of Reed's letters.

Estella,

Day one of summer baseball camp. The facilities are pretty sweet. All-you-can-eat meals in the cafeteria. We sleep in dorms, two guys per room, with a shared bathroom down the hall. I have a jackass for a roommate. There are guys on my floor from all over the country, and I get stuck with this loser. There's even one kid who traveled from the Dominican Republic. I guess they're serious about baseball there.

During opening ceremonies, the coaches threw out words like "legendary," "prestigious," and "tradition of excellence" to describe the training program. It was hard not to laugh. They sound like my dad. He still thinks he can get me to enlist. I'll skip the Winslow family tradition of excellence, thanks anyway.

xReed

BY THE FOLLOWING MORNING, MY TEMPER HAD cooled slightly. I wasn't in the mood to put on a dress and sit on a hard pew for an hour, but after spending most of the night stewing in a rage, I'd started to see things from a new perspective. Price wasn't going to lift a finger for me if I didn't show him I was trying to make things work with Carmina. Surely he knew me well enough to know I'd never go to church. Which meant if I did end up going, my willingness would become a powerful bargaining chip. Look, Price, I'd tell him, I'm giving this my best shot. I even went to church. But in the end, Carmina and I aren't a good match.

Ditto for Nebraska. But right now, I'd fight my battles one at a time.

Of course, there was always a chance they'd send me someplace worse. . . . Could things get worse than Thunder Basin? I cast a look full of disdain out my bedroom window. And had my answer.

I showered and flat-ironed my dark brown hair to sleek perfection. Standing before the mirror, I tousled my bangs. They were getting long, which I sensed was going to be a problem. I was better off trimming them myself, I decided, than letting someone at "Haircuts, 7.5 Owed" botch them.

Shortly before nine thirty, I trotted downstairs wearing a mint-green sundress and espadrille sandals that one of the deputies had hastily packed from my home. The shapeless muumuu dress Carmina had hung in the closet could hardly be called clothing. I was pretty sure the dress was the unspoken half of my punishment for taking the Mustang last night. Church *and* public humiliation.

"You look respectable," Carmina said somewhat stiffly when I came downstairs. She carefully avoided my eyes. She hadn't forgotten about last night, or forgiven me. We were on equal ground, then. What made me even angrier—what was extra painful— was that Carmina, a stranger, was mothering me when my own mother wouldn't.

"I don't want the dress you hung in my closet. Please remove it by the end of the day." Without breaking stride, I continued into the kitchen and poured myself a mug of coffee.

"There's a linger longer after church today," Carmina called from the hallway. "If you don't want to stay for it, you'll have to walk back here or catch a ride."

"I don't know what a linger longer is," I returned, burning my tongue on the hot black coffee. I would have preferred a heaping spoonful of sugar and a dash of cream, but I wasn't about to ask Carmina for help finding either. Instead, I sipped as much of the coffee as I could tolerate before I felt my insides start to curl.

"Potluck. Everyone brings a dish and a picnic blanket."

"Isn't that adorable. A country picnic. I'll pass." I put my mug in the sink and met her in the hallway. She was wearing a long denim skirt, a white blouse, and those same red cowboy boots. Her platinum hair was smoothed back in a nineties French braid. I tried to come up with a snide remark about her sense of style, but in the end, I just rolled my eyes. "Well, it's nine thirty sharp. Let's get this show on the road. Wouldn't dream of being late."

"With attitude to spare," Carmina murmured as she followed me out.

Oh, I was just getting started. I couldn't wait to meet her church friends. If I had anything to say about it, Carmina and her new foster daughter would be the gossip of Sunday dinner tables across town tonight. I fully intended to be the one who left her feeling humiliated. She was an ex-cop. People saw her as an authority figure. Their opinions might shift after today.

I was going to walk all over her.

Carmina's congregation met in a plain building that mildly resembled a large white barn. Arched windows ran along the sides of the church. A steeple capped the roof. A wide brick staircase led up to the double doors, which were open and letting out a stream of organ music. But what really caught my eye was the marquee sign on the lawn that read EXPOSURE TO THE SON PREVENTS BURNING.

I really hoped this meant the clergy had a sense of humor.

We were greeted at the door by a man wearing a crisply ironed black shirt and a clerical collar. His salt-and-pepper hair was parted on the side, and he smiled warmly at us. He was by all accounts so bland, it was impossible to be offended.

"Good morning, Carmina," he said, clasping her hand affectionately. "I see you've brought a visitor."

"Pastor Lykins, may I present Stella Gordon," Carmina said. "She'll be staying with me for the summer."

Before Pastor Lykins could ask a host of follow-up questions— and I could see by the stark surprise in his widening eyes that he wanted to—Carmina propelled me inside by my elbow.

"You're not even going to let me say hello to people?" I said as she steered me to a vacant pew. "Tsk, tsk, Carmina. Where are your manners?"

"You can open your mouth during the hymns." She set her green bean casserole for the linger longer between us. "Something tells me you've got impressive pipes."

Two silver-haired women shuffled into the pew in front of us, their gazes fluttering speculatively over me and Carmina. Just as one of them tried to catch Carmina's eye, she fixed her attention on removing a ball of lint attached to her skirt, putting true diligence into the task. At that moment I realized just how uncomfortable Carmina was with having me stay for the summer. I knew my supposed reasons for being in Thunder Basin, but I'd never thought about Carmina's side of the cover story. A reclusive and aging ex-cop fostering a seventeen-year-old? It was sure to raise a few eyebrows. I wondered why the U.S. attorney's office had picked her. Her background in law enforcement had undoubtedly made her a desirable candidate.

Probably, she was getting paid a boatload for taking me in. I wasn't an average foster—I was in WITSEC. The higher the danger, the steeper the pay. It was happening all over again: I was being used for money. The only reason my mom had fought for custody was so she could get child support from my dad . . . which she proceeded to use on drugs. And now Carmina was using me to pad her retirement.

Then again, Carmina didn't seem that interested in money. Everything she owned was on the fast track to the junkyard. I got the feeling she hated shopping more than putting up with me.

Whatever her motivations, I strongly sensed Carmina's game plan was to power through the summer by keeping her head down, dodging invasive inquiries, and praying the time passed quickly. I wondered what it felt like for her to lie to her friends and neighbors. After all, long after I was gone, she'd still have to live with these people, knowing she'd kept secrets and never been fully honest with them. I almost felt sorry for her.

But I wasn't ready to let her off the hook just yet. Not after she'd forced me to come to church. I should have been sleeping in. That's what the weekend was for.

"Why did you take me in?" I asked her, my tone a little bit demanding, a little bit suspicious.

"Pardon?"

"What's in it for you? What do you get from all this? What made you take in a seventeen-year-old girl you don't owe a thing to?"

"Now, that's one question I can't get off my mind."

Carmina and I turned in our seats as Chet Falconer sprawled comfortably in the pew behind us. He'd cleaned up for church, putting on chinos and a lightweight navy polo. He'd ditched the cowboy hat and grass-stained boots, and it had completely transformed his appearance. I'd say one thing for Chet: He knew how to put a little flutter in my stomach. His blue eyes glittered, and he raked his damp curly hair behind his ears. He smelled like soap and sun-dried laundry, and it was an irresistible combination.

"Good morning, Chet," Carmina said rigidly, then turned to face forward. Conversation over. I couldn't tell if Chet had done something to offend her—now or in the past—or if she was always this ornery. Given that she'd bought his Mustang as recently as last year, and that he mowed her lawn, I was leaning toward the latter.

"Aw, Gran, you know I'm not gonna give up that easily," Chet went on, leaning close to speak in her ear. "If you wanted help around the house, I could have loaned you Dusty. Kid's an angel. Wouldn't give you a single gray hair."

Carmina made a *harrumph* sound. "You're one to talk. You were just as much trouble at sixteen. Wasn't that about the time I first arrested you?"

"This conversation is finally getting interesting," I said, arching my eyebrows inquiringly at Chet.

"Outta luck, soldier," he informed me. "Carmina keeps all my secrets. She knows I'd stop mowing her lawn if she let my skeletons out."

"I made no such agreement," Carmina scoffed.

"Your hair looks different," Chet told me. "All dressed up, I almost didn't recognize you. 'Now, who is that pretty girl?' I asked myself when I came in."

I stuck my tongue out. "Speak for yourself. Are the pigs looking after your boots and hat?"

Chet grinned. "I bet this one's a real peach around the house, Carmina."

She gave another *harrumph*. Then her brow furrowed, and she fixed me with a probing gaze. "Am I to understand the two of you have met? When?" she demanded.

"Last night," I said. "Chet helped me start the Mustang at the library. I couldn't get it running. He's very good with cars," I added, twirling my necklace around my finger guilelessly.

The smile on Chet's face slipped. His face clouded with confusion before blanching with a certain sickened dread. *She knows?* he mouthed at me.

"She does now," I said sweetly.

Slowly, Carmina turned in the pew, giving Chet a dark, berating look. "You knew she stole my car last night, Chet Falconer? You helped her get away with it?"

"Yes, ma'am."

"Anything to say for yourself?"

"Carburetor was acting up again."

"I ought to have you both arrested."

Just then, the organist finished the final chord of the prelude music, and Pastor Lykins took his place at the pulpit. The congregation quieted, and all eyes turned to the front of the meetinghouse.

Carmina gave Chet a long, cool stare. Then she took the hymnal out of the seat pocket behind her and whacked it hard against his leg.

I bit my lip to stifle a giggle, just as Chet's breath tickled my ear. "Think that's funny, do you? My turn next."

I MUST HAVE BEEN IN A REALLY GOOD MOOD, BECAUSE
after church, I let Chet talk me into staying for the linger longer.
On the church's back lawn, he added two bags of potato chips to
the spread of salads, casseroles, and desserts on folding tables.
He hadn't brought a picnic blanket, so after separating ourselves
from the congregation, we made do with the grass in the shade
of a leafy oak.

Chet lay on his back, his arms folded under his head. "I'm
gonna get you back, you know."

I kicked off my espadrilles and sank languidly against the tree
trunk. "Someone wasn't listening to Pastor Lykins's sermon on
forgiveness."

"You always this self-righteous?"

I lifted an eyebrow. "Yeah. So?"

He rolled on his elbow, facing me. He dropped his voice to a secretive hush. "I remember what Pastor Lykins said about casting the devil behind us. Go on, girl. Get where you belong."

I kicked him in the leg.

"Before church, you and Carmina mentioned someone named Dusty," I said. "Who is he?"

"My kid brother." Chet's countenance darkened and the banter went out of him. "I'd formally introduce you, but I didn't get the pleasure of dragging his butt to church this morning. He never came home last night."

"Little brother?" When Carmina said Chet was man of the house, I'd envisioned him living alone. "Aren't you only nineteen?"

"Only? You're not that far behind."

"What I mean is, is it even legal for the two of you to live together?" I knew Chet's parents were dead, but I hadn't realized he'd taken on more than just ownership of the house—he was also his little brother's guardian. "How old is he?"

"Sixteen. Old enough to drive, not that he waited until he got his license to start. My parents used to try to slow him down by hiding the car keys, but necessity is the mother of invention, and he taught himself how to hot-wire cars at thirteen. Park your car on the street at night, and he's likely to borrow it. He'll bring it back by morning, a little lighter on gas." Chet made a sound of disgust. "When he finally does drag his butt home from whatever party he crashed, I swear I'm gonna lock him in the crawl space for a week."

"Crawl space?"

"Surprised you didn't have them in Tennessee. No? A crawl space is an underground tornado shelter. Just what it sounds like—a tunnel under the house with enough room to crawl inside on your hands and knees. Carmina has a newer shelter in her backyard, with two doors opening to a staircase that leads to an underground bunker. About ten by ten in size, lock on the door. Some neighborhood kids and I used to use it as a clubhouse—had a 'No Girls Allowed' sign and everything."

As a matter of fact, I had seen a set of low-lying doors, mounted at an angle, not far from her back porch. I'd just assumed the doors led to a storage cellar.

Chet said, "You'll get your chance to go inside one. It would be rare for a summer to pass without a tornado touching down in the area."

I shuddered. I sincerely hoped he was wrong about that. I'd weathered a few ice storms back home and gone without power for a couple of days, and that was where my tolerance for bad weather ended.

"Where are these parties your brother goes to?" I asked. My motive for asking was a little selfish. After spending three days in a government safe house, followed by three more under Carmina's watch, I was desperate for a nightlife. Thunder Basin definitely wasn't Philly, and I wasn't expecting trendy clubs, but at this point, I'd take anything. If Chet could point me in the direction of a party, I'd jump at the opportunity. I didn't want to spend every weekend this summer holed up at Carmina's house. I was dying for a social life.

"'The guy he was with last night is Cooter Saggory, so they probably found an empty boxcar on railroad property and drank until they passed out. Or maybe that's wishful thinking. With Cooter, who knows. That's the problem—he's a loose cannon, and now Dusty's mixed up with him. I've done my share of stupid things, and sure I spent a night or two in jail, but I never did anything that was going to potentially land me in prison."

"Cooter Saggory? Please tell me that's a nickname."

"Given name and it fits him," Chet grunted. "A lowlife and a redneck. As you probably noticed last night."

I frowned, tilting my head. "Hang on. The kid at the Sundown Diner last night. That was Dusty? And the man with him was Cooter?"

Chet's face revealed he'd thought I'd already figured this out. "Yeah. Sorry. I'm a little distracted. Long night. If I'd stepped foot inside the diner, Dusty would have bolted. And I wouldn't have known what he's up to. Having you there came in handy."

"You used me to spy on your brother?"

"And I'd do it again."

"Okay, but it's low and sneaky—and annoying. Give Dusty some room. He probably feels suffocated by you, and everything he's doing, all the bad stuff, is just to test you." I realized with a start that I was speaking from the heart. Rebellion had been my favorite tactic to push my mom's buttons. Skipping out on chores, siding with my dad on stupid issues, using foul language—I was a young lady, a descendant of genteel Southern folk, and was supposed to be courteous and mannered. It had worked. And then, of course, she'd started using drugs, and getting her attention was a worthless pursuit.

"Cooter Saggory deals drugs," Chet announced bluntly. "Dusty doesn't know what he's getting into. Even if he is trying to test me, this isn't the way to do it. Best case, he gets a record. Worst case, he winds up in prison."

Truth be told, I'd suspected drugs. The four-thousand-dollar start-up fee had been a bit of a giveaway. Dusty was going to try his hand at dealing. "Can you tell Carmina?" I suggested. "Maybe she can talk to Dusty, paint a realistic picture of what's in store for him."

"He'll know I'm behind it. It'll just drive him to do it. I'm gonna have to come up with another way to talk sense into him."

"Does he do drugs?"

"Haven't caught him, but I'm not going to kid myself. My parents' death wasn't easy on him. He'd drop out of school if I didn't keep dragging him through the doors. Last month, he got fired from the Sun Mart. What kind of person can't keep a job bagging groceries? He's doing something, I'm sure of it," Chet said with an upset shake of his head.

I wanted to tell Chet I knew how he felt. Living with someone who was using sucked. All the sneakiness and deception, and the never-ending string of excuses. How many times had I wanted to shake my mom and yell, "Stop acting like I'm stupid enough to believe your lies!"

But my mom's drug addiction wasn't part of my cover story. I was supposed to tell everyone in Thunder Basin she was dead.

That way, if she cleaned up and got out of rehab, we could relocate to a new town and start our lives over, this time together. It was the Department of Justice's goal for my future, and it was never going to happen. First, I wasn't holding my breath for my mom to achieve any measure of success in rehab. Second, I was never, ever living with that woman again. Now that I'd had a taste of life without her, they'd have to drag me back kicking and screaming.

I frowned, absorbing this declaration slowly. I still viewed Thunder Basin as a prison, and would for the next three months, but it stood to reason every prison had fleeting moments of freedom. A glimpse of blue sky, a singing bird on the windowsill. Or, in my case, not having the weight of caring for my mom dragging me under. What if Thunder Basin was my chance to come up for air?

Chet was waiting for my response. Even though I could tell he needed someone to talk to, Dusty's reckless behavior hit unnervingly close to home, and I needed to bow out of the conversation. It was wrong, but realistic. For my safety, I had to stick to my cover story.

"Who knew this parenting gig could be so tough," he said at last, kneading between his eyes.

"Yeah, good luck with that," I said lamely, hating the pang of guilt that followed. What Chet needed now was a friend and a sympathetic ear, not platitudes.

"Time to go, Stella." I hadn't seen Carmina approach. She stood over us, fanning away the growing heat with the church bulletin.

"Actually, I'll catch a ride with Chet," I said, glancing at him to make sure it was okay.

"I think it's best if you come with me." Carmina's tone was level, but as unbending as steel.

Chet nudged me with his knee. "I've got errands to run in town anyway. But I'll catch you later."

I felt heat creep up my neck. Chet didn't have errands. He was letting Carmina win, and it made me furious. Was I the only one with enough backbone to stand up to her?

"Then I'll run errands with you," I said, rising to my feet as he did.

"Not today," Carmina said. "Get in the truck, Stella. Go on, Chet. Don't let us keep you."

Chet nodded politely at each of us, then headed toward the parking lot. He glanced back once, but I couldn't read his expression. Disappointed? Apologetic?

I folded my arms stiffly over my chest and glared at Carmina. "You've really got the whole intimidation thing down, don't you?"

"I told you to stay away from that boy."

I gave a harsh laugh. "Because he's trouble? Open your eyes. Chet Falconer is as harmless as they come. Look at him." I gestured angrily at the parking lot where he'd retreated. "He was polite enough to let you chase him off rather than cause a scene. Trust me, I know trouble. And Chet isn't it. Even if he was, you don't get to tell me who I can hang out with. You're not my parent—you're a stand-in, a placeholder, a name on a government document, as far as I'm concerned."

Carmina's lips had thinned to a tight wire. "Get in the truck."

"No."

"Don't make me repeat myself, Stella."

"Nobody's making you do anything. You're the one bossing me around. I bet it kills you to have someone stand up to you. You used to be a big bad cop, and the town respects you for it. Well, you don't scare me. I'll walk back to the farm, but I'm not getting in your truck."

I started to turn on my heel, when Pastor Lykins crossed the lawn to us, waving his arms, signaling us to wait. "Carmina! I didn't get a chance to thank you and Stella for coming for this morning's sermon." Short of breath, he shook our hands again, smiling broadly. "I hope I gave you each something to reflect on this week."

Carmina smiled tightly. "You always do. Now, if you'll excuse us—"

"I hope to see you next week, Stella."

I didn't have much time to think up a response. Acting almost instinctively, I seized the moment and dropped my eyes, sighing forlornly. "I hope so. Of course, it's up to Carmina. I don't have a car or a bike, so she decides when I get to leave the house."

Pastor Lykins's smile faltered. "Oh. Well, I'm sure Carmina would want you to hear the Lord's word, isn't that right?"

Carmina rolled her eyes and exhaled a long-suffering sigh. "Stella is always welcome to attend church."

"Thank you, Carmina," I said, doing my best to appear sincerely grateful.

Pastor Lykins continued to glance between us uncertainly. At last his face brightened. "Stella, do you play softball?"

I didn't know where he was going with this, but I had a good feeling. "It's been a couple years, but I know the game."

His eyes lit up further. "Have you heard of our teen coed softball league? Games are Friday after sundown. I saw you talking with Chet Falconer earlier. He's in charge of the league. Why don't I see if he can squeeze you onto one of the smaller teams? I was new in town once too, and while it takes some time to feel like you fit in, the best thing you can do is dive in and make new friends. Carmina, surely you can do without Stella for a few hours a week?"

I turned to face her. "Please, Carmina?" My tone was hopeful, begging even, but my eyes blazed with smug triumph.

Carmina pinned me with a stern glare. "I'm sure that will be fine. Stella is allowed to come and go as she pleases, within reason. The child makes it sound like I'm a parole officer." When she caught us staring at her, she added adamantly, "I'm not."

Pastor Lykins patted Carmina gently on the shoulder. "I'm sure it's been an adjustment balancing your previous line of work with this new, exciting endeavor of raising a girl. Two completely different situations that require different, ah, approaches."

Carmina just stared at him blankly.

Pastor Lykins cleared his throat, then shook my hand. "Good luck, Stella," he said with heartfelt concern.

I waited until he walked away to smile contentedly.

My work here was done.

MONDAY MORNING I GOT A CALL FROM THE SUNDOWN
Diner. The owner, Dixie Jo, wanted to interview me for a carhop
position. The term "carhop" made me think of girls on roller
skates and the movie *American Graffiti*. I hadn't put on skates since
I was six or seven, and had distant memories of doing the limbo
on wheels, and a sore tailbone. If she made me skate as part of the
interview, I didn't stand a chance.

It was too hot for jeans, so I threw on cotton shorts and an
eyelet top. Not fancy enough to earn me a look of approval from
Carmina as I jogged down the porch steps on my way out, but I
was going for comfort.

Carmina had loaned me her bike, a lime-green beach cruiser
with balloon tires. A wicker basket was strung up between the
handlebars. Like everything Carmina owned, the paint was dinged

and chipped and the surface was coated in dust. But if the bike got me out of the house, it was as good as a Porsche in my eyes.

As I pedaled into town, the rush of hot air flung my hair off my shoulders. Instead of feeling oppressive, the heat felt energizing. I was overcome by the urge to release the handlebars and tip my face toward the sun. Cautiously, I tested the feel of the wind zipping through my fingers. I felt open to infinite possibility. This road, this morning, this summer belonged to me. No one else to worry about. My mom wasn't here. She wasn't my problem anymore. Imagining that every pedal stroke took me farther from her, I pumped my legs harder. A smile warmed in my throat, finally breaking on my face. I was free.

At ten, an hour before the Sundown opened, I propped the beach cruiser against a streetlight and rapped on the front door. My knock was answered by a willowy middle-aged blonde. Smile lines fanned from her eyes, and her hair had been combed into a loose braid. Short, messy strands sprang from her scalp like rays of sun. She had warm brown eyes and an open, honest face.

"You must be Stella. You know, I have a sweet spot for that name. One of my best girlfriends in grade school was a Stella. She had deep hazel eyes, just like you."

I shifted uncomfortably. It felt wrong to strike up a conversation around a name I hated and that wasn't mine to begin with. If I took that route, I'd inevitably have to make up more lies. It was my grandmother's name. Or, My parents named me after Stella McCartney. It didn't feel right to lie to a woman with such a sincere face. And the more lies I told, the harder it would be to keep everything straight in my head. So I settled on "You must be Dixie Jo. Thanks for the interview."

"Have you worked in food service before?" she asked, leading me across the dining area and through a pair of swinging double doors. The white-tiled kitchen gleamed, and smelled as clean as a bar of soap. I counted one woman chopping heads of lettuce, another slicing and battering onions, and a guy my age unloading an oversize, steam-spewing dishwasher. The air was already hot, their faces flushed.

Dixie Jo signaled for me to take a seat in a small office off the kitchen.

"I haven't." I sat in the chair across the desk from hers, deciding now wasn't the time to tell her I'd never had a job. "But I'm a fast learner, and I'm a people person." And I love AC.

"Can you work nights?"

"All but Friday." I still hadn't heard from Chet about the softball league, but I hoped it would work out. For one thing, I needed something to do on the weekends. For another, I could see myself hanging out with Chet for the summer. Annoying cowboy attributes aside, he had a good sense of humor and wasn't as backwoods as some of the people I'd seen in town. And if I was being completely honest, he wasn't the worst to look at, either.

"How many hours are you hoping for?"

"As many as you'll give me."

"I'm looking to hire someone part-time, twenty hours a week. You'd be responsible for some food prep, like milk shakes and adding the right dressing to our stock salads. But the primary

68

duties of a carhop are taking orders from curbside customers, sending the orders to the cooks, and taking the food out when it's ready."

"I can handle that."

"The nice thing about sitting smack-dab on the street corner is that we've got the parking spaces all down the left side of the building. Customers pull in and they don't have to leave their car to get food. We serve anywhere from twenty to fifty cars a night." She smiled slyly. "They don't take up tables in the dining area and there's no cleanup. Best of both worlds. Can you start tonight, Stella?"

I blinked. "Are you offering me the job?"

"If you want it."

It was an easy decision. Time away from Carmina, AC, and a little spending money? I smiled brightly. "You've got yourself a new carhop."

Dixie Jo rose from behind the desk. "Be here tonight at four thirty. It'll give you a chance to get the swing of things before the crowds arrive. I pay every other Friday. Still on board?"

"Definitely."

"Then we'll see you tonight, Stella." With a smile, she signaled me to see myself out.

I was halfway across the kitchen when I backtracked and poked my head through her door. "One more thing. Is there a uniform?"

She snapped her fingers. "Almost forgot. The new ones just came in. The old ones were pink-and-white-striped dresses with a lace hem. Reminded me of something Dolly Parton would've worn on tour in 1981. If you swing by the Salvation Army, they're selling them for ten apiece." She rifled through one of the boxes stacked along the back wall and held up a faux leather black skirt and fitted camo top.

"Better?" She arched her brows, asking my opinion.

I laughed. "You have to ask?"

"Top has to be tucked in for safety purposes, but you can wear whatever closed-toe footwear you choose. What size would you like?"

I took a medium and walked out with a bounce in my step. As far as job interviews went, I was 1–0.

Outside, Carmina's beach cruiser was gone.

I glanced both ways down the street. A few cars rolled along the brick streets of Thunder Basin's downtown, but the sidewalks were empty. No guilty-looking pedestrians making a break for it with an eyesore of a bike. So much for small-town safety. I still didn't have a cell phone, so I couldn't report the bike stolen. Nor could I call Carmina to pick me up—she'd be furious, and would probably force me to walk as punishment. Any way I looked at it, I was going on foot. I'd give her the good news first—that I was Thunder Basin's newest carhop. And hope it was enough to soothe over the loss of her bike. But it still didn't answer how I was going to get to work tonight.

Pinning my hair up, I crossed to the shady side of the street and started the long walk back. I'd only made it a few blocks when a banana-yellow vehicle rumbled up beside me. The passenger window was rolled down, and Chet Falconer grinned through it, tipping his tan Stetson at me.

"Hot morning," he observed.

"What do you want?" I said, feigning annoyance, but the truth was, I couldn't believe my luck. Maybe Chet was finished in town and I could bum a ride back to Carmina's.

"Did you walk to town? Quite a hike."

"Not all of us are lazy. Some of us like a little exercise and fresh air. What is this gas guzzler, anyway?" I asked, gesturing at his vehicle. I'd never seen anything like it. It looked like the love child of a jeep and a military truck.

"1977 International Harvester Scout. They don't make them anymore."

"Hazarding a guess . . . fifteen miles per gallon? You could give the environment a break and at least carpool. Find some lonely traveler who could use a ride . . ."

His grin widened. "You angling for a lift?"

"Just worried about the state of the world we're leaving for our grandchildren." For emphasis, I eyed his Scout doubtfully.

"Get in, already."

I glanced farther down the sidewalk, bit my lip, and tried to look conflicted. "But it's such a nice day."

Chet snorted. "It's ninety degrees out. Get in before I change my mind."

I tugged on the door and hauled myself inside. "Fine. You talked me into it."

The inside of Chet's Scout smelled like an earthy mixture of leather polish, old books, and grass clippings. No artificial air freshener dangled from the rearview mirror, and I hadn't caught a whiff of cologne. I hadn't expected to. Chet wasn't as fastidious about his looks as the boys I knew back home. He definitely wasn't as meticulous as Reed, who ironed his jeans. When Reed came to pick me up, his stiff hair held the telltale sign of maximum-hold gel, his clothes were fresh from the cleaners, and he smelled as fragrant as a department store. He probably spent at least an hour getting ready. Detail. I'd always appreciated his attention to it. But in retrospect, it did make him seem a little . . . fussy.

Chet hung his arm out the open window and put the Scout in gear. "Straight home?"

It was too early for lunch, but I wasn't ready to go back to Carmina's. Not unless I wanted a stern talking to. Seriously, how many people stole a green beach cruiser circa 1965?

"Know of any good bike stores in town?" I asked.

"Used or new?"

"Definitely used. I'm in the market for something pretty specific. A green beach cruiser with a basket between the handlebars. The paint has to be peeling. Scratches on the frame are vital. Oh, and it needs a wide padded seat. Think I can find one of those?"

Chet whistled thoughtfully. "Sounds like there's more to this story."

I tossed my hands up. "I lost Carmina's bike. I rode it to town this morning for a job interview, which I totally rocked, by the way"—I paused my story to give him a high five—"and when I came out, it was gone. Stolen. First the Mustang, now the bike. I'm not having any luck. She'll probably ground me. Having to stay at her place 24/7 is about the worst punishment I can think of."

"The Charlton Brothers," Chet mused to himself.

"What?"

"Jimbo and Billy John Charlton took your bike. Don't take it personally, they do it to everyone."

"Their names are really Jimbo and Billy John?"

"This is Nebraska."

He had a point.

"I know exactly where your bike is," Chet said, making a hard and illegal U-turn in the intersection. I grabbed the granny handle for balance as the tires clipped the curb. "Where?"

"Junkyard."

"They steal bikes and dump them in the junkyard?"

"Nothing better to do. They live in a trailer park near the railroad tracks. Dad's a drunk and on his way to join his wife, who died of cirrhosis of the liver a few years ago. The Charlton boys don't go to school, don't have jobs, and don't pay taxes. Rumor has it they've both made inappropriate advances on their little sister, Millie Sue."

"Ew."

"Town disgraces, Jimbo and Billy John."

Well. That's what happened when people got stuck in a place like Thunder Basin. Once the inbreeding started, it was all downhill. Drug dealers, bike thieves, and perverts, the whole lot of them.

* * *

Thunder Basin's junkyard was framed by a high chain-link fence topped with barbed wire. Chet parked at the rear of the sprawling acreage to avoid being seen by the attendant at the front gate. We weren't likely to get in trouble for trespassing, Chet assured me, but if we went through the front gates, we'd have to pay for any property we left with. I wasn't paying for a bike that was mine— Carmina's, technically—to begin with.

Chet walked along the outer perimeter of the fence and went right to the spot where the chains had been cut to form a hidden seam. "When Dusty was twelve, the Charlton brothers took his bike. Haven't changed their M.O. in years."

We slipped through the fence, walking down rows of old cars piled three high, and ancient appliances. We passed a mountain of tires, axles, and other car parts. Retired tractors and farm equipment had also made their way into the junkyard. Chet turned down a row, and at the end of it, I saw a large hill of dirt. Atop the hill was Carmina's green beach cruiser.

"That's it!" I said, quickening my pace.

I came to an abrupt stop at the base of the hill, dismayed to find the dirt had a sticky, mudlike consistency and was strewn with hay. It smelled awful. I was a city girl, but I didn't need to live on a farm to know that I was standing before a heaping pile of fresh manure.

"I'm going to kill the Charlton brothers," I muttered vengefully.

Chet clapped me on the shoulder. "First step's the hardest, kid."

I glanced at him hopefully. "I don't suppose . . ."

Chet flipped his palms up and backed away. "No way. You're on your own."

I took one tentative step onto the manure. My sandal sank easily. Wrinkling my nose, I let my thoughts travel to a myriad of gruesome ways I could dismember Jimbo and Billy John Charlton. Knives. Chain saws. An ice pick. My own two hands.

After slipping and sliding my way uphill, at last I had the bike in my hands. Digging in my heels to steady my footing, I sent the bike wheeling down to Chet. I got my hands dirty in the process, and had to close my eyes and count to ten to keep my composure. When I reopened my eyes, I risked a glance down, and was mortified to discover that my sandals had sunk completely into the manure; it was creeping up my bare ankles.

I couldn't help it; I shrieked.

"If it makes you feel better, cows are vegetarians," Chet called up cheerfully.

"What will make me feel better is a shower!"

Tamping down the queasiness rolling in my stomach, I jogged downhill as fast as I could without risking a fall. At the bottom, I kicked my feet at the air, flinging off any clumps of manure clinging to my heels, then took several deep, steadying breaths. After a minute, I'd managed to suppress my gag reflex.

"Where do they live?" I demanded, already striding toward the back of the junkyard, where Chet's Scout was parked. "Where can I find those two dirtbags?"

Chet waved me off, a strange gleam in his eyes. "Nah, let karma take care of them."

"I'm not waiting for karma. I'm going to take care of them right now." I bit off each word.

"They're mean boys, Jimbo and Billy Joe. If I were you, I'd take the bike and be glad they didn't stick it someplace worse."

I stopped in my tracks. "Which is it? Is his name Billy John or Billy Joe?"

Chet went a little pink at the ears. He coughed, clearly trying to disguise a laugh.

I stared at him for a few moments before realization dawned, and I narrowed my eyes. "Oh, no, you didn't. . . ."

"Oh, I definitely did." With that, Chet let out a whoop and took off running for the fence.

I grabbed the handlebars of Carmina's bike and chased after him, shouting a slew of creative and threatening curses. When I reached the fence, I was out of breath, and I could feel sweat trickling down my back. Chet stood on the other side, examining me distrustfully, but not without a slight and mocking smile.

"Told you I'd get you back," he said, smirking.

"Low blow, Falconer."

He pointed a finger at me. "I was just starting to get back in Carmina's good graces by mowing the lawn, and this was a big step backward. Did you see the way she eyed me when she found out I helped you start the Mustang? Tell me that's not worse than climbing a pile of manure."

"Well?" I huffed. "What got you in her bad graces?"

His eyes widened in disbelief. "We're still talking about Carmina, right? Does anyone need a reason?"

Point taken.

I stewed in my anger a minute, then heaved an irritated sigh. "The least you can do is give me a ride."

Chet held the broken fence open and helped me guide the cruiser through. Then he hoisted it onto his shoulder and carried it to the back of the Scout. I was still dusting myself off when he came around and held my door open for me.

"Now you decide to be chivalrous," I said, climbing in.

Another snort. "What kind of payback would it've been if I had rescued you?" After he swung behind the wheel, he turned to face me sheepishly. "Still friends?"

"Only if you make sure I get in the softball league. I need a nightlife. Has Pastor Lykins talked to you yet?"

"Matter of fact, he has."

"And?"

Chet thumbed his nose. "I figured I can squeeze you on my team. We'll have an extra player, but nobody will care."

"Good." I settled into my seat, content. "I was hoping we'd be on the same team."

"You were?" he asked, looking surprised and pleased.

"Rumor has it you're a good shortstop. I don't want to be on a losing team. Obviously."

"Right. Well, you're in luck. We're 2–0 for the season."

On the drive back, Chet grinned suddenly in recollection and said, "Still can't believe you bought that story about Jimbo and Billy what's-his-name."

"It was a legitimate story!" I protested. "Totally plausible!"

He gave an eye roll. "All small towns in America are filled with inbreeding, ignorant, Bible-spouting rednecks?" He wagged his head pathetically. "You can't really believe that. That's like me saying all city types are backstabbing, morally corrupt workaholics."

"The workaholic part is probably true. People go to the city because they have a dream—"

"You know what I'm saying."

I sighed elaborately and made a pouty face. "Okay, I admit I was wrong and perhaps prejudiced. Happy?"

"I'm not trying to coerce you into thinking one way or another, I just want you to consider my perspective. I've spent my whole life in Thunder Basin. This is my home. I like it here. But I'm not blind. I can tell you hate it. Fair enough. But I wish you'd hold off judging the town—and everyone in it—until you've given it a chance."

I bit my lip to hold in a smile. "I wish you could see your face right now. You look so serious."

"I was sort of hoping for hot, charming, ravishingly handsome, all of the above."

"First you've got to ditch the cowboy hat."

He flashed a crooked smile. "At least I don't smell like manure."

"Oh!" I threw my head back, laughing. "I can't believe you went there! Lower than low. That's it—I declare full-out war." I climbed across the seat and ran a soiled finger down his cheek. "A taste of what's to come. You're out of your league. Step up to the majors," I added, fluttering my fingers toward myself in a beckoning manner.

"All talk and no walk."

"Dream on."

"Game on."

We looked at each other and we both laughed.

When Chet pulled into Carmina's drive fifteen minutes later, he said, "I'll call you about Friday's game. Best number to reach you?"

"Just call Carmina and ask for me. I'm working on getting my own phone."

"When do I get to hear about the new job?"

I'd been so wrapped up in locating Carmina's bike, I'd completely forgotten to give him further details. "I'm the Sundown Diner's newest carhop. Tips will probably suck, but at least they've got AC."

Chet grinned. "Watch out for the drunk cowboys."

"Yeah, yeah, nothing I can't handle." I knew he was just trying to scare me. "First shift's tonight. Wish me luck."

"Don't need to." His blue eyes zeroed right in on mine, and unexpectedly, I felt strangely warm and a little breathless. "They're gonna love you. We should celebrate after Friday's game. Catch a bite, or see a movie. Up to you."

I broke away from Chet's gaze and collected myself. I'd crossed a line just now, and I didn't like how it made me feel. Chet was my friend, but I was devoted to Reed. *And you shouldn't need the reminder,* I chided myself.

I said, "Carmina has been stricter than usual after I took the Mustang Saturday night. I'll have to run it by her." I didn't care what Carmina thought, and I definitely wasn't running my plans past her; I threw in the comment to cover my bases. I didn't want to commit to giving my entire Friday night to Chet if better plans sprang up later. Assuming I met some people at the softball game, I might get a few more invitations. What I really wanted—what I really missed about home—was a weekend party. Lots of people, loud music, a good time.

Most of all, I didn't think it was wise to spend too much time alone with Chet. I knew the perils of a long-distance relationship. *The mice will play when the cat's away.* I wasn't going to be one of those girls. Reed and I had been through too much to throw it away on a summer fling.

"Carmina's used to having her way," Chet said. "But that house of hers is big enough for two opinions. She'll come around; it just might take time. You doing okay with her?"

"Yeah, we're peachy. So long as only one of us is in the house at a time."

"Must be hard, moving from one place to the next, never knowing who you're gonna land with."

"Hmm," I mused noncommittally.

"How long were you in your last foster home?"

"Long enough," I said vaguely. I hadn't expected to feel a moral twinge over lying to Chet. The U.S. attorney's office had given me a cover story for my safety, got it. But Chet and I were on good terms. He was the closest thing I had to a friend. It felt cheap to exploit that, even if I was only here for the summer. "Listen, I should get going. Catch a quick nap before my shift tonight. Well, that and plan my revenge."

"I'll sleep with one eye open."

My smile slipped. Chet had meant the words to be funny, but as my thoughts drifted to Danny Balando, who was out there searching for me, I realized Chet's joke was spot on for me, too.

Dead on.

AT FOUR THIRTY, I CLOCKED IN MY TIME CARD.
Clearly the Sundown was too cheap to upgrade to a computerized
system. Dixie Jo put Inny, another carhop, in charge of giving me
a tour of the kitchen and what I presumed was the diner's version
of basic training.

I couldn't help staring at Inny as she waddled across the white-
tiled floor with purpose, barking information over her shoulder
at me. Cooks' station, ice-cream machine, malt mixer, storeroom. Her black hair was cut in a choppy bob, and her small eyes
seemed permanently pinched in a scowl. She had gangly legs and
arms, and she folded the latter over her skinny chest. But below
that she was soft and round, her belly straining against the fabric
of her camo shirt. Inny, who didn't look seventeen, was pregnant.
Really pregnant.

Smacking her gum, she eyed me up and down. "Know the difference between French and ranch dressing?"

"Sure."

"Things gonna get real busy round here at six. You're not gonna have a mental breakdown on me, are you?"

I plastered on a false smile, because I knew what she was doing. She was trying to put me in my place, but I didn't feel intimidated by her. I wasn't intimidated by anyone in this town.

"Tell me what to do and I'll do it," I said.

Inny slapped an order pad in my hand. "Take down orders, give 'em to the cooks, then take the food out when it's done. Need me to repeat any of that?"

I took an apron off the row of hooks beside the swinging doors, tied it around my waist, and tucked my order pad in the front pocket.

"This here's the carhop door," Inny said, walking me over to a side door beyond the cooks' station. A rack of laminated menus hung to the left of the door, which had a porthole window encased in it that offered a view of the side street. "Stand here and keep an eye out. Someone should drive up soon."

I leaned a shoulder against the door and kept my eyes on the road. A couple of minutes later, a truck pulled up and honked its horn.

"The hungry beep—that's your signal," Inny hollered at me while balancing four salad bowls in a row up her arm.

I pushed through the carhop door. I was halfway to the truck when I realized I had no idea how to greet a customer, much less take an order. Since I wasn't in the mood to have Inny laugh at my ineptitude, or give me a General Patton–like dressing down, I tossed my ponytail over my shoulder and tried out an impromptu greeting.

"Welcome to the Sundown Diner. I'm Stella and I'll be your server today. What can I get you?"

"Two chicken fried steaks and an order of fries and coleslaw each. No drinks. You got that?"

"Got it," I said, scribbling it down as fast as I could. "I'll put that right in."

Inside, I clipped the order to the cooks' wheel, but before I could sigh in relief over getting through my first order smoothly, I heard two more hungry beeps from the curb.

"Let me know when your hands get full," Inny called from the other side of the kitchen. She stepped out of a large freezer, as big as a room, that shelved rows of frozen food in bags, canisters, and plastic buckets. Frosty air rushed through the open door, which she promptly shut. I had a feeling if the air conditioner didn't kick on in the kitchen soon, I was going to have to come up with an excuse to visit the walk-in freezer frequently.

By six thirty, I was too busy for nerves. Every parking space beside the diner was taken; the minute one car backed out, another shot into its place. My hand was beginning to cramp from furiously scribbling orders, and my shoulders ached from carting trays of food between the kitchen and the street. The standard tip was a flat two dollars, which would have been scandalous in Philly, but it wasn't like I could complain. Who was going to listen? Inny worked alongside me, methodically stuffing her tips into her pocket without comment. I wondered what she was saving for. It was probably judgmental, but I was sure she'd have no trouble getting some kind of government handout for teen parents.

Inny snagged me by the sleeve on my way outside. "I should warn you, that's Trigger McClure's truck that just pulled up."

I glanced at the carhop door. I was too far away to see clearly out the porthole window. "Who's Trigger McClure?"

For the first time all night, Inny's expression softened. Wagging her head, she gave me a sympathetic pat on the shoulder. "Don't let him scare you. And don't let him walk all over you."

I pushed through the carhop door and headed for the red truck parked nose-first to the curb. The guy at the wheel looked about the same age as Inny and me. Definitely high school. Based on Inny's warning, I'd expected someone older with crooked teeth and mean, alcohol-glazed eyes. One of Chet's drunk cowboys, maybe.

Trigger McClure had a lazy, impish smile that played across his bow-shaped lips. Bright red-gold hair fell into hot blue eyes. A few freckles dusted his creamy skin, and I found myself shaking my head to break out of a trance. He looked like a model for a sporting goods store. No wonder Inny had warned me about him. He probably had girls fawning over him regularly. Hard not to let that kind of attention go to your head.

Trigger leaned his gym-chiseled body out the driver's window and crooked his finger impatiently at me. "I'm next," he hollered.

85

I walked over, catching a whiff of male perspiration. That, along with his sweat-soaked T-shirt and the baseball glove on the bench seat beside him, told me he'd probably come straight from practice.

"Where's Inny?" he wanted to know.

"Inside. I'll be taking your order tonight." I held my pencil poised over the order pad, showing him I was on a schedule. Not that he noticed, but the car beside him had backed out and a new one had filled its place. Twin toddlers in the backseat whined and thrashed their legs while their mother tapped the steering wheel and fixed me with a hurry-up glare.

Trigger scratched his thumb across his forehead. "Listen up. . . ." His eyes perused the front of my shirt, and I couldn't help feeling like he was ogling my boobs. "No name tag?"

I shifted my pad higher. "Would you like to hear our drink list? Pepsi products, lemonade, sun tea—"

"Mountain Dew and a chicken fried steak, Miss No-Name." A sultry smile curved his lips as he addressed me with a hint of flirtation.

"I'll put that right in."

"You like this, don't you, making me work to get your name?" He flashed teeth as white and straight as piano keys. I couldn't say why, but something about him felt vaguely familiar. A ridiculous thought to have, since I'd never laid eyes on Trigger McClure before. But I couldn't brush the nagging thought, and it made my guard rise a notch.

"I like doing my job," I said, pulling on a bland mask of politeness. If Trigger wanted to learn my name, there were multiple ways—like strolling inside, cornering Inny, and asking her. It wasn't that I didn't want him to know my name. Despite how I was sure it looked, I wasn't being cagey. It was just that his strange familiarity had chased a chill up my spine, and until I had time to sort it out, instinct told me to keep my distance.

"You're a coquettish little thing, aren't you?" Trigger went on, ramping up the charm in his good-ol'-boy smile.

Coquettish. I had always hated that word. And while he wouldn't believe me, I wasn't stonewalling him on purpose. But—

The more I stared at him, the more rapidly the synapses at the back of my memory fired. I knew this guy. I just couldn't remember how.

Hoping to get away and clear my head, I skirted his truck and headed for the ragged-looking mom with twin toddlers.

"Making you nervous, aren't I?" Trigger drawled after me. "I'll get your name, girly-girl."

With only half my mind present, I scribbled down the mother's order, then hustled inside. It was going to drive me crazy, trying to place Trigger McClure. His name didn't ring any bells, but his face certainly did. It had changed since the last time I'd seen it—whenever that had been. He'd grown up a bit, trimmed out that baby face, which was why I hadn't recognized him at first—but at some point, Trigger and I had crossed paths. And I couldn't fathom how. When would I have met a country boy from Nebraska?

It would have been long before I became Stella Gordon. If I knew Trigger, he might know me—the real me. He was a potential breach in my cover story.

Unless he didn't remember me. It was a possibility. After all, it had taken me a moment to recall him. No, not recall. I still hadn't placed him. I was beginning to doubt I'd ever met him. Maybe, years ago, I'd sat across the aisle from him on a plane, and I was confusing a simple glance in passing with a deeper, more pro-longed connection. If I couldn't remember how I knew Trigger, there was a good chance he wouldn't remember me, either.

I knew I should tell Carmina. Deputy Price would want to know about this. But if they thought there was a breach, they'd probably yank me out. Thunder Basin hadn't grown on me, but the last thing I wanted was to relocate to another middle-of-nowhere town. I had a job here. I was beginning to learn my way around. And I had Chet.

The instant I thought Chet's name, I wondered why I had. Sure, he was friendly, but he wasn't a reason to stay. I supposed I liked how he had a funny way of making me forget I didn't want to be here.

I just had to make sure our relationship didn't stray over a certain line.

After hanging my new orders on the cooks' wheel, I picked up a food tray and started to carry it outside.

"He give you any flack?"

I glanced over my shoulder to find Inny dispensing vanilla ice cream into a malt cup. She put it under the malt machine, which kicked on with a high-pitched whir.

"Nothing I can't handle," I called over the noise.

"Don't be afraid to yell at him if he gets out of line. Dixie Jo wouldn't fire you over it. She hates him. Probably, she'd give you a raise."

"Food's getting cold," I said, hoisting my tray a notch. I wasn't sure about Inny yet. Instinct told me not to trust her, but there was something about her, something I couldn't name outright, that I liked. Or maybe admired. She didn't strike me as a girl who'd shy away from demanding her boyfriend use a condom, so I concluded it must have broken in the act. Her pregnancy was a genuine misfortune, not an oversight. Because this girl was as tough as concrete. Like me, Inny didn't back down easily.

As I delivered the food to a family of five in a Suburban, Trigger honked his horn. Leaning across the bench seat, he yelled through the passenger window. "Hey, No-Name! I wanna change my order. Scratch the chicken fried steak. I want a bacon-mushroom burger, medium rare. And fries. Bring me some of them, too."

I paused, making sure I could pull on a face of serenity before I strolled over. "As a regular customer, I'm sure you're aware of our policy. I apologize for any inconvenience, but once an order goes to the grill, you're stuck with it." With that, I strode toward the carhop door. I didn't want to give him time to argue with me.

No such luck.

"Hey!" Trigger hollered, slamming his truck door as he came after me. "Tell Inny to get her butt out here. I don't want you. I want her."

"Inny's working the dining room. You want her? Get a table inside. Either way, if your order's on the grill, and I'm betting more than that, it's probably almost done, you're paying for it."

And if you stiff me, I swear I'll do worse than spit in your food the next time you come around.

I pushed into the diner and let the door fall shut in his face.

The kitchen was hot. Steam from the pots and pans fogged the windows, and I blew my bangs off my forehead, which felt plastered to my skin. I'd have given anything for a reason to step inside the walk-in freezer, but Eduardo, the head cook, was dinging the bell for my next order. Trigger McClure's order, as fate would have it.

"I'll grab it in a sec!" I told Eduardo. Trigger McClure could stand to let his food cool. And his heels, if I had any say.

In the ladies' room, I grasped the sink and blinked at my reflection. My legs throbbed and I longed for a chair and stool to kick up my feet. I was only three hours into my shift, and already bed sounded pretty darn appealing. Turning on the tap, I splashed my face and wiped down the back of my neck.

"Trigger McClure is a self-important jerk who deserves a shot of urine in his next Mountain Dew," I murmured at the mirror. The thought brought a fleeting smile to my lips. It was a thought delicious enough that it just might, I decided, get me through the night. I exhaled, letting my clenched shoulders loosen, and that's when I heard the toilet flush.

Inny stepped out from behind the stall door. Just like that, the tension jumped back into my shoulders and the rest of me filled with sickened dread.

"I—" I began. But what could I say? She'd heard every word. Even though I would never pee in anyone's drink, I hadn't left much ambiguity as to my intentions.

Inny stepped up to the sink and scrubbed her hands. Eyes glued to the mirror, she tousled her black hair. Then she gritted her teeth, examining the cracks for food. "Urine?" she said at last.

"Please don't tell Dixie Jo—"

"Urine?" she repeated, louder. "You couldn't think up anything better than urine?"

Unsure where she was taking this, I ignored her baiting, even though a few more-disgusting options had sprung to mind. Perhaps discretion was the better part of valor.

"First time Trigger grabbed my ass on the job," Inny said, "I put a dead cricket in his hamburger. And all you can come up with is urine?" She shook her head. "Maybe I was right. Maybe he is gonna walk all over you."

Still cautious, I said nothing.

Inny bent over the sink, applying a fresh swath of lipstick. "I just told you I put a dead cricket in a customer's food and you've got nothing to say?"

I grazed her eyes in the mirror but didn't fully meet them. "What's his problem, anyway?" I asked carefully.

"Isn't it obvious? He has a small dick."

At last our eyes locked. Very slowly, we smiled.

"He plays baseball," Inny went on. "All the scouts got their eye on him. He's a pitcher, and a leftie at that. You oughta see his fastball. Ninety miles per hour with a little tail to it. Ball takes a sharp, cutting left-to-right curve just before it sails over the plate." She whistled with admiration. "And his change-up? 'Bout fifteen miles per hour slower than his fastball, but with a right-to-left sinking tail. The whole town is convinced he'll play in the majors—and with good reason. Believe it or not," she added cynically, "not many celebrities are born in Thunder Basin, so he's caused quite a commotion. Course, all the attention has gone to his head. And left him depleted in certain other areas."

"Sounds like you know a lot about Trigger."

She shrugged. "I know baseball."

"If he's headed to the majors, he'll be leaving town soon. That should give you—us—a reason to smile."

"Yeah," Inny said, but without the amused snort I'd expected. If anything, her tone sounded moody.

"He asked for you. I told him you're working the dining room tonight."

Inny grunted, snapping back to her sharp-eyed self. "I've worked here long enough to know what he likes. He doesn't have the patience to deal with anyone else."

I waited for her to say more, but she dried her hands and left the bathroom without another word.

Still pondering my strange, but not necessarily unwelcome, conversation with Inny, I gave her a minute's head start, then followed after. I picked up Trigger's order and carted it outside. Knowing Inny was on my side gave me the motivation I needed to face Trigger again. There was something to be said about solidarity.

"One chicken fried steak," I said, passing the take-out bag through Trigger's window, "and one ice-cold Mountain Dew."

He flung the bag back at me, nearly spilling the drink in my outstretched hand.

My temper took an edge. "I can place a second order for a burger and fries, but as I already explained—"

"Get Inny out here now."

It took all my willpower to speak calmly. "As flattering as your tone is, I can't do that. Inny is working. So am I. If you look around, you'll see there are five other cars waiting on their orders." I passed a faux-leather check folder with his tab through the window. "We take cash or credit card. No personal checks."

Trigger didn't accept the check folder. He grabbed the soda instead. The next thing I knew, the lid was off and the contents of the cup were flying at me.

I gasped, wiping ice-cold soda out of my eyes.

"Damn. There goes a perfectly good pop," Trigger drawled.

I counted to ten. I did it again. When I spoke, I made sure my voice was cool and level. "I've heard you're quite the baseball player. Pitcher, is it? Let's hope you handle your balls better than your drink."

Blotchy color flushed Trigger's face, but he merely grabbed himself, hitching his crotch blatantly, and said, "Wouldn't you like to know."

Then he slammed his truck in reverse and gunned down the street.

I don't know how long I stood staring at the plumes of exhaust rolling off the road, feeling my throat clench tighter. I squeezed my eyes shut, telling myself it was the soda that was making them sting. I felt a horrible and unwanted tickle in my nose, and knew I was close to crying. So much for being the tough girl from Philly. I was going to let that jerk make me cry. I hated him for it—almost as much as I hated myself.

Right when I thought I was going to lose it, Inny came up beside me.

"Here," she said, handing me a dish towel. "Just so you know, you've got a ways to go before you catch me. He's done that to me three times. Four if you count the chocolate milk shake. Man, that took forever to wash out of my hair."

I wanted to laugh, but my throat felt thick and slippery.

"Dixie Jo will get the money for his order from his parents, but I can't promise a tip. Trigger's mom and dad are his biggest fans. Probably he'll tell them you're a scorned lover and you dumped the drink on yourself to get his attention." Inny looked sidelong at me. "You'd be amazed how many girls in this town are scorned lovers of Trigger McClure."

"Because no way could a girl hate him simply because he's an asshole."

"Exactly."

"Want to grab a bite after our shift?" I asked Inny, the dampness finally leaving my eyes. The way this night was going, I could use a little company. And despite my earlier judgments, it was starting to look like Inny and I had something in common after all.

"Not tonight." She yawned, stroking her huge belly absently. "I'll be lucky to stay awake on the drive home. Third trimester's a kick in the pants."

* * *

When I got to Carmina's, she was waiting up. She sat on one of the faded blue corduroy sofas in the living room, flipping idly through a book. At the sight of me, she removed her reading glasses, letting them hang from the chain around her neck.

"How was it?"

"Busy."

"Legs hurt?"

"Not too bad."

"They'll hurt tomorrow. You should wear support hose."

I had my hand on the banister, and I tipped my chin tiredly upstairs. "I'm going to bed." Car-hopping was grueling work. Even if the library hadn't been closed by the time my shift ended, I wasn't sure I could have made the extra effort to pedal there and see if Reed had e-mailed me back. And that was saying a lot. Because I was basically living for that e-mail.

"Do you have a computer?" I managed to ask Carmina, pausing in my slow drag upstairs.

"An old laptop. But it's locked up," she quickly added, making it clear the laptop was off-limits.

"Let me guess. The Feds said it would be too big a temptation for me?"

"The people looking for you could track the computer's address straight to Thunder Basin," she pointed out gravely.

"It's called an IP address." But beneath my scorn, I felt icy bumps rise along my entire body. I had used a computer at the library to contact Reed. I'd been careful, so careful. But there was always a risk. Telling myself that if Danny Balando was on to my secret e-mail account, I'd be dead by now, didn't ease my mind. Maybe it was best to lie low for a while. But that would mean waiting even longer to talk to Reed, and I was desperate to plan our future. It was the hope of being with him again that pulled me from bed each morning.

"Chet Falconer called," Carmina said.

"What did he want?"

"To talk to you."

"Now that that's cleared up, can I use the phone, please?" I said with withering sarcasm.

"It's eleven, Stella. Too late for phone calls. You can try him in the morning."

I laughed quietly, but I wasn't humored. Unbelievable. She wouldn't give up—she was as determined as ever to keep Chet and me apart. Maybe I needed to tell her my mom had tried the same tactic with Reed, and look how well that had turned out.

"A mannered young woman doesn't make house calls after nine," she added.

"That's not what this is about. You couldn't care less about propriety. You don't want me talking to him. Admit it."

Carmina lifted her book, putting her nose in it, ending our conversation. Shutting me out. So this was how she dealt when things threatened to not go her way.

Well. At least I could say the mystery of where my first paycheck was going had just been solved. I needed a cell phone. Stat.

I WORKED THE FOLLOWING NIGHT. IT WAS INNY'S DAY off, and without her sharp-tongued and pithy observations about life in the kitchen, my shift felt overwhelmingly long. The Sundown locked its doors at ten, but the kitchen didn't fully wind down for at least another forty-five minutes. Sinks and floors needed to be scrubbed, the ice-cream machine needed to be flushed with hot water, and the garbage had to be taken out. Since I was lowest on the totem pole, the other waitresses took off early, leaving me to finish up the last of the cleaning. At a quarter to eleven, I ducked my head into Dixie Jo's office to say good-bye.

"You look tired," she told me, scrutinizing me with keenly observant eyes. "How you holding up?"

"Better." I sighed. "Didn't screw up any orders tonight."

"I heard about Trigger McClure."

"Figured you would."

She came around her desk, leaning back against it to look at me directly. "Can't stand that kid. Does this for my blood pressure—" She marked the air over her head.

"Yeah, Inny told me."

That earned me a cocked eyebrow. "Inny Foxhall? Talking to the new girl? What's the world coming to?" She went on to explain. "Inny's slow to warm to people. She's built up quite a few fences, as you might have guessed. Figures it's easier to hold the world at a distance than open herself up to ridicule."

"Because of the pregnancy?"

"It doesn't help. She's different in a world where fitting in is the only way."

High school. Got it. "How far along is she?"

"Seven months. Due the second week of August."

"I feel sorry for her."

Dixie Jo's eyes cooled and her posture stiffened. "Don't you ever say that again, Stella. Inny's tough as the hinges on the gates of hell, but I'll tell you what will break her. Pity. Want to help? Don't make her feel inferior. Treat her same as you would anyone else." She relaxed against the desk, trying to slow her breathing. "I'm sorry. I didn't mean for that to come out so harsh. But Inny's—how do I say this?—I feel a bit responsible for her. That girl could use a little kindness. That's all I'm trying to say."

I took her scolding to heart. And made a mental note to never bring up Inny's pregnancy again. But it did make me wonder. What else was going on with Inny? I sensed Dixie Jo's worry ran deeper than her pregnancy. What was the rest of the story?

"Now. Is the trash out?" Dixie Jo asked, her voice returning to its normal pleasantness. "Is the ice-cream machine clean?"

"Yes."

"Good. See you Thursday. Night, Stella."

While pedaling to Carmina's, I passed a lit-up convenience store with two cars in the parking lot. The Red Barn advertised gas, cigarettes, and hot sandwiches. My meals at the Sundown were discounted, but smelling frying onions and boiling chicken, mixed with the tang of human perspiration, for six straight hours was enough to halt my appetite at work. Now I was starving, and I propped my bike against a tree and rifled through my pocket, coming up with thirty dollars in tips. My blood sugar was so low, I would have willingly traded all my money for an ice-cold Coke.

I was halfway across the parking lot when I saw him. Trigger McClure leaned against the brick storefront, watching cars zip down the road with hawkish focus. One truck slowed and pulled into the lot. Trigger immediately straightened, staring at the truck greedily.

A man in ripped jeans slid out of the truck and ambled toward the Red Barn's doors, paging through his wallet for cash. At that moment, Trigger detached himself from the wall and greeted the man in friendly tones.

"What's it gonna take to get you to grab me a six-pack?" I heard Trigger say casually. "How's a twenty sound? You keep the change."

The guy uttered a throaty laugh. "Why not? I remember being your age. Sucks, don't it?"

Trigger clapped him on the back, and passed over the twenty. "I owe you, man."

"Just make us proud when you're in the majors, you hear?"

I pulled back into the shadows, watching the scene play out. Minutes later, the man came out with two bags of groceries. He handed the six-pack to Trigger, and the two exchanged jokes that were too quiet for me to hear, other than the occasional boom of laughter. Soon after, the man left. Trigger climbed inside his own truck and stayed there. With his lights off, it was impossible to see what he was doing. But I had a pretty good guess.

It didn't raise my opinion of him, but I shelved any remaining thought of Trigger. I didn't want to think about him; I wanted an ice-cold drink, and to sit under an AC vent with my hair lifted so the artificial breeze would whisper over my neck.

Inside, I grabbed a bottle of Coke from the icebox and browsed the sandwiches in the deli case. While I was making my selection, the cashier, a woman with bleached hair and messy eyeliner, took off her apron and hollered into the back room.

"Theo!"

A scrawny, bespectacled kid who had a constellation of acne dotting his chin stuck his head out the door. "Right here, Mom."

"I'm taking fifteen," she told him, reaching for the cigarettes and lighter in her back pocket. She'd lit up and completed a full drag before the exit doors closed at her back.

"Can I help you?" Theo asked me brightly, his voice cracking with puberty.

I set my food—I'd decided on a ham and Swiss sandwich—on the counter and gave him a conspiratorial smile. "How old are you?"

"Sixteen."

"Liar."

He swallowed, his Adam's apple bobbing nervously. "Fourteen. Are you gonna turn my mom in? I only work after nine when she's on break. Fifteen minutes here and there. Can hardly be called breaking the law. Otherwise I just hang out in the back room and play video games."

"I didn't hear any video games."

Theo looked ready to wet his pants. He glanced down and saw that his hands were shaking. Quickly, he folded his arms over his chest to hide his nervousness.

"What were you really doing in the back room?" I asked, thinking I already had a good idea. Assuming he had a computer, and wasn't playing video games, I could think of only one other reason a fourteen-year-old kid would be glued to a screen.

So he took me completely unaware when he whispered miserably, "Sewing. I was sewing." He dropped his chin and hunched his shoulders, as if bracing himself for my certain ridicule.

Not twenty minutes ago, Dixie Jo had scolded me for pitying Inny, but I couldn't look at Theo's despairing face and not feel sorry for him. "Sewing?" I said, trying to sound casual and interested. "What's so bad about that?"

Theo jerked his eyes around the store, but even after confirming we were alone, he motioned for me to lower my voice. "Y-y-you're not going to make fun of me?" He blinked owlishly up at me, clearly baffled.

"What kinds of things do you sew?"

His face softened fractionally. "Well, right now I'm working on a sports coat. It's hard to find an impeccably tailored blazer in Thunder Basin. I'm using a bright navy wool, and hope to have it ready to wear by autumn—" He stopped himself, chewed his lip, and examined my face earnestly, gauging whether to reveal more.

"I'd like to learn how to hem my clothes," I said. In Philly, my mom routinely used a seamstress. Inga was her name, I think. But Theo was right—things were different in Thunder Basin. I didn't know where, or even if, I could get my nicer clothes tailored. More important, would I even have an occasion to wear them here? "Maybe you could teach me sometime?" I suggested just the same.

Theo's entire face seemed to melt with happiness. "Of course! Anytime. It's not hard at all. And I'm a great teacher—honestly. I'm not tooting my own horn, even though it sounds like I am."

"It's a date."

Bumping his glasses up his nose again, Theo beamed. And then his eyes shifted behind me. The color drained from his face and he gulped. "Oh, no," he whispered hoarsely.

Before I could ask what was wrong, the door chimed and I turned to see Trigger swagger in, an open beer can in his hand. He saw me at the same moment, chuckled under his breath, and raised the can in a salute. Or maybe he was threatening me with a second dousing of liquid in my face. Either way, the gesture soured my mood.

"Theo." Trigger drawled the kid's name with enough insult to make it sound like the punch line to a crude joke. "Good to see you, my man. I was worried you weren't working tonight. Didn't see you when I stuck my head in earlier. You weren't hiding from me, were you? How many times I gotta tell you: I always find my man."

Theo's eyes dropped to the floor. His chin was tucked against his chest, and when he spoke, it was barely audible. "You got your beer. I saw that man give it to you. Can you please just go?"

"Go? We have a deal, Theo."

Theo blinked nervously at the side doors. "My mom will be back any minute—"

"Your mom's an alcoholic," Trigger cut in. "I saw the Smirnoff tucked under her arm. She's gonna pass out by the Dumpsters and be out cold for hours. It's just you and me. No mommy dearest to save you." The teasing left his voice. "You owe me a case of beer. Pass it over. Quick now. I'm behind schedule 'cause of you."

"My mom keeps meticulous inventory records. If you continue to come in every weekend, at the end of the month she's going to notice we're short four cases of Miller High Life."

"You're a smart kid," Trigger said. "Work it out."

"Someone has to pay for the beer," Theo insisted. "You're stealing from our store."

Trigger gave a sigh of exaggerated patience and walked over to jab Theo in the chest. "It ain't stealing if it's a donation. Get that in your head. Now grab me a case. Or you're not invited to the party."

"I don't care about the parties anymore. I made a mistake. I—d-d-don't want to go," Theo stammered. "You should leave. You really should go now."

Trigger dropped his smile and put an edge in his tone. He leaned heavily on the counter, causing Theo to shuffle backward two steps. "I'm gonna give you five seconds to gimme the beer, you zit-faced runt. Five. Four."

I watched Theo's lip begin to quiver, and I inwardly groaned. Damn my sense of moral duty. I'd dealt with Trigger last night, and while I wasn't in the mood to do it again, I felt I'd fare better than Theo, who looked moments away from crying. Trigger had caused enough tears this week. Plus, my Coke was getting warm. I hadn't stood on my feet for six hours, shuttling trays of food, to reward myself with a lukewarm soda.

Trigger had set his can of beer on the counter, and I slid it away from my sandwich and Coke. I did it with enough force to make it clear I was here first and didn't appreciate him cutting in line. "How much do I owe?" I asked Theo.

"You again," Trigger said to me, his mouth forming a swaggering smile. "Don't you got something better to do than follow me?"

"I was here first," I said simply.

"You always this prickly? A girl cactus, that's what you are." He stroked a finger down my arm, and I batted it away. If he touched me again, I'd break his finger.

"How much do I owe?" I repeated more firmly to Theo.

"Five ninety-seven," he said nervously.

"Here's ten. And how much does a case of Miller High Life cost?"

Theo's chin jerked up, and he watched me with amazement and guilt in equal measure. "Don't worry about it," he muttered, "I'll cover the cost."

Trigger chuckled, waving for Theo to be quiet. "I'm not gonna let a pretty girl buy my beer." He faced me. "But I'd love to get you a drink. Once Theo gets me that case, why don't you hop in my truck? Great party happening tonight at Lake Maloney. I'll show you a good time. Go on, Theo. Don't make this girl come to your rescue."

"Oh, I wasn't offering to pay for the beer," I chimed in. "Just curious how much you were trying to walk off with."

Trigger frowned at me. "What?"

"You have exactly five seconds to get out of here before I call the cops," I told him. I didn't have a cell, but I'd seen a pay phone out front and I knew 911 calls were free.

He shook his head, puzzled. "What?" he echoed.

"Let me make this simple." I pointed to the doors. "Walk that way. Don't look back, and don't come in here again."

Ignoring me, he tilted his head to one side. Through the tipsy glaze in his eyes, I saw a flash of something that made my stomach squeeze. "Have I seen you before?"

I swallowed, but kept the nerves out of my voice. "Yeah, yesterday. Remember? You threw your drink in my face."

"No, before then. . . ." His voice trailed off, but he eyed me with more intensity, as if trying to recall something from long ago. Whatever he was reaching for, I couldn't let him find it.

"You're drunk, Trigger. You can't see straight, let alone think rationally. You shouldn't be driving. Call a friend to pick you up."

"I swear, something about you . . ."

"Go." I gave him a light shove for emphasis.

A look of concentration still clouded his features, but to my relief, he let my shove propel him backward toward the doors. He pointed an unsteady finger at Theo. "I'll be back. Next time, no hiding behind your girlfriend," he slurred with a lopsided smile, the alcohol clearly starting to give him a serious buzz.

The minute Trigger was outside, I said to Theo, "Lock the doors and call the police."

He balked. "What?"

"If you're not going to, hand the phone over—I'll call."

"W-w-what are you going to tell them?"

"The truth."

"Trigger will kill me if I turn him in. If you call, it will make everything ten times worse. Please don't do it!"

"Stop being so dramatic. He's drunk. He shouldn't be driving. Anyway, he can't come after you—he'll be on record for harassing you, and the cops won't tolerate it." I plucked the cell phone from the chest pocket of his shirt and dialed.

Theo clenched his fists under his chin, his face greening by the second. I thought about reassuring him further, but didn't think he'd listen. I knew he'd be fine. Soon enough, he'd see that I was right.

Despite how much I'd complained about the constant supervision of the U.S. marshals, if there was one thing I'd learned about law enforcement during my three whirlwind days with them, it was that I could depend on them. Without hesitation, I made the call.

Ten minutes later a uniformed officer tapped on the glass and

I let him in. While Theo wrung his hands and shot me looks of deep uncertainty, the officer took my statement. When I implicated Trigger, the officer's brows swept up.

He held that mildly interested expression while I finished giving my whole account, then said, "You sure you want to stick with this story?" It almost sounded like he was advising me against reporting Trigger. Surely I was just misreading him.

"Um, that would be a *yes*."

"Did you see which way Trigger drove off?"

"He said he was going to a party at Lake Maloney."

"If this goes further and Trigger is arrested and charged, you may be subpoenaed to testify as a witness in court."

A cold shudder whipped up my spine. Would creating a case against Trigger bring me media attention I couldn't afford? Someone needed to stand up to him, but was it worth exposing myself? I remembered Danny Balando staring me down from behind the two-way glass in the police lineup. He hadn't been able to see me, but he knew I was there. His chilling gaze made no attempt to disguise what he wanted to do to me. Would this small-town case spread to national media? No, I decided. It was fear, cold and persuasive, trying to scare me away.

"No problem," I told the officer. He didn't know I was in WIT-SEC. Only Carmina and the sheriff knew.

Again, his eyebrows soared, as if to say, *Bad call, little miss.* I was amazed he didn't seem pleased, or even grateful, that one of his fellow citizens was stepping forward to do the right thing. Granted, I had my own selfish reasons for wanting to see Trigger busted, but the officer didn't know that. Either way, I definitely got the impression he was trying to get me to back down. Forget it. Trigger was a douche, and if he got a DWI or worse, it was his own fault—not mine.

"Anything else?" the officer asked.

"Yeah, thanks for being so helpful." I smiled when I said it, but it was probably a good thing he couldn't hear my thoughts, which weren't nearly as polite.

IT WAS FRIDAY AFTER SUNDOWN, AND CHET WOULD
be by any minute to pick me up. My first weekend on the town! I
never thought I'd see the day when I was this excited for a softball
game. But hey, beggars can't be choosers. A night out was a night
out.

I'd played softball in PE, and knew the basics, so I wasn't worried about making a fool of myself. Besides, Chet had told me
the league was slow-pitch. You had to be really uncoordinated to
not hit a ball the size of a grapefruit as it lobbed at a glacial pace
across home plate.

While getting ready for the game, which included dropping a
tee over my head and braiding my hair, I was seized by an unexpected punch to my gut. Out of nowhere, the sobering truth hit
me. I couldn't believe it had taken me this long to see it.

I would never play basketball again. Not at the collegiate level. My senior year of high school down through third grade, I'd spent every winter playing basketball. It was my sport. I was good at it. Sophomore year I'd been bumped up to play a couple of varsity games, and by junior year I was one of the starting five. I received offers to play for Babson College and Penn State, finally committing to Babson.

I lowered myself onto the edge of my bed. I gripped the baseball glove I'd taken from the closet, the one Carmina had said I could borrow. I clung to it like it was my lifeline. I was numb, my pain cutting too deep for tears. Gazing with hollow eyes at the wall, I let the truth swarm in. Before I'd been flown to Nebraska to start my newly incarnated life, I'd known exactly what my future held. A summer of fun and travel with my best friend, Tory, followed by college in the fall. Tory and I were supposed to be in Atlantic City right now. Did she know what had become of me? Did she think I was dead? I felt selfish and ashamed for taking so long to wonder how my friends might be handling my disappearance. As far as I understood, the detectives and U.S. marshals had not and would not explain what had become of me. It was their job to make me vanish. No bread-crumb trail left for anyone— good or bad—to follow.

Given everything that had happened since being whisked into WITSEC just over a week ago, I hadn't had a chance to mourn my old life. Or fully grasp how vastly different—how completely alien—my new future would be.

I struggled to quell the panic and dizziness that seemed to aim alternating blows at me. Those dreams of playing for Babson? Of donning a green-and-white jersey? Gone. My scholarship had dissolved with my identity. My career was finished, I'd never play for myself, my team, or the crowds again, and I'd given it up for what? To put Danny Balando behind bars. I'd done the right thing, and it had cost me everything.

Deputy Price had mentioned the government would create new records to help me get into college, but what college? In their suits and badges, the detectives had pretended to have all the answers, but could they tell me this—at seventeen, how was I supposed to start from scratch? The idea of fully accepting Stella Gordon's future gave me a deep, trembling fear of losing myself. Of becoming invisible.

"Stella!" Carmina called from downstairs. "Chet just pulled up."

I shook off my thoughts and breathed deeply until the numbness left. There was no use looking back. There was nothing for me in the past but heartache and remorse. It hurt too much to dwell on everything I'd lost.

I walked downstairs shakily, testing my smile. It felt strained and brittle, and I kept smiling until I got it right. If Chet saw even a suggestion of sorrow, he'd press me on it. If I wanted to avoid his inquiries, I had to pull off normal.

Get it together.

The outside lights were on, and I could see Chet making his way up the porch steps. He had on knee-length nylon shorts and a worn gray T-shirt that looked as soft as tissue. It clung to his body, highlighting his toned chest and shoulders. In Philly, the boys

I knew who had a body like Chet's spent hours at the gym after school. Since there wasn't a gym in Thunder Basin, it was safe to assume Chet earned his body the old-fashioned way: performing manual labor.

He saw us through the screen door and invited himself inside. "Carmina."

"Evening, Chet," she said in a measured tone. "You'll have Stella back by eleven thirty." An order, not a request. "Her curfew is nine, but I'm making an exception for the game."

"I don't have work tomorrow," I told Chet. "I can sleep in. We can stay out as late as we want."

"Curfew is eleven thirty," Carmina repeated firmly.

"It's Friday night," I said, giving her a look that said she was treating me like a child and needed to stop—immediately. "What if there's a party after the game?"

"Kindly tell your friends you won't be going."

"I don't have friends! That's the point. You keep me caged up in this house. You knew I was a teenager when you signed on for this, so why do you keep acting like I'm five?"

"All right," Chet said loudly, stepping between us. "The game starts in thirty. We should get going, Stella." He turned to Carmina. "I'll have her back by eleven thirty."

My jaw dropped. "You're letting her have her way."

He put his arm around my shoulders and steered me carefully out the door. "You got a mitt?"

He knew I had a baseball glove. I was holding it. He was purposefully changing the subject to distract me. And against the voice in my head that was screaming for me to turn back and have it out with Carmina, to give her the fight she seemed to want, I bit my tongue, choosing instead to fume in silence. I'd rejected most of my mother's early attempts to raise me properly, but in this one instance, I took her instruction and decided to spare Chet needless embarrassment. I'd wait to give Carmina my opinion of her actions in private.

Chet closed the screen door behind us and audibly let go of the breath he'd been holding.

"Someone needs to stand up to her," I argued, directing my pent-up frustration at him. "You're obviously afraid to, but I'm not. If there's a party after the game, we're going. What's the worst Carmina can do? Kick me out?" I shut my mouth to keep from saying more, but that didn't stop me from thinking it. *Go ahead, kick me out. Let's see how fast it takes Price and his friends at the DOJ to show up on your doorstep.*

Chet opened my car door, shutting it wordlessly behind me.

We didn't talk on the drive to the softball field, and I wondered if this was some secret ploy of his to give me time to cool off. Well, I didn't feel like cooling off. I knew there was history between Chet and Carmina, and I knew she strongly disliked him, or at least didn't want me around him, but this was getting ridiculous. She couldn't keep us apart by punishing me. I wouldn't tolerate it. But the real issue was that Chet should be taking my side. That's what I really wanted. He had a lot of things going for him, but his insistence on being polite to Carmina wasn't one of them. It was what I loved about Reed—he took my side, even if it meant going against my mom. He wasn't afraid of her. Of course, most of the time when he had come over, she'd been passed out in bed, but the point was, he was on my side. I couldn't say the same of Chet. The deeper this realization sank, the more betrayed I felt.

Chet parked and glanced at me warily.

I jumped out of the Scout and shut the door hard. I wanted him to know I was upset. Maybe it would give him something to think about. If he was trying to get on my good side, sweetening up to Carmina wasn't the way. She meant nothing to me. She basically *was* my parole officer.

Stadium lights blazed on the raked dirt of the infield and the thick green grass of the outfield. The foul lines were freshly chalked, and the concession stand had a line trailing down the sidewalk.

"You play before?" Chet asked as he led the way to our team's dugout.

"Wiffle ball counts, right?"

He gave me a startled rake of his eyes. "Uh—"

"Relax. I've played. But it's been awhile, so don't expect a home run on my first at bat."

Chet trotted down the steps to the dugout and cleared his throat to get the team's attention. "Everyone, this is Stella, the new player I told you about. Stella, this is the team. I won't bother with individual introductions—you guys can introduce yourselves better than I can—except to tell Stella to watch out for that guy in the Broncos hat. He thinks he's Don Juan."

Everyone laughed, apparently finding some truth in the joke.

"Don Juan's got nothing on me," the guy in the Broncos hat

said in a voice like silken chocolate. "I'm the real deal." He winked at me, puckering his lips to blow me an air kiss.

I blew a kiss back, then stared him down smugly, showing him I could handle anything he wanted to dish out. The team ate this up, laughing and teasing Don Juan.

When the laughing died down, I took a seat on the end of the bench, startled to find that the girl next to me was wearing perfume. It was so strong, it seemed to leak from every pore. I glanced furtively at her, noting she was wearing lipstick, too. Actually, she had a whole face of makeup. Leaning forward so I could see down the entire bench, I observed the rest of the girls. One had curled her golden hair into ringlets. Another wore denim shorts studded with rhinestones, and hoop earrings. I was the only girl who looked like she'd actually come to play softball.

Once upon a time, I'd been one of them. I'd cared what I looked like, especially when boys were involved. But I wasn't Estella Goodwinn anymore. I was Stella Gordon. I'd already traded my Manolo Blahniks for softball cleats, and now I was going to have to trade my expensive salon haircuts for the mom-and-pop barber shop version. I hadn't seen another option in Thunder Basin, and more importantly, I was on a monthly government stipend. Not wanting Danny Balando's cartel to trace my family's money from our bank accounts and use the paper trail to find me, the government had seized our assets and allotted me a monthly payout, which was about as generous as you'd expect from the government. Given my monetary restraints and my inability to care about keeping up Stella Gordon's facade, I didn't see the point in trying to be fashionable or pretty anymore. I didn't even know who I was anymore.

"I'm Sydney," the girl next to me, the one drenched in perfume, said. She had the sweet, translucent face of a milkmaid, and blond braids to match.

"Stella," I replied, thinking this conversation was a waste since she and I would never be friends. I had her figured out in all of thirty seconds: She was the sweet, innocent, country type. She'd probably marry straight out of high school and have a kid before her twentieth birthday. Of course, I'd been wrong about Inny, I had to remember that. Maybe I'd find I was wrong about Sydney, too. I remembered Chet's admonition to give the town—and those in it—a chance before blowing them off. I supposed I could take his advice.

"So you're friends with Chet?" Sydney asked. "I noticed he gave you a ride."

"I don't have a car, and he lives close by."

Her brow scrunched in confusion. "He lives out in the meadows on Sapphire Skies. He doesn't really have neighbors. Where do you live?"

"I'm staying at Carmina Songster's for the summer."

Her eyes went round, and she said, "Oh." I could tell by the tone of her voice that she'd heard of me. Whether from Chet or someone else, I couldn't say. "Just for the summer, though?" she confirmed.

"That's the plan." I decided it was more polite than Yes—hallelujah!

"I've known Chet a long time. When I was little, I had a crush on him, but I'm so over that now," she added with a laugh, then studied me a little too closely while she waited for my response.

"He seems like a pretty cool guy."

"Oh, yeah." She kneaded her hands uncomfortably in her lap.

Chet, who'd been going over the batting lineup with the team, crouched in front of Sydney and me. "Stella, you're batting third and playing right field. Sydney, you're batting seventh and playing center. Sound good?"

Sydney nodded, smiling eagerly—no, adoringly—at Chet. He didn't appear to notice, ruffling her hair like he would a kid sister's. When he shifted his attention to me, I pinned him with an unmistakable look of reprimand, then darted my eyes toward Sydney, who sat beside me unaware. I was very obviously trying to communicate to him that he had treated Sydney improperly and should give her a different kind of attention.

His brow furrowed and he shook his head slightly, indicating he didn't understand. With exasperation, I jerked my head more vigorously in Sydney's direction.

"Um, Sydney?" Chet began uncertainly, glancing at me for confirmation that he was proceeding correctly. "Would you . . . like to join me at the pitcher's mound for the coin toss?"

I beamed, signaling he'd done well, but he once again wagged his head in confusion, eyeing me like I'd sprouted alien antennae.

Chet and Sydney jogged to the pitcher's mound for the coin toss, then returned to tell us we'd bat first. The umpires took their places on the field, one behind home plate, the other behind first base. Don Juan was first up to bat.

"What's his real name?" I asked Chet, who had taken a seat on the bench beside me.

"Juan. Yeah, I know. Irony."

At bat, Juan swung powerfully and missed. Even from here, I heard him swear in Spanish. The umpire pointed a warning finger at him, spoke a few stern words, and the rest of our team giggled behind their hands.

"Showboat," Chet muttered, shaking his head, but he was smiling.

"Is he your best friend?" I asked.

"That's such a girl thing to say." He thumbed his nose. "But yeah. I guess that's what he is. He sat by me at lunch in kindergarten and split his Twinkie with me. The rest is history."

For the second time, I glanced down the bench to survey our team. "Anyone else you should warn me about?"

"Yeah, the shortstop. He's tough on the field, but he wears his heart on his sleeve." He nudged his thigh against mine, and the air around us seemed to grow heavy and harder to breathe. Chet's playfulness felt awfully affectionate. And his intentions way too direct.

I laughed airily, trying to lighten the mood, but felt the sudden urge to step out of the dugout and get some fresh air. Chet was flirting with me. It had to stop. Reed was my boyfriend. I made a mental note to swing by the library first chance I got, probably before work on Monday, and check the e-mail account. Surely he'd left a message by now.

But that didn't help me tonight. I needed to dispel any notions in Chet's head that I was willing to take our relationship to a new level, and I needed to dispel them *now*.

I also needed to get myself under control. Chet was being alarmingly direct, and I wasn't used to it. Reed had never overtly flirted with me; his way of showing he cared was always subtle. Touching my hand. Meeting my eyes across a room. Playing my favorite songs when we were driving in his car. He was secretive about everything he did, including revealing emotion, which meant I had to work a little harder to notice his affection. In contrast, Chet was straightforward and open. It made me feel almost uncomfortable—like stepping into noonday sun after a lengthy period indoors. It also made my heart yearn dangerously for more.

Juan had struck out and was walking back dejectedly to the dugout, and I seized my chance.

"Can't even make it to first base?" I quipped as he threw his bat down in self-disgust.

"With you, cariño, I'd go all the way to home." With fluid grace, Juan inserted himself between me and Chet, and draped his arm over my shoulder. "Don't be nervous. I'm a good teacher."

"Knock it off," Chet said, giving him a playful shove off the bench. But I noticed Chet's face had turned slightly pink.

Not giving up, Juan pulled me to my feet, pressed my body to his, and engaged me in a seductive Latin dance, humming a melodic tune in my ear. I played along, dancing with him, grateful that his comical routine had quickly defused the loaded moment Chet and I had experienced back there.

I laughed. "You're good, I'll give you that."

"I'm the gift that keeps on giving," Juan murmured tantalizingly against my cheek.

"Okay, break it up, Stella's next at bat," Chet reminded us. He handed me a bat and tipped his head at home plate. "Go get 'em, Slugger."

I took a few practice swings outside the dugout while the girl at bat hit a fly ball that was caught by the third baseman. The ump pronounced her out, and I stepped into the batter's box. In the dugout, I could hear Chet whistling and clapping for me. He was a good team captain, and was shaping up to be a good friend, and I told myself that's all we'd ever be—friends.

I settled my feet in the dirt and choked up on the bat. It was a little long, and I was only aiming for a base hit—no flashy tricks tonight. The pitcher rocked back on her heel, then sent the ball in an easy lob toward me. I went after the first pitch with an aggressive swing. I heard the crack of the ball, tossed the bat aside, and ran. I'd squeezed a line drive between shortstop and second, and easily made it to first base.

While our dugout erupted in cheering, I bobbed a curtsy.

Chet grinned ear to ear, but I quickly avoided eye contact, choosing to pucker up for Juan instead, who was drawing a circle in the air with his finger, a clear innuendo for "going all the way."

Chet followed me at bat, and pulled off a double after hitting a pop fly deep into left field. We played seven innings and won the game 5–4, bumping our season record to 3–0. After the game, both teams dispersed to the parking lot, and I watched anxiously as one by one the players got into their cars and drove off. Was no one going to invite me to a party tonight? Not even Juan? He seemed like a guy who'd be on the lookout for a good time and open to a tagalong. I knew Chet would try to talk me into going back to Carmina's, especially since it was after eleven, but that was the last thing I wanted. If I made it back on time, I was letting her win. And I refused to do that.

Feeling deflated, I walked with Chet to the Scout. He opened my door, even though I wished he hadn't. The gesture felt more than polite—it felt intimate. Like I was his date. I suddenly feared he might try to walk me to Carmina's door and get me alone on her porch. Whatever happened, I couldn't let him do that.

As we settled into our seats, I decided the best course of action was to keep things chummy—be one of the guys.

I kicked my heels up on the dash, smiling mischievously. "Sydney likes you." Halfway through the game, she'd cinched her jersey in a knot at her waist, showing off her curvy midriff. She'd also spent every free minute chatting off Chet's ear. Whether you lived in the city or the country, some signals were universal.

Chet glanced bemusedly at me. "What, Sydney?" He shook his head. "No way. She's got a boyfriend. Some bull rider from Hershey. They've been together awhile."

"She had her eye on you all night, lover boy."

"You're imagining things."

"Did you smell how much perfume she was wearing? At first whiff I thought it was Juicy Couture, but now I'm almost positive it was Pheromones to Attract Chet Falconer."

He groaned. "Stop."

"I've got a point and you know it."

"I know no such thing."

"Do you have a girlfriend?" I asked him directly.

He thumbed his nose some more and cleared his throat. "What?"

"You heard me."

"What would make you think I have a girlfriend?"

"Do you?"

"No, I don't," he said, sounding slightly offended that I even had to ask. "Why?"

With that one question our conversation took a sudden serious, and personal, turn, and I didn't like it. So I changed the subject. "When are you taking me out for that celebratory dinner?"

"Whenever you want."

"I was hoping you'd say that," I said, smiling triumphantly and wickedly in equal measure. "I want to go now."

Chet sighed and gave me a reprehensible look. "I promised Carmina I'd have you home by eleven thirty."

"Not even coffee?" I pleaded, batting my lashes persuasively.

His eyes flicked to the clock on the dash: 11:20. "A&W is still open. Drive-through root beer floats, final offer."

I frowned. "You drive a hard bargain."

"Me? You kidding? Mirror's right there," he said, gesturing at the fold-down visor. "You in or out?"

"In," I said, but I made sure to affect a sulky tone.

Chet drove across town, pulled through A&W's drive-through,

and paid for two floats. I couldn't remember the last time I'd had a root beer float. They used soft-serve vanilla ice milk, not the real stuff, but it was still surprisingly good. Chet drove to a nearby park, and we sat in the empty lot with the windows down. The air felt warm and sticky, but with a cold dessert in my hand, I didn't mind.

"Do you have a job?" I asked. "Besides mowing lawns."

He snorted. "You say that like mowing lawns is a lame job."

"You don't have to talk to anyone. You don't even have to shower or dress up," I pointed out.

"I only mow two lawns: Carmina's and my own. During the day, I work at Milton Swope's Ranch. I cut hay, maintain the pasture, and look after the cattle."

"Go on."

He gave me a sidelong glance, gauging to see whether I spoke out of genuine interest or to gain fodder I could tease him with. "It's hard work but never boring. I can be riding a tractor one day, mending a fence the next, and chasing down a lost calf the day after that. Best part, come rain or shine, I'm outdoors. Not stuck in some office hunched over a computer."

"The sun will prematurely age your skin," I pointed out practically.

His laughter turned genuine. "My mom worked in her garden most of her adult life. She had smile lines, crow's-feet, and sun wrinkles, and she was the most beautiful woman I've ever known."

"I'm sorry about your mom, Chet. I'm sorry about both your parents."

He shrugged. "I appreciate that. It gets easier over time. Maybe not easier. Just more tolerable. I think it helps knowing they're not completely gone. I don't believe in a God who creates beings only to let them stop existing. Matter isn't created or destroyed— just transferred, right? I can't see my parents, and I can't talk to them, but I feel them. They're out there. Knowing this makes the loss less painful." After a pause, he smiled slightly. "Knowing my mom is keeping an eye on me forces me to reconsider every time I'm tempted to whip the hide off Dusty's back."

"I don't believe in God," I said bluntly. "If there was a God, I don't understand why he'd let horrible things happen. A God who lets people suffer, who lets people behave abominably toward each other? That's not a God. That's a sadist."

"I know people who feel the way you do. Dusty is one of them. He doesn't understand why God would let my parents die. He thinks if God cared about us, he would have saved our parents. It's a valid viewpoint. I've asked myself the same questions, had the same doubts. But my parents' death has made me a better person. I care more about Dusty now than I ever did before. I don't think God took my parents from us to force me to be a good brother. I don't think he forces any of us—that's my point. He lets bad things happen because he doesn't control us. He lets us run our own lives, and our actions have consequences, good and bad. The drunk driver who killed my parents made a bad decision. If God had saved my parents, one person's bad decision—to drive intoxicated—wouldn't have had a natural and negative consequence. We all have to make mistakes, because it's the only way we learn." He exhaled slowly, pensively. "Some lessons are harder than others."

"That's a noble perspective, but I disagree," I said. "People drive drunk all the time and no one gets killed. If God really wanted to save your parents, he could have."

"Do you wish God had saved your mom?" Chet asked gently.

His question caught me completely off guard. For a moment, I didn't know what to say. He was baring his soul to me, and all I had to give him in return was a carefully crafted lie. My mom wasn't dead. I had nothing in common with Chet, and the fact that I was pretending like I did only made me feel more shallow and deceitful. I hated feeling this way. But what really bothered me, what hurt the most, was knowing Chet thought I was someone I wasn't. Was this how the rest of my life would be? Lying to people and never letting them get close enough to know the real me? I hated Stella Gordon. I hated her more than I'd ever hated anyone.

Except, perhaps, my mother.

"I don't believe in God, remember?" was all I said. Ready to switch the topic, I asked Chet, "Do you know Inny Foxhall?"

He'd taken a pull of root beer, and now he wiped his mouth with the back of his hand. "I think so. Short with dark hair?"

"Yeah. Did you know she's pregnant?"

"I did not."

"C'mon. Small town. News travels."

"It does. Toward people who tune their ear to it."

I made a face like he was being too superior. "Any idea who the father might be?"

"She's in Dusty's grade, I think. He might know."

"Do you know Trigger McClure?"

"Sure."

"Do you think he could be the father?" I didn't have any evidence to back up my suspicion, other than the depressed way Inny had reacted when I suggested Trigger might be leaving town soon to play in the majors. Well, that and the way Trigger seemed to prefer Inny over every other carhop when he came to the Sundown. I couldn't shake the feeling that there was more between them than a routine customer–carhop interaction.

Chet frowned. "Trigger and Inny? Instinct tells me no. But I could be wrong."

"What makes you say no?"

He thought about it, shrugged. "I guess she doesn't seem his type. Again, I could be wrong."

"What's his type?"

The look in his eyes changed from conversational to speculative. "You're not . . . ?"

"Asking for myself? Ew. No. Definitely no." I gave a dramatic shudder, proving my point. I was not interested in Trigger.

Chet seemed to relax in his seat. "If you believe the rumors, Trigger likes older women."

"How much older?"

"Old enough to be experienced." He looked uncomfortable talking about this, fidgeting with the keys dangling from the ignition. "There were rumors about him and a female teacher. Far as I know, they were just rumors."

"Oh, stop looking for the good in people," I said. "I wouldn't put fooling around with a teacher past him. What happened to the teacher?"

"She was moved to a different school mid-semester," he admitted reluctantly. "He was already eighteen when the alleged relationship happened, so the story didn't catch wind."

"See?" I said knowingly, then added with disgust, "Of course she took the fall for it." Just like it had been my fault when Trigger's Mountain Dew found its way onto my face. Every female who crossed paths with Trigger seemed to be at fault. Funny how that kept happening.

"He has a reputation for a nasty temper." There was a muted quality to Chet's voice. Part discomfort, part warning. "And he's physical."

"With girls?"

"With everyone. Maybe with that teacher. I don't know the facts. Just watch yourself with him." He eyed the clock. "I should get you home. Carmina's going to be pacing the doorway with a shotgun."

I made a pouty face, but he obviously had great self-control, because seemingly immune to my charms, he drove us back to Carmina's, parking in the drive at eleven-forty-five on the dot. The downstairs lights were on, but I didn't see Carmina's prowling silhouette through the curtains.

"Thanks for the root beer float," I said.

"Any time."

A notable pause followed.

Chet's eyes found mine, and the hot look in them made me wish I hadn't allowed myself to be alone with him. It was dark in the cab of the Scout, and while the bench seat had seemed roomy every other time I'd ridden beside him, it now felt just the opposite. He sat so close, I could feel heat radiating off his body. I could hear his slow, deep breathing. He rested his arm on the seat back, his hand draped inches from my shoulder. I was hypersensitive to the sweet, spicy scent of him, and even though he wasn't touching me, for one whirlwind moment I thought he might. I felt tipsy and nervous, my nerve endings electrified with anticipation.

And then I saw Reed's face. It popped into the back of my mind, and the image was so real, I almost believed he could see me.

I shoved out of the Scout, practically jumping onto the drive, feeling spooked.

Smiling as naturally as I could under the circumstances, I told Chet, "I'd better get the rest of this float in the freezer before it melts."

I didn't look at his face. I didn't want to see that slow heat again, and be forced to speculate what it meant. I already knew, but I wasn't going to give it another moment's thought. I had to remember I wasn't Stella Gordon, and I wasn't a foster kid who had a future in Thunder Basin or with Chet. I was Estella Goodwinn, and Reed Winslow was my boyfriend.

I dashed up the porch steps, thinking Carmina had better not be on the other side of the door, ready to have words with me. I couldn't handle it tonight. I wanted to clear my head of Chet and focus on what was important: my next trip to the library.

Reed was out there somewhere, and he was trying to contact me.

I was inside the house, with my back pressed to the door, before I heard Chet reverse down the drive. An image of his blue eyes, deep with yearning, drifted into my mind. He'd been easy on the eyes from the first moment I'd seen him, but I'd never found him as attractive as I had in the cab of the Scout tonight. I didn't want this complicated attraction. I didn't know what to do with it.

I wasn't the kind of girl who let a guy slip easily under my skin. I was in control here, dammit.

But I'd be lying if I said I didn't feel shaken by Chet.

"THERE'S A FUND-RAISER AT THE CHURCH TONIGHT,
if that sort of thing interests you." It was the following afternoon,
Saturday, and Carmina stood at the kitchen sink, plunging her
hands into soapy water as she scrubbed barbeque off our lunch
dishes.

"What kind of fund-raiser?" I purposefully kept my tone bland,
not wanting to give her the satisfaction of believing she'd piqued
my interest when she hadn't.

"To aid the women's shelter."

"More details? Is it a car wash? Are they selling popcorn? Over-
priced candy bars?" In past summers, my basketball team had
held weekend car washes when we needed to raise money. It was
the first thing I thought of when I heard "fund-raiser."

"Oh, I suppose you'd call it a carnival," she said, using her forearm to nudge a few white hairs that had strayed from her head-band off her face. "There'll be a ring toss, cake walk, corn-shucking contest, and that game where you throw darts at balloons."

"Will I know anyone?" I half wondered aloud.

"Reckon you will. Pastor Lykins asked several of the youth to help run booths. Plenty of them play in the softball league." She eyed me over her shoulder. "I imagine Chet Falconer will be there, if that's what you're getting at."

"I'm not getting at anything." And I wasn't. I had mixed feelings about seeing Chet again so soon. Last night before bed, I'd put him out of my mind, determined to end whatever complicated feelings I was developing for him. I wanted to keep our relation-ship simple. Friend-simple. Everything was fine until I woke in the dark, my body hot and clammy. And aching. I knew I couldn't control my dreams, but this particular one, involving Chet, the bed of his Scout, and his strong, *very* capable hands, seemed like a betrayal of Reed, and my resolve, just the same.

Frowning, Carmina said, "Don't think it slipped my attention he brought you home after curfew last night."

"I don't have a curfew. And are you seriously going to have a heart attack over fifteen minutes?"

Ignoring me, she said, "Fund-raiser starts at seven. I prom-ised Pastor Lykins I'd get there early to help set up. I'm sure he'd appreciate an extra hand, if you decide to come."

"Not really my thing," I said, yawning widely, which was rude, but I needed to make my point.

"Suit yourself."

And that was that.

But when six thirty rolled around and Carmina was backing down the driveway, I had a *what the hell* moment, grabbed my purse, and dashed down the porch steps. I felt like an idiot chasing her partway down the road before she thought to look in the rearview mirror. She braked, and I hoisted myself into the truck, heaving breath.

"What?" I panted in response to her arched eyebrows. "Maybe I'll die from boredom and be out of your hair for good."

"Or maybe you'll have yourself a good time," she said sweetly.

I gave her a cynical look. She smiled, self-satisfied.

The church parking lot was full. Carmina parked on a side street, and I helped her unload boxes of lollipops, gumballs, balloons, and air pumps, and a couple of bottles of drugstore wine for the wine pull. As we carted the boxes across the church's back lawn, we passed booths advertising pie throwing, face painting, and a myriad of carnival games. There was even a dunk tank. The sun blazed above the trees, the heat broiling my scalp. Sweat trickled down my spine.

I closed my eyes. It felt like summer . . . it just didn't feel like summer. Right now I should have been sunbathing at Tory's pool. Or helping her plan her guest list for her birthday party. She turned eighteen next Wednesday. I wondered if she still thought about me. Of course she did. We'd been best friends for years. Even if she believed I was dead, I would linger in the back of her mind, making her cry at random moments.

I squeezed the bridge of my nose, which was starting to tingle painfully. I couldn't do this. I couldn't keep going back. I was beginning to understand why Deputy Price had told me to start fresh in Thunder Basin. It hurt too much to keep one foot planted in the past. I wanted to hold on to it, but the only thing Philly had to offer me was danger or, worse, death. Keeping it close, pretending it was still an option, was a fantasy. A dangerous fantasy.

I grabbed Carmina's wine bottles and took them to Pastor Lykins, who bustled around the wine pull table, adding tags to the bottles already lined up in neat rows.

"Hello there, Stella," he said, bumping his sunglasses up his nose. He was one of those men who didn't have the face for sunglasses—his was blandly cherubic, and sunglasses looked out of place. They made him look like he was trying too hard. But the rest of his attire was exactly what I would have expected. Dockers, a white shirt, and scuffed loafers. His face shone with perspiration, and the underarms of his shirt bore damp circles. He shook my hand, but his eyes went past me, locking on Carmina. "Carmina sent you to give these to me? I'll have to seek her out as soon as I finish these tags and thank her."

I turned to go, thinking I'd browse the games before the carnival got under way, when I saw several girls my age clustered around a booth I hadn't noticed before. The booth was wrapped in red paper and decorated with large, heart-shaped cutouts. A boom box set on the window's ledge blared a female voice singing enthusiastically, "This kiss, this kiss! Unstoppable. This kiss, this kiss!"

"Who sings this song?" I asked one of the girls at the back of the group.

She stared at me like I couldn't be serious. "Uhh, Faith Hill. It's the song 'This Kiss.'" She watched me like she was waiting for something to click, but I'd never heard of the song. "Get it? 'This Kiss.' It's a kissing booth," she finished impatiently.

Before I could ask if she was serious, a wave of squeals rose up from the girls closest to the booth. A woman was writing names on a poster tacked to the booth's window.

"Trigger McClure!" one girl read aloud as the woman printed his name, followed by the seven o'clock time slot.

"Chet Falconer!" another said giddily.

I nudged the girl beside me a second time. "So this is, like, a real kissing booth. With actual kissing." It was more a declaration of incredulity than a question. Was this politically correct? Judging by the donations jar, the church was actually condoning the idea of buying, well, kisses. There were so many things messed up about this, I couldn't even start to list them.

"Uhh, yeah, obviously," the girl said. "The guy who raises the most money at the end of the night is crowned Mr. Hot Lips. He gets a tiara and a sash and everything. It's really funny. Chet or Trigger will win. Obviously. I mean, look at the other guys who volunteered," she said as the woman added the final two names to the poster. "Donovan Pippin and Theodore LeMahieu?" The girl wrinkled her nose in distaste.

Just then I saw Chet's yellow Scout rumble down the street, and decided it just wouldn't do to pass up an opportunity to tease him. Practically skipping across the yard, I met up with him on the sidewalk.

"Kissing booth?" I said sweetly, keeping step with his long, easy stride. He looked casual and comfortable in jeans, grass-stained boots, and a navy T-shirt that highlighted those striking jewel-blue eyes.

He grinned. "Keeping tabs on me?"

"Hard not to. When they wrote your name on the roster, girls within a ten-mile radius swooned and fainted flat on their backs."

"But not you?"

"I don't kiss friends," I quipped.

He gave a snort, but the playful glint in his eyes dimmed a little, and I regretted that I might have hurt his feelings. Still. I had to make my intentions clear. I wasn't going to give him false hope. Or encourage any more behavior like the kind he'd displayed in the Scout last night.

"Anyway," I added, hoping to repair his ego, "a kissing booth takes the serendipity out of the moment. I'm against them on principle. I mean, is there anything less romantic than paying for a kiss? It should happen when the time is right. It shouldn't be forced. It's the difference between kissing someone for the first time in Vegas . . . and Paris," I said in a burst of inspiration.

"Have you even been to Paris?" he grunted, shifting two crates of glass milk bottles in his arms.

For one half-moment, my heart raced wildly. I thought I'd said something that could jeopardize my cover. But no. The analogy was harmless. You didn't have to travel to Paris to know it was a million times more romantic than Vegas.

Even though Estella Goodwinn had. Traveled to Paris, that is.

"You know what I mean," I said.

"Did you happen to see what time slot they gave me?"

"Eight o'clock. All eyes, er, lips, will be on you." I dug in my purse for a tube of lip balm and tucked it in the front pocket of his tee. "A friendly deed for a friend in need. Halfway through your shift, you'll thank me."

He dug out the tube and read the label—crème de menthe flavored. "For real? This is as close as I'm getting to touching your lips tonight?" He wagged his head pathetically and heaved a sigh of disappointment.

I grinned. We were back to our old routine of kidding around and feeling easy with each other. This was what I wanted. It felt safe. "Just call me Little Miss Virgin Lips."

"At least stop by the booth and say hi—and donate a couple bucks. Proceeds go to new toys for the women's shelter."

"You just want my money so you can be the next Mr. Hot Lips."

I expected Chet to respond with a wisecrack of his own, but he stopped in his tracks. It was like he'd walked into a wall. His eyes fastened on something across the yard. A little color crept up his neck, and he smoothed a hand through his hair, almost like he was worried it might be sticking up. It seemed to take him a second to breathe.

"Chet?"

He jerked, like he'd forgotten I was there. He smiled, but his eyes were faraway and moody. "Yeah. Sorry. You were saying?"

I glanced at where he'd been staring, but wasn't sure what had distracted him. Surely he wasn't unnerved by the group of girls forming a line in front of the kissing booth. He had to have known what he was getting into when he'd volunteered. And anyway, Trigger had the first shift. Those girls might be gone by the time Chet took over the booth.

And then I saw her. A redhead in a Huskers hat and a white tank top. She had a hand on her hip, and the stance showed off her toned arms and shoulders. It was hard to tell if she had great legs, too, because her skirt was one of those billowy, hippie kinds that fell below the knees, but I was betting she did. She had a sprinkling of freckles, and she was pretty in an effortless and enviable way.

"Who is she?" I asked him.

But I had his full attention now, and he smiled at me, only me. "Who's who? C'mon. Help me drop off these bottles at the ring toss."

By eight I'd made the rounds, hitting most of the game booths. I thought it spoke volumes about how starved I was for a social life that I was able to amuse myself at a church carnival. In some small way it felt good to wander among strangers, but it also made me homesick. I missed Philly. I missed the life and the energy, the juxtaposition of the familiar and the anonymity of city life. I also missed Reed. In a way that made my heart feel like it had been squeezed into a box three sizes too small.

I wondered if there was any chance I could slip away from the carnival without Carmina noticing. On foot, a trip to the library and back would take about an hour. If she realized I'd left, she'd press me with questions later. Worse, she might heighten her patrol of me or start asking questions around town. In the end, I decided leaving was too risky. As hard as it was to be patient, I had to be. If Carmina discovered the secret e-mail account, it was all over. I'd lose my only way to contact Reed.

Across the carnival, Chet was relieving Donovan Pippin in the kissing booth. As promised, I headed that direction to donate a few dollars to the worthy cause of crowning him Mr. Hot Lips. On my way over, I bumped into Theo, the kid from the Red Barn gas station. He had his head down and was beelining with purpose through the crowd; he almost mowed me over.

I jumped back a step. "Where's the fire?"

His head sprang up. "Oh. Hey. Stella. What are you doing here?"

"Trying to look like I fit in. Want to hit a few booths together? Anything but the rubber-duck races—I've struck out twice on them."

"Uh . . . ," he began, glancing nervously behind him, almost like he was hiding from someone. "Afraid I can't. You haven't seen an older gentleman in seersucker shorts and a yellow polo, have you?"

"Nope. Why?"

"Oh, nothing," he said, still peering around anxiously. "He's my grandfather. I'm trying to, ah, avoid him for . . . reasons. I'll catch you later."

I grabbed his shoulder. "Who's that girl in the Huskers hat by the cake walk?"

Theo squinted through his thick glasses. "That's Lacy Parish. She must have come home for the weekend. She goes to UNL."

"That's in Lincoln, right?" Before I came to Thunder Basin, it was the only city in Nebraska I could have named from memory.

He nodded. "She graduated from high school last year. I heard she got a summer job in Lincoln as an au pair."

Lacy graduated last year. The same year Chet graduated. In a town this size, he would definitely know her. But the look in his eyes as he'd watched her was more than familiarity. It was the kind of look you got when someone punched you in the chest and your body forgot how to breathe.

"What's the deal with her and Chet Falconer?"

Theo considered. "Well. They used to date, but they're definitely not together anymore. He was supposed to go to school in Omaha, it's not far from Lincoln, so he and Lacy could basically still be together, but then his parents were killed in a car crash. He stayed here to take care of his brother and she took off for college. But first she broke up with him. I heard she told him she didn't want to wait for him and she didn't want a long-distance relationship, either. Before the car crash, everyone in town talked about how they were destined to get married. What do they call those kinds of people? A golden couple, I think? But now they're more like an old divorced couple—I don't think they've said a word to each other since she left town."

"That's a sad story," I murmured. Across the yard, Chet leaned out the window of the kissing booth, delighting a small girl with Shirley Temple curls as he pecked her on one rosy cheek.

In return, she dropped a dollar bill into the donations jar and skipped away. It was a sweet picture, and in spite of myself, I felt my heart melt a little.

As though sensing me watching, Chet turned his eyes toward mine. We held that gaze for no longer than three or four seconds, but in that moment, it felt much, much longer. I dropped my eyes to his mouth, which had more color from the repeated pressure of kissing, the same way slapped skin deepens with blood. Chet watched me back, a strange, wishful tension in his eyes. It put me on alert.

Uh-oh. I wasn't doing this.

I made myself flash him a radiant smile. Then I blew him a goofy kiss, puckering my lips and smacking them apart dramatically. I knew the distraction had worked when he grinned and crooked his finger for me to come over. The moment, whatever it was, had passed.

"Gotta run!" Theo gulped, dodging away before I could ask him any more questions.

Tempted by what Theo had told me, I sauntered over to the cake walk. Studying the cake designs, I listened to Lacy Parish and the girls huddled around. From their group rose the hush of gossip, punctuated by the occasional spurt of laughter.

"Have you talked to him?" one of the girls asked Lacy.

Lacy stared knives at the girl like, *Did you really just ask me that?* The girl blushed. "Stupid question," she mumbled.

"I saw him staring at me earlier," Lacy said, rolling her eyes. "Could he make it any more obvious? He still has a thing for me, but I'm so over him. Like, he can't compete with college guys, you know? It's harsh but true. They're doing stuff with their lives and he's"—she hesitated, searching for the word of impact—"a lawn boy."

A couple of girls snickered.

Lacy grinned, pleased with herself, then sobered her expression and added, "I mean, I felt super guilty when his parents . . . you know"—she gestured for her audience to fill in the blank—"but I'm not going to put my life on hold for some guy I made out with in high school. If he thought we were forever, he had the wrong girl. I'm doing something with my life. College is amazing. You guys will see. It's a different world. There's something happening every night. Parties, dances, football games." She laughed. "More parties."

"So do you have a boyfriend?" a girl with a red bandanna tying her hair back asked. She reminded me of Rosie the Riveter. Her voice was tough, a little challenging.

"Nobody dates in college." Lacy flicked her hair over her shoulder, all casual. But she was lapping up the attention. Her green eyes glittered and she spoke loudly and with authority. "It's less serious than high school. You don't feel pressure to belong to anyone. It's all about random hookups and having fun. You hang out with different guys every weekend. You don't do the same boring stuff with the same guy. Commitment is for, like, people who don't know better. Chet didn't get the memo," she finished, her mouth all twisted and wicked.

I'd heard enough. Originally I'd thought Lacy had a valid point in leaving Thunder Basin and Chet behind. She couldn't be expected to put her future on hold for him. But after hearing her talk, I was firmly on Chet's side. Lacy didn't feel bad about hurting him. Worse, she was talking crap behind his back and putting him down to build herself up. I hoped he wasn't in love with her still. She wasn't good enough for him.

I was about to walk away when Rosie the Riveter said, "Don't be so sure of yourself, Lacy. Maybe Chet has moved on. You should ask him to his face, instead of talking trash behind his back."

"Jealousy isn't very attractive on you, Dawn," Lacy shot back. "Who asked you, anyway?"

Dawn shrugged and walked off, but the smug little smile on her face never wavered. Inwardly, I sent her a high five.

"Who would go out with Chet now?" Lacy said to the remaining girls. "He knows you guys are my friends. He's gonna have to get his butt outta Dodge if he wants any lovin'."

Now I'd really heard enough. Striding past her, I shot her a black look, but she was too busy laughing at her put-down to notice.

I walked to the kissing booth and leaned an elbow on the window. "Happy to see your lips haven't fallen off yet," I told Chet. I eyed the donations jar, which was crammed with bills. "Looks like you're in the lead for Mr. Hot Lips."

Pastor Lykins, who was standing nearby, perked at my words. After confirming we didn't have any extra ears bent our way, he said in a hushed but excited voice, "He's raised over one hundred dollars. That's double what the first two kissers earned combined, but don't tell anyone I said so. We don't want to bruise any egos." He chuckled. "Suffice it to say, Chet is the star of the show."

Chet shrugged at me as if to say, *You can't argue with the facts, ma'am.*

"And to think he tried everything humanly possible to get out of volunteering when I said this would be the perfect place for him," Pastor Lykins pointed out.

Chet gave me another shrug, but this time the tips of his ears turned pink. He was the only guy I knew who could pull off modest and not be annoying. If anything, it made him more attractive. It was hard not to appreciate a guy who had a sensitive, vulnerable side, even if he tried to hide it.

"I haven't seen you in line yet, Stella," Pastor Lykins said. "I can't vet Chet as a kisser, but for what it's worth, I haven't seen one unhappy customer."

To my mortification, I felt my face warm. Was I blushing? Why was I blushing? I'd had no problem blowing off kissing Chet before, but something had changed. I didn't know what. Dammit, I *was* blushing! I fiddled with my earring. "Oh. Well. Actually—"

"Stella's saving her money for Theo," Chet provided. "He got the last time slot, and everyone knows that's a disadvantage, because by now most people have spent their money. She wanted to make sure he had something in his jar."

I cast Chet a look of sheer gratitude. He tipped me the slightest nod.

"Good thinking, Stella," the pastor said. He checked his watch. "Looks like your shift's over, Chet. Now, where is Theo . . . ?" Shielding his eyes from the setting sun, he searched the crowd.

"Can I get you a drink?" Chet asked me, coming around the booth.

"I think they've got fruit punch and lemonade at concessions."

Why not? I clearly needed something to cool me off. "Thanks for saving me back there," I said, once we'd walked out of Pastor Lykins's earshot. "I don't know what came over me."

He flashed a lopsided grin. "I guess if there's only one girl at church who doesn't want to kiss me, I can handle it."

I laughed, relieved he wasn't going to push the issue, and made a concerted effort to hide from my expression any hint that he might be wrong. I didn't want to kiss him. I really didn't. I had a boyfriend, a serious one, and I was committed.

The concessions table was picked over, only a few cups of punch and crumbled cookies left. I boosted myself onto the table and nibbled one of the cookie pieces. "I heard Lacy is here."

Chet watched me as he sipped his lemonade. "Who told you about her?"

"Small town. News travels."

"I could tell you I'm over her, but I'm not sure you'd believe me. No one else seems to. Whenever she comes home, everyone watches me closely, like they expect me to crumble."

"Does it hurt to see her?"

"Hurt?" He shook his head no. "But it flings me into the past. Takes a moment to remember I'm not back there anymore."

I understood with eerie perfection. When I was struck by flashbacks from that night, they yanked me back to Philly. No amount of reasoning or common sense could convince me I wasn't there; I just had to wait it out. In those instances, time couldn't move fast enough.

"She's pretty," I said.

He shrugged noncommittally.

"But she's kind of bitchy, too." I flipped a palm up before he could protest. "Just sayin'."

"I don't think she feels comfortable when I'm around. She knows some people blame her for the way things ended between us, even though it was inevitable."

I didn't tell him that she seemed perfectly comfortable making him the brunt of her jokes.

"I always wanted red hair like hers," I said wistfully.

He elbowed me affectionately. "I like your hair the way it is."

I could feel him watching me, could feel the pull of his eyes. He smelled earthy and enticing. Warm, golden light glinted off his dark curls. He was leaning back against the table, his hand not far from mine. He had amazing hands, strong and tanned and calloused from outdoor work. They were hands with purpose. The kind of hands a girl might dream about.

When I could avoid his gaze no longer, I saw something restless in it, and I struggled to not let it get to me. He was breaking down my barriers. This slowly building heat between us was trouble. I had to end it.

But it was Chet who broke the moment, not me.

With the familiarity of an old friend, he broke off a piece of my cookie and popped it in his mouth. "I should get home. Make sure Dusty's not causing trouble."

And with that, he left.

As I watched him drive away, I couldn't stop thinking about

him. I realized I must have known there'd been someone in his life. He was too good-looking to have gone unnoticed by girls. As far as I knew, there hadn't been anyone since Lacy. Despite the talk around town, I knew he was over her. When he saw her, he hadn't looked wounded. Startled, yes. Jerked into the past, yes. But not damaged. And that made all the difference.

I could think of another reason he'd moved on, but it made me uncomfortable, so I brushed it aside.

Deciding to make an honest man out of Chet, I went to find Theo at the kissing booth.

He was slumped on the stool, misery etched in every line of his face. He wore a pink bow tie that matched his flushed cheeks. When he saw me strolling over, he ducked his head and hid his face behind his hand.

"Hi, Theo," I said brightly. "How'd you get roped into this?"

"My grandfather volunteered me," he mumbled. "You don't happen to have a cyanide capsule?"

"I left it with the KGB when I resigned, sorry."

He dabbed his brow with a pocket square. "I still have twenty minutes of this torture." Seeing the empty donations jar perched on the window ledge, he snatched it and shoved it by his feet. "I want to help the women's shelter, really I do, but not this way. I could have donated something I'd sewn. A men's jacket. They could have auctioned it."

I opened my purse. "Put that jar back up here so I can add my donation."

Theo blinked at me in surprise. "But—I'd have to kiss you. You want me to kiss you?"

"If you're going to be direct, well, yeah. I do."

"But. Well. Ahem. You know I'm . . . I'm . . ." He cleared his throat, the flush deepening.

"Theo," I said gently.

"It's, well . . . it's awkward, isn't it? I mean—" He leaned closer, eyeing me intensely, as if he could transmit information directly to my brain. "Do you really understand what I'm trying to tell you, Stella?"

"Theo. We're friends. Are you going to kiss me already?"

"Um . . ." He scratched his cheek awkwardly. "I guess I could do that. . . ."

I leaned forward. He leaned forward.

He closed his eyes and brushed his lips tenderly across my cheek.

"That was the nicest kiss anyone's ever given me," I told him honestly. "Now put that jar back up here so I can donate."

With a sweet, almost bashful smile, he returned the jar to its place. I dropped a handful of bills into it—everything I had—and watched Theo's eyes widen with astonishment.

"Stella. What are you doing? You can't—"

"I can't guarantee you'll be the next Mr. Hot Lips, but it's enough to beat Trigger by a landslide."

Theo came around the booth and embraced me tightly. His was also the nicest hug I'd ever received.

THE FOLLOWING WEEK, I WAS ABOUT TO CLOCK OUT
after my shift when Eduardo, the head cook, stopped me on my
way out.

"You got a minute, Stells?"

I couldn't remember the exact day he'd given me the nickname, but it had stuck. All the cooks called me Stells now. Stells
Bells, Stelly Belly, and Stellow Mellow were variations, but I didn't
mind. They beat "Hey, new girl!" which was what I'd been forced
to answer to the first night on the job.

"Sure. What do you need?" I asked.

"Deirdre left early. Sick kid. Asked if I would refill her napkin
dispensers. Think you could grab me a stack of napkins from the
storeroom?"

Deirdre was a full-time waitress with two kids in day care. She usually worked days, but picked up a night shift now and then. From what I'd gathered, she had worked at the Sundown since Dixie Jo opened its doors over ten years ago. I was surprised she'd asked Eduardo to restock her tables and not me or Inny, who'd taken off a couple of minutes ago. As far as I knew, the cooks never helped waitresses with their tables. And I'd never seen Deirdre and Eduardo hang out during breaks, but obviously I'd missed something. It sounded like they were friends, or at least on friendly terms.

"No problem."

The storeroom was at the opposite end of the kitchen from the cooks' station, and down a narrow set of wooden stairs. I'd been to the storeroom several times before, and while it had the musty smell of damp concrete, it was always cool and I welcomed any opportunity to escape to it from the heat of the kitchen.

I flipped on the light at the top of the stairs and jogged down the wood planks. At the bottom, I rounded the corner and groped blindly for the light pull-chain. There were no windows in the storeroom, and at night, it was as dark as you'd expect a hole in the ground to—

The solid blow to my stomach knocked the wind out of me. Pain exploded everywhere, a sharp, excruciating sensation that left me wanting to writhe on the ground. I never got the chance; a pair of hands rammed me hard against the drywall. The shelves overhead rattled, and warm breath hissed against my cheek. My vision blurred gray.

I was still stunned from the hit—fighting to breathe, let alone scream—when he slapped his hand over my mouth. His damp skin reeked of leather and salt. Baseball glove and sweat. He snarled in my ear, and in the pitch-black space, the sound did exactly what he intended it to—I shivered in absolute fear. He felt my shudder and laughed softly.

Next thing I knew, pain blazed across my jaw. A sharp snap to my neck, and I went down on the floor, gasping for breath. I screamed—but the door at the top of the stairs had fallen shut behind me, and any noise I made was cut off when his boot drilled into my ribs. The air went out of me a second time, and my palms and elbows licked fire where I'd donated some of my skin to the floor. He kicked me again. And again.

I coiled my arms around my head and tucked my chin, but I couldn't protect the rest of my body. Intense pain seared through my legs and back. Each kick felt like a knife to the bone. Gulping air, I finally got a bloodcurdling scream out. It rang off the store-room walls; someone upstairs must have heard it.

Thinking someone would come running any minute, I found my courage and bucked my legs wildly against his assaults. My foot collided with something solid, and he swore viciously. His hand came out of the darkness, slapping my ears hard enough to make my head ring.

"This is how I want to see you from now on," he whispered harshly. "Head down, minding your own business."

I lashed out, fists flying wildly, but he'd already backed out of reach. I heard the stairs creak under his weight; he climbed at a leisurely pace. I understood. He wanted me to know he wasn't running away and he wasn't scared. He could stroll into my place of work and beat me up ten feet under my boss's office. He could find me anywhere.

Fading into the pain, I dimly noted that his feet landed on the steps at irregular intervals. It sounded like he was limping. Had I struck his leg? I felt a flicker of grim satisfaction, and then the door at the top of the stairs opened, casting a slant of light into the darkness. I squinted, watching his tall, broad-shouldered silhouette slip through the doorway before I was once again consumed by darkness.

My head lolled on the cement floor. I fought the haze of unconsciousness. I wouldn't have minded the blissful relief from the pain, but Dixie Jo would be locking up soon. She'd never notice my bike propped against a tree out back. She'd see the empty parking lot, assume we'd all left, and take off herself.

I'd stay here all night, in this horrible darkness, tasting blood.

With a moan, I rolled onto my elbow. The pain was so excruciating, I was past crying. I drew short, shallow breaths, alarmed by the strange gurgle that seemed to come from my lungs. Was something broken?

"Eduardo." I wheezed his name, wincing at the knife-edged pain it caused to rip through me.

In agonizing shoves and heaves, I crawled toward the stairs. He'd spared my arms from the beating, and I used them to drag myself up. I had no idea how I'd ever manage to climb to the top. I couldn't stand. My hips and back throbbed, and a wave of nausea surged through me. Swallowing, I ordered my stomach to calm. If

I were sick now, I might pass out. No one would find me until the diner opened tomorrow.

I felt weak, delirious. I knew it, and it made me cold with fear. Focus. Tears stung the backs of my eyes. *Don't you dare give up, Estella.* Was I strong enough to throw a can of sugar against the door? Would anyone hear it? I would not stay down here all night. He'd battered and bruised me violently, but I wouldn't give him the satisfaction of knowing he'd kept me cold, terrified, and isolated through the night.

Footsteps. I heard footsteps. The doorknob twisted and light spilled down the stairs. Eduardo breathed a slew of startled curses. In a fog, I heard the stairs rattle as he rapidly descended them. He knelt beside me, laying a quivering hand on my shoulder.

I faintly noted his wide-eyed and sickened astonishment, his warm brown complexion turning squeamishly pale.

He shouted over his shoulder. He was yelling at someone to call the police. I heard him rub his hands repeatedly over his thighs, drying the sweat.

For a self-proclaimed tough guy stamped head to toe with menacing tattoos, he was handling my condition worse than I was, I dimly observed.

Of course, I hadn't looked in the mirror yet.

14

ON THE AMBULANCE RIDE TO THE HOSPITAL, I
released myself to the haze. I remained awake but not alert—I
sent my mind to a separate place. I saw flashes of images, but
I felt no response to them. Blankly, I registered the paramedics
leaning over me, working quickly. Behind them I saw medical
equipment, tubes, and monitors. Again, no reaction. In my numb
and disoriented state, I heard fragments of commands, followed
by concise responses.

Nothing broken. I heard that, and felt some tense, quivering part
of me relax. If nothing was broken, I'd be okay, wouldn't I? They
gave me something for the pain, and once it dulled, it was easy to
sink into nothingness completely.

Carmina arrived at the hospital shortly after I did. Dixie Jo
must have called her; I couldn't remember telling the paramedics

who to contact. I still hadn't memorized Carmina's phone number. *I should do that,* I thought dimly. This was never going to happen again—I'd see to it—but just the same. It was good to have someone to call in an emergency.

Swatting aside the curtain, Carmina strode into the exam room. She looked as grim and formidable as I'd ever seen her. I wasn't ready to talk, so I turned my head away. Understanding the gesture, Carmina focused her attention on the on-call doctor. Instead of flying into hysterics like my mom would have, she kept her cool, weeding out information like a seasoned cop.

"What's her condition?"

"Bruised ribs, mild cuts, swelling."

"Have you given her something for the pain?"

"Lortab. We'll send her home with a bottle of ten tablets to get her through the next twenty-four hours, and a prescription. She's going to be tender for the next several days."

"I was told this happened at the Sundown Diner, during her shift. Have you heard anything about who was involved, who attacked her?" It occurred to me that Carmina might think there'd been a breach and that Danny Balando was behind this. But this wasn't the work of Danny's men. I had no doubt who'd done this.

"Where's the officer handling her statement?" Carmina continued to press the doctor.

"I haven't seen anyone from the department yet. They should be here soon. Why don't you pull up a seat by her bed? I'll have a nurse bring you—"

"Coffee? I don't need coffee. I need the damn police department to send over someone to take her statement. I want them out there looking for the individual, or individuals, responsible for doing this to her."

At the whiplike anger in Carmina's voice, a strange warmth seemed to build in my chest. Gratitude and relief. She'd take it from here. I put that worry out of my mind, and for the first time since arriving at the hospital, I felt a semblance of peace. Carmina would see to it that I was taken care of.

A second figure, a tall, dark-featured woman in trousers and a silk blouse, ducked behind the curtain and into the exam room. "Carmina," she said.

"Grace." Carmina stood, shook the woman's hand. "I'm glad they sent you. Was hoping they would."

"I'm sorry. So very sorry this happened."

"Tell that to her," Carmina said, nodding in my direction. "Stella, this is Officer Oshiro. I worked with her for a few years before I retired. She's a good cop. She's crosstrained to investigate any type of crime, including assault. She's going to ask you some questions. Let me know if you need a break at any point."

I sat up, leaning into my pillow. "I'm feeling better." And I was. Now that Carmina was here, bossing everyone around, the chaos and confusion didn't feel so overwhelming.

"Even so." Her eyes focused on Officer Oshiro, and with a businesslike nod, she gave the go-ahead.

"Hi there, Stella," Officer Oshiro said, speaking in that gentle but serious voice adults adopt in a crisis. "What happened tonight? Walk me through it. Be as detailed as you can."

I explained how Eduardo had asked me to get him napkins from the storeroom, how my attacker had waited for me at the bottom of the stairs, how he'd kicked, punched, and slapped me.

"He?"

"He talked to me. He said, 'This is how I want to see you from now on. Head down, minding your own business.'" I swallowed, unsure if the tingle in my fingers was from anger or the trauma of reliving the event in words. With perfect memory, I recalled his husky, loathsome voice. It sent chills down my spine.

"Did you see his face?"

"I was on the ground, covering my head while he kicked me. I didn't dare lift my head to look at him, in case he kicked me unconscious."

"Did you notice anything distinguishing? Like what he was wearing, maybe a watch, a tattoo, or a specific pair of shoes?"

"The lights were off. The storeroom is underground and doesn't have windows. It was pitch black."

"Any idea who'd want to do this to you?"

Trigger McClure was the first name that sprang to mind, and I told her so.

Carmina and Officer Oshiro locked eyes. Carmina nodded, and I got the feeling they'd just shared an entire conversation. One that didn't discount my suggestion that Trigger was behind this.

Officer Oshiro said, "What makes you think Trigger would want to hurt you?"

"He threw his drink on me last week at work. He was mad

because I wouldn't change his order after it had gone to the grill. I gave him a piece of my mind, and I don't think he liked that, either."

Carmina's mouth pinched. "You didn't tell me," she said disapprovingly, and I felt a twinge of guilt. I had made it a point to tell Carmina as little as possible. In hindsight, maybe I should have told her about Trigger. But I didn't think it would have prevented tonight's attack. I never would have guessed he'd go from throwing his soda at me to assaulting me. I doubted even Carmina would have seen it coming.

"Sounds like the two of you had a conflict," Officer Oshiro said, still speaking in that gentle, understanding voice. "I bet it made you pretty mad when he dumped his drink on you."

"He's an asshole."

"Stella," Carmina warned.

"What? It's the truth." I faced Officer Oshiro. "After he doused me, he took off without paying. Dixie Jo, my boss, had to go to his parents to get the money for his meal. The following night I saw Trigger bully a kid at the Red Barn. Trigger was pressuring the kid to give him free beer. He was also obviously drinking, so I called the cops—you guys. Needless to say, I don't think it really warmed him to me."

"You think he was humiliated enough by those two incidents that he decided to beat you up and put you in your place?" Officer Oshiro wanted to know.

"I think Trigger isn't used to being around a girl who does something besides stroke his ego or feel flattered by his advances."

Another brief glance passed between the officer and Carmina, and both their mouths pressed into a grim line of what I believed to be agreement. Apparently Trigger had made a name for himself—as something other than a baseball star.

I brushed my hair off my forehead, cringing when I accidentally touched the edge of my swollen eye. I'd had a black eye once before, during a game of Crack the Egg on a trampoline. I'd been eight, and clearly time had done a good job of erasing my memory, because I didn't remember it hurting this much. The dull pang of a headache was beginning to settle behind the blackened eye.

Carmina handed me a fresh ice pack and I dabbed it gently against the swelling. She said, "How long did he beat you?"

"A minute or two. It happened quickly, even though it didn't feel that way at the time."

"And then what happened?" Officer Oshiro asked.

"He left. He didn't run. He wasn't scared—he made that clear. He walked out leisurely. But I got a good solid kick in during the attack, and I must have hit him in the leg, because he was limping. It slowed him down."

Officer Oshiro wrote that down on her pad. "How do you know he was limping?"

"I could hear it. His gait was uneven. He favored one leg."

"And after he limped out?"

"There are three doors out of the kitchen. The carhop door, the swinging doors that lead into the dining area, and a back door we use to haul trash bags to the Dumpsters. I'm guessing he used that door. Eduardo was in the kitchen. He must have seen something. The door to the storeroom is easily visible from the cooks' station, where he would have been."

"Same Eduardo who called 911?" Officer Oshiro asked, quickly jotting down more notes.

"Yes."

"I'll touch base with him on that. Meanwhile, any other details from the attack stand out to you? Did the attacker say anything else?"

"He laughed." I shuddered unexpectedly as the snarling timbre of Trigger's voice drifted through me. "He thought what he did was funny. That I deserved it."

IT FELT GOOD TO WAKE UP IN MY LITTLE TWIN BED AT
the top of the stairs in Carmina's house. For the first time, I appreciated the familiar creak of the mattress and the hot sunlight streaming through the curtains. The room smelled like freshly laundered cotton and wood floor polish, and the smell was so much better than the sterile, recycled air pervading the hospital.

I pulled myself up to sitting, doing a quick inventory of my aches and pains. I was bruised all over, purple blooms splotching my legs, abdomen, torso. Deep down I was hurting, but the medicine—blissfully—masked the worst of it.

Carmina knocked and stuck her head inside. With a large lap tray held between her hands, she was forced to gesture with her shoulders. "I thought you might be hungry for a bite of breakfast. Should I leave it on the nightstand?"

A bite of breakfast included pancakes, eggs, hash browns, bacon, cubed honeydew and cantaloupe, and a tall glass of OJ. Carmina cooked meat and potatoes at nearly every meal, but this breakfast took things to a new level. I'd never seen her make so much food at once. And all of it for me. It had been a long time since I'd felt fussed over. The little girl inside me missed how my mom used to sit at my bedside and touch her cool palm to my fevered head. At the far reaches of my mind, there were still those memories. They were foggy, but they were real. Which made them that much more painful to remember. It's true what they say—you know keenly, cruelly, what you're missing after it's gone.

"Thanks," I said, clearing away the Walkman and cassette tapes from the bedside table. I was growing strangely attached to Van Halen, and usually fell asleep listening to their greatest hits. The cassette tape's audio quality was abysmal, but the music was decent. Anyway, it was good replacement music. I refused to listen to my favorite bands from home. Estella's life in Philly and Stella's life in Thunder Basin were two distinct entities, and I didn't want overlap. Estella had an inner jukebox that played fresh, undiscovered voices over and over until the lyrics became etched on her heart. When she left Philly, she wrapped her favorite songs in a box and placed them high out of reach. A wishful part of me still dreamed I'd get to go back and be her. I'd take down the box and let the music soar freely. But it could never be more than a fantasy, and with every passing day, the dream faded a little and reality brightened.

Estella was gone. Stella was my future.

Carmina set down the tray, then lingered by the window. She exhaled, as if she had something on her mind and was debating the wisdom of letting it out. "Chet stopped by this morning," she finally admitted somewhat stubbornly, and with that ever-present touch of disapproval.

"What did you tell him?"

"That you were sleeping and he should come back later."

"Does he know what happened?"

"Yes."

I sat up taller. "You told him everything—all of it?"

"When you didn't come home from work, I called Chet to see if he knew where you were. He didn't, and it worried him that I didn't either. He offered to help look for you," she said with an aggravated sigh. "He came over, and that's when Dixie Jo called to say you'd been attacked and were at the hospital. I told Chet to go home, but I suspect he tried to see you. He would have been turned away because visiting hours were over." She gave a fussy shake of her head. "He brought flowers this morning. Daisies and sunflowers from his mother's garden. She planted the daisies in the backyard years ago, and they've spread like weeds. Hannah Falconer always had the prettiest flowers. . . ." She trailed off, her eyes gazing vacantly out the window.

"I'd like to go see him after breakfast. I'll walk over, so it won't inconvenience you."

Carmina's eyes snapped back to me. "Walk? In your condition?"

"Dr. Simpson said I should walk if I felt up to it. And I do."

"I know you're anxious to see Chet, but don't overdo it. He said he'd swing by later."

"I really want to talk to him now. I need someone to talk to. I have to get this off my chest so I can stop reliving it."

When she turned back to the window, her chin turning up with a hint of pride, I knew I'd hurt her feelings. Something had happened at the hospital last night. Some of the animosity I'd built between us had eroded when Carmina strode into the exam room, determined to take care of me. My opinion of her had risen a notch, and I think she realized it. And while she might think we were in good standing now, I wasn't ready to confide in her yet. She'd have to accept that.

I ate the pancakes and two strips of bacon. I showered and dressed. I was too sore to flat-iron my hair, so I pulled it back in a simple ponytail, but even that was slow going and painful. I skipped makeup, opting only for a light swath of lip balm.

The doorbell rang. Thinking Chet had saved me from walking to his house, I slipped on my sandals and walked stiff-legged from the room.

I was coming down the stairs gingerly when Carmina opened the front door. She left the screen intact, keeping a barrier between her and the uniformed officer standing on the porch.

"Morning, Roger. To what do we owe this pleasure?" Her voice was pleasant, but not quite genuine. It held an underlying sharpness, a touch of suspicion.

The officer tipped his hat at Carmina. "I'm here on business."

"Business? What business?"

He cleared his throat. "The matter of Stella's statement."

"Where's Grace Oshiro? She took Stella's statement. This is her case."

"Chief assigned me to the case. I'll be handling things from now on. Thought we could have a nice conversation here, instead of a formal interview at the station."

"Interview? What on earth for?"

"Just double-checking a few facts."

"Last I checked, a fact is a known truth. What's to double-check?"

Roger cleared his throat again. "Mind if I step in?"

"Not at all. But first, I'd like to know the exact nature of your visit. Seems to me this conversation"—she put just enough emphasis on the word to make it sound like a euphemism—"might be better suited for the station. With our lawyer present."

Chuckling uneasily, Roger said, "There, there, Carmina. No need to bring out the attack dogs. We're friends, you and I. This is a courtesy visit. I thought the three of us—you, me, and Stella—could sit down and review Stella's statement from last night. Keep it friendly, of course."

"Of course," she said coolly.

Roger scratched his cheek, clearly uncomfortable. "Still got a jug of that sweet basil lemonade you make lying around?"

"Matter of fact, I do. But I'm saving it for company."

"Aw, come on, Carmina. Don't be like that."

"How should I be? Naive? I know what you're doing here. You forget I spent five years on the force with you, and another fifteen with your father. You want Stella to retract her statement. You

164

don't want us to press charges. Go on, admit it. It's a sticky mess for the department, arresting a promising young baseball star for assaulting a girl. Now tell me, does Chief Hearst still fish with Trigger McClure's daddy Saturday mornings? Come to think of it, don't they hunt pheasant in the fall, and watch Sunday night football at the chief's house?"

Color splotched the officer's cheeks. "It's her word against his. We talked to Trigger, got his side of the story. He said he accidentally spilled his pop on Stella at the Sundown Diner last week and she's had it out for him ever since. She follows him around, trying to trip him up. She followed him to the Red Barn last week and made up a story about him trying to steal beer."

Up until now, I'd let Carmina take the reins, but I wasn't about to keep quiet a moment longer.

"He said that?" I exclaimed, furious. "And you believe it? For the record, he dumped his soda on me—intentionally—after I insisted that he pay for his food. And every word I told the officer at the Red Barn was true!"

Carmina's eyes took a definite edge. "Stella saw Trigger threaten that boy at the Red Barn. And the boy corroborated her story. You have two solid witnesses. What's really the problem?"

"In her statement last night, she told Officer Oshiro she's positive it was Trigger who assaulted her. It's a hefty allegation." Roger rocked back on his heels, standing taller. His sloping belly made the buttons on his shirt strain; he looked to me like a peacock strutting with importance. "It's ruffling a lot of feathers, and before I go forward with this, I just want to make absolutely certain—"

"Any other kid, and you wouldn't be circling back." Carmina cut him off. "We both know Trigger did this. It isn't the first time he's been accused of hitting a woman. Remember the teacher? You shipped her off to a new school at midyear and told Trigger to play nice next time. I'll tell you what the problem is. This is the first time that boy has faced the risk of being accountable for his actions, and nobody wants to deal with him throwing a tantrum. We should have taken him into custody the first time the teacher called 911. We're no different from the parents in the grocery aisle who give their toddler whatever he wants to avoid a scene."

The officer looked more irritable by the moment. "I spoke with Trigger about the assault. He says he was at home when it happened. His parents concur. We've got nothing that puts him anywhere near the Sundown last night. Like I said, this is coming down to 'he said, she said.'"

Carmina chuckled softly, but the effect was menacing. "Arresting him is going to cause a scene, Roger, I can assure you that. His parents will be up in arms. They'll hire lawyers. Mr. McClure will lean on every friend he's got in the department. But it's the right thing to do, and it's your job. Now. If you ever come round here again and ask Stella to lie for you, or pretend that boy didn't hurt her, or even suggest she look the other way, I'll be forced to forever equate you with one of those castrated bulls at the back of Dell Chivalry's fields that's so passive and shameful, even the kids can't help take a poke at it as they walk by."

With that, Carmina closed the door. Leaning back against it, she exhaled. It took me a moment to realize she was shaking.

When she caught me staring, she widened her eyes as if to say, *Some people sure have a lot of nerve, now, don't they?*

I didn't know what to say. "Thank you" seemed like a good start, but I was too much in shock to open my mouth. Part of me wanted to laugh appreciatively at the ballsy way she'd stood up to the officer. Another part wanted to hug her. Maybe even shed tears of gratitude. She had my back. I wasn't alone.

At last I raised an inquiring eyebrow. "Once a cop, always a cop?"

"Damn that Roger Perkins," she said. "Sure has a lot of gall."

"I know it was Trigger who beat me up. I wasn't lying to get him in trouble."

"Oh, I know it. Just as surely as I know this is going to direct a heap of ill will our way."

I wondered if that's what was really bothering her—the shadow the community would cast over me, and her by association. I reminded myself that Thunder Basin was a small, tight-knit community, and one burned bridge was sure to create a lot of smoke. But then she waved herself off and said, "I'm too old to care what the gossips say; let them take a swing at us. They'll see I don't fall down easily. Something tells me you don't either."

I smiled at her, and she smiled back. It softened her face, and for one moment, the cop went out of her, and I saw something in her I hadn't noticed before. She looked kind, tender. Almost . . .

Likable.

DESPITE CARMINA'S CONCERNS, I INSISTED ON
walking to Chet's. I needed the quiet time alone to gather my
thoughts. I also had something to prove. I'd spent the past twelve
hours playing a reactive role, letting nurses and doctors poke and
prod me, allowing Carmina to tuck me in bed and administer my
medication, letting him treat me like his personal punching bag.
The next twelve hours were going to be very different. I was done
sitting back on my heels, letting everyone around me handle the
ropes. It was time I took back control. Starting with using my own
two feet to get me where I wanted.

I rang Chet's doorbell, and even though I wore dark sunglasses
to hide my shiner, I felt self-conscious. Nervous. He knew I'd been
assaulted, but I wasn't sure Carmina had given him more than the
necessary details. I doubted he knew just how bad a shape I was

in, and I worried how he'd react when he saw me in the flesh—
bruised and battered as it was.

Dusty answered the door. I hadn't seen him since that night
at the Sundown Diner when the Mustang broke down, but now
that I knew he was Chet's brother, it was impossible not to draw
comparisons. Dusty was almost as tall as Chet, but lankier, like
he hadn't quite filled out yet. He had the same wavy hair, but his
fell messily in his eyes and was in need of a good cut. Despite
their similarities, Dusty's features were harder and hollower, his
eyes closed-off and brooding. He slouched his shoulders, as if the
weight of the world rested on them.

"Yeah?" he said. He didn't seem to recognize me from the
Sundown, and that was okay with me. I didn't know if Chet had
told him about me, or disclosed my reasons for being in the
Sundown that night—namely, to spy on him—but either way, I
wasn't going to help Dusty put two and two together.

"Is Chet home?"

"Who wants to know?"

"Tell him Stella's here."

He scratched the back of his head, eyeing me head to toe. It
wasn't a leering examination, or meant to intimidate; he seemed
to simply be collecting information. For a moment I thought he
might recognize me after all, even with the cuts and bruises, but
he finally said, "What's the other guy look like?"

Limping, I thought. Definitely limping.

"Since he took me by surprise, and in the dark, I can't really say."

"If you're here to settle the score with him, you've got the wrong guy. My brother can't throw a decent punch to save his life. And he'd never smack a girl."

"Chet didn't beat me up. I just want to talk."

"Talking, on the other hand," Dusty said, shaking his head disgustedly, "now that's something he does very well. You know the nagging teacher in the Charlie Brown movies? Blah, blah, blah. That's my brother. 'Do this. Don't do that. Pick up after yourself. Get your butt outta bed. Don't leave the milk out.' Hang on, I'll go get him." And by "go get" he meant turn his head and holler his brother's name loud enough to make my ears ring. With his job completed, Dusty wandered deeper into the house.

A moment later, I heard Chet's feet descending the stairs. He came striding down the hall, his hair dripping wet, a dab of shampoo still clinging above his eyebrow. The top snap on his jeans wasn't buttoned, and he wrestled a T-shirt down his torso. He stopped at the sight of me.

His eyes drank me in, and they were raw with worry. His gaze flicked over the bruises on my face, and I didn't miss the tightening of his jaw. Lightning quick, his expression darkened with hatred for the person who'd done this to me.

"Stella." Before I could step back or hold my hands up to prevent it, he drew me against him, holding me tightly.

I made a soft squeal of protest, and he released me as though he'd been shocked on contact. "Did I hurt you? I didn't even think. I'm sorry—"

"Not hurt." I smiled to reassure him. "They've got me good and drugged. I just wasn't expecting a—hug."

He plowed a hand through his hair, his eyes assessing me, the line of his mouth grim. "Is that a—?" With care, he removed my sunglasses, his mouth compressing tighter at the sight of my blackened eye. And then he swore. Softly and with menacing effect. It took me by surprise, because I'd never heard Chet curse. I'd never seen him truly angry. "Who did this?"

"They're investigating."

"Did you see him?"

"Not his face. It was pitch black in the storeroom."

"Carmina told me he jumped you at work. Inside the diner, where someone should have stopped it from happening. You weren't alone. There were people around. Cooks, dishwashers, your own boss. You weren't in a deserted alley—you were at work." His blue eyes sizzled with fire. "This never should have happened."

"They're going to find him. And when they do, he'll pay."

"Who was with you? I want names. I want to talk to every last person who was in the diner last night. Someone knows something."

I couldn't do this. I'd thought I could, but I was wrong. I couldn't relive last night. Not now, when breaking down and losing it were still very real threats. I'd given my statement to Officer Oshiro, and I didn't want to rehash the details with Chet. Not because I didn't care about what he wanted or needed, but for my own sanity. I felt shattered, and I needed to collect the pieces and pull myself together. I wanted to feel strong again. I didn't want to go back to last night, to feeling helpless and victimized. Not only that, but the violent gleam in Chet's eyes unsettled me. *Payback*, it said. He wanted to handle this his way. If I let him—and even if I didn't—he would take this into his own hands.

As much as I appreciated, and felt flattered by, Chet's desire to protect me, this wasn't his fight. Carmina was going to use her weight to try to get Officer Oshiro put back on the case, and the three of us were going to prove Trigger's guilt. There would be no mistakes, no thoughtless screwups on our part. And no loopholes for Trigger to escape through. He wouldn't get away with what he'd done.

"Thank you for the daisies and sunflowers," I told Chet, hoping to defuse his anger. "They're beautiful. I can't look at them and not feel cheered up."

Chet exhaled, clasped his hands behind his neck, and bowed his head. He rolled his shoulders. He was trying to let go of the rage for my sake, I could tell. "You don't want to talk about it," he said. His expression was still stony, but the black heat had left his eyes.

"I don't. Honestly? I want to go for a long drive and not have to think about it."

He perked up slightly at the idea of having something to do, at having an outlet for his anger. "Anything. Name it. I'll drive you anywhere."

"Take me somewhere without a mirror." I gave a feeble laugh. "I'm sick of having to see myself this way. I already asked Carmina to cover my bathroom mirror. If I don't have to look at myself, I can almost forget it happened. There's also that whole vanity issue. I hate feeling ugly. Can you believe I'm worried about that?"

Chet's cool eyes stared past me, out the window. "You'll tell me when they find who did this?"

Something in his expression hinted that the fire hadn't completely gone out—it still smoldered under the surface—and despite Dusty's insistence otherwise, I had a feeling Chet was very good at using his hands in a fight. And that's when I saw a glimpse of who he was under that charming-boy-next-door exterior. Chet wasn't entirely harmless, and he wouldn't tolerate anyone hurting me. I wasn't going to tell him—I was hardly going to acknowledge it myself—but the fact that he seemed determined to protect me, and to right any wrong done to me, caused a heat that was equally uninvited and unavoidable to tingle through my body. I didn't know how to respond to his protectiveness. It felt so foreign, this notion of being cared for, that I instinctively rejected it.

I swallowed. "Thanks," I said softly, reaching for his hand and squeezing it.

He studied our laced fingers with a seriousness that made me realize my mistake. I dropped his hand.

I started for the front door, and not missing a beat, Chet was at my side. "Here, lean on me," he said, sliding an arm around my waist.

"Really, I'm fine," I said, but it felt good to have him close. I'd sworn off any hint at affection between us, but the aftershocks of last night were finally starting to tremble through me, all the fear and helplessness and terror, and I just wanted to let down my guard for one moment. With Chet's arm around me, I felt safe.

"How about we drive around the lake?" Chet suggested. "Or the park. I can grab bread to feed the ducks. Can't think of anything more relaxing than feeding ducks. No mirrors either. Even the pond's too murky to see your reflection."

"Can we stop by the library first? If I'm going to be sitting around for the next week or so, I could use a good book." I'd come to Chet's house because I wanted his company, and because I wanted to get out of bed and stop feeling sorry for myself, but I'd be lying if I didn't acknowledge that I had an ulterior motive. I didn't want to deceive Chet, but I needed his help with a task, one Carmina couldn't know about. Any guilt I felt over using Chet was overridden by the simple fact that I needed to contact Reed. I'd been in Thunder Basin two weeks and hadn't heard from him. Despite my best intentions, I'd only gone back once to check for an e-mail. I didn't like what that said about my priorities. Time to refocus. I had to know he was okay. And we needed to plan how we were going to get back together at the end of summer.

Outside, Chet helped me into the Scout.

"Want the AC on? I think it still works," he said, fiddling with the dials.

"No." I surprised myself when I turned down the offer. But the hospital last night had been temperature controlled, artificially chilly, and I didn't want to give my imagination any excuse to revisit that place. I associated it with pain, panic, and weakness. I was done with feeling that way.

"How's Dusty?" I asked.

Chet grimaced. "Slept in his own bed last night. It's a start, right?"

"Any further developments in his plan to strike it rich with Cooter Saggory?"

"I'm trying to prevent further developments by keeping Dusty too busy to get in trouble. I got him a job plastering swimming pools. He comes home caked in plaster every night, whining about how hard the work is, then inhales half the food in the fridge and crashes in bed. I know he's not sneaking out, because I've set my alarm to go off four different times during the night so I can check on him. I told him if he loses this job, I'll kick him out of the house. I won't, but don't tell him that. He's trying to stay on my good side because until he turns eighteen, I'm the trustee of the four grand my parents left him in their will."

"Then you can prevent him from getting this business off the ground—you control the capital."

"I can try." He gave a troubled sigh. "But Dusty's resourceful. If I stonewall him, he'll just find another way. Right now, I'm crossing my fingers he doesn't run out of pool jobs—or get fed up and quit—before the summer's over. Once he's back in school, it'll be easier to keep Cooter away from him."

"I admire how hard you're trying to take care of Dusty." I had dim recollections of my own parents taking a keen interest in me during the divorce, but after the dust cleared, and things like alimony and custody had been settled, both had moved on to other interests. Namely, work and drugs. I never visited my dad after he moved out. We'd been estranged for over two years. I think I blamed him for the divorce. The sad thing was, I couldn't remember anymore. My mom had a cabinet of prescription pills during the marriage, but segued into heavier drugs after the divorce. Drugs became her top—and only—priority.

"Sometimes I wish my parents were still here," Chet said. "They'd know how to help Dusty. He was close to my mom. Sometimes I think if he could just talk to her one more time—" He broke off. "I know it's a dangerous game to play, and I don't look back very often, but every now and then . . ."

He left his point unsaid, but I knew exactly how he felt. When I was really low, when it was all I could do not to feel sorry for myself, I played that game too. I knew I could never win, but some days, the dark days, the allure of playing "if only" was too strong to resist.

At the library, I stopped Chet before he parked.

"Can I ask a big favor? I could really go for a Coke. There's a Runza across the street. Would you mind?"

"Sure, no problem. I'll hit up the drive-through and meet you inside the library." He pulled up near the library's main doors and let me out.

Inside the library, I went right to work. Surely Reed had e-mailed by now. I checked our account. Thinking there must be some mistake, I refreshed the page. But no. There were no new drafts.

It didn't make sense. Something must have happened. Why else would Reed be waiting this long to contact me? For one moment I thought the worst, my imagination running wild with possibilities. Had Reed never made it to his new home? Had Danny Balando found him?

I drew a deep, reassuring breath. No. I was overreacting. Something was wrong, I had no doubt about that, but before I started picturing the worst, I needed more information. Reed was nineteen and living on his own. It seemed likely that he would have purchased a smartphone or computer by now, but maybe there had been a hitch. His funds might have been delayed. When it came to the government, nothing ran on time. I had to be patient a little longer, and see what information, if any, I could wheedle out of Carmina. I doubted she knew anything, but I could try.

I'd just closed the Internet browser when I saw Chet walking toward me. Empty-handed. He must have left the drinks in the Scout. Leave it to him to obey library rules. "Did you get your book?" he asked me.

"I had to look it up. It's over here." I led him to the fiction shelves, pretended to scan for a specific book, then plucked one at random.

After I checked out, he said, "Should we take the elevators? Here—" Seeing me lagging behind, he threaded his arm under my shoulders. I gave him a grateful smile and let him help me out to the parking lot.

Inside the Scout, I took a long drink of Coke. I'd tried swearing off soda as many times as my mom had attempted to give up the hard stuff, but I felt after everything I'd gone through today, I deserved a guilty pleasure.

I wondered if my mom told herself the same thing, and just like that, the Coke left a bad taste in my mouth.

No. I was being too hard on myself. I had nothing in common with her.

"Where to now?" Chet asked.

I eased back in the worn leather seat, which was unexpectedly comfortable. "Surprise me."

We drove through the park, stopping at the pond to feed the ducks. Chet's hair had dried, one stray curl falling idly over his forehead. I could still smell soap on his skin from when my arrival at his house had caused him to cut his shower short. It had probably taken him ten seconds to towel off and pull on a pair of jeans before he ran downstairs to meet me. Reed had frequently made me wait in his bedroom while he got ready in the adjoining bathroom. As much as Reed resented his dad, the army four-star general had left his mark: General Winslow's son was rigidly clean-cut and refused to go out in public looking thrown together. It was hard to think of someone more opposite to Reed than Chet.

Finding a shady bench near the water's edge, Chet tore the bread into pieces, letting me toss them at the ducks quacking frantically around our feet. One pecked my toe, and I drew my knee up with a squeal of laughter.

"Carnivores," Chet said, shaking his head reproachfully. "The whole lot of them."

Too late, I realized he'd slung his arm behind me. It rested on the back of the bench, impossible to ignore. My heart beat faster. Partly from irritation—I'd sworn I wouldn't let things go this far—and partly, to my great disconcert, from attraction. He smelled incredible. And those dimples. Not to mention the lazy curve of his mouth. I wondered what it would feel like to kiss him. . . .

I shook my head. I was not going there. I wasn't going to cheat on Reed, and more importantly, I wasn't going to let Chet believe a lie. And that lie was me. The girl he thought he was falling for didn't exist. She was a fraud. Chet was a good guy—a great guy. He didn't deserve the deception and heartache that would come from getting involved with me. My life was screwed up enough, and if I kissed him, I was giving him false hope. I cared about him too much to give him that. The truth was, I was taking off in August and he'd never see me again.

But I wanted to kiss him.

He traced the bandage holding the cut on my forehead closed. His touch made something inside me ache. Languid heat spread through my body, and it had nothing to do with the sun overhead or the wilting hot spell of its rays. I really had to stop this. If I needed more reasons, the last guy I'd kissed had had his future upended after getting involved with me. I carried my reasoning further. If I let Chet get close, and Danny Balando found me, Chet would become collateral damage. And when it came to damage, I'd done enough.

"Chet—" I protested.

I didn't get to finish. With a hunger I didn't expect from him, he cupped my cheek and drew my face to his. He kissed me, hard and solidly. Any thought of protest deserted me. I let go of my arguments and sank into the heat of him. Yes, yes, yes, my body screamed. I wanted this. I'd wanted it for a while and I was done fighting it. I pushed my mouth harder to his. With a drive completely fueled by reflex, I swung deftly onto his lap, straddled his hips, and surged my fingers through that thick, silky hair.

I grasped his shoulders, gratified by the cords of muscle that tightened as he drew his arms around me. Touching him only made my desire burn hotter. I kissed him recklessly, greedily. My body felt hot and alive, humming with a delicious ache, and I couldn't remember why I hadn't done this sooner. I couldn't remember anything outside of Chet and the feel of him pressed against me.

His teeth nipped my lip. I tasted his breath, warm and sweet. His hand was on my thigh, running over my bare skin. My whole body jolted with pleasure.

I heard giggling.

I tore my mouth away from Chet's, blinking at the sunlit path behind the bench. Two small girls stood there, pointing at us and laughing behind their hands. Their eyes grew round when they saw me; they gasped and raced away. It was enough of a distraction to pull me to my senses.

I climbed off Chet. I backed away. He reached to stop me, but I held up a hand. The heat was beginning to recede, and I felt ashamed.

I smoothed my clothes. Like I could pretend nothing had happened. We hadn't just made out, I hadn't felt his hands on me, I hadn't been overcome by hot, throbbing desire.

"I want to go back to Carmina's," I said. I couldn't look at him. If I did, I might run back into his arms. The way he kissed . . .

I shut my eyes. I squeezed them hard. I wouldn't think of it.

"Did I hurt you?" Chet asked, breathing heavily. He braced his hands on his knees and hunched his shoulders. He was trying to wrestle control of himself too.

Hurt? No. It wasn't that. Caught up in the moment, I hadn't felt any pain. Just electrifying sensation and longing.

"I can't do this with you."

"Is there someone else?" he asked roughly.

"Yes."

"In Tennessee?"

"Yes," I said again, miserably. I didn't want to lie to Chet or hurt him. I never should have kissed him. Looking at the pain on his face, I was terrified I'd ruined everything. How would I ever repair the damage? I couldn't lose Chet as a friend. The thought of enduring the summer without him filled me with a weight heavier than my shame or guilt.

"Will you see him again?"

"I don't know," I confessed.

Chet nodded slowly, but there was nothing accepting about the gesture. Behind the torment, I saw his eyes flare. "You're going to give up something with me for a guy who, let's face it, is probably out of your life for good?"

"I'm sorry." There was nothing more I could say. If I tried to explain, I'd have to tell him the truth. And I couldn't do that.

"I care about you, Stella," he said huskily.

Stella. It drove the point home. Chet didn't know me. He didn't even know my real name. He sat there looking frustrated and vulnerable, cutting himself open for a girl who didn't exist.

"I don't want to hurt you. I want to be your friend." My voice shook a little when I said it, and Chet laughed, but the sound was bleak and humorless.

"I guess we'll have to agree to disagree on that point." He pushed off the bench and stalked to the water's edge, his hands braced stiffly on his hips. The longer he stared into the distance, the bigger the rock in my throat grew.

I bit my lip, willing myself not to cry. My instinct was to be tough and coldly insensitive. I wanted to smother any hint of emotion. I longed for Estella, who'd learned to harden her heart and not care too much because of the risk of being disappointed or, worse, hurt. After the divorce, right about the time my mom started using, that's how Reed had found me. Cool, detached, distrustful, unimpressed by life. I had to find my way back there. It was the only way I knew to protect myself.

Wiping my eyes on the backs of my hands, I said, "Will you take me to Carmina's?"

On the ride, Chet did not speak to me. He didn't turn on the radio. I knew he wasn't trying to punish me, but that's what it felt like. The awful suffocating silence was the worst chastisement he could have given me. I wanted him to say something, anything. Even if it was just to complain about the weather. If he talked to me, I would know he didn't hate me, know he was still my friend.

He pulled up to a stoplight. The high, hot sun glinted off the hood of the Scout, and I could feel sweat beading at the small of my back. Waves of heat shimmered off the blacktop. It wasn't even noon, and the temperature was still climbing.

I gazed out my window at the baseball diamonds. Players were running laps around the outfield. Judging by the ruddy glow in their faces and the sweat stains on their shirts, they'd been out there awhile. I could only imagine how sunbaked and drained they must feel.

Farther down, in the batting cages, a few players swung bats to the rhythm of the pitching machines. Only one player sat on the bench, watching his teammates from a pool of shade provided by the overhang. He methodically tossed a ball in the air, his slouched posture bored.

The coach blew his whistle, and the team scrambled in from all corners. Practice was over. The benchwarmer stood up, his red-gold hair gleaming like fire. He hobbled toward his truck in the parking lot, noticeably favoring his left leg.

Trigger McClure, it seemed, had injured his leg.

ESTELLA,

SORRY I DIDN'T WRITE THE PAST TWO DAYS. THEY KEEP US BUSY. THERE'S A BIG BANNER IN THE CAFETERIA THAT READS "LIVE, EAT,

SLEEP, AND BREATHE BASEBALL." No SHIT. EAT A
CHEESESTEAK FROM LEE'S FOR ME, OKAY?

AND NO HOOKING UP WITH OTHER GUYS WHILE I'M
NOT AROUND TO DEFEND WHAT'S MINE.

KIDDING. SORTA. I DON'T KNOW WHAT I'D DO
WITHOUT YOU.

xREED

17

THAT NIGHT DURING DINNER, THERE WAS A KNOCK at the door. Carmina set down her fork and huffed a sigh of exasperation.

"If Roger Perkins is sniffing around here again, I'm driving to the animal shelter first thing and getting a watchdog. If I can't keep that man off my porch, maybe a pit bull will."

"Knock, knock, anybody home?" A familiar male voice drifted through the screen door, which Carmina used at night in the hope of luring a breeze inside. "Deputy Price here. I've brought a few acquaintances."

With an unfathomable look, Carmina pushed back her chair. "We're here, Deputy. Come on in."

I followed her into the hall, where, sure enough, Deputy Price stepped inside, trailed by a swarthy linebacker of a man, and a woman with a helmet of thick black curly hair. Detectives Ramos and Cherry from Philadelphia PD. They'd taken my statement at the police station the night I called 911—the night I was whisked into WITSEC.

Behind them, another man wiped his feet before crossing the threshold. He was lithely built, with a scholarly face that watched the world from behind wire-rimmed glasses. I couldn't remember his name, but I knew who he was. The head prosecutor handling the case against Danny Balando.

"Hey there, Stella—whoa. What happened to your face?" Price had been leaning forward to give my hand a shake, but stopped at the sight of me. "Looks like you got in a fight." He aimed a worried and questioning look at Carmina.

"Last night," she explained. "It happened last night. I was going to call you."

"You should have."

"Local boy. Has a temper. We're handling it."

"I don't like seeing my witness black and blue."

"I said we're handling it," Carmina repeated firmly.

"Why don't I ring you in the morning," Price said levelly, but there was no mistaking the displeasure flaring in his eyes. "You can explain it to me then."

Carmina nodded, but I could tell she was both annoyed by, and dreading, the call. I supposed, as a former cop she felt like he was questioning her ability to do her job. I felt bad that she was taking the fall for my condition, especially since none of this was her fault. Since the assault, she'd cared for me more diligently than my mom ever had.

Price turned to me. "Sorry this happened, Stella. We'll make sure it doesn't happen again, okay? When I said you'd be safe here, I meant it." His face warmed. "You've been spending time in the sun, I see. Getting a tan."

I stared at him, baffled, skeptical. Why was he making small talk? Why was he here, period?

"Good to see you again, Stella," Detective Cherry said. Her smile was pleasant, but behind it, her sharp eyes were furiously at work, sizing up me, Carmina, and the house—what she could see of it.

"What are you doing here?" I asked all three of them collectively. Was I in trouble? Had Danny escaped?

"Guessing you didn't get my message," Price said to Carmina.

"Message?" she echoed. "Haven't heard the phone ring all day."

"The special cell phone I gave you. I left a message on it. Said we'd be arriving tonight. I know it's a hassle, but you really need to keep the phone with you at all times."

Carmina patted her empty pockets, frowning. "Not used to carrying a mobile phone. Think I left it on the nightstand this morning."

"What are you doing here?" I repeated, this time addressing Price directly, since he seemed to be point man for the group.

"You remember Detective Cherry and Detective Ramos," he told me. "And the head prosecutor, Executive Assistant District Attorney Charles Menlove."

Mr. Menlove also stepped forward to clasp my hand, but his grip was tighter and felt much more formal. He wore a thin, frog-like smile.

"Where's the woman from Child Services?" I asked, thinking she was the only player missing from that long, harrowing night at the police station.

"Didn't bring CPU, figured Carmina could stand in for her," Price explained.

It clicked in my head. The only reason I'd needed Child Services at the police station was because my mom was too high to look out for my welfare when I met with the detectives. Instead, a woman I'd never met had been appointed to make sure I felt safe.

Price said, "There have been some developments in the case. The detectives haven't been able to get a statement from your mom, but even if she decides to cooperate, the defense will, in all likelihood, discredit her testimony. They'll play it so the jury views her as unreliable."

"Because she's a drug addict," I stated.

Price inclined his head tactfully. "And Reed, well, his criminal history makes his testimony iffy. People don't trust criminals."

"He isn't a criminal. He made a few bad decisions," I argued. "I know about the breaking and entering charge—he broke into that house on a dare. The people weren't even home! And I know about the prowling at nighttime charge. I can't believe that's even a law. So what if Reed made a couple mistakes? It doesn't change how I feel about him."

"Because you know him," Price said.

"Yeah," I jumped in defensively. "I know his dad was harsh and authoritarian, and his approach to parenting—if you can call it that—backfired, driving Reed to rebel. If you want to point fingers, maybe you should interrogate General Winslow. Ask him how he treated his son during the eighteen years Reed was forced to live under his roof. That man is an abusive sociopath."

Price's mouth pinched, but he didn't respond to my accusation. "To a jury, perception is everything. They have no reason to trust Reed. Right now, you're our best shot. Remember how I told you delay is the defense's best friend? That's because over time, witnesses forget their testimony. We need to make sure yours is rock solid."

"Detective Cherry and I reviewed the statement you gave us," Detective Ramos said, "and we have a few follow-up questions. We want to make sure your story is airtight. We don't want the defense seeing something we overlooked."

My knees swayed a little, but I ordered myself to keep it together. Follow-up questions. I knew my story. Stick to it, and I could get through this.

"Why don't we sit in the kitchen?" Carmina suggested. "Stella can finish her meal, and I can pour the rest of you sun tea."

"What was your mom's relationship with Danny Balando?" Detective Ramos asked, flipping out the coattails of his blazer as he lowered his muscled physique into the chair across from mine.

"I already told you. He was her drug dealer," I said, refusing to be intimidated by his hulking size, which I was sure was his intent.

"Meaning their relationship was strictly professional?"

I held his gaze without blinking, but my mind raced furiously. He was digging. Why? What did he know? "If you call buying and selling drugs professional, then yes."

"See, we believe he was more than that. We believe he was also her boyfriend. It's our belief that they were romantic."

I blinked once, reflexively, but other than that, revealed nothing. "Did Danny say that? Because we all know Danny can be trusted. He's such a great guy. I mean, it's not like he's in jail for murder or anything."

"Stella," Carmina said softly, covering my hand with her own. "Just the facts."

"We believe the reason your mom is refusing to cooperate with us is because she's trying to protect Danny," Detective Cherry explained.

"My mom's an addict. She was passed out when Danny Balando shot that man in our house. She isn't being uncooperative—she doesn't know anything."

Ramos flipped through the notepad in front of him. "When we asked her to tell us about that night, she said,"—he licked his index finger, finding the right page—"'Go to hell.' Those aren't the words of someone with no memory of events. Those are the words of someone who's defensive because they're hiding something."

"Maybe she's tired of being pestered for information she doesn't have," I shot back. Under the table, I wiped my palms on my shorts.

"Tell us about that night," Detective Cherry murmured. Her dark brown eyes were soft, sympathetic. Classic Good Cop. "Let's walk through it one more time."

"Again?" I said resentfully.

"Again," Charles Menlove said. Until now, he'd stood with his shoulder to the wall, watching the proceedings without comment. "I want to hear it again."

"It was after midnight," I began. I had rehearsed these words until I knew them by heart. My story was solid. "It was really late—or early, depending on how you look at it."

"What time? Ballpark," Detective Cherry said gently.

I shook my head, showing them I was at a loss. "I'd been out with friends. I lost track of time."

"Can you give us a range—between this hour and that?" Detective Cherry urged.

"I can't. I'm sorry."

She nodded. "It's okay. Keep going."

"I parked on the street because I didn't want to wake my mom."

"Because you broke curfew, isn't that right?" Detective Ramos clarified. "You were worried you'd get in trouble if your mom heard you. You were sneaking home. But you can't remember the exact time you got home? You weren't frantically checking the clock as you drove, sweating bullets as each minute ticked by?"

"I didn't have a curfew." Stay calm. "I was a little worried I'd wake her, but not overly. I knew there was a good chance she'd be passed out. I was right."

"At seventeen, you were allowed to come and go as you pleased? You don't find that unusual?" he pressed.

"She didn't allow me to do anything," I shot back. "She was completely unaware of me. When she was high, which was most of the time, the rest of the world dropped away. It didn't exist. I didn't exist. It was like . . . we were roommates. One roof, two different lives. I don't expect you to understand."

"What happened after you got home?" Detective Cherry asked.

Shutting my eyes, I let that night return to me. Every time I went back, I expected the nightmare to lose some of its grip, but that wasn't the case. I could see the past all too clearly.

I remembered the squeak of a rain-washed pavement beneath my shoes as I crept toward the back door. I remembered the hushed stillness of sleeping houses. The cool dampness of the night air.

I let myself inside. The kitchen light didn't turn on. Same thing in the dining room. In the dark, I felt my way through the house.

As I crossed in front of the library's glass doors, I saw my mom passed out in a chair. Her pills were spread on the side table. Before I could register disgust, my eyes were drawn behind her. I stared at the man's body. He'd been shot, execution-style.

I was too paralyzed to scream.

Scuffling sounds carried in from the street outside.

I turned to the window. A barrel of a man dragged a second, leaner man over to a parked Honda Civic. The man being dragged had a sack over his head. Something about him was remotely familiar, but I was too much in shock to pursue the thought.

The big man shoved the other man into the Civic's trunk, then beat him with a tire iron until his chilling screams fell quiet.

After closing the trunk, the big man stared at our house. His eyes glittered with something dark and disturbing. He didn't see me. But I saw him.

As much as I might want to, I would never forget Danny Balando's face.

"Your mother was unconscious when you entered the library?" Detective Ramos repeated, jolting me back to Carmina's kitchen table.

"Yes."

"And the man on the floor, the man who was shot, he was dead?"

"He wasn't moving. There was blood everywhere," I said shakily.

"Did Danny Balando attempt to enter the house at that point?"

"Reenter. No. He drove off."

"Did you see the weapon he used to shoot the man in the library?"

"No. He must have taken it with him. Why would he leave it?"

"What time did you call the police?"

"Right after Danny drove off."

Ramos paged through his notes. "Phone records show you placed the call at three twenty-two a.m."

"That sounds right."

"So it's safe to assume you arrived home about three fifteen a.m., wouldn't you agree?"

"I guess."

"You see, here's where we have a problem. We have some new information, and your statement doesn't jive."

New information? That had come to light while I was in Thunder Basin? My mind reeled frantically as I tried to guess what they knew. My hands felt damp with perspiration and I shifted in my seat.

Ramos went on, "In hopes of catching Danny Balando leaving the scene of the crime, we pored over hours of security feed obtained from cameras in the area. Banks, convenience stores, that sort of thing. We have a street cam showing your car driving through the intersection of Audubon and Eighth at two fifteen a.m. That intersection is only a handful of blocks from your house. You were driving in the direction of home. It stands to reason you should have made it home closer to two twenty. And yet, you didn't call nine-one-one for another hour." He propped his meaty forearms on the table, his eyes locking me in their hard gaze. "That street cam shows your car driving *toward* your house at two fifteen, then *away* at two forty. More perplexing, it shows you returning again at three ten. That's a lot of driving. What were you doing? Where were you going?"

I stared at him. My paralysis lasted only a moment. Finding my voice, I said, "I drove to Reed's. After I saw the dead man in my house, I panicked. I didn't know what to do. My mom was passed out—she couldn't help me. So I drove to Reed's, but he wasn't home."

"You drove to Reed Winslow's?"

"Yes."

"Why didn't you mention this in your statement?"

"I—" Tears burned my eyes. I wanted to look to Carmina for help, but she hadn't been there. She couldn't tell me what to say. "I didn't want to drag him into this. I—wanted to protect him."

"You weren't aware that Reed had just been at your house when you left to drive to his place?" Detective Cherry asked.

I shook my head adamantly, blinking against the hot sting in my eyes. "No. I didn't know Reed was in my bedroom that night, waiting for me to get home. I didn't know he would hear gunfire downstairs and go see what was wrong. I didn't know he'd walk in on a murder scene." My voice went up an octave. "Did I know my mom's drug dealer would drag him outside, shove him in the trunk of a car, and beat him with a tire iron to make him 'forget' what he'd seen? No! Why are we going over this again?" I cried. "I've already told you what happened! Why are you making me relive it?"

"Time for a break," Carmina said in that calm, yet adamant, voice of hers. Her chair scraped across the floor as she rose to her feet. "Detectives, Mr. Menlove, I know you traveled a long way to talk with Stella, but I'm calling it a night. She's had enough."

Detective Ramos dragged his hands down his face and Detective Cherry leaned back in her chair with a sigh of defeat.

It was Charles Menlove, the prosecutor, who spoke up. "Just one more question, Stella, and we'll be on our way. Can you tell me who the man in the library was? The man who was shot."

"He was my mom's former dealer, before Danny Balando."

"His name, by chance?"

"She called him the Pharmacist. She and her friends did. He supplied them with painkillers, I think. Prescriptions."

Charles Menlove's eyes were sure and steady, telling me he already knew this. "And what do you surmise he was doing at your house that night?"

"He'd fronted my mom prescriptions, and she owed him a lot

of money. He came to the house, demanding payment. He threatened her, roughed her up—we both saw the bruises."

A complying nod. "And Danny Balando? Where does he fit in?"

Angry now, I gave him my opinion with open defiance. "I think Danny Balando showed up, saw the Pharmacist assaulting his client, and shot him. Then again, I'm not the detective. Far be it for me to make sense of these mystifying—or not—clues."

Ignoring my jab, Charles Menlove said, "And that's when Reed came downstairs? Upon hearing gunfire?"

"That's right. Reed ran downstairs to see what was the matter, and Danny assaulted him, then drove him to the west side, where he dumped his body on the street without any care about what might happen to him."

"You seem to have your theory all worked out. I admit, it's well developed. Everything explained, no loose ends. You practically handed it to us on a gold platter."

"I'll put the bill in the mail," I said with withering sarcasm.

That night, I lay in bed listening to the stillness of the house. The air in my room was hot and placid, but I drew the sheet under my chin, shivering. It was after midnight before I got up the nerve to open the window. I leaned my back against the wall and shut my eyes. I rested a hand on the windowsill and let the cool air wash over my clammy skin. I breathed deeply, trying to plant my feet solidly in Thunder Basin.

I hadn't realized how tense I was until they—Price, Charles

Menlove, and the detectives—left. When they showed up tonight, it was as if they'd brought Philly with them.

The secrets I'd been running from had finally caught up with me.

But the detectives were gone now, and the world was beginning to slow. I felt the wide open spaces surrounding the farmhouse envelope me. My problems receded into the shadows and life seemed simple again. I felt cool, sweet relief.

Tonight Thunder Basin didn't feel like a prison. It felt like a set of open doors at the end of a long, painful road, beckoning me closer.

It felt like my sanctuary.

ESTELLA,

LAST DAY OF BASEBALL CAMP. I'LL FINALLY BE FREE OF MY ROOMMATE AND I GET TO SEE YOU. CAN'T WAIT. I'M GOING TO TAKE A CAB FROM THE AIRPORT AND STAY WITH A FRIEND IN THE CITY UNTIL THINGS BLOW OVER AT HOME. THAT'S RIGHT. MORE FIGHTING AT THE WINSLOW RESIDENCE, AND I WASN'T EVEN THERE TO START IT. I CALLED MY MOM LAST NIGHT AND SHE'D BEEN ARGUING WITH MY DAD. I COULD HEAR IT IN HER VOICE. MY DAD WANTS HER TO HOST A PARTY FOR HIS ARMY BUDDIES. BUT HER FIBROMYALGIA MAKES IT HARD FOR HER TO GET OUT OF BED. SHE'S

IN CONSTANT PAIN. How's SHE SUPPOSED TO PLAY HOSTESS? IN THE END, I KNOW SHE'LL DO WHAT HE WANTS. IT PISSES ME OFF THAT SHE WON'T STAND UP TO HIM, BUT I HAVE TO LET IT GO. I'VE WAITED SEVENTEEN YEARS FOR HER TO STAND UP TO HIM, AND look WHERE IT'S GOTTEN ME. IT'S A WEAKNESS TO CARE. WHEN YOU CARE, YOU HAVE SOMETHING TO lOSE.

xREED

BY THE FOLLOWING SUNDAY, I WAS FEELING MUCH
better—physically. I'd been medically cleared to go back to work,
and despite Carmina's insistence that I not rush things, I was
ready to see the Sundown again. As in all small towns, talk traveled quickly in Thunder Basin. If there was one piece of news
I wanted to reach Trigger's ears, it was that I was back at work.
He'd taken some skin and blood, but that was all he was getting.
I wasn't going to hide in Carmina's house, living in fear of him.

But since the Sundown was closed Sundays, I had one more
day of waiting before I donned my support hose, faux-leather
skirt, and camo top again. I woke first thing, beating Carmina out
of bed, and put a pot of coffee on. Then I showered for church.
That's right. Church.

I hadn't seen or talked to Chet since our disastrous kiss over a week ago, and despite the proverbial expression, time was not mending my heart—with each passing day, I felt worse. I needed to know things were okay between us. I needed his friendship.

I could pretend I liked him only because there was no one else around, but there was something about him. Something hard to resist. He was overpoweringly masculine yet incredibly sensitive. It was a dangerous combination. A dangerous, alluring, tempting combination. I staunchly refused to compare Chet to Reed—there was no point; I was happy with Reed—but an unwanted voice at the back of my mind whispered it was because I knew who'd win, and it wasn't who I wanted.

Or was it?

Despite my best-laid plans, I hadn't bumped into Chet in town, which I'd hoped would give me the perfect opportunity to gauge his feelings. Nor had I worked up the nerve to call him. I figured if I was aiming to cross paths with him, my best shot was at church. If I sat close enough to him to unavoidably run into him after the service, I'd get my excuse to talk to him. I had no doubt it would be awkward. I'd rejected him and had probably wounded his pride. He had every right to feel hurt. I just hoped . . .

I hoped for the impossible. That things would go back to the way they'd been before. But I'd settle for saying sorry. Which was another reason I was hell-bent on going to church this morning. If you couldn't make amends at church, where could you?

Carmina and I rode together. Climbing out of her truck, I straightened my skirt and squared my shoulders. *Here goes nothing.*

As we walked to the doors, we passed the marquee sign on the lawn. FORBIDDEN FRUITS CREATE MANY JAMS.

Talk about a guilt trip. No one knew I'd kissed Chet, certainly not Reed, certainly not any of the congregation, but just the same. I couldn't help but glance around nervously, half expecting to see huddled groups whispering and pointing at me like I was some kind of twenty-first-century Hester Prynne. Not that it was any of their business.

Carmina seemed to see the marquee sign at the same moment, and grunted her disapproval. "The flashy things pastors do these days to draw in larger crowds. That sign is just plain vulgar."

"We should rearrange the letters. Create an anagram. Create a dirty anagram. Let's see. . . ." I tapped my lip thoughtfully. "If an erect bride surfs on a fried car—"

"Oh, hush." Carmina eyed me reproachfully, but a hint of a smile touched the corners of her mouth.

"The expression on Pastor Lykins's face would be priceless," I said temptingly.

She rolled her eyes and gave a long-suffering sigh, as if to lament having to put up with me.

We reached the top of the steps, and Pastor Lykins greeted us by shaking our hands enthusiastically. He leaned in, his hushed voice turning grave. "Stella, I was grieved to hear about what happened last week. I sincerely hope you're feeling better. Did you receive my flowers?"

"Yes, thank you." In fact, he'd stopped by Carmina's house twice to check on me, but luck had been on my side both days and I'd been gone. A crying shame, as Carmina would say.

"I'm so relieved and delighted to see you at church this morning," he went on. "I hope you enjoy the sermon. Carmina, looking lovely as ever."

With a brusque nod that acknowledged his compliment, Carmina led me inside.

I waited until we were out of the pastor's range of hearing before I echoed, "'Lovely as ever?' Is there something you're not telling me?"

"Don't be nonsensical."

"He was hitting on you!"

Carmina paused in walking to give me a stern, reproachful eye. "Of all the harebrained things to suggest."

"Now I know what you do at Bible study," I said slyly.

"Lord help us," Carmina muttered, sliding into an empty pew.

I had just taken my seat beside her when Trigger and his parents strolled up the aisle. Trigger wore a navy-checked shirt and Dockers, and while he looked squeaky clean, I knew the dirty truth about him. He had a crutch tucked under one armpit, and hobbled into a pew two in front of ours. Before easing gingerly into his seat, he looked back and caught my eye. To anyone else, his expression would have seemed perfectly impassive. But I saw the taunting gleam in his rage-filled eyes as he leered at me. In that moment, he reminded me of Danny Balando. They shared the same untouchable arrogance and unstable temper—I could see it as plainly in Trigger's fixated stare as I had in Danny's crazed eyes all those weeks ago.

The woman seated in front of me leaned forward to speak with Trigger. "What happened, Trigger? Hurt yourself at baseball practice?"

He smiled, slow and easy. "Yes, ma'am. Took a stray ball to the ankle. Doc said I got a distal fibula fracture. Fancy talk for one broken bone, so I can still walk on it, I just gotta be careful. And I gotta wear this walking cast four more weeks."

"A shame. Were any scouts planning on watching you play this week?"

"Sure. They always are. But don't you fret, Mrs. Lamb. You throw an over-the-top sinker like I do, and nobody's going anywhere. Just giving them a chance to sit back and wipe the drool off their chins, that's all." He laughed and Mrs. Lamb joined in.

I glanced sideways at Carmina, and while her gaze was fixed forward, I knew she wasn't serenely listening to the organ prelude, as she appeared. At last I drew her eyes to mine. We shared a meaningful look. She patted me on the knee. I wasn't exactly sure what the gesture was supposed to mean, but I felt a measure of solidarity. She was on my side.

Chet wasn't in church, and I tried not to feel deflated as Carmina and I filed out of the chapel after the sermon. I wouldn't judge him if he'd gone out of his way to avoid me, but it didn't seem like his style. Chet was as likely to hide from me as I was to hide from Trigger. So where was he?

Risking arousing Carmina's suspicion, I said, "I didn't see Chet today. Does he usually miss church?"

"Why? Something happen between the two of you?"

I should have known there was no such thing as slipping one past Carmina.

I scoffed. "Of course not." Then, "What makes you think something happened?"

"You sound guilty."

Making a noise as though I were offended, I said, "Oh? And what do I sound guilty of?"

"Keep talking and I'll figure it out. Didn't spend thirty years honing my interrogation skills for naught."

A notable pause followed. At last I said, "If something did happen, do you think I should go over and try to set things right?"

She seemed to weigh my question. "I don't."

"But you don't like Chet," I protested. "Of course that's what you'd tell me. You'd like it if I never saw him again. Personal biases aside, what's the right thing to do?"

"I don't dislike Chet. That was you putting words in my mouth. I think you're looking at Thunder Basin as a pit stop on your way to something better. And I think Chet is looking for permanence. Feels wrong to encourage a relationship with no hope of catching wind in its sails."

"You're probably right," I said quietly. She had an uncanny way of seeing past the BS to the truth.

"What about the other boy?" Her eyes were set straight ahead, but there was something perceptive and shrewd in her voice. "I read your file. I know there was a young man in Philadelphia."

"Reed," I murmured, unsure how to deal with Carmina's

directness. Were we allowed to talk about this? I'd been ordered to stick to the cover story at all times, even with Carmina. Why was she breaking the rules?

"Perhaps you're hoping Chet will help you get over him?" she suggested quietly.

"No," I said automatically. Did Carmina think that little of me? I wouldn't use Chet that way . . . would I? Would I admit it if I were? Why did everything have to be so confusing?

"Chet has some flaws, but he's a good, hardworking, decent boy."

"Why are you telling me this?"

"So you believe me when I say I don't dislike him."

I felt a hot wave of guilt. "You think I'll hurt him."

"Chet's had a rough year since his parents' deaths. Getting involved with him is only going to end in heartache—for him, yes, but for you, too. You're gone in August, and you'll have to say good-bye all over again. Was it easy the first time? I doubt it was. Chet will be stuck here for another two years, raising that brother of his. I don't see a happy ending, Stella, and that's the truth. I think you'll hurt each other."

"Why do you suddenly care about Chet's feelings?" I wasn't being confrontational; I really wanted to know.

"Perhaps I've blamed him for things beyond his control."

"I don't understand."

"I knew his father. Chet resembles him in many ways. It can be hard to remember they're two different men."

"You didn't like Mr. Falconer?"

"Oh, it wasn't quite like that," she said with a troubled sigh. "But he's gone now. What does it matter?" Her eyes looked distant and deep with grief.

"You really think it's best if I end things?"

"I do."

I grew quiet. I wasn't sure I could do that. Chet was my only friend in Thunder Basin. Without him, the summer would stretch on agonizingly long. No more teasing or silly jokes. No more softball games, since what was the point? If I was going to break away from Chet, I had to make it a clean one. I'd miss the way he looked at me, with those warm blue eyes, as if it were just me and him and the rest of the world had dropped away. I'd miss his leggy stride when we walked together. I'd even miss his stupid cowboy hat. But I didn't want to hurt him.

Above all, I didn't want that.

"STELLA, CAN I TALK TO YOU? PRIVATELY?"

I was tying an apron around my waist when Dixie Jo poked her head out of her office and beckoned me inside. It was my first day back at work since the attack, and one glance at her concerned expression told me exactly what this was about. I tempered my exasperation. I was *fine*. No one seemed to believe me, but I was. With enough arguing, I'd finally persuaded Carmina to let me return to work; the way I saw it, everything was downhill from there. I'd make Dixie Jo see she had nothing to worry about.

"How are you feeling?" she asked, closing the door behind us.

"I know you're worried about me, but I'm ready for this." I pulled on a wide smile. "Trust me, it beats sitting at Carmina's house and counting the fruit flies in the peach bowl."

"I heard your doctor gave you the all-clear to come back to work," she said, sounding pleased, but I could tell she wasn't convinced.

I raised my arms from my sides, dropped them back into place. "Good as new."

"It's okay to be scared, Stella. It's perfectly fine to want more time. Inny and Deirdre are covering your shifts, so don't worry about us. Take all the time you need, and I really mean that."

"Thanks for the offer, but I'm fine. Really."

"That makes one of us," she said with a troubled sigh, and at that moment, I noticed how haggard and careworn her eyes looked. "I haven't had a restful night since you were attacked. I keep asking myself, how could this have happened? The Sundown is a family place. And I'm not just talking about our customers, but the employees, too. We look out for each other. The idea that someone could come in here and assault one of us is"—she shook her head, looking mystified and disconcerted—"unimaginable. Unthinkable. I'm sorry, so sorry."

She opened her arms to me, and even though I wasn't used to being hugged, I let her embrace me. I didn't want Dixie Jo to feel responsible for what Trigger did to me. She couldn't have prevented him. She kept the doors unlocked because this *was* a family place; we trusted each other. We felt safe here. And Trigger had taken advantage of that.

She held me at arm's length. "Let an old lady give you a word of advice. Sometimes it takes longer to heal here"—she laid a gentle finger against her head, just above her ear—"than here."

She touched that same finger to her heart. "Look me in the eye and tell me you're really ready to be here."

I met her gaze directly. I needed this. I had to send Trigger a clear message that I wasn't going to cower in fear. "Wouldn't want to be anywhere else."

Still not looking entirely persuaded, she turned me by the shoulders to face the door. "Then go give 'em hell."

I worked hard all night, shuttling trays of food to the street and leaving a trail of happy customers in my wake. I pocketed a five-dollar tip from a sweet older gentleman in orange suspenders who told me my smile was the best part of his meal. It felt good to smile, and I did it often. I wanted Trigger to hear that he hadn't left any permanent scars, inside or out. If he'd hoped to break me, he'd failed. In my mind, I drew up a scorecard. Stella one, Trigger zero.

That's right, you SOB. I came out on top.

At the end of the night, Deirdre took off early, leaving Inny and me to close up. Deirdre had seniority, not to mention two kids, so it didn't bother me. Inny and I worked side by side to clean and organize the kitchen for the morning crew. We refilled the salt and pepper shakers, wiped down the ketchup bottles, and swept the floors. Inny dispensed the remaining ice cream from the machine and made us cherry shakes. We went out on the back steps to drink them, not wanting to create any new spills to clean up.

"To the moron who laid his hands on you," Inny said, raising her malt cup in a toast. "May his balls rot and fall off, and be scavenged by vultures."

"Tell me how you really feel." I clinked my cup to hers, then took a long pull on my straw. "How's that baby of yours doing tonight?"

"Still kicking."

I wondered if Inny ever wished it would die. No one wanted to give birth to a dead baby, but then again, no one wanted to be pregnant at sixteen, either.

"Do you think the father will help out?" I asked, hoping I wasn't being too nosy. I had to tread carefully; as per Dixie Jo's directive, no pity parties were allowed.

"Yeah," Inny answered. "He'll help out financially. He's made that clear. He's taking his role as provider real serious. And he'll be at the delivery." She sounded certain, but maybe she was telling herself lies to make the idea of having a baby at sixteen seem less frightening.

We slurped our shakes in silence.

"I think I know who attacked me," I said after a beat. "I told the police my suspicion, but far as I know, they haven't arrested anyone."

Inny stared at me, wide-eyed. "How do you know who it was? I heard you never saw his face."

"When he was attacking me, I kicked him in the leg. Hard. As he left the storeroom, I heard him limp up the stairs."

"So we're looking for a bad leg."

I drew a deep breath, hoping my next words didn't ruin our friendship. I liked Inny and I had her back. But I also wanted to give her some much-needed perspective. Even if that meant telling her something she didn't want to hear.

"I think Trigger beat me up."

Inny thought this over. She set down her malt cup, planked her arms on her knees, and shook her head back and forth. To my relief, she didn't leap to his defense or yell at me for jumping to conclusions. "Well, I'll be."

"Trigger is the father of your baby, isn't he?" I asked cautiously.

That jolted Inny out of her reverie. Her face screwed up in puzzlement. "What? Seriously? Did you really just ask me that? Now, why would I willingly encourage a disgusting animal like Trigger McClure to put his genetic material into the gene pool? You ever make that suggestion a second time, I'll break your arm—and your nose for good measure."

"So . . . he's not the father?"

"No." She made a face, curling her lips back over her teeth like a snarling dog might. "Think I'm gonna vomit now."

"But he always asks for you," I protested. "And when I said he might be leaving town to play in the majors, you seemed depressed."

"Jealous, maybe, but not depressed. Trust me, no one wishes that hairy butt out of town more than me. Just seems unfair that a dirty butt hole like him gets a ticket out, that's all. He should have to rot in this place. What good is karma if it doesn't work?"

"So Trigger is definitely not the father," I confirmed one last time.

"Told you I'd break your arm if you asked me that again," Inny said threateningly.

"Then who's the father?"

She gave me a look that said my attempt at snooping was a waste of time. "If my parents found out who he is, they'd kill him—but only if his own family didn't kill him first."

I said, "You realize this is going to drive me crazy."

She barked a laugh. "That's been my master plan all along: drive you batty so after I have this baby, I'm not in the loony bin all by my lonesome self."

We resumed slurping our shakes. I felt dazed. I'd been so sure about Inny and Trigger . . . and I could honestly say I'd never been more relieved to be wrong. From where I sat, Inny's future had just gotten a whole lot brighter. Whoever the father was, he couldn't be as bad as Trigger.

Figuring nothing I could say at this point would offend Inny, I said, "I think Eduardo might have helped Trigger. I think he might have let him inside, then told me to go down to the storeroom, where he knew Trigger would be waiting."

She looked skeptical. "I've known Eduardo for years. He's not a bad guy."

"Right before I was attacked, he asked me to go to the storeroom for napkins."

Inny's frown deepened. "Why would he do that?"

"He said Deirdre asked him to fill her napkin dispensers."

"I filled Deirdre's napkin dispensers that night." Inny poked her straw repeatedly into her shake, thinking things through. "Damn. I like Eduardo. Have you told Dixie Jo?"

"No. I want to be certain before I do. I like Eduardo too. I don't want to believe he would help Trigger hurt me."

"Eduardo and Trigger aren't friends, don't run in the same circles. I can't see them having a single reason to go in on this together."

"Maybe I'm wrong." I hoped I was. But I couldn't ignore parts of that night that weren't adding up.

"Only one way to find out. Ask Eduardo. Spring it on him sudden-like, so he don't have time to throw you some act. He's an honest kid. You'll know right away if he was in on it."

"If I'm wrong, he'll never talk to me again."

"If you're right, he deserves what he gets. Tell me this. Do you want to be working the night shift with a guy who lets girls get the tar beat out of 'em? I sure as hell don't." She got to her feet, dragging me up with her. "Come on. Let's finish up here. Then I'm taking you to a party."

I perked up. "Whose party?"

"Ours. And did I mention you can drink as much as you want?" She rubbed her ballooning abdomen. "Got yourself a designated driver."

I drove Carmina's truck and Inny rode shotgun. Even though I'd felt strong enough to bike to work, Carmina had insisted I take her truck. She hadn't seemed too pleased when I reminded her of her promise that I'd never drive her truck. What could I say? I wasn't one to pass up an opportunity to be a pain in the butt.

Inny and I headed south of town, along the river. Houses thinned and the moon slipped behind a cloud, casting the streets in pools of darkness. After we turned onto a gravel road, dust drifted through the high beams like rising spirits. I'd be lying if I said it didn't send a chill up the back of my neck. You couldn't find a place in all of Philly as deserted or suffocatingly black as this. I kept a tight grip on the steering wheel, half expecting a creature from a horror movie to spring onto the road. At last I saw house lights ahead and my shoulders relaxed.

Trucks and cars were parked this way and that in the field in front of the Craftsman-style house. As we stepped out, I marveled at how dark it was behind us. And how brightly the stars shone overhead. They glittered like radiant, polished gems. Having spent my whole life in the suburbs, with the lights of the city only a few miles away, I'd never imagined how utterly black the sky really was. How black, or how vast.

Inny bypassed the house, heading instead toward a two-story white barn at the back of the property. Light flooded from the open doors, and there were people everywhere.

So this was Thunder Basin's night scene.

The barn smelled like sawdust and fresh hay, and it wasn't a bad smell. The roof was high and pitched, making the barn seem even roomier. Horse stalls at the far end, and a tractor just to my left. A ladder led up to the loft, which I could see stored neat, rectangular bales of hay. I could also see couples up there, flat on their backs, making out. I smiled, thinking some clichés would never die.

As Inny and I weaved through the crowd, she nodded her head in acknowledgment at a few people, but she never stopped to talk. Without breaking stride, she grabbed a plastic cup from the stack near the cases of beer in the middle of the barn and headed for the spigot. I had a designated driver, but honestly, I wasn't a drinker. When Reed and I went to parties, he limited himself to one beer and nursed it for an hour. He didn't like to impair his judgment, and I simply didn't like the taste of it. That, and I had a deeply harbored fear of turning out like my mother, whose switch to harder drugs could easily be blamed on excessive drinking during the divorce proceedings. So I followed Inny's example and filled myself a cup of water.

"I gotta pee," she told me.

"You just went before we left the Sundown."

"Try getting pregnant. I've got a five-pound baby sitting on my bladder."

"TMI."

"Gonna go find a tree to squat behind. Gonna tell me that's TMI too?"

While I waited for her to return, I decided to make the rounds. Maybe I'd see someone from my softball team. I wouldn't mind hanging out with Juan tonight—he seemed like he knew how to have a good time.

Shouldering my way through the crowd, I looked for a familiar face, and suddenly he was right there, standing directly in front of me. He saw me at the exact same moment, his blue eyes locking onto mine.

Slipping my hands in my back pockets, I rocked back on my heels, trying to pull off calm and collected, but really I was just trying to get my bearings. How many times had I practiced what

I'd say at this moment, and now that it was here, my thoughts scattered. All I could think of was how his body was doing that faded T-shirt a number of favors. He'd ditched the cowboy hat; his mussed hair fell sexily into his eyes. And then I remembered I wasn't supposed to be thinking about his body or his eyes. Friends didn't think about friends that way.

"Hey," I said, smiling brightly, just like pals would. "Is it just me, or are you avoiding me?" I laughed, letting Chet know I was teasing and I was all for sparing us both an awkward or humiliating moment by keeping our first official run-in since the kiss as light as possible.

"You look better," he said, his face politely stoic. Eyes carefully avoiding mine. "The cuts and bruises are healing."

"Yeah, and it kind of sucks. I'm afraid I'm going to lose the special treatment soon. Tonight was my first night back at work, and customers were standing outside the carhop door, ready to take their orders off my fragile, wounded hands. Going to miss that." I was joking, but Chet didn't laugh. Unlike me, it seemed he hadn't reached the point where he could joke about the assault. Which made my stomach do a strange flutter.

"I'm happy to hear you're feeling better."

"Yeah," I echoed, hating how formal and stilted our conversation sounded. I knew why that was, but I missed how easy it used to be to talk with him. Maybe if I kept talking I could lighten him up. "So. What are you doing here?"

"Keeping an eye on Dusty. And before you ask, yeah, I feel like an idiot. I graduated last year, and here I am, hanging out at a high school party." He rose up on his toes, scanning the crowd. He'd ditched the cowboy hat, but kept the boots. Oddly, I found myself liking them more and more. They fit Chet. Rugged, tough, broken in. I wondered why it had taken me so long to realize this.

"It's nice that you care so much, but he's not a kid anymore, and nothing you do is going to stop him from making whatever bad decisions he's planning on making. You'll just be around to witness it all."

Now he looked at me, with surprise and maybe even anger. It flashed in his eyes, but retreated when he saw from my face that I wasn't judging him—just trying to help him see clearly.

His stance relaxed. "What about you?"

"Why am I here? Oh, Inny talked me into coming."

"Where is Inny?"

"I'd tell you, but it would be TMI. Want to take a walk?" I suggested. "By the river? I can't promise we'll be able to see it—did I mention the country gets dark at night?" I waited for Chet to crack a smile, and when he didn't, I cleared my throat. "All joking aside, I have a few things I want to say, mainly apologize for being inconsiderate of your feelings the other day by the duck pond."

Chet watched me with those clear eyes that made me feel transparent. I didn't like the idea of him seeing more into me than I could into him. Right now, he was completely unreadable. It was like he'd put up a shield to protect himself from me, and it made my heart twist painfully. I didn't want to be the enemy. At last he said, "I don't think that's a good idea, Stella."

I tried to hide my disappointment, but his rejection stung.

Was he so angry he wasn't going to let me apologize? I couldn't imagine spending the rest of the summer with Chet mad at me. What if the end of August came, and I left without ever reconciling our friendship? The idea caused panic to bubble up inside me. I couldn't bear the thought of our last words being angry ones.

"Listen," I began with quiet remorse. "I'm sorry. I can't tell you how sorry I am. I didn't mean to lead you on. I really thought we were friends, just friends. I didn't see the kiss coming. When it happened, I—well, if I could take it back, I would."

His whole body went utterly still. I'd said the wrong thing.

"Can we please take a walk?" I quickly asked, sounding flustered. I reached for his arm, and he stiffened at my touch. What was wrong with me? I couldn't think with all this noise. I'd sworn I wouldn't let Thunder Basin, or anyone in it, grow on me, but Chet had gotten under my skin. I had to set things right before I lost my chance. I couldn't live with myself knowing we'd parted on bad terms.

"I need to keep an eye on Dusty."

"You know I won't take no for an answer." I tugged lightly on his sleeve. "Please?" I added more desperately.

His eyes met mine directly. They were flat and distant. "I don't want to take a walk because I don't think it's fair to your boyfriend. I made my intentions pretty clear on that park bench last week. I want to be more than your friend. I don't think I can be around you and stop from wanting that. I like you too much, Stella, to be anything less than honest. I didn't know you had a boyfriend. Had I known, I wouldn't have acted the way I did. I wouldn't have pushed for more. I wish I could be your friend, but I don't trust myself to be satisfied with that. I think it's best if I give you some space." He exhaled. "And I'm asking for some in return."

I stared at him, feeling my throat close off. This wasn't happening. After living in Thunder Basin for weeks, deprived of friends and family, I'd finally met someone I cared about, and I was losing him. I felt him slipping away, and my fear came fast and sharp. The world seemed to be swirling out of my control. I'd promised myself I would never feel this way again—desperate, dependent, needy. I'd let my defenses down with Chet. It had happened without my realizing. I'd let him in, and now I was paying the price for my mistake. Reed was right—it was a weakness to care. When you cared, you had baggage. You had something to lose.

My eyes dampened with emotion, and I was appalled to feel hot tears rolling down my face. Swiping recklessly at them, I said, "I understand. Will you take Inny home? I have to go."

Light-headed and disoriented, I pushed my way through the crowd. I thought I heard Chet call my name, but I couldn't be sure. My head felt swarmed with bees. I needed fresh air. I had to get away from this place.

Stumbling out of the barn, I fled for Carmina's truck.

I held it together on the drive to the farmhouse. But the moment I was through the front door, my lip started quivering and the tears I'd kept under control flooded out. I hurried upstairs before Carmina could come and find me—I didn't want her to see me like this. Shutting myself in my bedroom, I crawled into bed.

I buried my face in the pillow and cried freely.

I PUSHED BACK IN MY CHAIR AND LET GO OF A
frustrated breath. I was at the library, and there was still not a
single e-mail from Reed. Something had happened. By now I was
sure of it. I could come up with a hundred ways to justify his
silence, but deep down, I knew something had gone wrong. I tried
not to feel sick to my stomach, but how could I not? My boyfriend
was wanted—*hunted*—by a ruthless criminal (all my mom's fault!),
and he'd suddenly vanished? It was hard not to connect the dots
and form a terrifying conclusion.

Breaking one of my own rules, I let my thoughts travel briefly
to my mom. Thinking about her always left me feeling angry and
exhausted, which was why I shut her out. Call it unhealthy, call it
denial, but so far it had turned out to be a reliable coping mechanism. Days, even weeks, could go by without a single thought of

her. I was happier for it. And now here I was, doing what I knew would not end well.

Was she safe?

Almost reflexively, I cast her out of my mind like she was a toxic chemical. Who cared if she was safe? She'd gotten us into this mess. Actions have consequences—hadn't she always drilled that into me when I was young? If she was in danger, she was getting her comeuppance.

I could hear my breath heaving in and out, and I made a controlled effort to slow it. I sat rooted in the library chair until the heat drained from my body and I was in control once again. My mom's safety was no concern of mine. Why should I care about her, when she clearly didn't care about me?

To refocus my thoughts, I pulled out one of Reed's letters that I'd brought with me. I smoothed the worn paper. The familiar sight of his handwriting was enough to console me a little.

ESTELLA,

SOMETIMES I FEEL LIKE I CAN EXPRESS MY FEELINGS BETTER IN A LETTER, WHEN I HAVE TIME TO REALLY THINK ABOUT WHAT I WANT TO SAY, SO HERE GOES. FIRST, PLEASE KNOW THAT I WAS GOING TO KEEP MY MOUTH SHUT (I DON'T WANT WHAT I SAY HERE TO OVERSHADOW WHAT YOU TOLD ME ABOUT YOUR MOM LAST NIGHT), BUT IN THE END, I DECIDED IT WAS

IMPORTANT FOR YOU TO KNOW YOU'RE NOT ALONE. My mom's AN ADDICT TOO. You KNOW SHE HAS A DISEASE CALLED FIBROMYALGIA, BUT DO YOU KNOW THAT IT MEANS SHE HAS SEVERE MUSCLE PAIN AND FATIGUE ALL THE TIME? Her DOCTOR GAVE HER A NARCOTIC, OxyContin, TO CONTROL THE PAIN. She's SUPPOSED TO TAKE ONE PILL EVERY TWELVE HOURS, BUT I'VE SEEN HER CRUSH TWO PILLS AT A TIME INTO A FINE POWDER AND SWALLOW THEM. This WAY ALL THE MEDICINE GOES INTO HER BLOOD AT ONCE AND SHE GETS HIGH. She's BEEN ADDICTED TO THE DRUG FROM THE BEGINNING. She KEEPS HER ADDICTION HIDDEN FROM FRIENDS, NEIGHBORS, EVEN HER DOCTOR. My DAD KNOWS ABOUT HER PROBLEM, BUT PRETENDS HE DOESN'T. He DRIVES HER TO THE DOCTOR FOR A NEW PRESCRIPTION EVERY MONTH, BECAUSE IT'S EASIER TO SLAP ON A Band-Aid THAN TO OPEN A WOUND AND CLEAN IT OUT.

JUST WANTED YOU TO KNOW. Not SO YOU FEEL SORRY FOR ME, BUT SO YOU KNOW YOU'RE NOT ALONE.

If YOU NEED TO TALK, CALL.

xReed

* * *

Twenty minutes later, I pulled into Carmina's drive. She had the barn doors thrown wide open and was bent over a workbench, her brow furrowed in deep concentration. At the sound of the truck, she looked up and waved.

"What are you doing out here?" I asked, walking up to inspect her work. Canisters filled with various colors of stains, mostly reds and browns, littered the workbench, and there was a lineup of small jars of polishes, waxes, and vegetable dyes on the shelf. She had a pair of brightly colored cowboy boots in her hands. She buffed the boots with a bristled brush, polishing the leather to a lustrous shine.

"You've been in Thunder Basin one month today," she answered.

I did the math in my head, and was surprised to discover she was right. I'd religiously kept track of the days the first few weeks, ticking down until my birthday, but recently, the hot summer days had started to blur together.

"Decided we should celebrate," Carmina went on. "A fancy dinner for two. That, and I have a gift for you." She tipped her head at the boots. "If you hate them, you don't have to wear them. Just the same, thought you might like a little something country for the summer. I know you aren't one to blend in, but this is what the locals wear."

I carefully took the boots from her. I ran my hand over the soft, soft leather. Bright turquoise and dusty-pink flowers embroidered the chocolate leather. The boots were not new. Lines and wrinkles formed worn grooves in the glossy surface. Every line seemed to tell a story. I wondered where these boots had traveled. What they'd seen.

"I put a fresh lining in every pair," Carmina said, "so don't worry about where the former owner's feet have been."

"They're beautiful," I murmured. And I meant it. There was something dignified and special about the boots that made you sit up and take notice. Like a rare treasure you might find in some corner nook after spending all day popping in and out of vintage shops along the Main Line. "What do I wear them with?"

Carmina laughed, evidently pleased. "Wear them with anything. Jeans, dresses, I've even seen girls in town wear them with denim shorts, the kind you're fond of."

For a split moment, I wished I could show the boots to Tory. Tory had a thing for vintage. She'd gush about how jealous she was and then insist I get Carmina to make her a pair too.

And just like that, I'd crossed a line. The past did not belong in the present. Why did I keep doing this? Why did I have to ruin a perfect moment?

I put my focus back on Carmina. "Where did you learn to do this?"

"Refurbish boots, you mean? Been doing it for years. My grandpa, Papa-Dew, taught me when I was just a girl. He was a good cobbler. We'd sit at his workbench and fix up the whole family's boots. Resole them and polish them to a shine. Saved having to buy new ones.

"One year, I told Papa-Dew I wanted boots with flowers. He

laughed and told me boots and flowers don't go together. But sure enough, Christmas morning I had a pair of blue boots collared with leather flowers under the tree."

"I hardly ever saw my grandparents," I said quietly, still running my hand over the silken leather. "My dad's parents died before I was born. And my mother fought with hers constantly. She said we were better off not seeing them. They weren't worth the headache. They live in Knoxville, you know. I've never seen their house. I hear they live on twenty acres and keep horses. My mother refused to take me there. I only saw my grandparents during the few trips they made to Philadelphia. My mom made them stay in a hotel, so I saw even less of them than I might have. After a day or two, my mom would accuse them of trying to control her, and a huge fight would follow. Inevitably, the next morning, when I asked about my grandparents, my mom would tell me something had come up and they'd had to go home to Tennessee early."

"I'm sorry, Stella." Carmina laid her hand on my arm, and met my eyes with sadness, but not pity. It mattered a great deal to me that she respected me enough to not treat me like a charity case.

I didn't want to choke up in front of Carmina. Not because I didn't trust her to be sensitive, but because I didn't trust myself. I didn't want to be that poor little girl who was always hurting again. Carmina wasn't the only one who could make me into a charity case—I could do that myself if I wasn't careful.

"I'll go shower and get ready for dinner," I said.

Her hand still rested on my arm. I thought I'd feel more myself when I separated from her, but a strange hollowness filled me when her hand dropped away.

I walked back to the house feeling lonely and cold, despite the sweltering afternoon sun.

I wore a yellow sundress and my new boots to dinner. We went to Dirk's Burgers, which was fancy for Thunder Basin. You could order just about anything on your veggie burger: tomato, lettuce, and onions for the traditionalists; avocado, alfalfa sprouts, and mushrooms for the vegetarians; fried salami and ricotta cheese for those who wanted an Italian-inspired twist. They even had a burger that was 50 percent ground beef, 50 percent ground bacon.

In Philly, I definitely would have gone vegetarian. No offense to Thunder Basin, but they didn't do vegetarian well. Beef, on the other hand, they had perfected. We were in cattle country, after all. On this line of thinking, I ordered the 50/50 burger.

"Let's walk by the river," Carmina said, after we finished our meal. "It'll be shady this time of day, and peaceful."

A few blocks later, we strolled under the canopy of cottonwood trees clustered in dense groups along the water's edge. The shade was blissful, a breeze rushing with the current. Carmina's face grew serious as she tucked her hands awkwardly in her pockets. Matter-of-factly, she said, "Deputy Marshal Price called today."

With those five words, my heart seemed to still. I found myself clutching the eyelet ribbon on my sundress. Or rather trying to. My fingers had begun to tingle. Despite the heat, I felt clammy. My mind instantly shot in several directions, none of them good.

"I'm no good at softening the blow of bad news, so I'm just going to give this to you straight. Reed Winslow is missing."

"He—?" I shook my head. The river trail seemed to contract, expand. I looked at Carmina, her face going in and out of focus. I kneaded my forehead with the heel of my hand, trying to make the world stop spinning. I felt chilled, but I was sweating heavily.

"Stella." I felt Carmina's hand grasp mine; it was cool and steady. I clung to it almost involuntarily. She was the only thing that felt real at that moment.

"Missing?"

"Two days ago. U.S. marshals are working with local police to find him."

"Danny Balando—?"

Carmina exhaled and gave a sharp nod. "Right now, that's what they're forced to believe. Reed broke the rules, Stella. They found e-mails on his computer that were sent to Philadelphia. He'd installed software to reroute his IP address, but it wasn't foolproof. He knew the rules and he knew the risks. A neighbor noticed he'd left his outside water running, and called it in. Until we have more information, we have to assume Danny's men took him."

"E-mails to Philly?" I murmured, dazed. All this time he had a computer and he hadn't contacted me?

"They're analyzing them now."

I started crying softly. "They'll torture him. They won't kill him right away. They'll drag it out. They want him to suffer."

"I'm terribly sorry, Stella."

She didn't try to disagree. Then it was true. They'd break Reed in every imaginable way. I cried harder.

"They've got a task force looking for Reed. If he's out there, they'll find him. These men and women are the best in the business."

If he was out there. If he wasn't dead.

Carmina said, "The U.S. marshals have no reason to believe you're in danger. You or your mother."

"Of course they'd say that!" I lashed out. "They don't want me to run away and hide—they can't afford to lose another witness. I wish I'd never agreed to testify. I tried to do the right thing, and look what happened," I sobbed bitterly, burying my face in my hands. "I didn't make things better—I made them worse."

I hated them. All of them. Danny Balando. My mom for introducing him into our lives. The U.S. marshals for not watching Reed closely enough. Reed for sending stupid, careless e-mails to Philly but ignoring me.

Chet was right—it was impossible not to play what if. I was playing it now, wishing my life had taken a different path. Wishing I'd had some say in my future, instead of being at the whim of people I despised.

"It's okay to cry," Carmina said. She gathered me into her arms. She rubbed soothing circles over my back and stroked my hair. I didn't try to pull away. I leaned into her, needing to be comforted. I knew it made me weak, but I was hurting. For one moment, I wanted to pretend I knew what it felt like to have someone really care about me.

"Will Price tell you when they find Reed's . . . when they find his . . . his . . . ?" My voice shook as I broke down in earnest. Hot, wet tears tumbled down my face. When they find his body. These were the words I meant to say, but I couldn't bear to say them aloud.

"He will. I'm sure he will."

Reed's body would turn up soon. Danny Balando's gang wouldn't want to hide what they'd done. They'd leave the body where it would be found. They were making an example of him . . . and sending a very real threat to me.

I was next.

WHEN I PULLED CARMINA'S TRUCK INTO THE PARKING
lot behind the Sundown, and Eduardo eased his motorcycle into
the next stall over, I figured fate was giving me a nudge. I muttered a quick self–pep talk, then hurried to catch him before he
went inside.

"Eduardo! Wait up."

"Hey, Stells Bells," he said, turning back. His deep-set, melted-
chocolate eyes gave me a quick study. "Nasty shiner's almost gone.
Soon you'll be good as new."

"Actually, I want to talk to you about that. The night I was
attacked, you asked me to go down to the storeroom. I hope I'm
wrong, but I can't help but wonder if you set me up."

I sucked in some air. *This one's for you, Inny,* I thought. Couldn't
get more direct than that.

Eduardo's face froze. He opened his mouth, but if he was hunting for a lie, one never came. And I knew. He was as guilty as if he'd had blood on his hands.

"Why?" I asked, trying to keep the shake out of my voice. I'd trusted Eduardo. We were friends. How could he do this to me—and still look me in the eye?

He wagged his head from side to side. He swallowed, still searching for words. His face paled, and he licked his lips. The toughness went out of him, and what I saw in his eyes was genuine fear.

"I never knew," he said in a papery voice. "You gotta believe me. I had no idea you'd get hurt. If I had, I wouldn't have helped him."

"How did Trigger get you to do it?"

"Trigger? Is that who you think did this?"

That took me aback. "It wasn't Trigger?"

"I don't know." Eduardo shook his head again. "See, it went down like this."

He proceeded to tell me how he'd found an envelope with one hundred dollars cash on his motorcycle seat as he left for work that evening. A note with the cash gave one simple instruction: At ten forty p.m., send Stella to the storeroom. Alone.

"I didn't know he was gonna beat you up, I swear," Eduardo insisted. "I thought it was a prank, something like that. Maybe he was gonna surprise you with flowers. I didn't really think about it. I pocketed the money and did what the note said. If I'd known—You gotta believe me, Stella. I'd never hurt you. You know that. I was sick when I saw what happened. I haven't been able to live with myself since."

"And yet you never came forward."

"I thought I'd get arrested! I could be an accomplice. Jeez, Stells. Don't ruin my life over this. I'm begging you. I'll make it up to you, just swear you won't turn me in."

"You lied to Officer Oshiro."

"Just about the note and money. Everything else was true. I didn't see anyone come out of the storeroom. Maybe I didn't want to see." He wiped his hands down his face, the whites of his eyes becoming more pronounced. "Maybe I got a bad feeling and ignored it. I don't know. I talked myself into believing . . . I don't know what I believed. Not that this would happen."

"A hundred dollars didn't seem like a lot for a simple favor? It never crossed your mind that it might be hush money?"

"I don't know. Jeez. I don't know."

"You have to tell Officer Oshiro. Do you still have the note? It might help implicate Trigger. Right now, they're saying it's my word against his. He claims he was at home when I was assaulted."

"I tossed the note. Spent the money. Wish I hadn't. You aren't gonna tell Dixie Jo, are you? She'll fire my butt."

"Your butt deserves to be fired."

"Jeez, Stells. I gotta make a living. If I lose this job, it could take weeks to find a new one. I never meant no harm. I got a girl at home and a kid. Don't throw me under the bus."

Like you threw me, I thought.

"Tell Officer Oshiro the truth. Then we're even."

"No other way?" He was sweating, and it was starting to run down into his wide, petrified eyes.

"No."

He smeared his sleeve across his brow, wiping the sweat. "Think they'll bust me?"

"I think they'll be glad you came forward. They'll work something out. They're after Trigger, not you. Just make sure you talk to Officer Oshiro." She hadn't been reassigned to the case, but maybe this information would be enough to do just that. "And this time, tell her the truth—all of it."

"Yeah. Got it. Yeah."

"I'm not going to tell Dixie Jo."

Eduardo let go of some air. "Thanks. I mean it—thanks." He walked to the door and held it open. "Can't say enough how sorry I am. Really sorry, Stelly Belly."

I wanted to forgive him, but it wasn't that easy. He'd helped Trigger humiliate and batter me. I hated thinking what Trigger had done to me. I hated feeling weak and conquered. Without Eduardo's help, Trigger never would have beaten me.

So I said, "I hope you are."

Since the attack, Carmina had made it a habit to stay up until I got home from work. Tonight was no exception. I came through the front door to find her playing solitaire on the coffee table. Lately when I got off work, we chatted for a few minutes, or I watched a M*A*S*H rerun with her before I headed upstairs to bed.

I liked that she waited up. I liked relating anecdotes from the Sundown to her. It helped me unwind before bed, and I could tell Carmina, who knew a good portion of the Sundown's customers, enjoyed hearing the town news long before it became morning gossip. We didn't feel like roommates, sharing space and nothing else, the way my mom and I had. We had something more.

But as Carmina rose upon my entrance, her face sober, I knew we would be doing neither of those tonight. Something was wrong.

"What is it?" I asked. But I knew. They'd found Reed's body. The torture had been worse than any of us could have guessed. His funeral would be closed casket. It wasn't safe for me to attend.

"Your mother called."

It took a moment for her words to hit. I shut my eyes and exhaled. It wasn't the news I'd expected. I couldn't decide if it was better or worse. I wanted them to find Reed's body so I could put his suffering out of my mind. I felt responsible for his death. If he hadn't met me, he wouldn't have met my mom. He'd be in Philly. He'd be alive.

"I told her you'd be home shortly after eleven, but she isn't allowed to make personal calls past nine. Clinic's rules, she said."

"If she calls back, I don't want to talk."

"She's lonely. She misses you. She misses home."

My eyes flashed. "I do too. Did you tell her that? Did you remind her that she's in detox and I'm in Thunder Basin because of the stupid, thoughtless choices she made?"

"She's going to call tomorrow. I told her you have the night off."

"You shouldn't have done that. Anyway, I have plans tomorrow."

"Five minutes. Can you give her five minutes?"

"I don't know," I said angrily. "Can she give me my life back? My boyfriend? My friends? That's not too much to ask, is it?"

"Has she really dug a hole so deep that there's no hope of ever climbing out?"

"She stopped being my mom a long time ago—her choice. She chose drugs over me. I would have taken her back so many times. I wanted her back. I needed a mom. And then I got over myself and accepted that I can't compete with her pills. It's too late. I don't want anything to do with her. She's been to rehab before, did she tell you that? Failed every time. It's exhausting, sending her off, bringing her home. Rinse and repeat. She acts like I'm her rock, but how is a fifteen, sixteen, seventeen-year-old girl supposed to keep her mother clean? I was the little girl." I could hear my voice rising, but I couldn't control it. "She was supposed to take care of me!"

"Forgiveness is a tough wire to walk," Carmina agreed. "You have to balance letting go of what doesn't matter and holding on to what does."

"I don't want to forgive her!" I admitted furiously. "I don't want to let her back in, because she's going to hurt me again. Again and again!"

"Have you told her your fears?"

"She knows." I threw my hands up, frustrated to be having this conversation. There was a reason I never thought about, much less talked about, my mother. She brought to the surface all these emotions I didn't want. Being reminded I was still holding on to them only made me feel worse. Why couldn't I move on? It was the one thing I wanted, so what was holding me back?

"Maybe. Maybe not. Sometimes we have to say the words twice for them to get through. Sometimes we have to keep saying them over and over."

"I shouldn't have to."

"No, I don't suppose you should. Shoulda, coulda, woulda. Now, there's a game they ought to put in those Vegas casinos. Good people can't ever win. House has the advantage."

"Have you ever had to forgive someone?" I asked. "Really forgive? That's what I want to know."

Carmina pondered my question thoughtfully. "I'm a private person, Stella," she began cautiously.

"Don't give me that crap."

Her chin tilted up, and she drew a long, measured breath. "Yes. Yes, I have."

"How long did it take?"

"Years, I suppose. I dragged my feet. I chose to be ornery, letting my wounds fester, instead of letting go and finding peace. I thought I had a right to be angry. It occurred to me too late that I also had a right to heal. I could have fixed things," she said, with unmistakable grief woven into her voice. "I could have, but I didn't."

"I'm sorry about that. Really, I am. But forgiving means getting hurt. It means saying what you did to me was okay. What my mom did wasn't okay. It was never okay!"

"No, it wasn't. I suspect your mother knows that."

"Did the person you forgave ever hurt you again?" I pressed, because I suspected I knew the answer.

Her hesitation was confirmation enough.

"They did," I said. "They hurt you again. How can you stand there and tell me I should forgive my mom, knowing she'll only cause me more pain?"

"Because holding on to that bitter anger will hurt you more than your mother's failures." Carmina wiped her damp eyes, which glistened with deep and painful regret. She turned away from me, too dignified to let me watch her cry.

"I didn't mean to make you upset," I said, feeling pangs of guilt. I'd overstepped. Worse, I'd made an example of her for the sole purpose of proving I was right. She believed in the power of forgiveness; I did not. But I should have disagreed with her more respectfully.

"Not upset," Carmina said in a small, haunted voice. "We spend our whole lives running from our past, never realizing it's hitched to us—we can't ever outrun it."

I shifted uncomfortably, not knowing if Carmina wanted to be left alone. Her voice had changed—it sounded far off and lonely. I wasn't even sure she was speaking to me anymore. I said, "I should go to bed."

"I hear you," Carmina answered, trying to sound normal, but her voice was distant. "Go on up, I'll follow you in a minute."

"Do you want me to bring you a cup of tea?"

"Ah, no. Thank you, Stella. Go on, now. I'm gonna sit here a minute, listen to the radio."

With her back still to me, she eased herself down to lie on the sofa, moving slower than usual. She reached for the radio, her fingers stopping a few inches short of the dial. Her whole body looked stiff, as if braced for an unexpected—and unwelcome—blast of cold wind.

But it was summer, heat steaming off the pavement long after sundown. There would be no relief, no chill in the air tonight.

A LOUD CRASH STARTLED ME AWAKE. I BLINKED IN
the darkness, disoriented. Had the sound come from downstairs?
Had I imagined it? The clock showed just after two.

Danny Balando.

I clutched my sheet, paralyzed. Sweat flushed my body. His
men had found me. They were in Carmina's house, and they were
going to kill me.

Frozen in fear, I tried to think. How would I escape? My mouth
had gone dry. I could not think of a way out.

I waited for their feet on the stairs, but the house settled into
silence.

After several minutes, the fear lost its grip and my mind
cleared. Danny Balando's men were not here. They would have
found me by now.

I pushed off the sheets and padded to my bedroom door, opening it wide enough to peer down the hall. "Carmina?"

The living room light had been left on downstairs. It cast long shadows on the faded wallpaper. Had Carmina not gone to bed? It wasn't like her to stay up late or to forget the light.

I took the first several steps down the staircase. "Carmina?" I called softly. If she had fallen asleep on the sofa, I didn't want to wake her.

When I saw her, my mind seemed to sink into a fog, not really taking in the strange picture of her slumped forward on the coffee table.

I didn't know if it was really her, or if the flashbacks had seized my mind again. I saw my mom drooped in a wingback chair in the library, her skin blue, her eyes pinpricks. Human tissue sprayed the wall behind her. I saw Carmina, hunched over, her white hair hanging in her face.

"Carmina!" I broke into a run. I dropped to my knees beside her. I shook her hard enough that I should have been able to rouse her. "Can you hear me?" She didn't respond, and my heart began to hammer.

I eased her body back onto the sofa. Her eyes were shut, her face drawn tight in pain. She was breathing, her chest rising and falling in shallow, erratic spurts.

The phone. Where was the phone? I found it on the receiver in the kitchen and fumbled it; it clattered to the floor. Cursing, I tried again. With shaking fingers, I dialed 911.

"Nine-one-one. What is your emergency?"

"I think my foster mom, Carmina Songster, had a heart attack," I blurted. I willed myself to speak slower. I wasn't going to help Carmina if I couldn't keep calm long enough to give them directions to her house. I had to speak clearly. "I heard something crash, and came downstairs to find her slumped over on the coffee table. She's very pale and not breathing normally. I tried to wake her, but it's no use."

"What is your address?"

"Twelve Sapphire Skies."

"Emergency personnel will be there as soon as they can."

"How soon?" My voice climbed higher. "I don't know if she's okay. Please help me—I don't know what to do!"

"They'll be there as fast as they can."

I hung up and immediately broke into tears. I covered Carmina with the wool throw, tucking it gently around her body. I refused to think about death. Carmina would get better. The paramedics would come and they'd take us to the hospital, where doctors would know how to help her.

I nestled my hand in Carmina's chilled palm. She made no effort to tighten her fingers around mine. I didn't know if she was even aware of me.

I started crying harder. I felt sick with worry. I didn't have anyone else. If she left me, I'd be completely alone. They'd take me away, force me to start over somewhere new. I'd have to face my problems by myself, and at that moment, the thought seemed so insurmountable, it threatened to crush me. What would I do without Carmina and Chet? Without Inny? I felt safe in Thunder

Basin. I'd grown used to the faded blue sheets on my bed and Carmina's meat-and-potato dinners. When I needed to talk, she listened without interrupting or passing judgment. She didn't ignore me. She knew the real me, and I could be myself around her. I trusted her.

She was all I had.

Some time later, the paramedics arrived. I was in no position to judge how long it had taken them. It felt like a long, long stretch between when I called 911 and when I heard the ambulance sailing down the road. It must have only been a few minutes, because I was still crying when I ran to open the door for them.

"She's on the sofa in the living room." Frantically, I pointed which way they should go.

From there, the paramedics took over. With smooth efficiency, they lifted her onto a stretcher and wheeled her out to the waiting ambulance.

"Is she allergic to aspirin?" one of them asked.

"I don't know."

"Are you a family member?"

"I—yes." My answer just shot out. But it wasn't a lie. Carmina was the closest thing to family I had.

"How old are you?"

"Seventeen."

"Minors aren't allowed to ride in the ambulance. You'll have to meet us at the hospital."

"I'm not allowed? I just told you I'm her family!"

Turning the whole of his attention to Carmina, the paramedic climbed into the back of the ambulance and fit a blood pressure cuff around the soft flesh of her arm. The other paramedic closed the doors, and the ambulance raced toward town, leaving me staring at the back of it.

My mind was too full to think. In a haze, I tried to prepare myself for what might become of Carmina. What might become of me. I couldn't pinpoint the exact moment, but somewhere along the way, I'd started to view Carmina as someone who belonged in my life. Someone who'd pushed through my walls when it would have been easier to give up. But Carmina didn't give up.

I begged her not to give up this time.

I sat out in the hot night air, rocking slowly in Carmina's porch swing. I could hear insects whining around me, but I only dimly acknowledged them. Every time I tried to go back inside, my knees shook so hard I had to sit down again. I didn't know what time it was, but worrying about Carmina had sapped what little energy I'd started with, and now I felt not only dizzy, but exhausted. And my head throbbed a little.

I had to see her. I wasn't ready to handle the worst, but I would never forgive myself if I let her go without saying good-bye. I'd made a lot of mistakes in Thunder Basin, but this wouldn't be one of them.

I got up and walked inside by sheer willpower alone. My hand trembled as I picked up the phone. I didn't know what else to do, so I called Chet. His was the only number in Thunder Basin, besides Carmina's, that I knew from memory.

"Hello?" His sleep-roughened voice sounded deeper than usual.

"Chet." I swallowed to take the wobble out of my voice. "Carmina's hurt. She's not okay. They took her away in an ambulance."

His groggy voice came instantly alert. "Are you okay?"

"I'm fine, but I'm—worried about her. So worried about her." I could hear the high, quivering sound of my voice, and it was a foreign sound. I'd never felt so small. So small or in need of help. "Can you drive me to the hospital? I need to be with her."

"I'm on my way."

I WAS PACING THE PORCH WHEN CHET ANGLED THE
Scout into Carmina's drive. He left the engine running and
swung right out to meet me. His hair was mussed and his
clothes rumpled, but I hardly noticed either; it was those concerned blue eyes cutting right into mine that made me forget
about our fight and jog toward him. I didn't stop a safe distance away. I threw my arms around him and buried my face in
his shirt. I thought I'd cried all my tears, but a few more stung
the backs of my eyes.

"Oh, Chet. I'm so worried about her!"

"It's going to be okay," he murmured reassuringly, wrapping his arms around me. I let myself believe him, because
I had to. For Carmina's sake, I couldn't give up. I would be
strong for her.

"She was barely breathing. I didn't know how to help her. If she— If she—" I shut my eyes hard. I wasn't going to think it. Not until I had to.

It was my second time in Thunder Basin Regional Medical Center since the start of summer. I couldn't think of a darker place. Or one with less hope.

But hope was exactly what I clung to as Chet and I talked to the nurses at the ER desk. I wanted to be strong and take control, the way Carmina had when I'd been the one in the hospital bed. Instead, I stood there with red-rimmed eyes and a runny nose while Chet peppered the nurses with inquiries.

Carmina had had a heart attack. She was breathing again, but in critical condition. Her heart muscle had been damaged, and the doctors were going to perform coronary angioplasty to reduce the damage and restore blood flow to the heart. They'd know more after the procedure.

In the meantime, all we could do was wait.

I'd fallen asleep in the waiting room. When I woke, morning sunlight streamed through the windows. My head rested on Chet's shoulder. He was paging through a copy of *Sports Illustrated*, but turned his attention to me when he felt me stir.

"The doctor came out while you were sleeping."

I sat up straighter. "You didn't wake me?"

"She just wanted to tell us that the procedure went well. They moved Carmina to a special care unit. She has to stay there for a few more hours to recover. You should be able to see her soon. The doc—I think she said her name's Dr. Zielke—will come get us as soon as they've moved Carmina to a private room. Stella . . ." He waited until I met his eyes. "You saved her life. You found her before it was too late."

My stomach started to churn with nervous relief. She was okay. They'd let her go home soon. I'd take care of her and get her back on her feet. I could stay in Thunder Basin as long as she needed me.

I still had a place to call home.

Chet grabbed us a breakfast of pretzels and cran-apple juice from the vending machines, and as he was carting the food back, a doctor pushed through the double doors behind the ER desk and walked over.

"Hi, Stella. I'm Dr. Zielke. I performed Carmina's angioplasty, and I'm happy to report it went as smoothly as these things can go. I hope you got a few minutes of sleep, though I doubt it was very restful. Hello again, Chet," she said, nodding at him.

"How is she?" I asked.

"She's asking for you," Dr. Zielke replied with a friendly smile. "She's a little out of sorts, and very tired, but anxious to talk to you."

"When can she come home?"

"Tomorrow. When you pick her up, we'll give you all sorts of instructions to aid her recovery. I've prescribed her medication to prevent blood clots from forming, and it's very important that she take her medicine as directed. You can help with that." Another smile. "She's going to be okay, Stella. In about a week, she'll be up and about, back to her old self."

"I want to see her."

She waved for me to follow.

I felt the rapid flutter of nervous anticipation as I followed Dr. Zielke through the double doors and down the beige-toned corridor. Chet was beside me, and he squeezed my hand. I listened to the hollow tap of our feet on the tiles, trying to figure out what I'd say when I saw her. Carmina would be formal, dignified, greeting me not without a little reservation. She didn't like fanfare or fuss. I couldn't decide how she'd want me to act.

Carmina's door was open, and Dr. Zielke led us into the room. "I've brought you something better than flowers and balloons," she told Carmina cheerfully.

I stepped around the partition dividing the room and felt my self-control abandon me.

I wasn't a crier. Estella Goodwinn wasn't a crier, and I hadn't wanted Stella Gordon to be one either. But when I saw Carmina on the bed, her white hair matted and her eyes smudged with rings of exhaustion, my emotions slipped beyond my control. I moved toward her bed, stunning myself when I threw my arms around her.

"Now, there's a face I've missed," she said, her voice cracking. Stroking my hair, she pressed me firmly against her chest. "Oh, how I've missed you."

"They said you can come home tomorrow," I choked.

"That's right. Tomorrow I'll come home. No more doctors, no more hospital. Just you and me, Stella-girl."

CHET AND I TALKED ABOUT THE WEATHER ON THE RIDE
home. We talked about Carmina and Dusty. He brought up Major
League Baseball, and threw in a few comments about the high
quality of our softball team. During the twenty-minute ride, we
seemed to touch on every subject except the one that was burning
a hole in my chest.

I listened to the gravel pop beneath the tires as we left town
and took the long stretch of unpaved road that led to Carmina's.
The corn in the fields was a lush green, and the stalks seemed
to have shot up overnight—they were nearly as tall as Chet, and
topped with wheat-colored tassels. The sky spread over us, not
a single cloud to break up the soft denim blue. We passed cattle
grazing behind wind-battered fences and fields of leggy sunflowers. The scenery was far different from the bustling streets of

Philly. Different, but not bad. It just took time to get used to.

Finally I could stand our meaningless talk no longer.

"Where is Milton Swope's Ranch?" I asked. I would let him decide when he was ready to talk about us, but I had to make real conversation. An awkward silence here and there was one thing. Riding next to Chet and suffering through all the uncomfortable and unspoken things waiting to be said while he rambled on about the forecast, well, that was pure torture.

"North of town. Heading toward the Sandhills."

"What are the Sandhills?"

"They're sand dunes," he said, giving me an unfathomable look. "Have you never seen sand dunes?"

"Not in Nebraska." I closed my eyes. "Paint me a picture."

"I guess you could call them rolling hills made out of sand."

"More description, please."

Chet let go of some air, but I could tell he wasn't exasperated. If anything, there was a hint of smile behind it. "I'm not a poet."

"Do your best."

He let a lengthy pause pass before he began in that deep and soothing voice of his, "Hundreds of years ago, maybe thousands, the wind whipped the sand into rolling drifts. Imagine an ocean of sand—a prairie ocean. Indian grass and wildflowers wave above the drifts. When you drive through the Sandhills, you can go for hours without seeing another car. You feel like you're the only person left in the world. But it's not a scary feeling, because you're surrounded by a peaceful quiet you'll never find anywhere else. If you park your car and walk away from the road, something magical happens. The wind begins to whisper to you. You have to listen carefully, but it will tell you that you're not alone. You see a heron standing stock-still on one leg at the edge of a lake. He's watching you. He's as curious about you as you are about him. You're new and strange, and he's not used to your kind.

"You walk farther. Pelicans drift lazily on shimmering lakes, dipping their heads underwater to scout for fish. In the spring, prairie chickens stamp their feet and leap into the air to attract a mate. The courtship rituals are comical at first—but the longer you watch, the more impressed you are. The dances are complicated. They remind you of the tribal dances of the Sioux or Lakota. When you finally walk back to your car, you feel like you're saying good-bye to an undiscovered land. You can't help but think it was only by a miracle that this place escaped discovery. You leave with a picture in your mind of what the world must have looked like hundreds of years ago, before it was soiled by human hands."

I sighed contentedly. "That was beautiful. I want to go there someday." I opened my eyes and looked at him. "Will you take me?"

Chet pulled into Carmina's driveway and parked. He turned off the engine, and I ordered myself not to speculate what it meant. Would he walk me to the door? Would he come inside? Was he finally ready to talk? There were so many questions I wanted to ask him, but I had to deliberately keep my mouth closed and let him do this his own way.

"The other night at the party, I was frustrated when I said what I did. Disappointed, too," he admitted. "I thought you liked me as more than a friend. I'd created this story in my head where we could be together. I built up the fantasy too far, and then when you turned me away, well, I had a long way to fall.

"I told you I didn't trust myself to be your friend, but I was wrong. If that's what you need, I can be that person. I'll be your friend as long as you want. No strings attached. I'll never ask for anything in return, won't even expect it. Who knows?" he said with a faintly ironic smile. "Maybe we'll be the first guy and girl on record to keep our relationship purely platonic."

I tried my best to smile in agreement, but a strange sensation swirled through me. It was a mix of disappointment and regret. I knew it was shallow and wrong, but I wasn't sure I wanted Chet to stop having feelings for me. I was flattered by his attention. And then there was that tiny issue of my attraction to him. Could we be friends? Strictly friends? He trusted himself to uphold his end of the bargain, but now that I was being forced to take a stance, I wasn't so certain I had that kind of faith in myself.

I remembered Reed.

It had the right effect; it sobered me up and killed the mood. What was the matter with me? How could I entertain ideas of being with another guy when my boyfriend's life was in question? I was committed to Reed until I knew for sure he was dead. And even then, I wanted to grieve for him properly. Chet was right. We'd make this platonic thing work.

"Thanks for taking me to the hospital," I told him. "I was in no condition to drive myself, and I don't think I could have handled sitting in that waiting room for hours alone."

"It wasn't even a question. Of course I wanted to be there for you."

His words put a stir in my belly. Determined to ignore it, I said, "Will you come with me to pick up Carmina when they release her tomorrow?"

"Absolutely."

"I'll call you as soon as I know what time."

"Do you work tonight?" Chet asked.

"Yeah. Last shift this week. I get off around eleven."

"I'll meet you here at the house. It'll make me feel better knowing you made it in safely. I can walk through the house too, if you want. Nobody likes coming home to an empty house."

"Are you accusing me of being scared of the dark?" I quipped. I wasn't usually scared, but ever since Trigger had assaulted me, I'd been a little less comfortable with dark spaces. I felt safe in Carmina's house, but just the same, I wouldn't mind having Chet do a quick sweep of the place.

"Just trying to make you think I'm a gentleman," he said.

"First you hang out all night at the hospital with me, now you're sweeping my house for things that go bump in the night. You're almost too good to be true."

"I'll do a walk-through and be on my way. I won't hold up your plans."

"No plans," I told him. "You're welcome to stay for some of Carmina's highly touted basil lemonade if you want. And of course, you'll have my company. You could do worse," I teased.

"I'll be the envy of the neighborhood," he said casually enough, his swirling gaze framing me in his vision. He had remarkable eyes. A sultry blue that stood out against his dark hair. I meant to look away, but then I saw myself reflected in those mesmerizing eyes. Warm liquid flashed in my veins, and once again, I felt a dangerous tug to my restraint.

The harder I fought my attraction, the weaker I felt. In some ways, it was exhausting trying to avoid something that felt almost . . .

Inevitable.

Deciding there was no sense in flirting with temptation, I hopped out of the Scout.

"Let me walk you to the door," he said, coming around to meet me. "No, I insist. I don't believe in dropping a girl off in the driveway. Blame it on my mother, but she raised me to walk a girl to the door."

Since I could see I was going to have a hard time talking him out of it, I let him have his way. But the minute we were on the porch, I said a quick thank-you, unlocked the door, and hustled inside.

I could do this. I could fake platonic. I could guilt-trip myself over Reed all I wanted, but the real issue weighing on my heart ran deeper, and I knew it. I was falling in love with Chet. And I wasn't going to get involved with him only to break his heart in August.

Work was hectic and blissfully busy. In the chaos of the kitchen, I didn't have time to think about seeing Chet later tonight. I told myself it was no big deal that we'd be alone in the house together—we were friends—but even I could tell when I was trying to convince myself something was less significant than it really was. There was nothing completely harmless or innocent about being alone with a very hot guy.

After work, I drove Carmina's truck home. For once, I didn't push the speed limit. I took the long way, hitting every red light I could, hating the foreign churning in my stomach. I was nervous. There, I said it. Estella Goodwinn, Stella Gordon, whoever the hell I was, was still capable of getting butterflies over a guy.

Chet's Scout was already parked in the drive. No surprise he'd beaten me, since I'd taken the scenic route. I pulled Carmina's truck in behind his, then realized I was blocking his exit. Not wanting him to think I was cleverly trying to keep him here over-night, I reversed, then scooted up beside the Scout, giving him plenty of room to leave whenever he wanted. Which would be soon, I was sure. After all, he was only here to check the house and give me peace of mind.

I found Chet leaning against the porch railing, his arms folded casually over his chest. Even though it was nearly midnight, the air felt sultry. The soft breeze couldn't seem to stir the hot mugginess of the night. The moon glowed high above us, casting filmy yellow light. Shadows cut into the hollows of Chet's face, making his eyes and cheekbones more prominent.

"How was work?" he asked.

"I set a personal record for tips earned."

"Sounds lucrative."

"At the end of the night, Inny and I line up our pennies and see who has the one with the oldest mint date. She won tonight—1938. Right before World War II. It's almost overwhelming to think how many people have touched that penny since. How was the ranch?"

"I like the penny tradition. The ranch was good. I had to rescue a couple stray calves out of a mud hole. Like I said, never a boring day."

"Isn't that sweet. A cow's knight in shining armor."

"I had to wash my hair three times before I was presentable enough to come over. I was head to toe in mud. Worse, the sun baked it onto me before I could rinse off. Had to scrub so hard, I must've taken off at least a couple layers of skin."

"I think you missed a spot." Before I realized it, I brushed my thumb near his eyebrow. There wasn't any mud. I just wanted to touch him. His hair was still damp from his shower, and he smelled clean and earthy, like rain. He'd put on jeans and a button-down denim shirt rolled to the elbows, and he looked great in both. The jeans accentuated his long legs, and the shirt was snug enough to show his muscles. Paired with chiseled cheekbones and those stunning blue eyes, his attractiveness was hard to ignore.

"Did I?" he asked, rubbing his thumb self-consciously over the spot. "Didn't mean to come over muddy."

The mosquitoes were beginning to land on me, so I said, "Let's go inside. I hope you brought your own baseball bat to fend off any monsters lurking in the shadows. I don't think Carmina owns one."

"She does. She keeps it in the umbrella stand. Don't ask how I know."

I unlocked the front door, but I didn't reach for the hall light right away. I could feel Chet standing close behind me. My limbs felt loose, and a slow, liquid warmth filled me. It was so quiet, I heard the steady rise and fall of his breathing.

I closed my eyes and willed everything inside me to slow. If I let him in, I had to promise myself to keep my head.

"I like the outfit," Chet told me, his voice drifting through the darkness. "Camo and leather. It suits you."

"Why's that?"

"Tough. Feisty. Sexy." He cleared his throat. "I shouldn't have said that. What I meant was—"

I turned. "You think I'm pretty?"

I still hadn't switched on the light. My eyes were beginning to adjust to the darkness, distinguishing the outline of Chet's body. Broad, athletic shoulders stood directly in front of me. He was so close, I could have touched him. I could have curled my fingers into his shirt and pulled our bodies together.

"No," Chet said, his voice low, husky. "Not pretty."

My breath caught.

"Stunning," he continued in that same low voice. "Mesmerizing. Smart. Sassy. I haven't been able to think straight since I met you. I can't think of a day when you haven't been in my thoughts. There are a hundred other things I should be thinking about, but I think about you. What you're doing, when I'll see you next, what you're thinking."

"Do you want to know what I'm thinking?" I asked softly.

"Yes."

That slow, liquid heat swirled faster in my belly. I felt dizzy, unsteady. I could come back from it now, I thought. It wasn't too late. I could step outside and clear my head.

But at that moment, I didn't want a clear head. I didn't want control. I wanted to touch Chet, and I wanted him to touch me.

I looked up at him. He watched me just as closely. I was sliding into him. I felt the draw, that slippery pull, that wonderful, wild sensation of falling fast.

My restraint unraveled in a flash. Chet lost his at the same moment.

He pushed me inside, kicked the door shut, and flung me back against it, his mouth hot and fervent on mine. I locked my arms around his neck, drowning in sensation. He felt warm, solid, and tough. His weight crushed me, delicious and real. I'd imagined this moment. I'd dreamed about it, but my imagination was a poor substitute for the real thing. My blood seemed to melt, pouring through me in throbbing surges and leaving me light-headed.

He ran his hand up my arm, and I quivered.

At my response, his arms, which had been braced on either side of my shoulders, tightened around me.

I hung my fingers on the waistband of his jeans, trying to balance myself. My knees felt slippery, weak. Desire washed over me, each new wave quicker and sharper. When my fingertips brushed the smooth skin where his jeans rode his hips, he shivered and kissed me harder.

He picked me up, carrying me to the sofa. I felt the cushions under my back, his body braced above mine. He kissed me deeper, sliding his hand up my thigh in a tantalizing caress. His mouth was warm and wet, unabashedly doing things to me that made me want to scream out. I felt like I was on fire. I could feel myself spinning wildly, but no amount of willpower could bring me back to that still, rational place. I let myself soar, leaving it behind.

Chet stopped. His eyes were deep and full as he stared at me.

"What's wrong?" I panted.

He bowed his head, pressing his face to my neck. His breath sounded ragged in my ear. "This feels wrong, doing this on Carmina's couch."

I let go of a little moan.

"Carmina will kill me," he added.

"Only if she finds out." If he didn't start kissing me again in five seconds, I felt like I might wither up and die.

"It doesn't seem sneaky to you? Disrespectful? She's in the hospital. She's depending on me to look out for you."

Now I let out a full-on groan. "Why do you have to be so ... moral?"

"I want to do this the right way. I don't want to look back and wish I'd treated you better."

I tipped my head back against the pillows, not sure if I should laugh or cry. "You are the most confusing guy I've ever met. I'm right here, and I'm willing."

"Don't do this, Stella," he said, nuzzling his face deeper into my neck. "If you don't tell me to stop, I'm not sure I have it in me to walk away on my own."

His body felt rigid, all that desire held in check with quivering restraint, and I believed him. If I said yes, he wouldn't stop.

I sighed, letting my body slacken. "I feel like I've been transported to a parallel universe." I plowed my fingers through my hair, which had tumbled out of its ponytail sometime in the middle of all that kissing. "This is a first for me. I've never had a guy say no." I studied him quizzically. "Are you a virgin?"

Chet rolled off me, exhaling slowly to release some of the built-up energy. "Yes."

"Now I *know* I'm in a parallel universe. A guy who admits to being a virgin? We have definitely left earth behind."

He looked at me sideways. "Are you?"

I hadn't expected him to ask me so bluntly. Which I supposed was unfair, since I'd just hit him with the same question. "No."

"Your boyfriend. In Tennessee."

I swallowed. My lies haunted me, and at the very least, I had to be honest now. "He was the only one."

"Did he treat you right?"

More questions I hadn't anticipated. "What kind of question is that? When you're in the throes of passion, you aren't really thinking about the other person."

"I was thinking about you just now," Chet said quietly. "If I'd been thinking only about myself, I wouldn't have stopped. I wouldn't have cared if you really wanted to be with me. I would have taken what I wanted." He paused. "I don't want you to say yes because you feel sorry for me, or because you're lonely and there's no one else around."

"That's not why I kissed you tonight." It wasn't, was it? I didn't think I was trying to get over Reed or exorcise his memory. I *was* lonely, but less so than when I'd first come to Thunder Basin. I was attracted to Chet. That's why I wanted to be with him tonight. Because I cared about him. Because it hurt to keep so many secrets from him; for once, I wanted him to know something intimate about me. Sharing this with him—this physical connection—felt like giving him something of me, the real me.

"I feel like you're keeping something from me," Chet said. "I don't know what it is. But I feel it there, under the surface."

I ached to tell him everything. To finally come clean. But it was too risky, and so I forced myself to bite down the words.

"It's stifling in here," I said, gathering my hair off the back of my neck. "I wish Carmina had AC. It's too hot outside to open the windows, but I feel like I need fresh air. It's too hot to think."

"I have an idea," Chet said after a moment, a daring smile glinting in his eyes. "If you're game."

"That sounds like a challenge."

"Ever been to a swimming hole at night?"

"I've never been to a swimming hole, period."

"Hot air, cool water. Not a bad combination." He made a weighing gesture with his hands. "But if you'd rather stay here and try to sleep in this heat . . ."

"I'll grab my swimsuit now."

Upstairs, I changed into my suit, a solid black number that was as classy as I could find at Kmart, and selected a faded towel from the linen closet that I didn't think Carmina would worry about getting soiled.

While I located my sandals in my closet, I thought about what Chet had said. With my head cleared, I tried to remember my first time with Reed. It was a little rough, a little flawed. When we finished, I remembered hoping I'd done it right. In fact, every time we had sex, I hoped I was good enough that Reed didn't go looking elsewhere.

I'd never once wondered about my own fulfillment.

And he'd never asked.

THE COOL WATER OF THE SWIMMING HOLE STILL
tingled on my skin when I crept to bed later that night. I left the
lights on downstairs, but it didn't make the house feel safer. Suddenly I wished I'd asked Chet if I could sleep at his place. A spare
room or the sofa, it didn't matter. I didn't want to be alone.

Lightning flashed outside, followed by a rumble of thunder.
The wind picked up, knocking branches against the house. A few
raindrops splashed the window. I shuddered and wrestled the
sheets higher.

I wondered how Reed had felt moments before Danny Balando's
men ambushed him. Had he felt ice in the pit of his stomach, like
I did now? Did every creak and thump in his house cause him to
freeze, and bring his senses to full alert?

It was impossible not to wonder what they'd done to Reed. I

tried to squeeze all speculation from my thoughts, but the worst ideas flooded in. Had they butchered him? When his body was found, would I recognize him?

Did Danny dream of doing the same things to me?

I had no way of knowing if he was any closer to finding me. I had to try to make a life outside that constant and relentless fear.

I knew Danny dreamed of me. And I dreamed of him.

I feared my dreams.

The following afternoon, Chet helped me drive Carmina home from the hospital. As we rounded the tall hedge bordering her driveway, her eyes went wide with surprise.

"What on earth have you two done?"

A small crowd was gathered on her lawn, and as Chet bumped into the drive, they sprang to life, waving balloons and flowers, and scurrying forward to meet us. Pastor Lykins led the way, instructing Chet where to park with a few arm gestures and a jovial smile.

"This wasn't my idea," I said, excusing myself of any responsibility. But I felt a twinge of annoyance—and jealousy. I should have been the one to throw Carmina a welcome-home party.

"Nor mine," Chet said.

He'd barely parked when the Scout's doors were flung open from the outside, and the little group began cheering and clapping. I could see now that there were casseroles, salads, and desserts in their hands as well.

"Welcome home, Carmina," Pastor Lykins said, stepping up to take her hand and help her down. "You missed Sunday's linger longer, so we decided to throw another pot luck, right here on your lawn. We hope you don't mind."

"Nonsense," Carmina said, flushed. "As long as Stella has left the house in a state befitting company, we can set the dishes in the kitchen and eat on the back lawn—plenty of shade at this hour. Chet, would you get the front door?"

Carmina's home was filled with sounds. Happy voices, silverware clanking, laughter. The chirping of birds floated in through the open windows. Under Carmina's direction, Chet spread picnic blankets on the lawn and set up folding chairs in a wide circle. The potluck dishes were arranged on her kitchen table, which was conveniently close to the screen door leading out back.

I piled my plate with a roll and the fixings for a ham sandwich, then went to the fridge for mustard.

"I suppose you heard what happened to Trigger McClure," a woman said, coming up behind me and cornering me against the fridge. She leaned in and kept her voice hushed. I could tell she'd been eating from one of the platters of barbeque; sauce smeared her cheek.

"I haven't," I confessed, trying to hold a neutral, if not indifferent, tone. It wasn't public knowledge he'd beat me up, so I couldn't fathom how she knew. But the mere mention of Trigger's name had soured my mood.

"The police department kept it hush-hush," the woman continued in a quietly excited voice. "Fact is, only a select few know they took him in. My sister works as a court reporter and gave me the scoop. Trigger was arrested for what he did to you. Charged him with simple assault, they did. Not aggravated, 'cause there was no deadly weapon or serious bodily injury. The judge gave him five hours of community service, and he's required to take anger management classes. What do you say to that?" she asked, her eyes sparkling with gossip.

I was shocked they'd arrested him and failed to mention it to Carmina and me. I'd pressed the charges. I wondered if they'd taken advantage of Carmina's heart attack to slip this under the carpet while we weren't looking.

"Makes you feel a little better, right, hon?" the woman nudged.

"I'd say they went lenient on him. Excuse me." Not bothering to come up with an excuse, I walked away. Simple assault. Trigger's feet and hands didn't count as deadly weapons? And I suppose my bruises and cuts hadn't been severe? Given that Trigger was seventeen and his case had likely been handled in the juvenile justice system, it didn't surprise me that they'd gone easy on him, but five hours of community service and anger management? Where was his restitution? I would have preferred they make him apologize to my face. It would have hurt him more than picking up trash on the weekends.

I went to the table and poured myself a glass of lemonade. I felt shaken, and nearly dropped the pitcher. I had to pull myself together. I could feel the woman's eyes sticking to me, carefully analyzing my reaction to her news. If I showed any sign of weakness, word would trickle back to Trigger. He'd won all right. But his victory wouldn't feel half as sweet if I didn't show any sign of defeat.

"You must be Stella."

I set down the pitcher and looked up, recognizing a different woman from church. She sang in the choir and had the most ample arms I'd ever seen. Saddlebags hung from her elbows, which were nothing more than dimples lost in folds of soft flesh.

Apparently having no sense of personal space, she grasped my shoulders and held me at arm's length, nearly causing my lemonade to slosh over the rim. "Aren't you a pretty thing? Such prominent eyes, and hazel to boot. I bet you have to swat the boys away." She had a hearty, rumbling laugh that grated on my nerves.

"I'm sorry, have we met?" I said, detaching myself from her grip.

"Mavis. Call me Mavis. Carmina and I have been friends for ages. Went to school together, graduated the same year. I never would have thought Carmina could pull a fast one on me, but lo and behold that woman has a few tricks up her sleeve. A foster child! Who would've seen it coming?"

I said nothing, hoping she would lose interest and leave me alone.

"I hear you've been running around with Chet Falconer," she babbled on. "Now, there's a boy who has turned his life around. Mark my words, I used to say, that Chet will turn out okay. No one believed me, but I have a way with people." She tapped her head knowingly. "I can look past a rough exterior. I can see a heart of gold masked under teenage rebellion." Another exuberant laugh.

I eyed the back door impatiently. "Yes, well—"

"Of course, it must be hard on Carmina, having you run

around with Hannah Falconer's boy. Old wounds." She wagged her head with pity. "Never got a chance to heal, and here you are, reopening them. Not to say it's your fault, dear. It's just the way things are. Poor thing, Carmina."

I stared at her, aggravated. "I'm sorry?"

"I'm sure by now you've heard how hard the death of Hannah Falconer, Chet's mother, was on Carmina. They were best friends, you know. Childhood best friends. As I recall, Carmina liked Thomas Falconer first. I remember the two of them went to dances at the high school together. And then Hannah took a liking to Thomas, and for a while, it threatened to destroy Carmina and Hannah's friendship. In the end, Carmina backed down and let Hannah have her way. Carmina was maid of honor at their wedding. Had to break her heart, seeing the two people she loved most dearly married to each other. To this day, I can't help but think Carmina must feel short-sticked. I'm not saying she does—she's a good Christian woman—but when she looks at Chet, who's a spitting image of his father, mind you, I wonder if he stirs up old feelings of betrayal and the sting of unrequited love. No matter," she said with an airy and dismissive gesture. "I'm sure that's just the gossip in me rooting around for a story to tug the ol' heartstrings. I do know Carmina and Hannah remained best friends until the day the Falconers died. And Carmina holds Chet personally responsible for his parents' deaths."

"Why would she blame Chet?" I asked, annoyed by the woman's delivery of this story, and annoyed at myself for asking a question that would encourage her to go on telling it. But it was a lot of information to digest, and I'd asked without thinking.

"When Hannah and Thomas were hit by that drunk driver, they were on their way to pick up Chet from the police station. He'd been caught doing some such nonsense, and was cooling his heels behind bars. Chet was a hellion, always looking for the next bout of trouble. Had he not gotten into trouble that particular evening, his parents never would have been on the road that fateful night. Course, that's only half the story. Carmina's grandson, Nathaniel, was Chet's best friend. He was riding in the car with the Falconers that night, on the way to give his friend a much-needed talking to. He died with the rest of them. In one fell swoop, Carmina lost her first love, her best friend, and the grandson she'd raised from birth."

I went very still. So this was why Carmina held Chet at a distance. Seeing him brought back memories of her grandson—She *had* a grandson? Was it his room I'd inherited?—that were painful. With Chet around, it was impossible not to remember Nathaniel. Nathaniel, Hannah, and Thomas.

I wished Mavis—was that her name?—hadn't told me. I felt a strange heat flush through me. Resentment. I resented her for prying in other people's business. Was this what the people of Thunder Basin went around doing—digging up the past and flinging it in each other's faces?

"You're wrong," I told her, my voice shaking slightly with anger. "Carmina doesn't blame Chet. She's a better woman than that. She understands people make mistakes. And that's exactly what Chet did—he made a mistake. One mistake that will haunt him the rest of his life, because people like you can't seem to let him put it in the past, where it belongs!"

"Oh, dear," Mavis said, covering her mouth, which had taken the shape of a fat, lipsticked oval. "Oh, my."

"Really? Now you're at a loss for words?"

"You've hardly had time to get to know Carmina," she stammered. "I thought a little backstory might shed some—"

"I've had enough time to gauge Carmina's character. It's amazing how little people have to say for us to really know them."

Her hand went to her lacy throat, and her shocked expression pinched with offense. "I dare say."

"Oh, you've said enough," I said, disgusted.

With another gasp at my rudeness, Mavis tilted her nose upward and waddled outside.

I stayed in the kitchen, fuming in silence. I felt sick. Absurdly, I also felt like crying. I wanted to find Chet, pull him aside, and hold him tightly. How could he stay in a town that was so decidedly against him? If I were him, I would have run at the first chance. Why hadn't he bolted long ago? And then I remembered.

Dusty.

Chet was stuck here until his brother graduated. To his credit, I'd never heard him complain. He had compassion for Dusty, who'd given him every reason not to. He stayed in Thunder Basin because it was the right thing to do. His family meant more to him than the idle talk of nosy men and women.

Family. I had a family, but unlike Chet, I'd turned my back on mine long ago. My mom was a mess and I couldn't stand to be near her. I was better off without her. Those were the words I told myself, but Chet's example caused me to pause and take a hard look at what I was doing.

Was I a horrible person? Would Chet still want to be with me if he knew the truth about me and my family?

Something unexpected happened then. My throat grew slippery and my hands turned clammy. As hard as it would be, I had to call my mom. Before it was too late, I had to swallow my pride, forget the deep sense of injustice I felt, and set things right.

If something happened to one of us, I wanted her to know I didn't hate her. I hadn't forgiven her, but I didn't hate her either. It was a start.

While no one was looking, I scrolled through the caller list on Carmina's phone. I wouldn't call my mom today; I had to plan what I'd say, and I had to buy my own phone. I couldn't let Carmina know I was making the call. If I lost my temper with my mom, I didn't want Carmina to be disappointed or, worse, think less of me.

The only number in the call list that didn't have Thunder Basin's area code was an 800 number. It had to be the clinic's. I scribbled the digits on a Post-it note and shoved it in my pocket. My hand shook as I did, and I was even more grateful Carmina wasn't there to see it.

I WAS RIDING SHOTGUN IN THE SCOUT, AND CHET
refused to tell me where he was taking me. We'd left town a few
miles back and were picking up speed on a wide open stretch of
highway. We passed lone mailboxes on the side of the road, and
when I squinted into the distance, I could just see the houses
they belonged to, and the blinding glint of sunlight on alumi-
num barn roofs. We passed windmills, too, and low rolling hills
speckled with grazing cattle. The wheat-white of prairie grass
whizzed by.

At last Chet slowed, turned off the highway, and drove through
a tall gate constructed of timber posts that flanked a narrow dirt
road. An iron sign hung down from the highest post and clued
me in to our destination. MILTON SWOPE'S RANCH.

"You brought me to work?" I asked, trying to figure out what I was missing. It was evident by the smirk on his face that he was up to something. "On a Saturday?"

"Work barbeque. Boss said to bring a friend. Plucked a random name from my Rolodex, and you're the lucky winner."

I rolled the window down and stuck my head out to catch the breeze. It whipped my hair around my face and whisked the sweat off my neck.

I wrinkled my nose. "What's that smell?"

Chet grinned. "Money."

"I'm serious. It stinks."

"Cattle have to do their business too."

"We're eating barbeque with that pleasant aroma in the background?"

"Hold your horses. We've still got a ways to drive. The ranch's entrance gate we passed through back there? Marks another five-mile drive to the house. You won't smell cattle by the time we get there."

The next five miles gave me a view of some of the prettiest countryside I'd seen in Nebraska. The land was rolling hills slashed by narrow and winding creeks, and low golden bluffs loomed on the horizon. When we pulled up to the ranch house, the driveway was already filled with cars and trucks. Chet was right; the only thing I smelled now was meat sizzling on the grill.

"Eat all the burgers and potato salad you want," Chet said, "but you might want to lay off the Rocky Mountain oysters."

"I like oysters. I've never had freshwater, but I'm up for trying anything."

He thumbed his nose. "You might not be up for these." He was hiding a smile, and that was my first clue.

"What's wrong with them?"

"Rocky Mountain oysters aren't oysters. They're bull calf testes." I just stared at him.

Grinning, he said, "Still up for sampling?"

I lowered myself out of the Scout slowly. "I think I'm going to be sick."

"Ranchers have to castrate all but a few select bulls with superior genes. Most bulls are inferior, and you don't want them breeding. If you leave them intact, they turn mean. They'll break down gates, barn doors, loading chutes, and any other pen you put them in to get to a cow in heat. I'm not joking. I've seen them destroy trucks, water tanks—"

"That doesn't mean you have to eat their . . . their you-know-what!"

"Waste not, want not," he said dryly. "Here—I picked you up a little gift." Reaching over the backseat, he produced a straw cowgirl hat with a thin chocolate-colored ribbon. "Come here."

When I leaned forward, he set the hat gently in place. His eyes met mine, and I felt a little whirl of dizziness.

"Do I look like a local?" I asked, modeling for him.

"Get you atop a horse, and nobody would suspect otherwise."

"I went to horse camp once, just outside Philadelphia. My grandparents paid—" I stopped abruptly, horrified by my mistake. I couldn't believe I'd almost rattled off the truth—that my mother's parents had paid for horseback riding camp the summer before

I turned sixteen. I'd almost told him about Philadelphia. About Estella.

Quickly amending my story, I said, "My grandparents paid for me to spend two weeks learning to ride horses. They died shortly after. My mom followed them, and that's when I went into foster care."

"Wish you hadn't had to go through that," he said solemnly. "Do you mind if I ask what happened to your dad?"

"Oh, he's dead too."

"You've had a lot of deaths in your family. Must be hard."

"Yeah, well, you get over it. Let's go get burgers and potato salad, okay?"

The look in his eyes told me he wasn't fooled, but to my great relief, he let me have my way. He wouldn't push for answers. At least not yet.

After lunch, Chet and I strolled behind the ranch house to a cement pad with two basketball hoops at either end. There was a ball on the ground, and Chet picked it up, spinning it skillfully on his finger.

"Up for shooting hoops?" he asked.

I walked to the top of the key, spray-painted in black, and held my hand out for a pass. He lobbed the ball gently in my direction, like I might shatter on contact. I had to refrain from rolling my eyes. Squaring up, I sank a clean shot. Nothing but net.

He stared at me, his expression dazzled. "You've played before."

"Oh, you mean this?" Showboating, I accepted his rebound

pass, dribbled under the basket, powered up on my left foot, and nailed a tricky hook shot.

His stupefied grin stretched wider. "No offense to your softball skills, but you're better at basketball. Way better."

"Played back home," I said, taking another pass and sinking a jump shot.

"Varsity?"

"Yep."

"How many scholarships you pick up?"

I almost fumbled while dribbling. Recovering quickly, I held my voice steady and fastened my sights on the basket, as though I were intently gauging from where to take my next shot. "None."

"Don't believe it. You're too good to get passed by."

"I didn't play last year—senior year," I lied.

"Injury?"

"Just busy. Other stuff."

"Other stuff, meaning what?" he asked ludicrously. "I can tell you love the sport. It shows in your face, your body language. And you're good, really good. What could have been more important?"

"I don't want to talk about it." I felt suddenly defensive. And nervous. I wasn't afraid Chet would discover the truth—I'd see to it he wouldn't. It was just—

I was tired of lying to him. The more we talked about this, the more pressure I would feel to make up more excuses and stories. I was sick and tired of making Chet believe I was Stella Gordon. A fake. A fraud. An ever-shifting lie. "Let's just shoot, okay?" I said more tersely than I meant.

"I got a scholarship," Chet said, rebounding my shot and putting it back up. "Creighton."

It was my turn to gaze with wonder. "They've got an impressive program. I talked with a scout from there my sophomore year. You must be really good."

"Was good. Haven't kept it up. I was banking on that scholarship to pay my way through college. I was going to major in biology, maybe work for the Red Cross, get a little life experience, then go back for my graduate degree."

"You didn't take the scholarship because of Dusty," I realized out loud. "Your life plans got derailed because of him."

"Yeah."

"Do you regret it?"

"Nah. But sometimes I think about the guy they gave the scholarship to after I turned it down." He flashed a smile, but it didn't quite ring true. "Hope he's putting it to good use."

"What's your plan now?"

"See to it that Dusty walks across the high school stage with a diploma in hand a year from now. Then I'll take classes at the community college. After that, I'll try to transfer to Lincoln. I'll get my degree, just might take a little longer."

"What position did you play?"

"Forward."

I'd guessed as much. He was tall enough to play forward, but not big enough for center. By my estimation, he weighed right around 200.

"You?" he asked.

"Point. I always wanted to play under the basket but was too short. Ready?" I lofted the ball up by the rim, and with stellar reflexes, he jumped and tipped it in. It was a pretty impressive alley-oop.

I said, "Nice vertical."

"Not too bad yourself. You've got great form."

Beating him to the rebound, I sent him a wink. "So that's how a girl catches Chet Falconer's eye? Great shooting form?"

"I can think of a few other attributes that make it higher on the list." He held his hand up for the ball and I passed it.

"Such as?"

"I've got a weakness for hazel eyes."

"That so."

"Dark brown hair. Smart-alecky. Knows how to put me in my place."

I made the sound and gesture of a cracking whip.

He laughed. "Up for a little one-on-one?"

I took the ball to the top of the key. I dribbled in for a right-side layup, then spun and attempted a showy left-handed hook. Before I could execute the move, he scooped me by the waist, lifting me off the ground and swinging me around. I lost the ball in the process, and it rolled out of bounds.

"Foul!" I cried, but I was giggling hysterically, because he was using his free hand to tickle me. "I—get—two—shots!" I gasped.

He set me down and backed me against the pole. I was short of breath from running—and from finding myself so close to him. I watched him intently, my heart beating faster.

He slid his hand behind my neck and drew my face up, his mouth hot as it brushed mine. Closing my eyes, I let myself feel. My head was spinning wildly and my legs felt wonderfully unsteady.

Chet drew back, short of breath himself. "You're hard to resist."

"How hard are you trying?"

"Not very." And he kissed me again.

At that moment, I could think of nothing but how right it felt to be with Chet. I was happy, deliriously happy, filled to the brim.

ON OUR WAY BACK TO TOWN, CHET STOPPED AT A
dairy bar. The sign above the shack said it was established in 1951,
and the faded purple paint was a testament to the truthfulness of
the claim. A carousel with white ponies twirled idly on the side
lawn. The carousel reminded me of the Parx Liberty Carousel at
Franklin Square in Philly.

When I was little, my parents would take me there on hot summer evenings, and let me ride and ride until they ran out of quarters. It's true, what they say. You never know what you've got till it's
gone. Before going into WITSEC, had I known I'd never return to
Philly, I would have taken one more ride. Not for old times' sake,
but to savor the memory, to really hold it tight, so when I looked
back, I could clearly see the three of us happy and smiling, genuinely caring about one another.

I found a booth inside the dairy bar and slid in with my back to the window, scanning the menu above the registers. Chet had gone outside to grab cash from the ATM. I was debating between mint chocolate chip and birthday cake, when his voice startled me like a knife to the back.

"Mind if I sit?" Without waiting for me to tell him I did in fact mind a great deal, Trigger dropped into the seat opposite mine. He set his baseball cap on the table and combed his fingers through his red hair. "What's on the menu today? Black eye? Split lip?"

"Get the hell away from me."

He drew his fist toward me suddenly, then stopped short, chuckling when I shrank back in fear. "Touchy, touchy."

"That's it. I'm calling the cops."

"You can't have me arrested for talking," he drawled, sprawling comfortably in the booth, as if making it clear he wasn't going anywhere.

"You're threatening me."

"Who, me? In this nice, friendly voice? I don't think so."

"I'll get a restraining order."

"Who's gonna grant you one? Haven't you heard? I'm taking anger management classes. I'm reformed." He leaned forward, folding his hands on the table. I gripped the bottom of my seat hard enough to feel the blood leave my hands.

"I'm asking you to leave," I said firmly.

"What if I don't? What are you gonna do then?"

"I'll kick your ass. This time I'm ready."

"Now, that was a threat. See, I've been chatting with my lawyer, and it turns out assault is one of those fuzzy, blurry matters of the law. You don't have to lay a hand on me to be charged with assault. If you threaten me with words and I feel reasonable apprehension, that's enough." He leaned even closer into my space, his eyes black with hate. "So tell me again, Stella, what you're going to do to me if I don't move off this public seat."

I was so angry, I was shaking. It took all my control to speak calmly. "You think you own this town—"

"I do."

"No, you don't. You beat me up—your rules—and I had you arrested—the rules of the real world. You got off with community service and anger management, but next time, they won't go light. They can't. I don't care if your daddy goes fishing with the president of the United States, if you lay a hand on me again, you'll serve time."

"It's funny you say that. See, on my way over here, I was thinking to myself, 'Damn if I don't own this town. Damn if I don't make the rules. Damn if I'm not this close to putting Stella in her place.'" His gloating smile was more than an intimidation tactic. He had something. He knew something. And I couldn't fathom what, but it made me extremely uneasy.

"What are you talking about?"

"Something isn't right about you," he said, shaking his finger at me. "You're bristly, secretive. You act like you've got something to hide. What are you hiding, Stella? Whatever it is, better hope you hid it real good, 'cause I'm digging. Haven't found what I'm looking for, but I will."

I grew cold. The chill settled on me as thick as winter snow. I had to tell Carmina right away. Drawing up all the bravado I could, I said confidently, "You're fishing in an empty lake."

"Don't think I am."

"You're in my seat."

Trigger and I looked up at the same time. Chet stood at the head of our booth, his stance relaxed but his eyes as hard as I'd ever seen them.

Trigger flipped his palms up. "Didn't realize it was taken."

"It is." Chet spoke casually, but his words were lit with fire, hot and dangerous. "You mind?"

"Naw, me and Stella are all finished here."

As Trigger slid out and rose to his feet, Chet grabbed a fistful of his shirt, stopping him. "You're finished, period. Are we clear?"

Pulling on that lazy smile, Trigger said, "Sure, bud. Whatever you say."

"Remember it. Because if I find out you approached Stella, we'll have to have this talk again. And I don't like repeating myself."

Smoothing his shirt, Trigger backed away, holding his smile, which had soured. "Y'all have a nice one."

When he left, Chet took the empty seat and reached for my hand. "You okay?"

I nodded.

"You looked pissed. And maybe a little shaken."

I was, I thought, both those things.

"What was that about?" he asked.

"Just Trigger being Trigger."

"I got the feeling it was more."

I thought about telling him the truth, but I didn't trust Chet. If I told him that Trigger was responsible for beating me up, and that just now he'd come back to rub it in and intimidate me further, Chet would go after him. I didn't doubt Chet would win that fight, and as satisfying as it would be, I worried what might follow. Chet was nineteen. If Trigger pressed charges, the matter would be handled in criminal court. I wasn't going to risk tainting Chet's name with a record, or sending him behind bars, for a little ego-stroking.

"Trigger gave Inny a hard time at work last week, and I stood up to him," I said. "He's just trying to intimidate me. It'll blow over, and he'll forget about it. You'll see."

AFTER CHET DROPPED ME OFF, I WENT TO FIND Carmina. She sat in a rocker on the back porch, staring into the distance, the line of her mouth pensive. An untouched glass of basil lemonade was perched on her knee.

"What is it?" I asked right away. "Is it your heart?"

"No, no, not that. Just thinking. Wishing the summer didn't have to pass so quickly. Every year it goes by faster and faster." She patted the empty rocker beside hers. "How was your date with Chet?"

I gave her arm a ribbing poke. "That sounds so old-fashioned. It was fun. I saw my first real live ranch with cows and everything. Caught some trouble on the way home, though."

"Oh?"

"Trigger."

She stopped rocking, planting her red cowboy boots firmly on the porch. "Go on."

"He knows I'm keeping secrets. He threatened to dig around."

"That boy has nowhere to dig," she said decidedly. "The U.S. attorney's office notified the sheriff upon your arrival in town, standard procedure for WITSEC, but he's under strict authority not to disclose anything. I know the sheriff, he's a good man. Honest and fair. He wouldn't break the law or put you in danger. I'll touch base with him just the same, but I can see this for what it is. Trigger's trying to ruffle your feathers. What'd you tell him?"

"I told him I'd kick his ass if he threatened me again."

She sighed, vexed, but I thought I saw a gleam of pride in her eyes. "That's no way for a lady to behave."

"You're right. Empty threats are very unladylike. I should've just kicked his butt on the spot."

This time she reached out and squeezed my hand. "Wouldn't we all like to."

"Carmina? Can I ask you a question? It's personal, so I understand if you don't want to answer."

"Mmm?"

"My bedroom. Who did it belong to? Before I came, I mean."

For a half second, the soft squeak of the rocking chair halted. Then it started up again, though not quite as slow or steady as before.

"My grandson. Nathaniel." She took an absent sip of lemonade. "His favorite color was blue. Bet you couldn't guess."

"You must miss him."

"Oh, I do. He was a firecracker. Told the funniest jokes. Whip-smart, too. He'd debate anything with me. Even if he didn't believe his argument, he'd defend it with everything he had, just for the sake of the debate. Was a daredevil, too. Wasn't anything he wouldn't try, so long as he was fifty percent sure it wouldn't kill him. Once, I came home to find him and Chet—" She broke off abruptly.

"What were they doing?" I prompted softly.

Her voice heavier and strewn with sorrow, she said, "They were on the roof. Two stories up. They were taking turns doing flips off it. They'd pulled one of those big trampolines close to the house and were using it to land on." Wiping away tears, she chuckled. "About made me wet my pants. And that while dressed in full police blue."

"I bet you were a good grandmother."

Her smile fell away. "He's dead, Stella. A year ago."

"I know."

"Chet?"

"No. One of the women from church. I wanted to hear the truth from you. Do you mind if I ask about Nathaniel's parents?"

"My daughter, you mean."

"Where is she?"

Her face cramped with anguish. "I've made mistakes, Stella. I wasn't a good mother. My daughter abandoned Nathaniel the day he was born. I did right by him, but I failed her. She was sixteen years young when she had Nathaniel. She was addicted to horrible things. Drugs, alcohol, boys. I was always at work. My career was important to me—the most important thing. She fell in with the wrong crowd. I punished her. I grounded her. Rules—I enforced every one in the book. I was a cop, and a damn fine one. I wanted to make her fall in line. But I never did the one thing she needed. I never listened. I never showed up for her. I was never around. Don't you see? I expected her to grow up just fine without my love. It's no surprise she left. It's no surprise she never came back."

I digested her confession slowly. I tried to reconcile this negligent version of Carmina with the strong, clearheaded woman I'd learned to care about so deeply. It was difficult to think Carmina had anything in common with my mom. Absent, unloving, selfish—those were not words I could imagine using to describe Carmina. It hurt to see any similarity between her and my mom.

But the fact that she was being honest made it hard to hold her mistakes against her. How many times would I have forgiven my mom if she'd only told me the truth? Carmina was not the same woman she was describing to me. Stern and duty driven, yes. But not harsh, callous, and negligent. Unlike my mom, she'd changed. Her past and her future were not the same.

"What became of your daughter?" I asked.

"Angie? The last time I saw her, she was giving birth to a baby boy. The next morning the hospital called to say she'd vanished, and what did I want done with the baby? You can't know how many times I've wished she would come back. I need to apologize and make amends. More than that, I need her in my life. But I was never there when she needed me," she brooded into her lemonade.

"I'm sorry."

"Me too. We've all got our troubles, haven't we?"

The phone rang.

Carmina started to ease out of her rocker, but I jumped to my feet. "I'll get it." I was trying to help out around the house as much as possible, especially with her weakened heart. I didn't want her back in the hospital.

I grabbed the phone in the kitchen. "Songster residence, Stella speaking."

"Estella? Is that you? Is that really you? Oh, baby! I've missed hearing your voice."

I went still. Utterly still.

"Baby? You there? Say something to your mama," she chided me. "I've waited so long to talk to you. I can't wait another minute!"

Panic fluttered in my throat. I'd made up my mind to call my mom, but on my terms. I hadn't planned for this. Caught off guard, I couldn't control my emotions. I hadn't seen her since the night of the murder. The night I was whisked into the protection of the U.S. Marshals Service and blissfully, blissfully separated from her. I'd managed to all but forget about her. And now here she was, causing months of buried anger and resentment to flash to life in an instant.

I found my voice. "Why are you calling?"

"Why on earth do you think, silly?" she went on, her voice as sugary and bubbly as soda. "I'm aching to catch up! Anyway, can't a mama call her baby just because?"

Just because? I didn't believe it for a minute. "I can't talk. I'm busy," I said flatly.

Disappointment swept into her voice. "Too busy for the woman who endured twenty-four hours of excruciating labor to bring you into the world? They pulled you out with forceps. Most painful thing I've ever endured. Getting a case of the wobbly-woos just thinking about it."

"I'm on my way out the door," I said in that same bland tone. "I have to go to work."

"Now, hold on a minute, Estella. I'm not finished. I called for a reason."

That's more like it.

"What's this nonsense about you testifying against Danny? Those detectives from Philly came to see me. At least one of us was smart enough to tell them to eat dirt. You can't do it, Estella. I won't let you. It's dangerous business. The men Danny works with? Believe me when I say they aren't to be taken lightly. They're bad men, sweetheart. Real bad."

"And you let them into our life."

If my remark rattled her conscience, she recovered quickly. "It's in everybody's best interest if you tell that frog-faced prosecutor from the federal courts that you're scared silly of Danny, and while you appreciate the government's protection, your life means more to you than their conviction."

"They're protecting me because I agreed to testify. That was the deal. It's the reason they're protecting you, too."

"Oh, darling. Don't let them hustle you. This is the U.S. government, for crying out loud. They aren't going to leave an itty-bitty seventeen-year-old girl at the mercy of a powerful cartel, even if you refuse to testify. And that's what you're going to do. Refuse," she said, the last word coming out almost threatening.

"Do you even care about me?"

"I— What? What kind of question is that? I'm your mother. What do you think I'm doing? I'm trying to save your life."

"Has there been one moment during all of this that you actually thought about me first?" I asked, my chin trembling.

"What are you getting at, Estella?" she said irritably. "If you have something to say, come out with it. Right now."

"I'm your daughter. You should be protecting *me*, not Danny. He doesn't care about you. Don't you get it? You were his income source. He let you believe whatever you liked about him, because he wanted your money. He didn't love you," I said, my voice pitching higher at the ludicrousness of the idea. How could she not see what I saw? How could she be so desperate and blind?

"I should have known you'd refuse to listen." She cut me off, sounding flustered and indignant. But beneath that, in some small, human way, I heard her shame. For one moment, I thought I might get through to her. Deep down, a part of who my mother once was still struggled to survive, and I clung to it. "You never listen. Not to me. I did everything for you, gave you the best money can buy. . . ."

I covered my face with my hand. I swallowed the unwanted and wavering tickle in my throat. It hurt, hearing her gloss over the real issue. Why couldn't she just confess her mistakes? I wanted an apology. I wanted my old mom back! I thought about telling her, but my anger was ebbing away, leaving hollow heartache. I felt completely drained.

I said, "I can't listen to this. I'm done. Don't call back."

"You listen to me. Do *not* testify against Danny. For once in your life, listen to your mama. This is not a man you want to cross. If you step foot in that courtroom, he will find you. He will use every resource in his organization to hunt you down and he will kill you. He knows people. Violent, nasty men—"

Men she allowed into our life. Into *my* life.

Trembling, I hung up.

I would not let my mom follow me here, to my haven. I would not let her make me more afraid than I already was.

That night, I dreamed of Danny Balando. I woke up panting heavily, sweat drenching the back of my nightshirt. I told myself it was just a dream, I was safe here, he'd never find me. But no amount of rational talk could calm my trembling.

Light spilled under the door.

"Stella?" Carmina said, knocking lightly.

"I'm awake."

She came in. "I heard you cry out."

"I had a nightmare."

"Trigger?"

"Danny Balando."

Still fragile from the heart attack, she lowered herself with care to sit on the bed. As she patted my knee, her fingers were blissfully cool to the touch. "Have you talked to anyone about the night-mares? I've heard you cry out more than once."

"No. I live with them."

"Would you like to talk to me?"

I met her eyes. "What do you want to know?"

"In my experience, sometimes you have to flush the bad stuff out before you can heal. Getting it out hurts, but it's better than holding on to the poison."

I thought about this. "I could go back to the beginning. I could tell you about my mom."

Carmina spread her hands as if to say the stage was mine; she would listen as long as it took.

I don't know how long I sat there, trying to find the right words. I harbored so much anger at my mom, it should have been easy to let it spill out. I felt filled to the brim with that anger. But when confronted with the option of getting it out, it seemed I'd buried it deeper than even I knew. Carmina was right. It was poison. It was in my system; it had taken root.

"She drank before, at social events, or she'd have a glass of red wine before dinner," I began slowly. "But during the divorce, she started drinking a lot. Sometimes right after she woke up in the morning. I think she drank to forget how sad she was. I don't think she was still in love with my dad, or mourning the loss of him. It was more personal. She saw the divorce as an attack on her, as a personal failure. My dad was cheating on her, and the divorce was his way of saying she wasn't young enough, or beauti-ful enough, or good enough for him anymore."

"How do you know your dad was having an affair?" Carmina asked.

"Affairs. Plural. My mom hired a private detective to follow him. There were photographs."

"She shared them with you?"

"She wanted to hurt him. He wasn't ashamed to admit his indiscretions to her, but she thought he'd be humiliated if I knew." I paused, remembering that awful night when my mom had dragged me out of bed well after midnight. I was already awake—I couldn't sleep through the shouting—and she marched me right up to my dad and shoved the photographs at us, demanding that he explain himself to me. He hadn't. Without looking at me, he walked out, slamming the front door behind him. The next day, he had his assistant come by to collect his clothes and a few other personal belongings.

"When I agreed to testify against Danny Balando for the prosecution, the U.S. attorney's office offered to put my dad in WITSEC with me. After all, he was family. He declined. He didn't want to quit his job, and WITSEC doesn't allow you to do the same line of work after you're relocated. They told him I'd never be able to contact him again, not in person, not through e-mail, nothing. I guess he was okay with that."

Carmina guided my head down against her shoulder. She said nothing, but I could feel a change in her breathing. It was slow and deep, and troubled.

"My mom started hanging out with a woman named Sandy Broucek right after the divorce. My mom complained the only friends she had were the ones she'd met through my dad, and who still moved in his social circles. She wanted to break away from that world and make her own friends—the old friends were polite to her face but gossiped bitterly behind her back.

"She was on meds for depression, and when she went out with Sandy and her new friends, she'd come home smelling like pot. Then she started abusing prescription drugs. She and Sandy talked about a dealer they called the Pharmacist. I don't know if he was a real pharmacist, but prescription bottles of OxyContin labeled for other people started popping up around our house. She tried to hide them, but I knew. After a while, she stopped talking about the Pharmacist and I stopped finding prescriptions. Somehow she met Danny. He became her new dealer and gave her heroin. She was really happy at first. In the days after she'd had a night out with friends, she'd laugh and joke with me. She seemed interested in my life. She was depressed, but the drugs masked it. I think she thought they made her the person she wanted to be—happy, fun, relaxed. But she was none of those things. She was still depressed, and the drugs only distorted her perception of herself for a little while."

"It was easier for her to drink and do drugs than face her problems and get help," Carmina said.

"After her initial happiness, things got bad. I tried to get her help. I drove her to the city early every morning to wait in line at the methadone clinics. Methadone was supposed to help her get off heroin. The clinics were in bad parts of the city, and we'd wait outside, in the cold or heat, surrounded by unwashed, desperate-looking people. Sometimes fights would break out in line and I'd beg my mom to leave, but she had to have enough medicine to get through the day.

"When the methadone didn't work, she reverted back to heroin. She lost so much weight she was almost unrecognizable. She stopped eating, showering, or leaving the house, except to party with Sandy. She refused to get out of bed unless it was to get more drugs. Over time, her partying isolated her from me. She wasn't there when I needed her. She broke every promise she made. It got to the point that I was so scared, I called my grandparents— her parents. That made things worse. She got really angry and wouldn't talk to me. Her parents put her in rehab, but the center told us going in that withdrawal is extremely painful and that she'd probably relapse. She did."

"How many times did she go to rehab?"

"This is her third."

"In my whole time as a cop, I only saw a handful of abusers recover. Drugs bring out the bad in people. Sometimes it's hard to remember that addiction is a disease—it doesn't define the person who's suffering. Behind the addiction is a real person, a human who deserves respect."

I shook my head fiercely. "Don't take away her accountability. She chose this life. She had me, but she chose drugs. She's a coward. I don't ever want to be weak like her."

"She needs your faith, Stella."

"You think I should believe that this time she'll get better," I said, my spine stiffening. Was Carmina listening? This was my mother's third attempt. The longer she stayed on drugs, the harder it was to quit. I'd given up on her. It hurt too much to care. When you cared, you had something to lose all right.

"Before believing comes faith. Before faith comes hope."

"I don't want to hope."

"Because it hurts?"

I couldn't hold the tears back any longer. My lip quivered and my throat burned. When I spoke, my words sounded thick and fragile. "It hurts when she lets me down. It hurts knowing drugs are more important to her than me."

"It's easier to ignore her, wish her away. If she doesn't exist, she can't hurt you."

"Yes," I choked.

"Oh, Stella. My sweet Stella." She gathered me into her arms and rocked me while I cried.

When the worst of my tears had subsided, I said, "Before she called today, I'd actually given some thought to calling her." Sniffing, I wiped my nose on my sleeve. "I thought it would make me feel better to tell her I don't hate her anymore, and that I'm ready to move on. I can't decide if that makes me stupid or just naive."

"Brave, Stella. That's what it makes you."

"I don't want her to think I'm weak or that I caved. She wants me to call back. I don't want to give her what she wants."

"What about what you want? Why not look at it that way?"

I considered this. I wanted to be brave. I wanted to heal. Most of all, I wanted Carmina to be proud of me.

I said, "Why did you take me in? Why would you do that? You didn't know me. You didn't owe me anything."

"Well," she said, "the short answer is, because they asked me."

"The long answer?"

"I suppose you should know I was appointed to the U.S. Marshals Service when I was thirty-four. I was getting ready to head to Glynco, Georgia, for basic training. Training was seventeen weeks long, and Angie, my daughter, was going to stay with Thomas and Hannah Falconer while I was away. Days before I left, I found out Angie was pregnant. She was fifteen and due in six months. Well, I stayed. I took care of her, then I took care of Nathaniel. Never ended up a U.S. marshal. But I must have stayed on their radar, because they called me and said they needed me to take in a girl who'd been placed in witness protection, keep her safe for the summer."

"You sacrificed your own success to take care of your family, and then you gave up your retirement to take me in."

"You make me sound like a good woman, Stella. But I figured it out too late. A few years too late," she echoed. "It was hope that kept me afloat in those dark weeks after Angie ran away. Hope that I could change. Hope that she'd someday forgive me."

Even though my eyes felt raw, tears surged back. "I don't want to hope. I'm terrified my mom will prove me wrong. She's let me down too many times. That night—the night I went into WITSEC—I swore it would be the last."

"Tell me about that night. Tell me the worst of it. Get it all out. Tell me, then let it go."

I wanted to tell her. I wanted it more than anything. To let go of the poison and move on? It was all I thought about. But I was afraid. The fear and shame and guilt coiled around me like a snake ready to strike. If Carmina knew what really happened that night, if she learned what I did, I was terrified she wouldn't like me anymore.

She'd turn her back on me. And hand me over to the authorities.

BEFORE WORK I STOPPED BY RADIOSHACK. AFTER a little searching, I found a cheap, no-frills, pay-by-the-minute phone.

The guy working the register scanned the bar code, whistling appreciatively. "Got yourself a real dinosaur here."

"I'm on a budget."

"You said it. Anything else?"

"Yeah, how much would a cell phone plan for an iPhone cost?"

"Looking at around seventy a month."

"Is an Android any cheaper?"

"Same ballpark."

I calculated a rough sum of my saved tips. Maybe it was better to hold off getting a cell phone plan until my birthday, when I left Thunder Basin and settled somewhere permanently. Recently,

I hadn't given much thought to how my life would change after I turned eighteen, but here it was a few days shy of August. I'd served over half my time in Thunder Basin, and while the realization should have thrilled me, I felt a strange pang of misgiving. In four weeks, I would be leaving Thunder Basin for good, and I hadn't told Chet. Nor had I discussed my plans with Carmina. I cared about them both deeply, and didn't look forward to saying good-bye, but the rational part of me knew Thunder Basin wasn't my final destination. Maybe it was the kind of place Stella Gordon could settle down in, but changing my name didn't erase Estella Goodwinn from my blood. Could I feel complete here, content? Or was I destined for bigger, better things? I'd always clung to the fantasy of running away with Reed and starting our life over together, of having him nearby to take care of me, but that was no longer an option. Nor was I sure I'd want it if I could have it. This summer had changed me.

I wanted to find my own way.

At work, we were short staffed. Inny had called in sick, and Dixie Jo was on the phone frantically trying to reach Deirdre to see if she could help out through the dinner rush.

"Any luck?" I asked, peeking my head in her office.

"No." Dixie Jo rubbed her temples. "And this on a Saturday night, of all the bad luck."

"I'll do my best to keep up with the cars."

"Oh, I know you will. That's not what's bothering me. It's Inny," she admitted. "I can't reach her. She called and left the message hours ago telling me she was sick. She left a message on the machine. It isn't like Inny. She'd tell me to my face she wasn't up for a shift. She'd offer to help find a sub. I can't shake the feeling she's avoiding me on purpose. Now, why would she do that?"

"She's due any day now," I reminded her. I had a baby gift at home ready to take to Inny the minute I heard she'd gone to the hospital. "Do you think she went into labor?"

"Thought of that and called the hospital. She hasn't checked in. She isn't answering her cell phone. What if she's on some lonely road, in the back of her car, trying to deliver the baby herself?"

"Would she do that?"

"She's worried she can't pay the hospital bills." Another temple squeeze. "She's picked up extra shifts for months now, saving up. Her parents don't support the pregnancy, said they'd have nothing to do with her if she kept the baby. Even threatened not to pay the bills. Legally they'd have to, of course, but it's a matter of pride now. Inny won't accept their help. If she's afraid she can't afford the hospital, I wouldn't put it past her to deliver the baby in a field. Anything but ask her parents for money. She should've come to me. I told her to come to me."

"She wouldn't do that." In the two months I'd known Inny, I'd never seen her ask for help. Even with swollen ankles and her belly protruding to the point where she looked like she'd swallowed a beach ball, she refused to sit down for a breather at the end of the night and let me fill her salt and pepper shakers. She was bound and determined to do everything herself.

"Foolish girl," Dixie Jo snapped. She pushed out of her chair, pacing the office. "Stubborn, pigheaded girl." A tear trickled down her cheek. "I need to be alone, Stella. I need to think where she'd go to have this baby."

"I can help you look. Now or after my shift. Just tell me what you want me to do." I was worried about Inny too, especially now that I knew more about her situation. If her parents weren't on board with the baby, Inny would have turned her back on the idea of asking them for help long ago. No matter how desperate, she'd do this on her own. Even if it killed her.

"I appreciate that," Dixie Jo said, grief weighing heavily on her face, "but I'm worried either way we'll be too late."

After work I found a note under the windshield wiper of Carmina's truck. It was from Chet, and the news he had to deliver didn't lighten my mood.

Dusty hadn't shown up for work today. Chet had been at the ranch until sundown, and hadn't played the message Dusty's boss left on his phone until late. Worse, Dusty had raided the emergency stash of money Chet kept in the house. It was gone, all of it. Chet was out looking for him, and would call me at Carmina's the minute he knew something.

I didn't want to think bad of Dusty, but I had a hunch he was feeling desperate to get his business with Cooter started—even if it meant cheating his brother. It was hard not to draw a parallel with my mom. Only once, but still once, she stole money from me to fund her habit. The cash was in my wallet before I went to bed.

She went partying with Sandy, and in the morning the money was gone. She might have stolen again, had I not learned to hide my money.

I'd fallen asleep with the window open, tempting any trace of a breeze inside my bedroom, and the deep rumble of the Scout pulled me instantly awake. In the dark, I tugged on a pair of shorts and hurried downstairs.

Chet climbed out of the truck, his movements heavy, his shoulders hunched and his eyes dead. He was looking at me, but he didn't seem to see me. He stood dazed and blinking, almost like he was lost. Right away I knew it was Dusty. Something horrible had happened.

"Chet?" I slipped my feet into Carmina's garden clogs and jogged down the porch steps. The night air was thick and hot, but the look on Chet's face chilled me to the core, and I wished I'd brought something to wrap around my shoulders. "It's Dusty, isn't it?"

He sank down on the driveway. He leaned his head back against the Scout. His face, which had always appeared strong and certain to me, reflected sheer exhaustion. "He spent it. All of it. His college savings, the money he earned this summer, our emergency fund. Nearly five thousand dollars. Gone."

"Drugs?" I asked quietly.

He laughed sharply, and the ice in his tone made me shiver again. "I wish he'd blown it on drugs. Drugs he could sell. Drugs would be profitable. He used the money to hire a midwife. His girlfriend was pregnant. I didn't even know he had a girlfriend."

Now it was my turn to blink. I stared into near space, her name rolling involuntarily off my tongue. "Inny."

"They're keeping the baby. Did you hear me? They're keeping the baby!" he shouted angrily. "Don't tell me I should be grateful he did the responsible thing. For once, I don't want him to be responsible. I want him to be selfish. Like I'm being now."

"Have you tried talking to him?"

"He told me they couldn't afford the hospital so they hired a midwife. He said they're keeping the baby, and the minute those words sank in, I started yelling sense at him. I told him he was putting the baby up for adoption or I'd kick him out. He hung up." Chet's breath heaved in and out, his eyes dark and blazing. "He doesn't want to listen, but he knows I'm right. If he keeps the baby, it's over. He'll never go to college. He'll stay here, plastering pools until his back gives out, and then he'll get a job on the railroad in North Platte. It's not what my parents wanted." He scrubbed his hands through his hair. "I'm not cut out for this. I failed. I let everyone down. This is why Dusty wanted to partner with Cooter Saggory—to support his girlfriend and their kid. I never saw it. I was oblivious. And now it's too late. Everything is falling down around me."

I didn't know what to say. I took his face in my hands and tipped his forehead to mine. My hands were steady, but I felt my strength start to crumble. What Chet hadn't said, but knew as well as I did, was that if Dusty couldn't support the baby like he thought he could, Chet would step in. He was angry now, and threatening to kick Dusty out, but he wouldn't. When he calmed, he'd accept that he was Dusty's guardian, and he'd see this through—at the expense of his own future and dreams.

"Oh, Chet," I said, feeling my heart break for him.

"Her parents already kicked her out," he said roughly. "She doesn't have anywhere to go. If she'll give up the baby, they'll take her back."

"She won't do that."

His eyes found mine, and they were swimming with bewilderment. "Does she have any idea what it's like to be a parent? Dusty said he knows it won't be easy, but he has no idea what's in store. It isn't that it isn't easy. It's that it's the hardest thing he'll ever do. He isn't ready. He thinks he is, but he's a kid. He hasn't lived his own life, so how is he going to take care of someone else's?"

I held him tighter; I didn't have answers, but the last thing he needed right now was to feel alone. I could give him that at least. My companionship and a listening ear.

"I told Dusty she couldn't live with us," Chet said, his tone morose. "I laughed when he suggested it. I called him a fool and a few other things. I told him, 'Don't show up at the house with her or the baby, because I won't let you in.'"

"Here's true irony," he went on. "This week at work we were castrating bulls, and I'm not usually squeamish, but I took a moment to wince—feel a bit sorry for them, you know? And then this happened with Dusty, and my first thought was, Nope, castration isn't a bad thing at all. Apply it to humans."

He was aiming to amuse me, but I couldn't bring myself to laugh.

"I'm going to let her move in, aren't I?" he realized quietly. "I don't know if it's the right thing, or the worst idea I've ever had, but I'm scared out of my mind that I'm going to go through with it and let her and the baby live with us."

"What would your mom have done?" While I waited for his answer, I asked myself the same question. What would my mom have done if Reed had gotten me pregnant? It didn't matter. I would have run away with him. I would have moved out, not staying long enough to see her reaction, because the reality of the situation was that she wouldn't have cared. That's what drugs did. They took away your ability to care about anything but more, more, more drugs.

"If I don't take her in, Dusty will drop out of school and get a full-time job. He'll have to take care of rent, food, bills, all of it. His life will stop here."

"All probably true."

He sighed again, but this time his body relaxed, and I guessed that meant he had his answer.

"I'm here to help, you know," I said.

I rested my cheek against the slope of his shoulder. He smoothed my hair absently and let go a rueful sigh. "What did I ever do to deserve this?"

"You gave Carmina hell," I said, smiling faintly. "Some might call this karma."

He pulled back, looking at me directly. "I meant you. What did I do to deserve you, Stella? I've made mistakes. I've screwed up enough times. So how does a guy like me end up with you?" There was genuine wonder and amazement in the way he looked at me, and if I thought I'd known guilt before, I was wrong.

When he guided my head against his chest, I drew a quiet but deep breath. I had to tell him I was leaving Thunder Basin.

I couldn't hold off any longer.

30

A FEW DAYS LATER, I WAS KNEELING IN CARMINA'S rose beds, absorbing myself in the mindless task of pulling weeds while I worked up the courage to call my mom back and tell her: First, that I was going to testify, and second, that I didn't hate her anymore.

After hanging up on her during our last call, I'd sworn I'd never speak to her again. But that was the poison talking—it wanted to stay rooted inside me and turn me black with bitter rage. I had to call her. This time on my terms. I had to exorcise the past and move on.

I'd never forgiven anyone—not officially, like to a priest in a confessional—and was having a hard time figuring out how to balance what I wanted her to hear with what I wanted her to feel.

I didn't want her walking away from our conversation feeling excused for her behavior or without guilt. I supposed I wanted her to know I wasn't going to let her hurt me anymore . . . but if she wanted to kick herself over her bad choices, so be it.

Carmina wouldn't approve, but I had to start somewhere. Maybe down the road I'd decide to fully forgive my mom. I still didn't believe in God, but it made sense that if there was a supreme ruler of the universe, he wouldn't expect these kinds of harbored emotions to be dropped in an instant. Forgiveness took time, I decided. It was a process. Better to start slowly than not at all.

I heard the Scout approaching down the road. Rocking back on my heels, I peeled out of my garden gloves just as Chet angled into the drive.

"You busy?" he asked, hanging his arm out the driver's side window. His cowboy hat was tipped low, shading his eyes, which sparkled mischievously.

"You're in a good mood."

"Agree to come with me, and make it even better."

"What do you have in mind?"

"Ever been to a rodeo?"

"Like cowboys and clowns?"

A smile danced at his mouth. "Yeah. And bull riding, steer roping, chuck-wagon racing, and mutton busting."

"No," I said cautiously. None of the above sounded like my thing, even if half the words were foreign.

"Hop in." He inclined his head at the seat next to him. "You're about to get a culture lesson."

"See, I don't think you know what the word 'culture' means. Where's Dusty?" I asked, playing for time.

"At the house with his girlfriend and the baby. Come on. Time's a-wasting."

Inny had moved in with Dusty and Chet over the weekend. I'd stopped by to visit and deliver a gift for the baby—a girl they'd named Beatrix—but Inny had been asleep. I was dying to talk with her and catch her up on the latest gossip from the Sundown.

"I don't know," I hedged further. It wasn't that I didn't want to hang out with Chet. But a rodeo? Weren't rodeos consistently getting panned by animal rights activists? Plus, I had visions of fried bull testes being sold alongside churros and funnel cakes out of a dirty food truck.

"You're overthinking this," he said, smiling at my expression, which must have appeared deeply conflicted.

"No bull testes," I finally said. "Final offer."

"Deal."

"And if it rains, we seek shelter." Dark clouds cloaked the horizon, but the evening sun blazed hot overhead, and while I hadn't seen rain in the forecast, I needed to cover my bases.

"No wet T-shirt contest today, you got it."

"Carmina's at the store. Let me change clothes and leave a note for her."

Inside, I zipped myself into my yellow sundress, left a note for Carmina on the kitchen counter, and snagged two chilled Cokes from the fridge.

"Am I wearing proper rodeo attire?" I asked Chet, twirling

in a circle. I'd paired the sundress with the boots Carmina had given me.

"You look like a local."

I tossed him a Coke and climbed in.

"I have to drop off some rodeo gear first, but it shouldn't take long," Chet said, reversing down the drive. "Milton Swope referred me to a neighbor who has a couple saddle and bareback bronc riders competing tonight. I'm delivering their gear."

Thirty minutes later, we pulled up behind the rodeo arena. Trucks and horse trailers clogged the dusty, rutted road looping the arena. We were opposite the stands, and I could see they were starting to fill, even though the rodeo didn't start for another half hour. As Chet drove past the loading chutes, he pointed to a string of cowboys stretching their legs.

"Those are the bareback bronc riders warming up. Have to tie their spurs, do squats to stretch the groin, and of course chew tobacco, drink beer, and talk trash to the other riders."

"What are the crushing in their gloves?"

"Rosin. They rub it quickly along the rope they are going to use to ride to make it tacky."

"They look nervous."

"Some of that, sure, but mostly concentrating. Running through best- and worst-case scenarios in their heads. Dreaming of the purse. There's nearly a hundred grand up for grabs tonight."

"Wow." It was more than I would have guessed from small-town entertainment.

Next we drove past the bull pen. The gates were high, but I

caught a glimpse of black hide stretched over meaty haunches, and sharp horns.

"How does bull riding work?" I asked. "You said Sydney's boyfriend is a bull rider. Is he here?"

"Might be. If there's one rodeo sport I wouldn't try, it's bull riding. Too risky. When I was a kid, I saw a rider's leg, right up near the groin, skewered by a bull horn. That tempered my curiosity real fast. But it's an exciting sport to watch. A ride is scored from zero to one hundred points. Anything above seventy-five is impressive. A rider has to stay mounted on the bull for eight seconds to get any points; if he falls off, the bull gets the points. If the rider touches the bull, the rope, or himself with his free hand—the hand you always see a rider holding in the air—he's disqualified."

"I always thought riders held up a hand for balance."

"Riders are judged on style and control, things like synchronizing their movements to the bull's, and on how the bull performs. If the bull is unusually aggressive and gives the rider a hard time, extra points are awarded. After eight seconds, a loud buzzer sounds, and the rider can jump off."

I'd seen pictures of cowboys in chaps and boots, their bodies twisting and convulsing like a rag doll on the back of a bucking bull. I was with Chet—probably not something I wanted to try any time soon.

Chet parked a distance from the bucking shoots and unloaded a couple of boxes from the back of the Scout.

"Can I help?" I offered.

"Nah, I'll be less than ten."

After he disappeared, I propped my boots on the dash and watched the bull riders stretch in the rearview mirror. I wished I'd thought to grab the cowgirl hat Chet had given me. I could have taken a country selfie with the bull pen directly behind me.

But since I didn't use social media anymore—the government had shut down my accounts—it wasn't like I could post the picture anywhere. And there was that whole issue of not having a phone with a camera.

I took the pay-by-the-minute phone out of my purse and turned it over in my hands. I still didn't know exactly what I was going to say to my mom. Even once I came up with a script, I was afraid I'd abandon it in favor of yelling or, worse, crying.

For days now I'd searched for the right words, but I was beginning to accept that this wasn't the kind of conversation you could rehearse. I was never going to settle on the perfect lines. Maybe it was time for a new approach. Dive in and have faith the words would flow when I needed them.

I could call her now. While I waited for Chet.

With the help of a deep breath, I dialed the number for the detox clinic. Before I could squash the butterflies in my stomach, a receptionist answered.

"Savannah Gordon please," I said, since Carmina had told me that the DOJ had given my mom the same last name I was going by—Gordon.

"One moment." After a pause, her voice came back on the line. "I'm sorry, Savannah Gordon is no longer with us."

"What?"

"She checked herself out this morning."

"That can't be right. There must be a mistake. Check again."

"It's right here, in her file. She voluntarily left the program."

"Where did she go?"

"Patients aren't required to leave that information. Miss? There's another call coming in. Would you mind holding?"

"Yes, I'd mind," I snapped. "I need to know where Savannah went." I knew getting upset wouldn't help, but I was too shell-shocked to be polite. Had my mom only left rehab, or had she left witness protection too? I knew WITSEC was voluntary, and she could leave at any time, but surely she wasn't stupid enough to return to her old identity. Was the U.S. attorney's office aware of what she'd done?

"It isn't our policy to track patients after they leave the program," the receptionist said stiffly.

"Gee, thanks for the help," I said, and hung up.

I stared into near space, dazed. Why would my mom leave rehab?

Because she needed drugs. It was the reason she always left. And if she'd returned to drugs, she'd returned to Philly.

I couldn't believe she'd do something this dangerous. Had she given any thought to the risks? If Danny's men found her, they'd kill her. It didn't matter that she wasn't cooperating with authorities; Danny didn't know that. And he certainly didn't love her. Was chasing the next high worth her life? Had she spared a single moment to consider how her recklessness might affect me?

It stood to reason the U.S. attorney's office had told her my new name—Stella Gordon. If Danny's men got her high, she might give me up. They could string it right out of her. I didn't want to think she'd betray me sober, but I wasn't sure. When it came to my mom, nothing was certain.

I had to think. Now that Danny was behind bars, who would she call when she got to Philly? Sandy.

If my mom was back in Philly, Sandy would know. My mom would want to party with her.

I'd been warned not to contact anyone from my former life, but I wasn't going to sit back and let my mom get herself killed. And I wasn't going to let her put me at risk.

I slowed my racing thoughts deliberately. I had to be smart about this. Danny Balando's gang could be watching Sandy, hoping my mom would eventually reach out to her. Deputy Price had told me it would be one of Danny's (and the cartel's, if they were backing him) strategies—to keep an eye on our family and close friends, waiting patiently for us to slip up and contact them. I had to be very, very careful. I couldn't raise even a hint of suspicion.

Reed had once told me the best way to avoid having a call traced was to use a disposable prepaid phone, because they could only be tracked when turned on. I knew calling Sandy wasn't completely risk free, but I could greatly reduce my chances of being caught if I turned the phone off and trashed it immediately after using it. To find me, Danny Balando's gang would have to be monitoring Sandy's calls, they'd have to recognize my voice, and they'd have to know what phone I was calling from. The odds were on my side. Not completely in the bank, but on my side.

Feeling a pounding of nerves, I called Sandy. Her number was fresh in my mind. Back in Philly, on the nights when my mom didn't come home, I knew to call Sandy. They were always together. If they hadn't passed out, one or the other could usually give me an address. Then it was up to me to find my mom and drag her home. I shut my eyes, feeling tears slip through my lashes. It hurt to remember.

"Hello?" Sandy answered, sounding cranky but sober.

"May I please speak to Sandy Broucek?" I affected a slightly deeper voice, but I wasn't worried she'd recognize me. We'd only talked a handful of times. Sandy hadn't visited our home frequently. I'd known from the first time I met her that she had no interest in me.

"Who is this?" she wanted to know.

"My name is Mary Dutton. I'm responsible for several accounts owned by Savannah Goodwinn, and I've had trouble reaching her. She listed you as her primary contact. Would you be willing to provide her most current contact information?"

"You a debt collector?"

I didn't know if real debt collectors had to be up-front, but I didn't have to follow the same rules. "I'm with Keystone Financial Services. There have been some important updates made to Savannah's accounts that will affect future transactions. It's very important that I notify her."

"Why would Savannah list me?" Sandy demanded, sounding more irritated.

"Part of my job is to track her down, and until I have her most current phone number and address, I'll have to keep calling this number."

That seemed to give her food for thought. She didn't pause long before saying, "Yeah, all right. I can give you her new number. Lucky you called when you did—I haven't heard from Savvy in months, but she rang this morning. Hang on a sec, here it is. Ready?"

"Ready." I tried to sound calm and not overly anxious.

"Area code two-one-five . . ."

I scribbled down the entire number, repeated it back, then ended the call.

The next call was harder to make. When my mom answered, it was going to take all my willpower not to yell. I was furious—and disgusted—but if I wanted her cooperation, I was going to have to keep my cool. If I kept my head, maybe she would too. Maybe I could reason with her and talk her back to rehab.

The phone rang and rang. With each passing moment, I felt my anger drain, and worry fill its place. What if something had already happened?

I stepped out of the Scout, pacing in front of it. A few raindrops splashed my arms, but the sky looked like it would hold. Chet was taking an awfully long time. I could hear the rodeo announcers in the distance, introducing the lineup of ropers.

Sitting on the bumper, I forced my nerves to settle. I wasn't going to panic until I had a reason to. My mom could be too high to answer her phone. I couldn't leave a message—too risky. I'd have to keep calling back. But if she didn't answer tonight, if she still didn't answer tomorrow . . .

I hated myself for feeling the first prick of tears. I would not cry for her. She didn't deserve it.

"Thomas Dickerson speaking." The man's voice on the other end of the line startled me.

"Um, yes, is Savannah there?" I adopted the same deep voice as before.

"Who?"

I repeated my mom's name.

"I'm sorry, you must have the wrong number."

I double-checked the number. I'd entered it correctly.

"I don't know anyone named Savannah," he added.

I couldn't believe it. Sandy had given me a fake. I should have seen it coming.

Hanging up, I immediately turned off the phone and tossed it into one of the barrel trash cans.

I hoisted myself back into the Scout, feeling duped. I had a list of choice names for Sandy running through my head. Now I was going to have to think up a new way to reach my mom. I feared I was running out of time. She wouldn't be able to evade Danny's men for long. Especially if she was high, which would impair any reasoning she had left at this point.

I had to tell Carmina. Handling this on my own was out of the question—I was in over my head. When Chet came back, I'd explain that something urgent had come up and I needed to go home. Carmina would call Price, and they'd organize a team to go after my mom.

It was my final thought before the door was wrenched open from the outside. I had one shoulder braced against it and nearly tumbled out. Catching myself from falling, I found myself face-to-face with Trigger McClure.

31

"HEY THERE, LITTLE LADY," HE SAID IN A VOICE that was honey on the surface—and black ice beneath. A ruddy glow stained his cheeks, and his eyes were slightly glazed. A beer bottle dangled from his fingers.

"Stay away from me, Trigger."

He tipped the bottle to his lips. "Nah. I don't think so."

"Then I'm going to get out of this car and I'm going to kick your ass."

Flipping his palms up, he said, "No harm here. I just wanna talk."

"Talk? Are you kid—"

"I'm not finished. It's my turn. Then it's yours. That's the way this works."

"The way this works is I'm about to shove my fist into your

jaw." To show it wasn't an empty threat, I rammed my foot into his leg, knocking him off balance.

There was a flash of anger in his eyes, immediately controlled. A sloppy smile bowed his mouth. "I finally figured out where I know you from, why you look so familiar. The pictures. Baseball camp. You were his girlfriend. He had lots of pictures of you. You look different now, it's why I didn't recognize you right away."

"What?"

"Baseball camp. Two summers ago. I bunked with your boyfriend. Reed Winslow."

Like I'd gotten a punch to the stomach, I felt the wind go out of me. I stared open-mouthed at Trigger, a flush of surprise and shock creeping up my neck. He knew Reed? Could he be the "jackass" roommate Reed had complained about? Was that why Trigger had seemed so familiar the first time I saw him? Because Reed had shown me pictures from baseball camp?

Yes.

Trigger had figured it out before me.

Pulling myself together, I pinned him with the most ludicrous and outlandish glare I could muster. "I don't know what you're talking about."

"Reed wasn't half bad. At baseball, or as a roommate." He bounced his shoulders. "I meant to keep in touch. Never did. How is good ol' Reed? The two of you still—? Nah, couldn't be. You're giving it up to Chet Falconer these days." Before I could tell him what I thought of his asinine and tasteless speculations, he continued conversationally, "The Phillies were Reed's favorite team because he was from Philadelphia. He spoke with an accent. Kinda like the New York accents you hear on TV, but not quite. You have the same accent. Looking pale, Stella. Can I offer you a drink?" he asked, feigning concern as he touched my shoulder as though to steady me.

I slapped his hand away.

"What's a girl from Philadelphia doing all the way out here in Thunder Basin? Is that part of your big secret?"

I snapped my head up. "I'm in the system, you idiot. I'm a foster kid. Yeah, I came from Philly. So what?"

"Foster kid?" He shook his head in disagreement. "That's not how I remember it. I distinctly remember Reed saying you came from money. Your mother was one of his best clients. She had a nasty habit. Yeah, I know about that. Sure you don't want a drink? You look like you could use one. No? I suppose that makes sense. Scared of turning out like your mom, isn't that right? A drunk and an addict. They say addiction can be passed down—it's genetic. But let's not get off on tangents. You're no more a foster kid than I am. Unless, of course, your mom overdosed and kicked the can. But then you'd be living with family now. That rich extended family of yours. So what are you really doing here?" he grilled me. "What's a privileged rich girl like you doing in my little corner of the world?"

"What did you say about my mom?" My voice was shaking. With anger or fear, I couldn't say.

"Oh." He showed the whites of his eyes. "You didn't know? Well, now I feel like a piece of crap. It isn't my place to tell you

Reed was dealing your mom OxyContin. He specialized in the stuff. Was quite the businessman at camp—selling it to the other players. Bragged that he made enough at camp to earn back what he'd paid in registration fees. Bragged about how he was saving up to buy his own place. He was gonna move out of his parents' house and live with his girl." His eyes zeroed in on mine. "You."

Lies. Trigger was telling lies. I knew Reed. I'd spent two years of my life in love with him. During those two years, there was no one in the world I was closer to. I would have known if he was dealing. I'd confessed to him my mom's addiction, and he'd been so sympathetic and understanding. He'd had my back. He'd loved me. There was no way he was dealing. There would have been signs.

All those nights I'd come home to find him at my house, he'd been waiting for me. I refused to even consider the possibility he'd been there for her. The night Danny Balando beat him with a tire iron, Reed had been at my house waiting for me. He wasn't there to sell my mom OxyContin.

But it was her favorite. It and heroin, which Danny supplied.

One dealer for OxyContin. And one for heroin.

No.

Oh, God, please no.

I knew Reed's mom had taken OxyContin to manage the pain from fibromyalgia, but now it was looking like he'd either sold off some of her supply, or at least discovered what the drug was capable of by watching her abuse it. How could he have hurt me this way? Tears welled in my eyes, but I refused to blink, afraid it would set them free.

Trigger leaned close, reeking of alcohol, his voice hushed with secrecy. "Don't worry, darlin'. Your secret's safe with me. Fact, I think I'll stop looking into your past altogether. Your secrets don't pique my interest in the least. I mean, you've given me no reason to want to hurt you . . . have you? Let your pretty little head think on that." His eyes hardened. "That's right, Stella. I always win."

I was trembling. The wind had picked up, cooling the air, but my chill came from inside. Secrets were starting to unravel, and I'd been selfish enough—self-absorbed enough—to think I was the only one keeping them. How could she? How could he? I must have looked like such a fool—to both of them. Stupid, gullible, blind. My shock was starting to crumble, replaced by surging betrayal and humiliation. They'd worked behind my back. Reed wasn't my ally. He was her dealer. Had he used me to get close to her? Or had he actually liked me first, and her addiction had been a fringe benefit, an opportunity to seize?

Thunder clapped and I jumped in my seat. The world had grown so dark so suddenly. A gust of icy wind whipped through the open windows, but a hot, queasy feeling roiled in my stomach. I wanted to push past Trigger and run. I wanted to run and run, but there was no escaping the truth.

A startled exclamation from Trigger jerked my attention back to him.

He stumbled sideways, trying to catch his footing. Chet stood behind him, his dark hair blowing wildly in the wind. His eyes were cold and hard, his face outlined by flashes of lightning.

"Touch me again and I'll break your hand," Trigger snarled, drawing up to full height. The two were equal in size, but there was a severity to Chet's eyes that made him look far more frightening.

"I told you to stay away from her."

"It's a free country, I can talk to whoever I want," Trigger drawled.

"True," Chet agreed, his jaw clamped tightly. "But there's a difference between talking and harassing, and having to explain it to you is testing my patience. We had an understanding, you and I. You and Stella are finished. You don't approach her. You don't look at her. You don't so much as think her name. When she's in the room, you make yourself disappear. As far as she's concerned, you don't exist."

"I'm not real keen on threats," Trigger sneered.

Before I knew what was happening, Chet slammed his knuckles into Trigger's jaw. Another brutal punch to the ribs left Trigger howling. Trigger swung his fist wildly at Chet, who turned to the side, dodging the blow, then grabbed Trigger's arm and struck his elbow joint. Chet finished his assault with a strike to Trigger's nose, taking him down.

"What the hell's wrong with you?" Trigger blubbered, scrambling to get up.

"Stay down," Chet barked. "You get up, I'll hit you again."

"I'll have you arrested," Trigger growled. But he stayed on his haunches.

"You do that. Tell the police how you got your ass kicked. I'd love to see that in the report. Course, you'll want to wait until morning to squeal, after you've sobered up—cops are touchy about underage drinking. But that's going to raise more questions, like why you waited. Not to mention the bad press. I bet pro scouts like a guy with a temper, a guy who's hard to control. A guy with loose fists."

"More threats?" Trigger spat, his face as dark as the thunderclouds overhead.

"I'm helping you see your options. These things always play out one of two ways: the hard way, or the easy way. You pick."

"You think there's a chance in hell I'll take the easy way, let you intimidate me?"

Chet laughed softly and wiped his bright red knuckles on his jeans, as though dusting them off for round two. "I hope you choose the hard way. I'm just getting started."

"You must have a death wish, you crazy sonofa—"

"Not crazy. Angry. I've got more unresolved anger than you can imagine. Hitting you is helping to release it. So tempt me, Trigger. Get back up and give me what I want."

Something changed in Trigger's face, as if he'd figured out Chet wasn't bluffing. He inched backward. He held a hand out, signaling Chet to keep his distance. His other hand cradled his jaw, which glowed violet with a fresh bruise.

"Your girlfriend isn't who you think," Trigger said, pointing accusingly at me. "The foster-kid story is a cover. She's got a mom—a strung-out mom in Philadelphia. And that's only one of her secrets. I'm digging. I'll find more. Something about her just ain't right."

"When I'm finished here, people will say the same about you," Chet said, advancing toward him.

"Ain't you listening?" Trigger yelped, scrabbling away. "I just told you your girlfriend is lying to you. To all of us."

"So she's got a few secrets, does she? What the hell does it matter to you?" Chet leaped to my defense, but I could hear an underlying pain in his voice. It hurt him to know Trigger was right. I'd lied to him, and while he apparently wasn't going to hold it against me, he wasn't ready to forget, either. His eyes flashed. "Why does she matter so much to you? Why can't you leave her alone?"

"All right, man, calm down. I'll stay away from her."

"You'll give her every opportunity to forget you exist."

"Yeah. Yeah, that too. Whatever, man."

"She won't see you again."

"Not on account of me." Trigger backed up cautiously, making no sudden movements. "I'm leaving now. Just stay away from me, you hear?"

As soon as he was a safe distance from Chet, Trigger turned and limped hurriedly away. Chet and I ducked out of the gale-force winds, shutting ourselves inside the Scout. But the wind was blowing so hard, even after we'd rolled up the windows it continued to rock the car.

Chet shook his fist, flexing his fingers. "Been a while since I hit someone. Forgot how much it hurts."

"Why did you hit him? It was so—" I searched for the word. It was so—*unlike* Chet.

"He beat you up at the Sundown, didn't he? He was your attacker," he said quietly.

I swallowed. "Chet—"

"You didn't tell me. You knew, but you kept it from me."

"I was scared you'd go after him. I was scared of seeing you in trouble. I didn't want Trigger to be the cause of a black mark on your record. Or worse."

"Yeah?" His eyes turned fiery. "Well, I'm scared of seeing you in trouble. It kills me to think of him hurting you. Nobody—not Trigger, not anyone—touches you that way. You were bruised and broken, Stella," he said, his voice climbing. "How could that not affect me? How could I not go after him? When you love someone, you look out for them. You fight their battles."

I frowned. "I don't need you to fight my battles. I'm not a fragile little girl. I can take care of myself."

His head cocked as he scrutinized me. "You're angry that I hit him."

"No."

"Like hell you're not."

"Take me home." I said it with my face to the glass, not looking at him.

"Now I get the cold shoulder?"

"I said, take me home," I said through my teeth.

"Tell me why you're pissed. That I can deal with. The cold shoulder? Silent treatment? I've lived with a guy the last year, Stella. I don't do passive-aggressive. Tell me what you're thinking.

Don't punish me with silence. Don't treat me like I'm one of your girlfriends."

"You condescending bastard."

"Tell me what's bothering you," he said, louder than before.

Tears of rage stung my eyes. I wanted to tell him I resented him for thinking I was weak. I'd been looking out for myself for years. He had no idea what I'd been through or how strong I was. But most of all, it scared me to think he was falling in love with me. I wasn't going to let him fight my battles, only to leave him. It wasn't fair. It was a cowardly thing to do, and I was done being a coward. Leaving him would be easier if I didn't have to deal with knowing he loved me.

He tried again. "You're pissed that I fought over you. You don't like male aggression. Or violence. Did someone hurt you? Someone in your past? Is that it?"

I turned on him, furious. "Shut up, Chet. Just shut up."

At the sight of my face, he stopped abruptly. "What's wrong? Dammit, just tell me. I won't fight anymore, if that's what you want. I just need to understand you."

Plowing my hands through my hair, I tried to calm my thumping heart. I wanted to tell Chet the truth. It hovered on the edge, just like my tears. I could tell him. It would feel so good to be honest with him, to have someone to share my burden, to open the floodgates and finally be free of these toxic secrets.

But telling him the truth would only give me momentary relief; it wouldn't solve my problems. In fact, it would compound them. And it would entangle Chet in a web of danger that wasn't of his making. So I locked down my pain and ordered myself to swallow the words I desperately wanted to get out.

Sitting stiffly, Chet spoke first, his voice flat. "Fine. I'll take you home."

I found Carmina in the backyard, latching the storm shutters while tumbleweeds and leaves pelted the house.

"Bad feeling in the air," she called over her shoulder as I ran to help. "This storm isn't holding back." She saw my face. "What on earth's the matter, Stella?"

Even though I wished I didn't have to tell her, I didn't see an option. Between doing what I wanted and doing the smart thing, there was only one answer. So I told her that Trigger had figured out I was from Philadelphia. Then I told her my mom had left rehab. She didn't ask how Trigger had pieced together my past or how I'd gotten the clinic's number; she immediately went in and called Deputy Price.

Trigger's discovery was a threat to my safety. A minor one, but he would keep digging. Eventually he might find something that could genuinely endanger me. I wasn't safe here anymore.

I was leaving Thunder Basin.

32

THAT NIGHT, I LISTENED TO THE STORM HOWL AND
rage. Gusting air lashed the windowpanes and hail bombarded
the roof. From my bedroom window, I watched the frozen pel-
lets paint the lawn white and turn the road to ice. The world was
so dark, it took flashes of lightning to illuminate the landscape.
Cattle and horses had vanished from the pastures, and prairie
grass flapped like the waves of an angry sea.

The wild tempest mimicked my own raging heart. I thought
of my secrets, trapped there, dashing themselves like wild
birds to get out. Even now, I felt them overcoming me, and I
wondered where Estella's vicious strength had gone. Months
ago, I'd made the decision to lie to the authorities. I'd told the
detectives the story I wanted them to believe. Even if I hadn't
fully realized what I was doing, I'd trusted myself to be strong.

I'd promised myself I'd guard my secrets until I died.

I did not know they would kill me.

The violent thrashing outside made my ears ache, and at last I put my headphones on. But tonight the throbbing, guitar-heavy music of Nathaniel's cassette tapes didn't distract me.

The next morning, the sky was a brilliant shade of sapphire. Trash and branches littered the yard, and puddles of mud pocked the road, but they were the only evidence of last night's storm. Birds sang merrily and the dew on the grass caught the morning sun. The air was calm, enveloping my shoulders like a warm, thick shawl.

A note on the kitchen counter told me Carmina had gone to the grocery store for milk, but I wasn't fooled. She was buying food for my trip. I imagined crusty sourdough rolls, roast beef, cheese, and chips would find their way into a brown paper sack with my name on it. In Carmina's mind, nothing was worth doing without food, especially meat, potatoes, and bread.

Deputy Price was scheduled to arrive tomorrow night to transport me to my new living quarters. This time, I was determined not to resent him for it. It was his job. My job was to let him keep me safe. End of story. No attitude this time, and no longing to stay where I could not. To prove my point, I reminded myself I would have been leaving Thunder Basin in a couple weeks anyway. So what if the date had been pushed up? Get over it.

I inhaled deeply. I would not think about tomorrow. I had nearly thirty-six hours left in Thunder Basin, and I wanted to make the most of them. Chin up, be brave. That was my strategy. But deep down, I was scared of so many things. Of leaving this place I'd learned to love. Of breaking Chet's heart. Of letting go of Carmina. Of facing the world without both of them. I didn't want, or know how, to say good-bye.

Maybe it was better this way. When Deputy Price came for me, there wouldn't be time for a sappy, drawn-out farewell. We'd have to keep things quick, tidy. I'd be in the car, Thunder Basin miles behind me, before the loss and heartache hit. I'd deal with it alone, like I always had.

Outside, I fingered the petunias in Carmina's whiskey barrels. I drank in their fragrance, searing it to memory. I ran my bare feet over her warm grass. I felt the sun on my face and listened to the sweet, friendly song of the meadowlarks.

I was padding barefoot up the drive, sifting through the morning mail, when I heard tires chew the road behind me.

Sunlight glinted off the car's windshield as it pulled into the drive. The driver swung out, shielding her eyes as she sized up the white clapboard house. She wore a floral dress—cleaned, ironed—and sandals. Her soft brown hair swung over her shoulders; it was freshly washed and full of bounce. The hollow look in the woman's eyes was gone. When her gaze came to rest on me, I saw an eagerness, a brightness, that whirled me into the past.

"Mom?" I said, stunned.

"Baby doll!" She sashayed toward me, her arms stretched wide. The next thing I knew, I was smashed against her chest. "Oh, honey. Your mama's missed you!"

I detached myself. "What are you doing here?"

She pinched my cheek. "Is that any way to greet your mama? Let me have a look at you." She held me by the shoulders, her eyes drinking me in. "I can't believe how dark you are! I see how it is, me cooped up under fluorescent lights all summer while you're out here sunbathing." She clucked her tongue. "Hardly seems fair."

I just stared at her. Seeing her here, washed and sober—it didn't seem real.

"Well," she said, plopping herself down in Carmina's porch swing and crossing her slender legs prettily. "Tell me about your summer. Tell me everything." She glanced around the yard with a smirk. "I'm impressed you lasted as long as you have. What do people do for fun around here, anyway?"

"How did you find me?"

She let out a hoot. "How do you think? I'm your mother. Those Feds had to tell me where they were keeping you. I demanded to know right from the start. Did you think I'd let them drag you off and hide you without my knowing?"

"I called the rehab center. They said you checked out. I thought—"

"Surprise!" she said, throwing her hands up and wriggling her fingers. "I checked out early. What kind of boring suss would I be if I told you I was coming? I wanted to surprise you. Anyway, don't worry a thing about me. I'm clean. My whole outlook has changed. Much as I hated that place"—she wrinkled her nose—"I'll be the first to admit it was what I needed. You were right, sweet baby girl. I needed help. Well, I got it. This is our chance to start fresh. A do-over. Things are going to be different this time, Estella."

"Stella," I corrected automatically. But she was right. Things were different. Way different. Who was this overly affectionate woman? Two years ago, my mom had taken a path that led her straight to the intersection of depressed and strung-out. It was hard to remember her as anything but lost, disinterested, and, intentionally or not, very cold and indifferent toward me.

She flapped a hand dismissively. "You're Estella to me. And I'm Mama to you. The Feds and their documents don't change that."

"I—What are you doing here?" I repeated, still dazed.

"Would you stop asking that? Makes me feel unwelcome. You don't have to stay here anymore, baby girl. We're done with this place. I came to pick you up. It's me and you again. We're going to buy a house, get jobs, put down roots. Oh, we'll miss Philly, but we'll find something almost as good. I know you love Boston." Her tone was rosy, full of hope. "Just a hop, skip, and a jump away from our old life. Now, tell me you don't like the sound of that."

"Boston," I echoed.

"That's right, sweetheart. We're moving to Boston."

Stunned, I found myself unable to draw up a response. Before I could draft one, Carmina's truck rounded the drive. She braked at my mom's car, clearly not expecting it, then backed up and parked alongside it. I didn't know what it said that my first reaction upon seeing her was sweeping nervousness, a strange tingle in my bones of wanting to step away from my mom, to dissociate myself from her. I'm ashamed of her, I realized. I felt uneasy at the thought of introducing her to Carmina. I didn't know how to explain what she was doing here. Carmina hadn't planned for this. She didn't like surprises.

Carmina hopped out, her red boots landing solidly on the drive. She looked between me and my mom, and her face changed. It grew watchful. I guessed she saw a resemblance, because her first words were "You must be Savannah."

"That's right. And you are?" It seemed to me that my mom's voice was unnecessarily cool, and I cast a quick glance of apology at Carmina.

"Carmina Songster. Welcome to Thunder Basin."

"I'm here to pick up Stella. This shouldn't take long. Stella, darling, why don't you go on inside, pack your bags?"

I eyed Carmina, whose expression was unflappable. "I wasn't aware you were coming to fetch Stella today," she said.

"I wasn't aware I needed your permission," my mom returned, her voice tainted with something subtle. Resentment, perhaps.

"Permission? Heavens, no. Not from me, anyway. You're her legal guardian."

"I'm her mother."

"Yes, of course. I wonder, though," Carmina mused patiently. "Have you thought this through? If you take Stella from Thunder Basin, you'll have to notify the U.S. Marshals Service. They need to keep tabs on her, since she's agreed to testify for the prosecution. This was all explained in the contract you signed with the marshals upon entering WITSEC."

"I don't need to tell them anything," my mom said loftily. "The program is voluntary. We can leave witness protection at any point. If Estella and I go, they can't tell us what to do."

"Would you do that?" Carmina asked, her voice still measured. "Would you put Stella in that kind of danger? If you leave, you'll have to return to your old identities. The U.S. marshals will no longer be responsible for your safety. I know you want your old life back, but it's no longer safe. It isn't an option. I know moving on is hard, but you have to try. You need to think about your daughter now. What she needs."

"I know how to keep my daughter safe," my mom said, clutching my shoulders protectively. "I'm not taking her back to Philadelphia."

"You're making a mistake," Carmina told her bluntly.

"Go on, Stella," my mom repeated more firmly, her eyes flaring as they locked with Carmina's. "Our flight leaves at noon."

"You bought tickets?" Panic seemed to close my throat. She was really going through with this. What about rehab? She was clean now, but how long would it last? Would she even make it to Boston before relapsing?

"You still have weeks of rehab left," I said.

"I told you I'm clean," she said, flustered and irritated. That Southern charm was chipping away, revealing the anxious, defensive woman I remembered. "I always said I'd quit when I was ready. And I've quit. Now, get your bags. We don't have a lot of time."

I suddenly feared I wouldn't have time to say good-bye to Chet. To Inny and Dixie Jo. I couldn't go without letting them know how much they meant to me. How could I leave Chet without apologizing for last night? Without setting things right? This wasn't how I wanted to remember him: hurt and frustrated while I shut him out. It wasn't fair to him. It made me ache just thinking about it.

"Why don't you come in and I'll make you both breakfast," Carmina suggested to my mom. "You can't travel on an empty stomach. Have you eaten, Stella?" she asked me, before my mom could reject the offer.

I shook my head no, grateful for the opportunity to slow time. Everything felt rushed. How many nights had I lain awake in my cramped bedroom upstairs, counting down the days until I was back on the East Coast, surrounded by strangers in a city brimming with energy and opportunity? I'd dreamed of returning to Estella's life. But that was a fantasy. A secret wish you kept inside, because it didn't belong in the real world. I couldn't go back and I couldn't leave WITSEC. But I also couldn't abandon my mom.

"Carmina makes the best breakfast," I told my mom. "Pancakes and eggs and bacon. It won't take long."

"I had coffee on the drive," she answered brusquely. At my fallen face, she sighed impatiently. "A couple minutes, Stella. Then we really need to go."

Carmina showed my mom to the downstairs powder room to freshen up, and I went upstairs to pack. One bag was all I needed. I hadn't amassed much in the way of belongings over the summer. Most of what I'd be taking, I realized, were memories carefully collected and stored inside me. For no apparent reason, a surge of tears brimmed my eyes.

The door opened. "Stella," Carmina said gently.

I drew my sleeve across my eyes. "I'm okay. Really. I'll be fine. Everything will be fine," I blubbered. "This won't take long. I don't have much to pack. I've hardly gained anything." I glanced at the meager spread of clothes I'd placed on my bed. My yellow sundress. The boots Carmina had made me. Chet's hat.

"Funny," she said, sitting on the edge of the mattress, "I was just thinking how much I've gained by having you here this summer. You were a blessing, Stella. I went to bed every night, my heart filled with a little more joy. I thank God for the time I had with you."

Unable to contain myself, I threw my arms around her. "Oh, Carmina. Do you really want me to go?"

"I don't want you to go," she said, blinking, but not fast enough to keep her eyes from dampening. "Oh, Stella. I don't want you to go. Can't you see that? Deep down, I don't think you want to go either."

"I don't want to take care of my mom, but if I don't, who will? She'll never make it alone."

Her smile was sweet and sad. She bent my head to her shoulder and ran her worn, loving fingers over my hair. "Stella, if you leave, there is nothing stopping Danny Balando from finding you and your mother," she said gravely, the first note of concern seeping into her voice. "She may tell herself Boston isn't Philadelphia, but she's walking as close to the fire as she can without getting burned—or so she tells herself. You can't get in that car with her. Do you understand? Legally I can't stop her from taking you. She's your guardian, and as much as I don't want to, I have to follow the law. Deputy Price and I can help you file for emancipation, but it will take time. If you go with your mom, the clock will work against us."

"What are you saying I should do?"

"Go to Chet's. Go out the back door. Stay there until I come get you. Let me deal with your mother. I'll try to help her see the danger in her plan."

Three months ago, that's exactly what I would have done. Run away. Dodged my problems rather than solved them. Wished my mother away. Pretended she didn't exist, then resented her for doing just that. Running away hadn't worked three months ago, and it wouldn't work now.

For once, I had to be honest. And show her how strong I'd become. I needed to tell her I wasn't going to Boston and I hoped she didn't either. If she really wanted to try to make things work between us, she had to finish rehab. I knew it wasn't the be-all and end-all, but it was a step. A show of good faith.

"No. I should be the one to tell her," I said.

"Are you sure?"

"Yes."

Carmina squeezed my hand. "Do you want me to come with you?"

I shook my head no. My mom would be more defensive if she thought this was Carmina's idea.

I moved down the staircase, my hand slick on the worn banister, feeling the weight of each footfall. I didn't know how my mom would react. Or maybe I did. And that's why my legs felt watery and my stomach tight. I tempered the feeling of nerves and dwindling confidence, and entered the living room to see my mom bent over Carmina's purse.

"What are you doing?" I sputtered.

She jumped. In one swift movement, her hand was out of the purse and in her own pocket. When she turned, her smile was as smooth and sweet as candy. "Hi, sweetheart."

"What did you put in your pocket?"

"Listen, darling, I was thinking we could stay in the city tonight. Play tourists through the weekend, then start looking for an apartment in the suburbs the following—"

"What did you put in your pocket?" I demanded, striding forward. I tried to grab her, but she swatted my hand away.

"Don't touch me, Estella. I'm—I don't like the way you're looking at me."

"What did you take from Carmina's purse?"

"I thought I dropped a hairpin—"

"Money. Is that what you took?" My voice was edged with anger. "So you can buy drugs? I knew you didn't clean up. Too easy." I could have kicked myself for believing her—no, for *want-ing* to believe. We were rewinding the clock. My mom was back to being a fountain of lies. I was back to being undeserving of any respect. "You checked out early because you couldn't go another day without getting high!"

"Hush, Estella," my mom snapped. "Don't you say those things about your own mother. It's not nice."

"You stole from Carmina." My jaw was quivering. "After

everything she's done for me. She took me in when no one else wanted me."

"I wanted you, baby—" she began, reaching for me.

I threw my hands up, shielding myself. "Stop it. Just—stop." I closed my eyes, tears squeezing out. "You have to leave. You need to go. Back to rehab, somewhere else, I don't care. But you're leaving. And I'm not going with you."

I felt ill. My knees were doing a poor job of holding me up, but I had to keep it together and get her out. It was the only thought drumming in my head. I gripped the wall, trying to flush out the worst of the nausea. I didn't want to remember all those times I'd come home to find her lying in a puddle of vomit, her skin blue, her pupils tiny pinpricks. I'd wonder if she was dead, secretly hope she was. . . .

"I need you, baby." Her voice cracked.

"Stop. Leave. Please. Just go." I was begging now.

Her eyes were wet. But all those nights before, her eyes had been dry. She'd stared vacantly at her bedroom ceiling, and I'd pulled off her shoes and covered her in blankets, then watched over her through the night. Would she live? What would become of me? I'd spent hours pondering those questions.

For years now, I'd taken care of her. I'd wanted to believe I was helping her. It had taken coming to Thunder Basin to see the truth. I wasn't helping anyone. Least of all her. The longer I protected her, the more people she would hurt.

"I can't go alone," she whispered, her face a blotchy mix of pink and translucent white. In that moment, she really did look like a child. Small and frightened.

"If you stay, I'll tell Carmina."

"You can't do this to me."

"I won't let you steal from Carmina."

My mom made a bewildered sound. "Where will I go?"

"If you're smart, back to rehab."

Now her eyes flashed. "Don't look at me like that. Don't judge me. Don't stand there all self-righteous and look down at me. You have no idea what it was like for me. I kept the perfect house, I hosted the best parties, I made his friends laugh. I gave him a beautiful baby girl. I did everything right, and he left me!" Her voice was inflamed, bordering on hysterical. In the next moment, it tumbled to weeping despair. "It wasn't supposed to be like this. I had dreams. I had—I had—" She covered her face with her hands. "I have nothing. It's all gone," she sobbed. "If you leave me too, what will happen to me?"

My head was pounding. I didn't want her to have this power over me—to draw me in, then cast me away. Then suck me back in. I hated being caught in her tide. I'd spent years at its mercy, feeling moments away from capsizing.

And then I'd come to Thunder Basin. The tide had receded. This summer had been a secret treasure. A guilty, selfish, gratifying escape. I'd been a fool to think it would last. Carmina was right. Our pasts were hitched to us; we couldn't outrun them.

I felt the tide tugging at my heels, but this time I would not surrender to it. She was my mom. I wanted her to get better. Deep down, I cared about her. But I had to remember that she was the mother. Not the other way around. I couldn't make her do anything.

"You need to leave." I pushed the words out from someplace deep inside. A stronger version of myself was speaking now.

"You can't do this."

"I can't protect you anymore. I can't lie." I wanted to confront her about Reed, too, but given everything else, her relationship with him seemed insignificant. I let it pass. But I would not ignore that she wasn't better, wasn't ready to be my mom again.

Her face blank, she turned to the door. I shut my eyes and listened to her uncertain steps moving farther away. My chest was painfully tight. I felt a heavy loss inside me that was both sorrow and relief.

The door shut behind her, and I sank to the floor.

The drag of the tide released me.

THE SETTING SUN DRAGGED AWAY THE DAY'S HEAT,
and as I rocked in Carmina's porch swing, drinking a glass of her
sweet tea, the night air felt almost balmy as it whispered over my
skin. The weather was changing, shifting toward autumn. Summer
was drawing to an end. So was my time here, in this quiet,
beautiful refuge. Tomorrow was coming, and it was painful to
think about. Tomorrow meant change. It meant saying good-bye.
Starting from scratch all over again.

When I tried to imagine where Deputy Price would take me,
what my new bedroom would look like, what my new job would
be, everything went blurry. I wanted to stay here. I wasn't ready
to leave. Part of me, a very small, unrealistic part, daydreamed
about what it would be like to stay permanently. To make Thunder Basin my home.

But even if Trigger hadn't jeopardized my cover, could I ever feel satisfied here? Or would I grow bored, restless, and resentful? More importantly, could I make a life here when I'd lied to everyone?

No. No, I could not.

I had to be realistic. It was time to move on. Sooner than I'd planned, but guess what? That was life. I could cry over it, or I could be a big girl and tough it out.

I tucked my knees to my chest and drank in the candy-like fragrance of the August lilies. A swollen yellow moon drifted on the horizon. It could have swallowed ten Philadelphia moons; it was that large. Crickets sang in the bushes, lulling me until I felt heavy and drowsy.

The screen door squeaked and Carmina's boots sounded on the wood planks. "Look at you, lazy as a pet coon."

I smiled up at her, raising my glass. "Your tea is really good. I wish I'd thought to have you teach me the recipe. Now it's too late."

Carmina took a moment to answer. "Don't fall asleep out here. You'll give the mosquitoes a feast."

I eyed her denim skirt and starched blouse. "Where are you going?"

"Bible study. I'll be home by ten."

"Don't come back early on account of me."

"I'll go to Bible study and then I'll come directly home, like I always do," she said practically.

"Or you could ask Pastor Lykins out for a drink."

She narrowed her eyes in disapproval. "Pastor Lykins doesn't drink."

"Then invite him over for tea."

"All the caffeine? He wouldn't sleep a wink. You shouldn't be drinking it this late either."

"Trust me, if Lykins comes over, he won't want to sleep. I've seen the way he looks at you. He might not drink with those holy lips, but I bet he uses them to—" I made obnoxious smooching noises.

"Stella," she chided, then continued on her way—but not before I saw pink stain her cheeks.

"You only live once. Bring him home, and I swear I'll stay out of the way. You won't even know I'm here."

"Why would I care if you're here?"

"Oh, Carmina." I tossed my hands in the air. "You're hopeless."

"Goodnight, Stella. Behave yourself while I'm gone."

"Not if I have anything to say about it!" I called as she climbed into the truck.

She waved me off, and I watched her taillights bounce down the road.

I sprawled in the porch swing, feeling the caffeine from the tea stir my blood. I wasn't in the mood to watch TV. I felt restless and uncontainable. It was a perfect night. Fat moon. A sea of stars. Just the right amount of heat rising off the ground. A good night to take care of long-delayed business.

Upstairs, I changed into my swimsuit and twisted my hair into a high bun. Glancing in the mirror, I noted my mom was right.

My skin was honey brown, almost the same shade as my eyes. And my arms and legs were toned, shapely. Even my shoulders had muscle definition. A summer's worth of shuttling trays of food would do that.

I thought of my best friend, Tory, and all the hours we'd spent scrutinizing ourselves in the mirror. Front pose, side pose, glancing-over-the-shoulder pose. Our ideal body had been long, lanky, and as iridescent as a pearl. We dieted religiously and we never worked out, because we didn't want to bulk up.

A slow smile dawned on my reflection. I'd been clueless. Or maybe my perception had shifted. Either way, I liked the image before me. I felt strong, confident, and newly discovered.

Since I hadn't brought my cover-up from home, I tugged on a pair of frayed denim shorts and looped a towel around my neck.

Then I headed to Chet's.

For nearly three months our lives had intersected, each of us spinning madly around the other like planets in orbit. How did you break that kind of gravitational force without someone getting hurt? This morning, I'd considered leaving with my mom. No painful good-byes. Cut my losses and run. It was easier to leave than be left.

Without realizing it, I had slipped into Estella's tough, impenetrable armor. This perfect summer with the perfect guy? Wouldn't last. Nothing ever did. Fold while you were ahead, damn everyone else.

But when I'd nearly left with my mom, I wasn't worried Chet was a summer fling.

I was terrified he was more.

A moment later I was on his porch. He answered my knock, standing shirtless and barefoot before me. His damp hair hung in his eyes and he smelled of soap and late-night coffee. He leaned a hard, sculpted arm on the doorjamb and peered down at me.

"I'm sorry about last night," I said. "It was unfair of me to shut you out. Can we put it in the past? Can we be friends again?"

The tension went out of those strong, set shoulders. "Never stopped."

My smile was part relief, part hopeful. "Want to go swimming?"

He studied me, his eyes keenly fixed on mine, as if he saw something in them I myself wasn't aware of. His face changed, grew discerning.

I wondered if he could sense the strange, restless stirring inside me, or read the thoughts burned on my mind. Thoughts of him. The hard grip of his hands. The solid press of his body. The pressure of his mouth tasting mine. His breath, rough and hot, in my ear. The unquenchable ache in me that only he could satisfy.

He didn't bother to change out of his jeans. He took my hand and led the way, and that's when I knew the urgent stirring in my blood wasn't mine alone.

I stood on the dock at the edge of the swimming hole, watching Chet monkey-walk up the thick, sloping tree trunk that jutted over the water. A ribbon of moonlight ran to shore, and I slapped at mosquitoes whining in my ears.

At the top of the tree, Chet reached into the leafy branches and took a rope in both hands. Feeding it no slack, he maneuvered his feet onto the side of the trunk, putting himself in a position to rappel down. With a forceful push, he sprang and dropped, sailing over the swimming hole in a graceful crescent. When his heels swung above the deepest part of the swimming hole, he let go of the rope, plunging into the water—but not without first letting out an enthusiastic whoop.

His head resurfaced, and he shook his hair like a dog would. "Water feels great."

Bending my knees, I dove off the dock, squeezing my eyes tightly as that first blast of cool liquid electrified my skin. After a few underwater strokes, I came up for air. The water was deep; I had to tread to stay afloat. Chet was a couple of feet away, doing likewise.

Slowly, slowly, he swam closer.

I didn't move, shivering with excitement. His eyes were alert and hungry, and it made my body pulse with a wild, reckless thrill. I felt the seductive whisper of his fingertips brush my stomach. A tempting, teasing, underwater touch that made every nerve ending dance and burn.

I searched for his hand in the murky water. His fingers locked around my wrist, reeling me close. In the cool water, his skin shed heat. It licked up my body, dissolving my fears, my heartache, and all the guilt that had been yoked to my shoulders. This was why I'd gone to Chet tonight. I needed him. I felt his heart pounding, urgent and alive. He needed me, too.

I'd made up my mind. I wasn't leaving Thunder Basin without sharing something real with him. A true part of myself. No more pretending to be someone I wasn't. I was ready to exorcise the past and give him the real me.

My legs tangled with his; I felt his strong, powerful kicks churning the water. His knee slipped between my thighs and it made the breath go out of me.

"It's deep," I said, my toes scraping cool, empty nothingness.

But I wasn't sinking underwater. I was sinking into Chet, floating weightlessly as his mouth found my throat, nipping and grazing, each taste causing a riot of heat to stir my blood faster. I clutched his hair and arched backward, my knees coming to rest on his thighs. The water rushed everywhere, a potent contrast of cool and heat. Chet held me up, that wet mouth roaming lower. My breath caught as his tongue teased the elastic of my swim top. I felt myself go hard in some places, melting in others. Only half aware, I realized this was pleasure. Selfish, greedy, wondrous pleasure.

We bumped against the dock, the post hard at my back.

He looked straight into my eyes. They were filled with a question. And a promise.

And when I didn't stop him, his mouth came down on mine. The kiss wasn't soft or restrained. He pushed deeper, his hands guiding my legs to lock around his hips. Those rough, strong hands skimmed over my legs. They spread, touching everywhere.

"I want you." His gravelly voice tore me with longing.

This time he didn't stop me when I reached for him. His teeth sank into my shoulder, muffling a groan. He pressed my back to the post, the hot, ravenous look in his blue eyes the only warning I had to hold on tight.

Later, I hauled myself up the dock ladder and sprawled on the weather-beaten wood. I was deliriously exhausted. Chet lay beside me, gathering my body to curve against his. He kissed my bare shoulder.

"Wish we could stay here all night," he murmured.

"Carmina will wait up for me."

He tasted my ear. "I don't want to stop holding you. I put clean sheets on the bed this morning."

I smiled. Truthfully, sleeping here with Chet sounded wonderful and perfect. I loved the feel of him. I loved being with him.

Until that whispering voice reminded me this was still a lie. I'd given him a part of me, but I hadn't given him the whole truth. Chet was falling in love with a shadow version of me, someone who was real and not real at the same time. Someone who was gone tomorrow.

When he kissed me again, letting his mouth linger, I knew it was time to tell him.

I rolled over. "Do you believe what Trigger said yesterday? That I'm keeping secrets?"

The moon was bright enough that I could see my reflection swimming in his eyes. Something in them changed at my question; I saw a flicker of unrest, unease.

"Everyone has secrets," he said, not quite answering my question.

"Do your secrets eat away at you? Do they keep you up at night?"

He gazed at me a long time. "Do you want to tell me your secrets?" he finally asked quietly.

I swallowed. I had to tell someone, because my secret was carving away at me, piece by piece. I was in danger of losing myself. Still, I felt myself stalling.

"Then I'll tell you mine," he said.

I sat up. "Your secret?"

"Are you cold?" He fetched our towels and tucked mine around my shoulders, rubbing briskly. Scrubbing off with his own towel, he sat on the dock facing me. He cleared his throat.

"Last year my parents died in a car crash," he began. "You already know that. What you don't know is that my best friend was in the car with them." He gave a throaty, trembling laugh. "My best friend, Nathaniel, was Carmina's grandson."

I uncurled his balled fist and cradled it to my cheek.

"I don't talk about that night with anyone," Chet continued. "I know what people would say: That I can't blame myself. I couldn't have known the three people I loved most would be hit by an oncoming car. And they're right—I didn't know. But I wasn't in jail that night for no reason. I put myself there. I'd had too much to drink and I was speeding. I got picked up. I can't blame Carmina for arresting me. I was the one who chose to pick up that bottle. I made a mistake that will torment me until I die. I haven't taken a drink since that night. Doesn't appeal to me—makes me sick. I make myself sick." He scrubbed his hands over his face, his voice turning haunted. "That was Carmina's last night on the police force. She asked for an early dismissal, and since she was only a couple months from retirement, they gave it to her. They knew she needed time to grieve. She's the only one who knows I was drinking. She took great care to make sure the truth didn't come out. I suspect, in part, because she felt responsible to my parents. She couldn't save them from me, but she decided to save my future. She gave me a second chance when I didn't deserve one. Yeah, Stella, it eats away at me. Yeah, it keeps me up at night. People think I'm a victim. A selfless brother who sacrificed his future to raise his brother." He wagged his damp head, water dripping down his cheek like tears. "I'm a guy who's desperately trying to make amends, but a lifetime of amends won't bring my parents and Nathaniel back."

I held him tightly, but I didn't try to contradict or console him. He didn't want me to make him feel better or chase away his demons. He simply wanted me to listen and try my best not to judge. I knew, because it's exactly what I wanted.

"You don't have to tell me your secret, Stella," he said, "but I wanted you to know mine. If you hate me for it, I understand. God knows I hate myself."

I stared at him, my heart aching. I felt closer to Chet than ever. We had something in common. Not Chet and Stella, but Chet and Estella. We both had a shameful, destructive secret. And we were both ready to let it out, no matter how ugly the aftermath. Lying had not solved my problems—it had made them worse. I couldn't speak for Chet, but my secret had rotted me on the inside. I felt cold, black, and empty where I wanted to feel genuine, hopeful, and alive.

"I have a secret too." I didn't pause to ask myself if this was a mistake.

"Stella—"

"No. Don't try to stop me. I know you want to make sure I'm ready, but if I look for excuses, I'll keep this secret until it poisons me. I need you to listen." My voice wobbled, and I drew a stabilizing breath. "My name isn't Stella Gordon. And I'm not a foster kid from Knoxville. Before I came to Thunder Basin, I lived in Philadelphia with my mom. I—my real name is Estella Goodwinn. I witnessed a crime and now I'm in the federal witness protection program."

I couldn't meet his gaze. I was afraid he'd look at me with new eyes, as though he'd never seen me before, and the past three months would be erased in an instant. Moments ago, I'd known exactly how Chet felt about me. Now I couldn't be certain of anything. Except, maybe, how I felt about him. I was afraid of losing him. The thought sliced me with a fear that ran deeper than the fear of being discovered by Danny Balando.

I felt his arms encircle me and heard him murmur, "Come here."

Because I didn't want to feel alone, I let him gather me in his arms.

"You're in witness protection," he repeated, his voice mostly steady. "And your name's not Stella. Am I allowed to ask questions? Because I've got a few. But they can wait. If you're not ready, I can wait."

He had questions. I hadn't thought about those. My hands were shaking and I squeezed them into fists. Opened, closed.

He said, "I don't know much about witness protection, but I'm thinking the crime wasn't run-of-the-mill. I'm thinking drugs, human trafficking, weapons, terrorism—something serious. Organized crime. Run by dangerous people."

I nodded, and while Chet tried to keep his expression normal, ice-cold fear seized his eyes.

I said, "The U.S. attorney's office sent me to Thunder Basin to hide. Because the man who's hunting me? The man I agreed to testify against? He's very dangerous."

"This man—he's in Philadelphia."

"Yes."

His eyes were glued to mine, and the worry hadn't faded. "Is he Mafia?"

"Cartel. One of the largest controlling drug trade on the East Coast."

"Are you safe?"

"I think so. Carmina thinks so too. She's part of my cover story. I'm sorry I lied to you. I wanted you to know the real me, but I was scared."

Chet shook his head. "Don't say that. I know the real you. I haven't spent the entire summer with a stranger. You may think you're a good actor, but no one can keep up a charade for that long. I know you," he repeated, each word spoken with confidence.

"I'm glad you think so," I said quietly. "But there's more I lied about. A lot more." Dredging up courage, I drew a supporting breath. "The crime I witnessed was murder. In my house. I had come home late, very late, and there was blood everywhere. A man had been shot—in the head." I squeezed my eyes to flush out the horrific, unwanted memory. "There were pieces of him splattered on the wall. All that blood . . . it painted the walls." My breath came choppy and quick.

"Breathe," Chet instructed me. He took my hands, squeezing them gently, rubbing circles over my knuckles. "Nice and easy. Deep breaths. You're not there anymore. You're here with me."

"The dead man—I knew him. He was my mom's first dealer. She called him the Pharmacist. He'd fronted her a lot of prescriptions, but she'd never paid him back. She dropped him hard and fast when Danny Balando came into her life. Danny supplied her with heroin and put on a show of being interested in her, probably to get her to buy more. She thought he was her boyfriend. The night the Pharmacist was murdered, he came to our house demanding money. My mom left the room, pretending to get cash, but instead she called Danny. Trigger was telling the truth, Chet. My mom's an addict. She isn't dead. She spent the summer in rehab."

I paused, giving him a moment to reply, but he watched me in silence, a ghost of something dark and strained shadowing his eyes.

"My boyfriend, Reed, was at my house that night too. He was upstairs, asleep in my bed, waiting for me to come home. He heard the shot and ran downstairs. Danny dragged him outside and beat him to make him forget what he'd seen and threaten

357

him into silence. At least, that's what I used to think." I pressed my fingers to my eyes, trying to alleviate the sting. "Now I'm not sure. I'm not sure of anything. Part of me thinks Reed might have been selling my mom OxyContin and Danny found out. If Reed was selling my mom OxyContin, it would have competed with Danny's heroin. What if Danny beat Reed to scare him off his turf? That's how he viewed my mom—as property. She thinks he was her boyfriend, but he wasn't. He was a criminal. A dangerous, manipulative, lying criminal. He was the worst thing that ever happened to her."

Chet dragged his thumbs over my cheeks, drying them. "That must have ripped you up, seeing your mom treated that way. And it must have angered you to watch her allow it."

"I knew Danny Balando was dangerous, but after I called the police to report the murder, and they took me to the station, I found out they'd been trying to catch him for years. They believed he was deeply embedded in the cartel, but they didn't have proof. They'd never been able to make a case stick."

"You helped them catch him."

A new wave of shame rolled through me. "When I came home that night, the night of the murder, my mom was sitting in a chair, feet away from the Pharmacist's dead body. Her face was sheet white. Mascara had run down her eyes. She was shivering. And she was holding a gun in her lap. The murder weapon.

"I panicked. There wasn't time to think. I didn't want to lose her—I was scared of being alone. And in some messed-up, twisted way, I was used to taking care of her, so the urge to protect her was my first instinct. The gun—I took it. I got in my car and drove. I knew where the remains of an old colonial mansion were. Downhill from the ruins, deep in the woods, I knew there was an icehouse cut into the hillside. An iron grate barred the entrance, and vines and weeds had grown to cover the facade. No one played there, not even children. I tossed the gun through the iron bars. No one would ever find it. Then I drove home and called the police. I told my mom to take whatever drugs she needed to pass out. For the first time, I wanted her high. I told her that when she woke, the police would question her, and she should say she knew nothing. I told her I would handle everything. I called the police, and when they came, I—I—"

"You told them Danny Balando shot the Pharmacist."

"I lied to the police to cover for my mom. I never imagined they'd put us in witness protection. I never imagined I'd have to lie to the prosecutor, the U.S. marshals who risked their lives to guard me, and a whole townful of people I'd grow to care about. Over and over I had to lie, each time feeling more guilty and ashamed and trapped. I thought the police would arrest Danny and he'd be out of my mom's life for good. There wasn't time to think it all through. I had to act. Danny Balando was a horrible person. It seemed fair that he should go to prison. I told myself I was doing the right thing." I looked into Chet's eyes, too lost in my grief to see what emotions were playing out on his face. "Danny Balando is a terrible man, but he isn't guilty of this crime. My mother is."

"You covered for your mom because she was all you had. You

loved her, and you wanted to protect her. That's what love does, Stella. It makes us loyal. Fiercely loyal."

"I lied to the police. I could be charged with perjury. I could go to prison. If I come forward, my mom will definitely go to prison." I stared helplessly at him, wishing he could tell me it wouldn't happen that way, but I'd had the entire summer to think it through from every angle. I was backed into a corner. There wasn't a trapdoor I could help my mom escape through. She'd committed murder. If I came forward, she would go down for it.

If I didn't come forward, she'd continue hurting people. She would steal, lie, and cheat. Anything to get high. If the cravings became bad enough, I feared her crimes would become more dangerous and destructive. I was being forced to choose between my mom and strangers I might never meet. But those strangers were someone's daughter. Someone's boyfriend. Someone's loved one.

Chet took my face in his hands, resting his forehead against mine. I could feel the sweet softness of his breath. His hands were cool and steady, and as he stroked my hair behind my ears, I had no choice but to look at him. "I wish I could make it go away, or take it from you and deal with it myself," he said. "I wouldn't think twice—if I could take this off your shoulders, I would. It's agony to see you hurting, especially since all I ever wanted was to make you happy. To love you."

"How can you love me?" I said, crying softly. "I'm a liar."

"Don't," he warned. "Don't say that again. Early on this summer, back when you and Carmina used to fight every chance you got, I stood quietly by. Because I knew the two of you would work it out. You didn't need me. Well, you need me now. You need me to tell you the truth, because you're in too deep to see what's plainly in front of you. Your mom made some lousy choices. I don't know the whole of it, but I've heard enough to know she made your life hell. It scarred you and messed you up. I'm not going to tell you what I think of her, because nobody deserves to hear those things about their own mother. I don't care how sorry or pathetic her life was—she had a responsibility to you. You were a kid, a girl who needed her mom. She shouldn't have put that weight on your shoulders."

"Carmina told me her addiction is to blame, it's the disease—"

"Yeah?" he said harshly. "Carmina's a better person than me. The hell with your mom. She hurt and neglected you. She put you in this position, and it kills me to see you in pain."

"Tell me what to do, Chet. Please help me."

"You know what you have to do."

I shook my head sorrowfully. "If I tell the truth, they'll arrest her. She'll go to prison. And I'll be alone. I'll be completely alone."

"Hey," he said, his voice gentling as he tilted my chin up. "You have me. You have Carmina. You have people who care about you here in Thunder Basin. Did I mention you have me? In case I failed to make it clear, you can count on me. Not just today, but always. I'm here for you, Stella."

Through the tears, I felt choking guilt. He was here for me, but I was gone tomorrow. Why couldn't I tell him?

Because I didn't want to break his heart. No. Because I didn't want to break my own. I was still searching for some way to avoid it. Tonight, I reminded myself, was for exorcising the past. Tomorrow I would face the future. Tomorrow I would be strong enough to tell him.

He said, "I'm sorry your mom put you in this hard place. I know you think you can't do the right thing, but I've seen you be brave too many times to doubt you."

Exhausted, I climbed to my feet. I rubbed the back of my neck, trying to loosen the knots of tension. Chet rose too and wrapped his arms around me from behind. He kissed the base of my spine softly, then nestled his chin on my shoulder, his eyes seeming to pinpoint the same part of the swimming hole where I was staring absently.

"Going home?" he asked.

"I have to tell Carmina the truth. All of it. Tonight. Before I lose my courage."

Despite the somber mood, he smiled. "Well, hop on, then. I'll give you a piggyback ride home."

It felt wrong to smile back, but I felt myself do it anyway. Chet had a way with me. I was going to miss him, really miss him. I jumped on his back, and he grasped my legs and hiked me higher. I took a mostly deep breath. Everything was going to be okay. At least for tonight. I believed it, because when I was with him, all my fears seemed to fade.

CHET AND I SAUNTERED HOME, OUR CLOTHES AND
bodies dripping water. He took my towel, tossed it over his shoulder, and reached for my hand. After everything we'd done tonight,
it seemed silly to feel a thrill over such a small gesture, but I
wanted to remember the little and big things equally.

As we walked under the boughs of the cottonwood trees, their
leaves rustled and whispered like old ladies gossiping at the
sight of late-night lovers sneaking home. Earlier, I'd promised
myself there would be no regrets tonight, and I'd kept my word.
I'd wanted to share something true and real with Chet before I
left. And I'd wanted something real from him, too. I'd wanted
him. He was the only one I wanted. Even now, as I glanced at
the moonlight dancing in the hollows of his cheekbones, I felt

a warm stirring of desire. I'd never felt like this before, and the contrast between Chet and Reed was as clear as comparing summer to winter.

I'd been attracted to Reed because I was lonely and scared and I needed someone to help me forget about my problems at home. He'd listened and taught me how to be tough—by example. In return, I slept with him. Looking back, I thought it felt more like a business transaction than a wild, heart-stopping romance. Fear and desperation weren't reasons to love someone. Love shouldn't need a reason, I decided. It was a deep bond, a commitment. It should steal your breath away. It should never make you compromise yourself.

When we reached Carmina's, her truck wasn't in the drive.

"What time is it?" I asked Chet.

"Nearly ten."

I exhaled, nodding to myself. I'd hoped she would already be inside so I wouldn't have time to lose my nerve, but I wouldn't have to wait long. She'd be home from Bible study soon.

He walked me to the door, then took both my hands, twining our fingers. "Want me to stay until Carmina gets back?"

"No. I need a minute to gather my thoughts."

He laid a hand on my cheek. "Tell her what you told me. You've already done it once. Hard part's over."

Logically, I knew he was right. If only my thundering heart felt the same. This was it. I was coming clean and owning up to the consequences. I was relieved and maybe even a little proud to discover it was nervous anticipation I felt, not fear.

"I'll come by tomorrow. Take you to breakfast," he offered.

"That would be nice." And at breakfast, I would tell him. I would not spoil tonight. It was the last of the selfish things I would do for myself, and I wasn't compromising. Weeks, months, years from now, I wanted to remember this as a perfect night. My perfect night with the first guy I'd ever loved.

Leaning me back against the door, he kissed me softly. "I'm not going to sleep tonight."

"Because of earlier, at the swimming hole?"

"Because I'm worried about you. But yeah, what happened at the swimming hole? I'm not going to forget it any time soon. It's seared in my memory. Thank my lucky stars."

I laughed in spite of myself. "You did that to make me smile."

"I like making you smile. You'd be amazed at the things I'd do to keep you happy."

"You're awfully good to me, Chet."

"Just getting started." He kissed my hand, and once again, I quashed my guilt. I would not let it rob me of this moment. I watched Chet walk away until the darkness closed around him.

Flopping in the porch swing, I pressed a hand to my chest. I wondered if I was entitled to feel this happy. This deliriously, wondrously, steal-your-breath happy. Everyone deserved to feel this way at least once, I decided. A light to cling to when things got dark. One sliver of happiness, to give a person hope that the light would come again.

Shortly after, I let myself in, fumbling for the light switch several paces down the hallway. Still basking in the afterglow of being with Chet, I didn't register right away that the lights didn't turn on.

When it finally hit me, the hairs on my scalp rose.

Suddenly I was back in Philly; it was late; it was dark. Something was very wrong.

I heard a soft wheezing behind me.

I spun around to see Trigger. He sat in the chair Carmina kept at the bottom of the staircase, his breathing shallow, his chin slumped on his chest. He clutched his abdomen, blood trickling out between his fingers.

He lifted his head, his face screwed in a tight grimace of pain, his eyes blazing with hate. "It . . . shoulda . . . been me who . . . killed you," he gasped.

I didn't understand. But I knew I was in danger. I could feel it vibrating all around. I stumbled toward the front door, my body shaking with fear. I had to get out. Chet. I had to get to him.

But a dark, looming shape stepped into the hall, blocking my path.

35

"ESTELLA, ESTELLA," THE MAN SAID. HE DIDN'T SPEAK
with the flat, gliding accent I'd grown accustomed to hearing in
Thunder Basin. His was Eastern European. One of a hundred
accents I'd heard on the streets of Philly.

I shrank back.

"You do not trust me?" he said, his tone amused. "You think
I am a bad man? Why would you think a bad man is hunting
you?" His voice turned taunting. "Maybe you have been a bad girl.
Maybe you screwed with the wrong people."

My blood ran cold. No. No, no, no.

I had to get out. I had to run. But my legs felt slippery, watery.

"You called Sandy Broucek," he chided. "Tsk, tsk. They did not
tell you not to do that?"

I shook my head in disbelief. I'd turned off the phone

immediately. I'd done everything right. It was a stab in the dark for Danny Balando's man to find me.

"Technology is sophisticated, yes? I tapped the phone of your mother's friend. I traced your call. I came to town and showed your picture. This boy"—he gestured dismissively at Trigger—"led me right to you. Easy, so easy."

"Shoulda killed you . . . at the Sundown," Trigger rasped.

The man turned and fired on him. It happened so fast. The bullet was quick and popping. Trigger's body sank sideways and the wheezing sound stopped.

Black dots crowded my vision. I felt myself sliding into shock. I had to stay alert. But Trigger's body was right *there*, dead. This was just like Philly. Death was everywhere. I could smell it, hear it rushing in my ears.

"I'm not going to testify against Danny." My voice quivered. "I know he didn't kill that man, the man they called the Pharmacist. I'm going to tell the prosecutor the truth and they'll let Danny go."

"Ah, but I do not believe you."

I shuffled backward, deeper into Carmina's dark, dark house. The blinds were closed and the drapes drawn for night; there was very little light for our eyes to adjust to. "Please. Don't do this."

He rushed forward. I had my house keys in my hand, and I slashed them at his face.

He made an enraged, animal-like sound and doubled over.

He fired at me, but I was already fleeing out the back door.

Outside, moonlight bathed the yard. There was nowhere to

run. He'd find me in the open fields. The barn door didn't lock. Chet's house was too far.

I heard him staggering through the house, knocking into furniture as he came for me.

In a state of blind panic, I ran. I tripped over a low structure that materialized out of the darkness. The storm shelter.

My hands slid the bolt on the doors leading underground. I lifted one, then the other. The smell of cold, wet earth wafted through the opening. A stairway of railroad ties descended into utter darkness.

Climbing in, I shut the doors noiselessly behind me. With each downward step, the ice in the pit of my stomach expanded. Down, down, down. It was so inescapably black at the bottom. I couldn't see. But neither could he.

Feeling my way through a second door, I felt a lock and turned it behind me. Carmina would be home any minute. I just had to hide for a bit. I tried to slow my panicky, racing thoughts. I could smell sweat. My sweat.

The metal doors above groaned open. I felt dizzy with dread. Next came footsteps, methodical and heavy, descending. When the doorknob on the door rattled, my breath turned to hard, dire pants.

In dry-mouthed terror, I listened to him bang the door. He was kicking it in. I heard the splinter of wood, louder with each thrust.

And then I was listening to his soft breathing.

"Estella," he called softly. His shoes scuffed over cement as he felt his way inside. "Do you remember Mr. Balando's promise after you identified him to the police?"

How could I forget? Danny's words had ripped through the one-way glass at the police station. Even now, his crazed voice growled in my ear. *I will kill you. I will find you and I will kill you. You'll never be safe.*

Danny's voice had risen above the officers' shouting to have him hauled away. Even after the guards wrestled him from the small room behind the one-way glass, I could hear him shrieking my name in that awful, bloodthirsty snarl.

"Danny would prefer to be here," the man cooed chillingly. "But no matter. He gave me instructions. I know exactly what to do to you."

Every part of me rattled with fear.

A deafening *bang!* split my ears.

I cupped a hand over my mouth, willing myself not to whimper, not to make a sound. I pressed my back to the wall, my legs shaking too hard to hold me up. Dread and blind, wild desperation coursed in my veins.

"Maybe I start shooting bullets, yes? This way and that. All around the room. You will scream when I hit you. I will find you, Estella Goodwinn."

Bang! Bang! Bang!

Tears streamed down my face. I hugged myself tightly. I was trembling to the bone. He was going to find me. Just like he'd found Reed. Just like he would someday find my mom.

Danny Balando would keep his promise.

"Put the gun down."

Chet's voice sliced through my dizziness. I lifted my head, eyes searching the black, black room. Had I imagined hearing him?

"I've got a twenty-two long pointed at you," Chet told the man. "Put down your gun and kick it over here."

The man chuckled. "I cannot see you. So how do I know you are speaking the truth?"

"You don't."

"Do you know how to use that rifle, boy?"

An ear-splitting blast erupted, followed by a casing clinking on the floor. "Looks like I know how to use it," Chet said. "Gun on the floor, kick it over here, nice and easy."

"Okay, okay," the man said. "I am putting it down." There was a skidding noise as the gun slid across the floor.

"Got a phone?" Chet asked him.

"In my motel room, yes."

"Then that's where we're going. You're going to call the people you work for. Tell them you killed Stella, job's over. If you want to walk out of here alive, make your story convincing."

The man laughed smoothly. "And then what? You kill me? My employer will know if I do not return to Philadelphia. He will send more men. He will not stop until he finds her. Now or later, it makes no difference, she will die. She is—how do you say it?—a ticking clock. You are putting your life in danger unnecessarily. Forget the girl and save yourself." He made a casual grunt. "What I do with her is not your concern."

"That's where you're wrong. Step over to the wall."

The man exhaled a troubled sigh, as though telling Chet he was making a big mistake.

"The wall," Chet ordered.

"Yes, yes, I am going."

"Stella?" Chet said. "You okay?"

"Yes," I croaked.

"The Scout's in the drive. Key's in the ignition. Drive to the police station. Don't leave until Carmina comes for you. Stay there and don't come out for anybody else."

Pushing to my feet, I felt my way across the room. A fresh wave of tears tumbled down my cheeks, but these were tears of relief. Chet had found me. I was going to live. I was going to see him and Carmina again.

With one hand on the wall, I moved through the darkness. Just a few more steps to the door—

I heard a scuffle of feet and felt fumbling hands. Before I could move away, he grabbed my arm, yanking hard. I whirled, stopping with my back to his chest. His breath panted against my cheek. Something cold and sharp dug into my throat. I gasped as the pain cut deeper.

"I have a knife to her throat," the man snarled. "Lower your gun. Put it and the one you took from me on the floor. Slide them over."

"Stella?" Chet called out.

"Three seconds before I cut her throat," the man growled.

I heard Chet set his rifle on the floor. The smaller gun followed. They scraped over the cement as he kicked them toward us.

The man barked, "In the corner. On your knees. Head down. Speak to me as you do these things. I hear your voice and know where you are."

"I'm moving," Chet said. "I'm on my knees. Head down." The sound of his voice confirmed his location.

"You next," the man ordered me, shoving me in Chet's direction. I scrambled to him, pressing close. I grappled for his hand, locking mine around his. He felt warm and solid, and while he wasn't shaking, I knew he had to be afraid.

I heard the man feeling the ground for the guns.

Chet pulled me into his arms. We were on our knees, holding each other tightly.

"I'm sorry. I'm so sorry," I sobbed quietly.

He kissed my forehead and nudged my damp hair off my face. I shut my eyes and imagined I could see him. Dark curly hair, sizzling blue eyes. A chiseled, handsome face. One I associated with strength, intelligence, and tenderness. "Shh, don't say that," he murmured. "No matter what happens now, we think about each other. We remember the good. Until this is over, we cling to that. No regrets."

The man picked up the rifle. I gripped Chet tighter.

"Estella first," the man ordered. "Stand up."

Before I could even process his request—or realize this was it, we were out of time, he was going to shoot us, one and then the other—Chet shoved to his feet. "I'm going first."

"No!" I cried, scrabbling to get up and stop him. I couldn't find him. It was too dark. "Chet, no!"

I heard the man push Chet toward the stairs. Next thing, I felt a strike to my chest, sending me sprawling backward on the hard concrete. All breath left me in a whoosh. It took several moments for air to burn down my throat again.

I listened, dazed and horrified, as the metal doors above shut and locked between Chet and me.

"Chet!" I screamed.

"Remember what I said," he yelled through the doors.

I dragged myself after him and pounded on the metal doors. It was no use. The bolt was secure. I couldn't get to Chet. I couldn't stop this from happening. I drew up a mental image of him and played it in my head, over and over.

Folding my hands over my ears, I wept. I didn't want to hear the shot. I didn't want to know when he was dead. Stumbling downstairs, I put distance between me and that horrible sound I knew would come.

I still had things I wanted to tell Chet. There were things—important things, life-changing things—we'd never done together. I'd been wrong about tonight. I was haunted by regret. This was not how our story ended.

The sound of the gunshot ripped me open.

And I knew.

IN THAT INSTANT, I KNEW CHET WAS GONE. I FELT
numb and groggy. The next thing I knew, I'd emptied my stomach.

My extremities shook uncontrollably. Even my lips felt like
they were vibrating. I couldn't see straight. I couldn't see. It was so
black. So cold. The air was stale and muggy, but I was cold. Bone
cold.

I should have wept. I wanted to. But there was nothing inside
me. Dry and hollow, I sat with my back braced against the wall,
smelling vomit.

He was gone. Never coming back. I'd killed him. It wasn't an
exaggeration or dramatics. He was dead because of me. Because
he fell in love with me. Because he did the honorable thing and
tried to save my life.

I rewound time in my head, going back to the beginning.

If I hadn't gone to the library that night to e-mail Reed. If the Mustang hadn't stalled. If I hadn't agreed to let Chet help me.

I wouldn't have known him, or spent the best three months of my life with him. But he would still be alive.

I was so deep in my grief, I almost didn't hear the sound of feet thundering down the stairs. Beams of light darted erratically around the room. In quick succession, they all came to shine on me.

"Stella!"

Carmina's voice caused my chin to jerk upward. "Carmina?"

She rushed forward, yanking me to my feet and pinning me in a tight embrace. The force of her hug squeezed the breath out of me. "You're okay. You're okay," she murmured, her voice shaking with relief.

I sank into her, my knees dissolving.

"Everyone, stand back. Give her some room." Her hand touched my forehead. "She's cold. Eyes are unfocused. Someone give me a water bottle!"

Water trickled past my lips. As soon as I realized it was real, I drank greedily. The tears started flowing then. I wept freely. "Chet. He—he—"

"Oh, Stella. No. He's alive. He's right outside. Being questioned by local PD."

"I—What?" I stared at her blankly. "I heard the shot."

Her voice turned solemn. "I shot the man who tried to kill you and Chet. Chet called me a few minutes ago saying he thought he heard gunfire here at the house. I told him to stay put, but he came for you. Right away I called local PD and headed home."

"Deceased's name is Yevgeniy Polishchuk," one of the uniformed officers said, stepping forward to address Carmina. "We're running him through the system now. Driver's license gives an address in Philadelphia, Pennsylvania."

"I have to see Chet," I said. Everything else could wait.

At that moment, he pushed his way inside the storm shelter. His searching eyes zeroed in on me, and they were stripped raw. The next thing I knew, he was tugging me against him. He guided my head to his chest, where I felt every ragged breath. I clutched fistfuls of his shirt, unwilling to lose him again.

"You've alive," I said. "It's really you."

"I heard the shot and thought I was gone," he said roughly in my ear. "Couldn't figure out why I didn't feel pain. And then I saw the blood. He was on the ground, covered in it. Carmina's a hell of a shot."

"You went first," I said. "You tried to buy me time, hoping she would make it here."

"Doesn't matter. Didn't need the extra time."

"It matters to me."

He kissed me once, twice. Burying his face in my hair, he held me closer than before. "It was never a question. Of course I was going first. Let's get out of here. You need a place to sit and let it all go."

"First I have to tell Carmina what I told you earlier tonight. I should have told her ages ago. If I had, none of this would have happened."

"Tell me what?" Carmina said, turning away from the officer speaking to her.

The scattered light from the flashlights illuminated her strong, unflinching features. As I met her eyes, I felt no fear. If anything, I wanted to be like her. Courageous. I wanted to do the right thing, even though it was also the most difficult.

I glanced once at Chet, who gave an encouraging nod. He believed in me, and I clung to that.

"Let's go up to the house," I told her.

37

THE FOLLOWING MORNING, CARMINA AND I WERE
swaying idly on the porch swing when Chet strolled up the drive,
blooms of long-stemmed sunflowers in his hands. His button-
down shirt was rolled to the elbows and open at the collar. The
summer sun had bronzed his skin as it had mine. His hair was
dark and unruly, his eyes midnight blue.

He tipped his hat when he saw us watching him, then leaped
up the steps gracefully.

"One for the lady who saved my life," he said, delivering a bouquet to Carmina's hesitant hands, "and one for my girl."

"Did you hear Carmina was on the news this morning?" I
asked him, inhaling the yellow blossoms' nutty fragrance.

"In fact, I did," he said, stretching those long legs as he sat on
the top step. "What I want to know, Carmina, is, when you aimed

your weapon at that man, did it ever cross your mind you might hit me instead? It was awfully dark. What if I'd moved at the last second? What if he'd moved? What if you'd flinched and lost your aim?"

"Lost my aim, my foot," she scoffed.

He laid his cowboy hat solemnly over his heart. "Not that it's happened to me. But I'm younger." He grinned. "Better eyesight."

"Maybe I ought to have put a hole in you," she remarked. "Deflate some of that pride keeping your head afloat." Her tone grew serious. "We can joke all we want, but I'm glad you're both here, both okay. I'm just—glad we're together. Don't know about the two of you, but I didn't sleep last night. Can't imagine what Trigger's family must be going through. Say what you want about him, but no parent deserves to bury their child." Her eyes misted and she blinked them dry. "I think it's going to take a long while for his parents to accept what he did and how that poor, foolish boy's life ended. It'll probably take me a similar length of time to move on. No use in thinking what might have been—how last night could've ended—but if I'm not careful, my mind strays there just the same."

Yes, it does, I thought. Like Carmina, I hadn't slept last night. I'd replayed those final minutes before she shot Danny Balando's hit man over and over. The terror, the fear—both were still so fresh. When I hadn't been imagining how those minutes might have ended differently, I'd thought about my mom. Was she safe? Would I see her again? I'd also thought about Reed. Looking back, I think I'd always known that when we went into WITSEC, that was the end. We would never see each other again. Out of self-preservation I'd let myself believe otherwise. I'd desperately needed to cling to any hope that my old life—and those who'd mattered most—weren't gone forever. Even if Danny's men hadn't caught up to Reed, he wasn't looking for me. He'd moved on.

And so had I.

"I'll pour you a glass of basil lemonade, Chet," I said, rising from my perch.

"Don't you two have anything better to do than hang around with an old woman?" Carmina fussed, shooing us with her hands. "Take a walk. It's too pretty a day to lounge around here. No, Stella, I don't want to hear a word. I've got the paper's crossword puzzle to keep me busy. Go on, now."

I bit my lip to hold in a smile. It seemed she'd finally warmed to the idea of me and Chet. Took her long enough. "All right. But only if you promise to put my flowers in a vase."

"As if I'd let Hannah Falconer's sunflowers go to waste," she said exasperatedly, snatching my bouquet, then using it to slap me on the bum. "Take a walk and work up your appetites. I'll have lunch fixed by the time you get back."

I grabbed my cowgirl hat off the milking stool Carmina used as a doorstop and dropped it on my head. Then I let Chet take my hand and escort me down the drive.

I swung our joined arms lazily and said, "Carmina and I had a long talk last night. We stayed up most of the night. I told her everything. The detectives working the case are flying out. I'll have to give them my corrected statement. My lies will come out, but

I'm not afraid. I'd rather deal with the consequences than keep living that horrible lie. Carmina said prosecutions for perjury are incredibly rare, and while I'll most likely be off the hook in that regard, I've punished myself with enough guilt to last a lifetime. I could have avoided everything if I'd told the truth from the beginning."

"You were scared. You were protecting your mom."

"I justified my actions. I told myself it was okay to lie, because Danny Balando was an evil man who belonged behind bars. Maybe he does. But not for this crime."

"Have they released him?"

"They're holding him on conspiracy charges. After they got a warrant from the original arrest, they found evidence linking him to the cartel. He's not getting out any time soon."

"Are they worried he'll send someone else to hurt you?"

"I'm a discredited witness. The prosecution can't use me in court. Nothing I say will hold up because I lied before. Anyway, he's no longer being charged with murder. I'm not a threat to him anymore."

"And your mom?"

"The marshals are looking for her. Sooner or later, they'll find her. Until then, I think she'll go back to stealing and using," I said, my tone turning melancholy. As much as I didn't want to care about her, I did. I wanted her to get better. Maybe she some-day would. But it would be a long, hard road back. "It's what she knows."

"What about you?" Chet said, stopping us under the shade of

an expansive cottonwood. He leaned his forearms casually on the split-rail fence, but a closer look revealed his hands were clamped tightly. He worked them opened and closed, those strong, sure fingers tense. "Will you go back? To your old life?" He seemed to hold his breath while his eyes studied mine closely.

I considered his question carefully. So many things had changed this summer. I had changed. I could never go back to the person I once was. I was not Estella Goodwinn anymore. "I don't have happy memories there. That scared, desperate, hurting girl in Philadelphia? She's not me. Not anymore. This is my home now. This feels right."

Slowly, his eyes cleared. They lit with a spark of hope. "You'll stay?"

I eased my elbows back against the fence beside him, smiling. "See, there's this guy here, a really sweet, sensitive, sexy guy, and I'm not ready to let go of him just yet."

Chet moved in front of me, positioning his legs around mine. He braced his hands on the fence, trapping me between him and it. Lowering his head, he spoke with his mouth inches from mine. "You're going to have to tell this guy you're taken. Because I don't share."

"Should I let him down easy?" I murmured, leaning in close to play this game. When my mouth skimmed his jaw, I heard his breath hiss, low and hot.

"Doesn't matter. When I finish with you, you aren't going to remember his name."

"Mmm, is that a promise?"

He slipped my denim jacket off my shoulders. It landed in the dandelions with a whisper of fabric. His long-lashed eyes gave me an unhurried once-over. I felt their trailing heat like a physical caress, and warmed with anticipation.

Chet was nothing, I'd learned, if not a man of his word.

Read on for a sneak peek at
Becca Fitzpatrick's chilling thriller . . .

From the author of the bestselling *Hush, Hush* series

BECCA
FITZPATRICK

BLACK
ICE

Danger is hard to resist . . .

Hot. Cold. Deadly.

PB ISBN: 9781471118166
EB ISBN: 9781471125119

The door chimed and my fake boyfriend strolled inside. He was even better-looking up close. And his eyes were most definitely brown—a weathered brown that reminded me of driftwood. He reached into his back pocket for his wallet, and I grabbed Calvin's arm and hauled him behind a shelf stacked with Fig Newtons and Oreos.

"What are we doing?" Calvin asked, staring at me like I'd sprouted two heads.

"I don't want him to see me," I whispered.

"Because he's not really your boyfriend, right?"

"That's not it. It's—"

Where was a third lie when I needed it?

Cal smiled devilishly, and the next thing I knew, he had shaken off my hand and was ambling toward the front counter. I trapped a groan between my teeth and watched, peering between the two top shelves.

"Hey," Calvin said affably to the guy, who wore a buffalo-check flannel shirt, jeans, and hiking boots.

With barely a glance up, the guy tipped his head in acknowledgment.

"I hear you're dating my ex," Calvin said, and there was something undeniably smug in his tone. He was giving me a taste of my own medicine, and he knew it.

Calvin's remark drew the full attention of the guy. He studied Calvin curiously, and I felt my cheeks grow even hotter.

"You know, your *girlfriend*," Calvin prodded. "Hiding behind the cookies over there."

He was pointing at me.

I straightened, my head surfacing above the top shelf. I smoothed my shirt and opened my mouth, but there were no words. No words at all.

The guy looked beyond Calvin to me. Our gazes locked briefly, and I mouthed a humiliated I *can explain* . . . But I couldn't.

Then something unexpected happened. The guy looked squarely at Calvin, and said in an easy, unruffled voice, "Yeah. My girlfriend. Britt."

I flinched. He *knew my name?*

Calvin appeared similarly startled. "Oh. Hey. Sorry, man. I thought—" He stuck out his hand. "I'm Calvin Versteeg," he stammered awkwardly. "Britt's . . . ex."

"Mason." Mason eyed Calvin's outstretched hand but didn't take it. Then he crossed to me and kissed my cheek. It was a no-frills kiss, but my pulse thrummed just the same. He smiled, and it was a warm, sexy smile. "I see you haven't gotten over your Slurpee addiction, Britt."

Slowly I smiled back. If he was game for this, then so was I. "I saw you pull in, and needed something to cool me off." I fanned myself while gazing up at him adoringly.

His eyes crinkled at the edges. I was pretty sure he was laughing on the inside.

I said, "You should stop by my house later, Mason, because I bought a new lip gloss that could use a test run . . ."

"Ah. Kissing game?" he said without missing a beat.

I shot a covert glance at Calvin to gauge how he was handling the flirting. Much to my enjoyment, he looked like he'd caught a mouthful of lemon peel.

"You know me—always spicing things up," I returned silkily.

Calvin cleared his throat and folded his arms over his chest. "Shouldn't you be heading out, Britt? You really should get to the cabin before dark."

Something undecipherable clouded Mason's eyes. "Going camping?" he asked me.

"Backpacking," I corrected. "In Wyoming—the Tetons. I was going to tell you, but . . ." Ack! What possible reason could I come up with for not telling my boyfriend about this trip? So close to pulling this off, and I was going to blow it.

"But it seemed unimportant, since I'm heading out of town too, and we won't be able to spend the week together anyway," Mason finished easily.

I met his eyes again. Good-looking, quick on his feet, game for anything—even pretending to be the boyfriend of a girl he'd never met—and a frighteningly good liar. Who was this guy? "Yes, exactly," I murmured.

Calvin cocked his head at me. "When we were together, did I ever take off for a week without telling you?"

You took off for eight months, I thought snidely. And broke up with me on the most important night of my life. Jesus said forgive, but there's always room for an exception.

I said to Mason, "By the way, Daddy wants to have you over for dinner next week."

Calvin made a strangled noise. Once, when he'd brought me home five minutes after curfew, we'd pulled into the driveway to see my dad standing on the porch tapping a golf driver in his palm. He'd marched over and smacked it against Calvin's black Ford F-150, leaving a nice round crater. "Next time you bring her home late, I'll aim for the headlights," he'd said. "Don't be stupid enough to need three warnings."

He hadn't meant it, not really. Since I was the baby of the family and the only girl, my dad had a grouchy streak when it came to the boys I dated. But actually, my dad was a lovable old bear. Still, Calvin never broke curfew again.

And never once had he been allowed to come to dinner.

"Tell your dad I could use a few more fly-fishing tips," Mason said, continuing to hold up our charade. Miraculously, he'd also correctly guessed my dad's favorite sport. This entire encounter was starting to feel . . . eerie. "Oh, and one more thing, Britt." He combed his hand through my hair, pushing it off my shoulder. I held perfectly still, his touch freezing my breath inside me. "Be safe. Mountains are dangerous this time of year."

I gawked with amazement at him until he pulled out of the gas station and drove off.

He knew my name. He'd saved my butt. He knew *my name*.

© Krista Sidwell 2014

Becca Fitzpatrick lives in Colorado. Hush, Hush was her first novel, followed by Crescendo, Silence, Finale, Black Ice, and Dangerous Lies. When she's not writing, she's most likely to be found prowling sales racks for reject shoes, running, or watching crime dramas on TV. You can visit her on **www.beccafitzpatrick.com**, or on Twitter: **@becfitzpatrick**, or Facebook.